I0831376

Patriot's Farewell

A Boston Brahmin Novel

by

Bobby Akart

Copyright Information

© 2017 Brahmin Merchandising Inc. All rights reserved. Except as permitted under the U.S. Copyright Act of 1976, no part of this publication may be reproduced, distributed or transmitted in any form or by any means, or stored in a database or retrieval system, without the prior written permission of Brahmin Merchandising Inc.

Other Works by Amazon Top 50 Author, Bobby Akart

The Doomsday Series

Apocalypse

Haven

Anarchy

Minutemen

Civil War

The Yellowstone Series

Hellfire

Inferno

Fallout

Survival

The Lone Star Series

Axis of Evil

Beyond Borders

Lines in the Sand

Texas Strong

Fifth Column

Suicide Six

The Pandemic Series

Beginnings

The Innocents

Level 6

Quietus

The Blackout Series

36 Hours

Zero Hour

Turning Point

Shiloh Ranch

Hornet's Nest

Devil's Homecoming

The Boston Brahmin Series

The Loyal Nine

Cyber Attack

Martial Law

False Flag

The Mechanics

Choose Freedom

Patriot's Farewell

Seeds of Liberty (Companion Guide)

The Prepping for Tomorrow Series

Cyber Warfare

EMP: Electromagnetic Pulse

Economic Collapse

DEDICATIONS

To the love of my life, you saved me from madness and continue to do so daily. Thank you for loving me.

To the Princesses of the Palace, my little marauders in training, you have no idea how much happiness you bring to your mommy and me. Seeing your wiggly butts at the end of a long day behind the keyboard makes it all worthwhile.

To the Founding Fathers, whose vision and bravery built America. My apologies for what we've become.

ACKNOWLEDGEMENTS

Writing a book that is both informative and entertaining requires a tremendous team effort. Writing is the easy part. For their efforts in making Patriot's Farewell, a Boston Brahmin Political Thriller a reality, I would like to thank Hristo Argirov Kovatliev for his incredible cover art, Pauline Nolet for her editorial prowess, Stef Mcdaid for making this manuscript decipherable on so many formats, and the Team—whose advice, friendship and attention to detail is priceless. A special thank you to Stewart McLaurin with the White House Historical Association and the White House Museum for their extensive background material on the White House, as well as insight into the daily life of our presidents.

Thank you all!
Choose Freedom!

About the Author

Bobby Akart

Author Bobby Akart has been ranked by Amazon as #55 in its Top 100 list of most popular, bestselling authors. He has achieved recognition as the #1 bestselling Horror Author, #2 bestselling Science Fiction Author, #3 bestselling Religion & Spirituality Author, #6 bestselling Action & Adventure Author, and #7 bestselling Historical Author.

He has written over twenty-six international bestsellers, in nearly fifty fiction and nonfiction genres, including the chart-busting Yellowstone series, the reader-favorite Lone Star series, the critically acclaimed Boston Brahmin series, the bestselling Blackout series, the frighteningly realistic Pandemic series, his highly cited nonfiction Prepping for Tomorrow series, and his latest project—the Doomsday series, seen by many as the horrifying future of our nation if we can't find a way to come together.

His novel *Yellowstone: Fallout* reached the Top 50 on the Amazon bestsellers list and earned him two Kindle All-Star awards for most pages read in a month and most pages read as an author. The Yellowstone series vaulted him to the #1 best selling horror author on Amazon, and the #2 best selling science fiction author.

Bobby has provided his readers a diverse range of topics that are both informative and entertaining. His attention to detail and impeccable research have allowed him to capture the imaginations of his readers through his fictional works and bring them valuable knowledge through his nonfiction books.

SIGN UP for Bobby Akart's mailing list to receive special offers, bonus content, and you'll be the first to receive news about new releases in the Doomsday series:

eepurl.com/bYqq3L

VISIT Amazon.com/BobbyAkart, a dedicated feature page created by Amazon for his work, to view more information on his thriller fiction novels and post-apocalyptic book series, as well as his nonfiction Prepping for Tomorrow series.

Visit Bobby Akart's website for informative blog entries on preparedness, writing, and a behind-the-scenes look into his novels.

BobbyAkart.com

EPIGRAPH

It doesn't take a majority to prevail but rather a tireless, irate minority, keen to set brush fires in the people's minds.

~ Samuel Adams

*****

I get red, white, and blue sometimes.

~ Walt Disney

*****

One flag, one land, one heart, one hand, one nation evermore.

~ Oliver Wendell Holmes

*****

To restore harmony, to render us again one people acting as one nation should be the object of every man really a patriot.

~ Thomas Jefferson

****

Liberty, once lost, is lost forever.

~ John Adams

*****

The duty of a true patriot is to protect his country from its government.

~ Thomas Paine

*****

Choose Freedom!

~ Henry Winthrop Sargent IV

AUTHOR'S NOTE TO THE READER

Patriot's Farewell is written as a standalone novel based upon my six book Boston Brahmin series. Knowledge of the characters and back story of the Boston Brahmin series will be helpful as you read Patriot's Farewell.

Whether you've read the Boston Brahmin series already, or if you decide to pick up the story in this time frame, I suggest you read "Previously In The Boston Brahmin Series". This will enable you to familiarize yourself with the characters and the events which led to Patriot's Farewell.

Previously in The Boston Brahmin Series

Dramatis Personae

THE LOYAL NINE:

Sarge – born Henry Winthrop Sargent IV. Son of former Massachusetts governor, godson of John Adams Morgan and a descendant of Daniel Sargent, Sr., wealthy merchant, and owner of Sargent's Wharf during the Revolutionary War. He's a tenured professor at the Harvard Kennedy School of Government in Cambridge. He is becoming well known around the country for his libertarian philosophy as espoused in his *New York Times* bestseller—*Choose Freedom or Capitulation: America's Sovereignty Crisis*. Sarge resides at 100 Beacon Street in the Back Bay area of Boston. Sarge is romantically involved with Julia Hawthorne.

Steven Sargent – younger brother of Sarge. He is a graduate of the United States Naval Academy and a former platoon officer of SEAL Team 10. He is currently a contract operative for Aegis Security—code name Nomad. He resides on his yacht—the *Miss Behavin'*. Steven is romantically involved with Katie O'Shea.

Julia Hawthorne – descendant of the Peabody and Hawthorne families. First female political editor of the *Boston Herald*. She is the recipient of the National Association of Broadcasting Marconi Radio Award for her creation of an Internet radio channel for the newspaper. She is in a relationship with Sarge and lives with him at 100 Beacon.

The Quinn family – Donald is the self-proclaimed director of procurement. He is a former accountant and financial advisor who works directly with John Adams Morgan. Married to ***Susan Quinn***

with daughters ***Rebecca*** (age 7) and ***Penny*** (age 11). Donald and Susan coordinate all preparedness activities of The Loyal Nine. They reside in Brae Burn Country Club in Boston.

J.J. – born John Joseph Warren. He is a direct descendant of Dr. Joseph Warren, one of the original Sons of Liberty. The Warren family founded Harvard Medical and were field surgeons at the Battle of Bunker Hill. J.J. was an Army battalion surgeon at Joint Base Balad in Iraq. While stationed at JBB, J.J. saved the life of a female soldier who was injured saving the lives of others. He later became involved in a relationship with former Marine Second Lieutenant Sabina del Toro. He finished his career at the Veteran's Administration Hospital in Jamaica Plain, where he also resides. He is affectionately known as the Armageddon Medicine Man.

Katie O'Shea – graduate of the United States Naval Academy who trained as a Naval Intelligence officer. After an introduction to John Adams Morgan, she quickly rose up the ranks of the intelligence community. She now is part of the President's Intelligence Advisory Board. She resides in Washington, D.C. Katie is romantically involved with Steven Sargent.

Brad – born Francis Crowninshield Bradlee, a descendant of the Crowninshield family, a historic seafaring and military family dating back to the early 1600s. He is the battalion commander of the 25th Marine Regiment of 1st Battalion based at Fort Devens, Massachusetts. Their nickname is *Cold Steel Warriors*. He is an active member of *Oathkeepers* and the *Three Percenters*.

Abbie – Abigail Morgan, daughter of John Adams Morgan. United States senator from Massachusetts since 2008. A political independent, with libertarian leanings. She resides in Washington, D.C. She has been chosen as the running mate of the Democratic nominee for president. She briefly became romantically involved with her head of security, Drew Jackson, aka *Slash*, on the Aegis team.

Drew Jackson – a/k/a ***Slash***. Former SEAL Team member who worked briefly for private contractors like Blackwater. Born and raised in Tennessee, where his family farm is located. He has excellent survival skills. He was assigned to Senator Abigail Morgan's security team that works with her Secret Service detail.

THE BOSTON BRAHMIN:

John Adams Morgan – lineal descendant of President John Adams and Henry Sturgis Morgan, founder of J.P. Morgan. Morgan attended Harvard, obtaining a master's degree in business and a law degree. Founded the Morgan-Holmes law firm with the grandson of Supreme Court Justice Oliver Wendell Holmes Jr. Among other concerns, he owns Morgan Global, an international banking and financial conglomerate. Extremely wealthy, Morgan is the recognized head of The Boston Brahmin.

Walter Cabot – direct descendant of John Cabot, shipbuilders during the time of the Revolutionary War. Wealthy philanthropist and CEO of Cabot Industries. He is part of Morgan's inner circle. Married to Mary Cabot.

Lawrence Lowell – direct descendant of John Lowell, a federal judge in the first United States Continental Congress. Extremely wealthy and part of Morgan's inner circle. Married to Constance Lowell.

Paul Winthrop – descendant of John Winthrop, one of the leading figures in the founding of the Massachusetts Bay Colony, his family became synonymous with the state's politics and philanthropy. The Winthrops and Sargents became close when Sarge's grandfather was governor of Massachusetts and his lieutenant governor was R. C. Winthrop. The families remained close and became a valuable political force on behalf of The Boston Brahmin. They have a French bulldog called Winnie the Frenchie. Married to Millicent Winthrop.

Arthur Peabody – Dr. Arthur Peabody is a plastic surgeon in private practice. He is the youngest of the Boston Brahmin at age fifty-five. His wife is Estelle, affectionately called Aunt Stella. They are Julia's aunt and uncle. They're direct descendants of the Hawthorne and Peabody lineage.

General Samuel Bradlee – former general and Secretary of Defense. A direct descendant of Nathaniel Bradlee, one of the key participants in the Boston Tea Party. He is Brad's uncle.

Henry Endicott – great-grandson of former Secretary of War William Crowninshield Endicott. The Endicott family name is synonymous with warfare throughout the world as one of the largest manufacturers of advanced weapons systems in America. His third wife, Emily, is younger than some of his children.

SUPPORTING CHARACTERS:

Malcolm Lowe – John Morgan's trusted assistant. Former undersecretary of state during Morgan's tenure as Secretary of State. He *handles* sensitive matters for Mr. Morgan.

Sabina del Toro – former Marine second lieutenant deployed to Iraq, assigned to the 6th Marine Regiment under the 2nd Marine Division based at Camp Lejeune. The 6th was primarily a peacekeeping force deployed throughout the Sunni Anbar province, which included Fallujah, just west of Baghdad. Sabs, as she prefers to be called, was seriously injured protecting children from a car bomb blast. She lost her left arm and left leg as a result of her heroics. She was in a relationship with J.J. She died in *Martial Law*, book three, during a confrontation with local residents.

Citizen Corps Governor James O'Brien – former president of the Boston Carmen's Union—one of the oldest and largest public service employees' unions in the city. O'Brien is a staunch supporter of the President and is known to have organized-crime connections. He is a fierce political opponent of Republican Governor Charlie Baker. He was named the new governor of Region I. His office is located on High Street in Boston.

Governor Charlie Baker – Governor of Massachusetts. First Republican in decades to be endorsed by the left-leaning Boston Globe newspaper.

Captain David Morrell – Part of the security detail assigned to Prescott Peninsula and a sergeant in 1st Battalion, 25th Marine Regiment based in Fort Devens.

Primary Scene Locations

100 Beacon – Renovated residential building located in the heart of the Back Bay area of Boston. Located on the lower end of the Boston Common, just to the south of Cambridge and the Charles River, the top three floors of the eleven story building were renovated as a veritable fortress. The top floor housed Sarge's residence, and the Prepper Pantry. The floor below it, was intended to provide housing for The Loyal Nine and The Boston Brahmin. The ninth floor contained an armory, a small medical trauma center, a jail cell, and large storage area. The rooftop provided three hundred and sixty degree views of the city, and overlooked Storrow Drive and Cambridge.

73 Tremont – historic building in downtown Boston located at 73 Tremont Street. (Pronounced "trem-mont") Formerly a historic hotel, the building was purchased by John Morgan to house the top floor offices of The Boston Brahmin. 73 Tremont overlooks the gold dome of the Massachusetts State House and Boston Common.

Fort Devens – is a United States military installation located in northern Massachusetts. It is the home to First Battalion, 25th Marine

Regiment, headed up by Lt. Col. Bradlee. It is also the location of a Federal Bureau of Prisons Medical Facility.

Prescott Peninsula (1PP) – The largest land mass in the Quabbin Reservoir, Prescott Peninsula was completely surrounded by the reservoir and was largely unimproved except for an abandoned radio astronomy observatory where the old town of Prescott Center once stood. The observatory was renovated by the Quinn's to create a state-of-the-art bug-out location, known as 1 Prescott Peninsula, or 1PP. Bungalows were built around 1PP to house The Boston Brahmin and the soldiers from Fort Devens who were tasked with protecting 1PP.

Quabbin Reservoir – the largest body of water in the State of Massachusetts. Located in the central part of the state, it was formed by the creation of dams and dikes in the 1930s, and became federal government owned and was largely undeveloped. The largest land mass, Prescott Peninsula, was completely surrounded by the reservoir and was largely unimproved except for the abandoned radio astronomy observatory which was renovated to create 1PP.

Book One: The Loyal Nine

The Boston Brahmin series begins in December of 2015 and the timeframe of *The Loyal Nine*, book one in The Boston Brahmin series, continues through April 2016. Steven Sargent, in his capacity as Nomad, an Aegis deep-cover operative, undertakes several black-ops missions in Ukraine, Switzerland, and Germany. The purposes of the operations become increasingly suspect to Steven and his brother, Sarge. It is apparent that Steven's actual employer, John Morgan, is orchestrating a series of events as part of a grander scheme.

Sarge continues to teach at the Harvard Kennedy School of Government. He begins to make public appearances after publishing a *New York Times* bestseller *Choose Freedom or Capitulation: America's Sovereignty Crisis*. During this time, he rekindles his relationship with Julia Hawthorne, who is also celebrating national notoriety for her accomplishments at the *Boston Herald* newspaper. The two take a trip to Las Vegas for a convention and become unwilling participants in a cyber attack on the Las Vegas power grid. Throughout *The Loyal Nine*, Sarge and Julia observe the economic and societal collapse of America.

The unraveling of society in America is evident as the chasm between the haves and have-nots widens, resulting in hostilities between labor unions and their employers. There are unintended consequences of these actions, and numerous deaths are the result.

Racial tensions are on the rise across the country, and Boston becomes ground zero for social unrest when a beloved retired bus driver is beaten to death during the St. Patrick's Day festivities. In protest, a group of marchers descend upon Copley Square at the end of the Boston Marathon, resulting in a clash with police. The protestors are led by Jarvis *J-Rock* Rockwell, leader of the unified black gangs of Dorchester, Roxbury, and Mattapan in South Boston. The march quickly gets out of hand, and J-Rock's pregnant girlfriend is struck by the police, resulting in her death and the death of their unborn child.

The Quinn family—Donald, Susan and their young daughters—are caught up in an angry mob scene at a local mall, relating to the Black Lives Matter protests. Donald decides to accelerate the Loyal Nine's preparedness activities as he gets the sense America is on the brink of collapse.

The reader gets an inside look at the morning security briefings in the White House Situation Room. Katie O'Shea becomes a respected rising star within the intelligence community while solidifying her role as a conduit for information to John Morgan.

John Morgan continues to act as a world power broker. He manipulates geopolitical events for the financial gain of his wealthy associates—the Boston Brahmin. He carefully orchestrates the rise to national prominence of his daughter, Senator Abigail Morgan.

As a direct descendant of the Founding Fathers, Morgan is sickened to watch America descend into collapse. Morgan believes the country can return to its former greatness. He recognizes drastic measures may be required. He envisions a reset of sorts, but what that entails is yet to be determined.

Throughout *The Loyal Nine*, the Zero Day Gamers make a name for themselves in the hacktivist community as their skills and capabilities escalate from cyber vandalism to cyber ransom to cyber terror. Professor Andrew Lau and his talented graduate assistants create ingenious methods of cyber intrusion. At times, they question the morality of their activities. But the ransoms they extract from their victims are too lucrative to turn away.

The end game, the mission statement of the Zero Day Gamers, is succinct:

One man's gain is another man's loss; who gains and who loses is determined by who pays.

Book Two: Cyber Attack

But who else loses in their deadly game? *Cyber Attack*, book two in The Boston Brahmin series, begins with the Zero Day Gamers testing their skills by taking over control of an American Airlines 757. Throughout *Cyber Attack*, the Zero Day Gamers conduct various cyber intrusions, including compromising a nuclear power plant in Jefferson City, Missouri. But one of the Gamers, in an attempt to impress a young lady, makes a mistake. His cyber snooping into the laptop of Abbie Morgan following the Democratic National Convention is discovered.

Meanwhile, over the summer, the Loyal Nine increase their

preparedness activities. Through some legislative maneuvering, John Morgan acquires Prescott Peninsula at the Quabbin Reservoir in central Massachusetts. The Quabbin Reservoir is the largest body of water in the State of Massachusetts. Located in the central part of the state, it was formed by the creation of dams and dikes in the 1930s and became federal government owned and was largely undeveloped. Prescott Peninsula is completely surrounded by the reservoir and was largely unimproved except for an abandoned radio astronomy observatory where the old town of Prescott Center once stood. The entire acquisition encompasses nearly forty square miles. He immediately tasks Donald and Susan Quinn with renovating the property into a high-tech bug-out location for the Boston Brahmin.

While Donald, Susan, J.J., and Sabs focus their attention on Prescott Peninsula, Sarge is making a name for himself on the speaker's circuit as a straight-talk libertarian. His relationship with Julia Hawthorne has grown, and they continue to observe world events with an eye towards preparedness.

After the hack of Abbie's computer, through some excellent cyber forensics on the part of Katie O'Shea, the Zero Day Gamers are located and contacted by Steven Sargent and Malcolm Lowe, acting on behalf of John Morgan. The three orchestrate a ruse upon Andrew Lau and his team of cyber mercenaries for hire.

Morgan has determined that America is descending into collapse, both socially and economically, and is in need of a reset. The Zero Day Gamers are the perfect tool to accomplish this purpose.

Morgan has conducted several private meetings with the President, culminating with a face-to-face discussion in August of 2016. The two agree—a reset is necessary, and each will play a vital role in bringing America to its knees only to build the country back in their respective images. These two powerful political players navigate a complex game of chess, not realizing the unintended consequences on the people of America.

As *Cyber Attack* closes its final chapter in early September 2016, Andrew Lau is forced to make a choice. Does he watch his young proteges die by a gunshot to the head at the hands of Morgan's men, or does he push the button that will result in the end of life as we know it?

Book Three: Martial Law

Lau makes his choice, and his sophisticated cyber attack causes a cascading collapse of the Western and Eastern Interconnected Grid representing ninety percent of America's electricity. Only Texas, whose grid is not connected to the rest of the nation, is spared.

The Loyal Nine are scattered throughout the country. Each faces their own set of unique circumstances and challenges.

John Morgan, despite his meticulous, well-thought plans, makes one critical mistake—he loses track of his daughter's whereabouts. Despite his efforts, Morgan is unable to call off the cyber attack. This leads him to frantically arrange a trip to Florida to extract his daughter and bring her to safety. Just before, and immediately following the grid collapse, he communicates with Abbie's chief of staff to insist that Abbie meet him at Camp Blanding.

Abbie Morgan is in Tallahassee to give a campaign speech. Under the watchful eye of her ever-present protector, Drew Jackson, Abbie addresses a packed crowd at the Donald Tucker Civic Center. Then they are thrust into darkness. Within moments, thirteen thousand people are informed, via text messages and cell phone calls that America has been attacked and the power grid is down.

Drew, Abbie, and some of her entourage attempt to travel several hundred miles east to Camp Blanding, where John Morgan will meet them in his helicopter. First, they have to flee the inner city of Tallahassee, where nearly one hundred thousand people have congregated for the concert and a college football game.

During this night of terror, Drew and Abbie fight their way through looters, marauders, and the throes of Hurricane Danni. Within thirty miles of their destination, they run out of fuel near the small town of Lulu. This small community has been ravaged, not by the hurricane, but by escaped inmates from three of the worst prison facilities in Florida.

Daylight approaches, but the feeder bands of Hurricane Danni continue to obstruct visibility. With a borrowed car from an elderly victim of the inmates' violence, Drew and Abbie make their way to the rendezvous point. Within fifty yards of the helicopter, and safety, they are overrun by a group of attacking inmates. Drew pushes Abbie to the safety of her father, but he is savagely beaten and left for dead. As Drew reaches toward the helicopter, shouting, Abbie and Morgan leave him behind, much to the devastation of Abbie, who had fallen in love with Drew.

In Boston, Sarge and Julia are having drinks on the rooftop of 100 Beacon, having a deep conversation, when the transformers begin to explode. As the lights go out in waves throughout Boston, they immediately recognize this as a possible grid-down collapse event.

They immediately begin to implement their preparedness plan. First, they secure their perimeter. Next, they establish various means of communications and information gathering.

The first call Sarge makes is to John Morgan, who at the time is traveling to the heliport by private car. Morgan's orders are clear: gather up the Boston Brahmin and keep them safe. Sarge knows that this is his call to duty. But something else bothers him about the conversation. Morgan's words weigh heavily on his mind—*widespread, long-lasting*. For the past seven years, somehow Sarge knew this moment would come. What bothers him is the fact that so did John Morgan.

Sarge successfully gathers up the executive committee of the Boston Brahmin, but it does not go without incident. During his last pickup, Sarge is involved in a high-speed chase, with gunfire, through Chinatown. He unknowingly leads them right to the front door of 100 Beacon.

Steven and Katie are in Washington together, enjoying a few beers and shooting pool at a local hangout near the White House. As the grid collapses, they also recognize the need to get out of the major population center and return to Boston. But for Katie, work calls. She ignores her instructions to report to the Situation Room in the White House. She cannot, however, ignore the phone call from John Morgan with instructions to contact General Mason Sears, the chairman of the Joint Chiefs. Katie makes a choice to remain with Steven and loyal to her friends.

Katie is prepared for a bug-out scenario, and the two embark on a road trip through the Poconos toward Boston. They quickly learn that bugging out isn't easy, even when you are armed and prepared. They are attacked near a toll-booth exit and Steven is almost killed. Katie repels their assailants and nurses a badly injured Steven back to health.

But now their car is destroyed. Their gear and communications are lost. They only have their handguns and limited ammunition. They have to enter survival mode in a world without rule of law. Finding a car dealership, they commandeer a Range Rover and begin their trip northward. But another unexpected confrontation occurs.

Within miles of the last encounter, they see a young girl running in fear from a group of men who are chasing her through an industrial park. Steven and Katie give chase and save the girl, leaving four dead bodies in their wake.

At various junctures of their trip, the two meet people familiar with Sarge and his book. Some have tattoos of the Rebellious Flag—five red and four white vertical stripes. Several use the phrase *choose freedom* as a way of showing solidarity. Steven begins to see that Sarge's message is resonating throughout the country.

Finally, driving a FedEx delivery truck, the two make their way to Boston and the safety of 100 Beacon only to find it under assault by four Asian men. Steven, who quickly morphs into *Nomad*, despite his injuries, takes out the four attackers. The only thing standing between them and the top floors of 100 Beacon is a group of frightened residents firing wildly out of the front entrance. Not a problem for Nomad.

At Prescott Peninsula, the detailed preparedness plan implemented by Donald and Susan Quinn is on full display. They had successfully built a state-of-the-art bug-out facility on the old radio observatory site. J.J. and Sabina had grown close over the past several weeks and were officially a *couple.* Along with the Quinn's young girls, the four are enjoying a quiet Labor Day weekend away at the Quabbin Reservoir facility.

When the power goes out, the four are enjoying drinks and dinner in front of 1PP. Because of the lack of surrounding, ambient lighting, they don't realize the grid is down. Once they discover the situation, they begin to implement their preparedness plan.

Their first arrivals come in the form of the Morgan Sikorsky helicopter. Abbie is still upset over the loss of Drew and mourns for several days. As she calms down, Donald introduces Abbie and John Morgan to the sophisticated 1PP facility, which includes a gold and silver vault worth hundreds of millions of dollars.

Brad beefs up security at Prescott Peninsula. After a visit from a representative of Homeland Security, he senses that the President is about to declare martial law. Brad goes rogue and rallies the Mechanics led by Gunny Falcone, Chief Warrant Officer Shore, and First Lieutenant Branson. They systematically divert assets and like-minded troops to Prescott Peninsula. They are nearly at company strength in gear and numbers.

In the process of building up the military assets at Prescott Peninsula, Brad has to send a platoon to Boston. He gathers up the Boston Brahmin from 100 Beacon to take them safely to 1PP. Sabs, over J.J.'s objection, takes up the slack and joins the security detail at the gated entrance to the Quabbin Reservoir complex. In a confrontation with locals, she is shot.

J.J., with the assistance of Susan and Donald, tries valiantly to save his new love, to no avail. Sadly, Sabs dies on the table, together with his unborn baby, of which he has no knowledge. Susan and Donald wrestle with telling him, but the arrival of the Boston Brahmin and the upcoming address by the President puts the issue off for another day.

On the fifth night following the collapse, the President is set to speak to the nation through whatever means of communications are available. Susan overhears a conversation between two of the Boston Brahmin that leads her to believe there is something nefarious going on. Abbie, who has been having nightmares, finally comes to the realization of what happened the morning they left Drew behind. He was shouting, "He knew, he knew." *What did that mean?*

The President addresses the nation, but not with an uplifting message of hope and perseverance. It is divisive, condemning, and declarative. Through executive orders, the President quickly sets up a massive militaristic occupational force called the *Citizen Corps.* In conjunction with regional FEMA governors, the Citizen Corps will establish local Citizen Corps Councils that will fall under the control of the President and FEMA.

Then the President instructs General Sears to read the Declaration of Martial Law, which suspends the constitution and essentially revokes all freedoms guaranteed to American citizens by the Bill of Rights. *Freedom, liberty, and independence are lost.*

After General Sears reads the declaration, he receives a phone call from John Morgan. The four words that General Sears hears from John Morgan are plain and simple—yet chilling.

The end begins tomorrow.

Book Four: False Flag

As book four, False Flag opens, Sarge stands atop 100 Beacon alone, reflecting on the President's Declaration of Martial Law. In just a matter of days, the country was rapidly descending into collapse. He was surprised at how rapidly the President reacted to the events, and the level of governmental overreach contained in the Declaration.

But Sarge's thoughts were interrupted by a series of massive explosions as the Kendall Station Power Plant malfunctioned. The blasts rocked the city, and caused the collapse of the Longfellow Bridge. The deaths and casualties were numerous.

Julia insisted on helping the injured by volunteering at Massachusetts General Hospital. Unknowingly, she and Sarge assisted with a severely burned patient—Andrew Lau. Later, Katie and Steven discover that Lau is alive.

Prescott Peninsula, and 1PP, was now inhabited by The Boston Brahmin and their wives, the Quinn family, Abbie, and a platoon of Marines dispatched by Brad. J.J. was still distraught over the loss of Sabs, and insisted upon going back to 100 Beacon. News of the Kendall Station explosion gave him an excuse to leave.

As part of the President's Declaration of Martial Law, the former FEMA regions were re-designated to fall under the purview of the newly created Council of Governors appointed by the President. With the expansion of the Citizen Corps, the President named former Carmen's Union President, James O'Brien, as the new governor of Region One, which consisted of Massachusetts, and upper New England. His offices were in the FEMA location at 99 High Street overlooking the Boston Harbor.

O'Brien is thrilled at his new appointment, but not out of pride. He is an opportunist. He sees the collapse as an opportunity to enrich himself, and his friends. He also intends to right many perceived social wrongs. He surrounds himself with men willing to work outside the law to achieve this purpose.

The White House assigns for Federal Protective Services Agent, Joe Pearson, to be the liaison between O'Brien and the President. Pearson, who has had heated conversations with Brad on two prior occasions, is prepared to assist O'Brien achieve his goals.

However, for the more nefarious jobs, O'Brien enlists the employment of an old friend, and notorious Union thug, Marion La

Rue. La Rue orchestrated the walkout of the union transit workers during the St. Patrick's Day event last March. The walkout inadvertently led to the death of a black man named Pumpsie Jones, which caused social unrest throughout the city.

Pearson is tasked with training forty-four of O'Brien's trusted union associates. The first order of business is to raid all of the Massachusetts Guard Armories across the state. Via inside information, The Loyal Nine are aware of the details of the raids, and provide a surprise for O'Brien's men. Throughout the night, Steven and Katie coordinate ambushes of O'Brien's men using The Mechanics. They apprehend O'Brien's men and imprison them at Fort Devens under Brad's watchful eye.

O'Brien, thinking the men betrayed his trust, looked for an alternative to carry out his plans. He instructs La Rue to arrange a meeting with Joaquin Guzman, head of the El Salvadoran MS-13 gang, and Jarvis Rockwell, a/k/a J-Rock, heads of the unified black gangs in Boston. Their task is a simple one — loot. They are provided assurances that no one under O'Brien's command will impede them as they enter the wealthiest neighborhoods of Boston and take what they want.

Meanwhile, The Loyal Nine seek out an ally of their own to counteract O'Brien. They meet with John Willis — The White Devil, head of the Asian gangs in Chinatown. A celebrity of sorts, having been interviewed extensively by Rolling Stone magazine, Willis is hesitant to to deal with Sarge, Julia and Steven at first. But an alliance is formed for the purposes of thwarting MS-13 and the black gangs of Dorchester, Mattapan, and Roxbury.

The Loyal Nine also begin to organize their modern day insurgent arm — The Mechanics. Meeting under cover of darkness at the location of the original Liberty Tree, 630 Washington Street, Sarge and Steven rally their trusted militia. Steeped in historic precedent as the predecessors to the Sons of Liberty, The Mechanics are ordinary Bostonians who are answering the call of duty to protect and defend the Constitution and the United States.

At 1PP, Morgan, who is exhibiting signs of stress, grows

concerned that the President is ignoring his phone calls. Morgan advises the President that it is time to consider rebuilding the country but he is rebuked by the President, who responds "You'll make your money now let me finish what I started." The President is surly and combative, prompting Morgan to contact General Sears suggesting the nation was in a constitutional crisis. He seeks to remove the President from office, but Sears refuses such drastic action as a coup d'état.

Following the shooting death of Sabs at the front gate, the residents of Belchertown, located just west of Prescott Peninsula, became enraged. They insisted their newly appointment Chairman of the Board of Alderman, Ronald Archibald, take action. For Belchertown, supplies are quickly running out and there haven't been any new provisions from the Federal government in weeks. They are panicking. Partly out of revenge for the death of their neighbor, but mostly out of need, they concoct a plan to attack the inhabitants of Prescott Peninsula and confiscate their provisions.

O'Brien begins to suspect that Brad is working against him. After a brief period of mistrust (courtesy of Brad) in Agent Pearson, O'Brien enlists Pearson's support in contacting the White House for reinforcements in the form of a United Nations occupying force. Along with La Rue and Pearson, O'Brien watches as tanks, and artillery, together with thousands of U.N. soldiers roll off the ships lined up in Boston Harbor. "Boys, now I've got my army," he quips.

The Loyal Nine come together at Prescott Peninsula for the first time since the cyber attack. Their first order of business is trade notes on the events which led up to the power outage, and to make a determination of who is responsible. The conclusion becomes obvious — John Morgan.

Without notice to Abbie, Sarge is tasked with confronting Morgan with these facts. While Abbie and Steven watch, Morgan and his godson, Sarge, engage in an epic debate about the use of the cyber attack as a means to reset America from its downward path into economic and social collapse.

As the argument intensifies, Morgan suffers a stroke. J.J. is called in to assist and is successful in savings Morgan's life. After surviving the ordeal, and contemplating his future, Morgan calls in his trusted friends, Cabot and Lowell. Then Sarge is summoned to Morgan's bungalow. The conversation went like this:

"Come, sit with me, Henry," said Morgan, who took a deep breath before continuing. "I promised your father that you would do great things. I promised to be your guardian, your mentor, and protector. For all of these years, I have ushered you through life, keeping a watchful eye over you as if you were my son."

"Yes, sir, I know," said Sarge, who was welling up with emotion.

"I am not a dying man, but I am tired. A tired man can do nothing easily, and we still have work to do, Henry." Morgan attempted to push himself up again, and he was assisted by Sarge.

Morgan continued as he addressed the room. "I thank God that I have done my duty in upholding the ideals and vision of our forefathers. I've done all of the business I am capable of doing on this earth." He turned his attention to Sarge.

"Patriotism is not enough, Henry. I see compassion in you I never had. You recognize that our fellow man must not be forgotten."

Morgan again looked into the faces of the Boston Brahmin. "I intend to live, my friends. You can't dispatch me that easily.

"We must finish what we started, but it requires a younger man. It needs a different vision, one capable of looking beyond the creation of wealth, but to the creation of a new nation. My role now is that of teacher—the grand master to the student." He turned his attention to Sarge and struggled as he reached out to grasp his shoulder.

"It is time for me to step aside. The Boston Brahmin must be led by the next generation of patriots. Henry, I am entrusting you to take the reins and accept your destiny as the new head of the Boston Brahmin."

Book Five: The Mechanics

How do the weak vanquish the powerful?

Sarge takes the reigns and immediately decides to take the fight to Governor O'Brien and his new friends—the United Nations occupying forces. But first, they face the residents of nearby Belchertown as Ronald Archibald, the appointed Citizen Corps leader of the town, undertakes an ill-fated attempt to assault Prescott Peninsula.

Experience and preparation wins the day as Steven Sargent leads a gun battle on the waters of the Quabbin Reservoir which displays the benefit of planning and superior firepower. Brad's men are efficient in their ability to defend the shores of Prescott Peninsula and repel the three pronged attack. A valuable prisoner in the form of Archibald's son, is taken into custody and plays a pivotal role later.

With 1PP once again secured, The Loyal Nine now face the bigger threat posed by the tyrannical O'Brien and the UN *peacekeeping force.* Sarge is firm in his resolve when he announces to a secret meeting of The Mechanics, "Gentlemen, it's time to start poking the bear."

Using resources from Fort Devens, Brad and Steven undertake a two-pronged attack. The first was designed to distract the UN troops, as well as eliminate their superior firepower in the form of two assault helicopters. Brad retrieves Stinger missiles which were supposed to be used for a training exercise and decimates the air power of the UN.

During the attack at the Seaport District, UN troops are called away from their post at the Greater Boston Area Food Bank where Governor O'Brien was hoarding relief supplies for his own benefit. Steven liberates the food and hauls it away to be disbursed throughout the city.

Once again, The Mechanics prove themselves as a force for freedom, but there is still work to be done. Sarge, in his newfound position as head of The Boston Brahmin, begins to learn from the master—John Morgan. Morgan imparts his knowledge and experience upon his godson who learns the extent of The Boston Brahmin's wealth and power.

Morgan's intricate planning is paying off for his friends as he reveals to Sarge that The Boston Brahmin now control seventy percent of the gold mining operations in the world. With the collapse of the dollar and the world's economy, gold, coupled with political influence, will assist Sarge in his endeavors.

In the meantime, sitting Governor Charlie Baker attempts to reconvene the legislature. Men and women from across the state arrive at the Massachusetts State House, including Sarge and a security detail. Shortly into the Governor's speech, the detail notices something is wrong. They alert Sarge and barely escape as O'Brien and the UN troops storm the State House. Governor Baker and the legislature are taken hostage.

O'Brien proposes a swap. He offers the legislature and State House in exchange for his forty –four men being held prisoner at Fort Devens, which he wants as well. The proposed trade is to take place on November 8, Election Day.

After Sarge's announced *promotion* to head of The Boston Brahmin, a festering sibling rivalry began to form between Sarge and Steven. This conflict between the brothers was fueled in part by Steven's envy, but largely due to the inciting rhetoric of Katie. As Steven took the reins of The Mechanics, he formulated a plan to double-cross Governor O'Brien without Sarge's knowledge. It was going to be his opportunity to show John Morgan his worth.

On the day of the prisoner exchange, Steven covertly led his team into the State House with the intention of freeing the hostages. Unfortunately, two members of his team had ulterior motives. Isaac Grant and Rory Elkins conspired against Steven and during the mission, the cowardly Elkins stabbed Steven in the back.

Grant is killed, but Elkins slithered away into the bowels of the State House. Sarge reached Steven in time to hold his brother in the midst of a firefight. Fighting for his life, Steven managed to speak with Sarge.

"*Steven, I can't do this without you. Can you hold on?*" asked Sarge.

"*Fuck me. I can't feel anything.*" He coughed up more blood and grimaced. "*It's karma, you know.*"

"*What is?*" asked Sarge.

"*My whole life has been in the shadows. I killed, and they never saw it coming.*"

He coughed again and his eyes began to roll back in his head.

"I love you, brother," said Sarge, ducking as a rapid burst of bullets sailed over his head. "*Hold on for me.*"

Steven was whispering now. "*You know what they say?*"

"*What's that?*"

"*Karma is just a polite way of saying ha-ha, screw you.*"

And Steven slipped into the darkness.

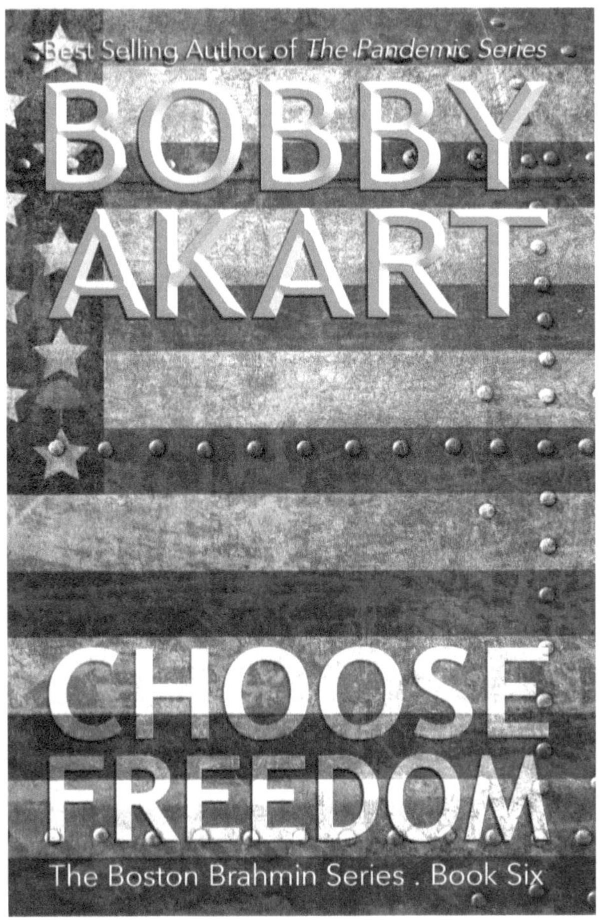

Book Six: Choose Freedom!

Following the death of his brother, Sarge buries him at sea and vows to avenge his murder. He addresses the issue of Katie's admitted betrayal by assigning her the task of hunting down the two men who betrayed the trust of The Mechanics.

The loss of Steven left a hole in Sarge's heart and also a gap in the group's operations. Sarge steps up as the leader of The Mechanics against everyone's protests, but he promises to rely heavily upon Donald as his chief advisor and Brad for military strategy.

As John Morgan recovers from his stroke, he and Sarge become closer. Morgan has mellowed and Sarge is anxious to take the reins of

The Boston Brahmin. The two men discuss how to use the considerable resources of The Boston Brahmin to facilitate the recovery of America. They both agree, however, that any approach to making a better post-collapse world starts at the local level, which means they most deal with the tyrannical Governor O'Brien and the United Nations occupation forces.

With the assistance of Drew Jackson who returns to Prescott Peninsula to the delight of Abbie, the Battle for Boston begins. By coordinating the resources of the New England states, Sarge marshals the regions assets to mount an offensive against the UN.

To her credit, Katie has stepped up and found the hideout of the elusive Gov. O'Brien. A surprise in the form of Andrew Lau was also uncovered and the two men were quickly placed in the stockades below 1PP. O'Brien was later exiled to Campobello Island in the frigid North Atlantic. Lau was give the option of death by firing squad, or joining The Loyal Nine in their fight against the President who has convinced four states to secede from the Union — Hawaii, California, Oregon, and Washington.

After the rest of the Zero Day Gamers were rounded up and provided a work space, every aspect of Sarge's plan was implemented. First, the United Nations forces were driven out of Boston. Next, Drew leads a team to recapture Logan Airport from the brutal MS-13 gang. This opened up New England to receive relief supplies from around the world via Sarge's efforts.

With New England under control, Sarge looked to the next aspect of the recovery effort — How to take the movement nationwide? He hopes to spread the success attained in New England to the southern states. This became a team effort and once again, it was successful with Sarge being given full credit for the turnaround.

The mid-Atlantic states of Virginia, Pennsylvania, and New York were a tougher nut to crack but by reaching across the political spectrum to the son of the deceased Vice President, Sarge successfully created an alliance which resulted in the tyrannical Mayor of New York being ousted.

Sarge's successes in the recovery effort did not go unnoticed by the President in Hawaii. Once easily manipulated by power and money, the President hoped to carve out his own fiefdom in the western states. He also chose to use the military power at his disposal to silence Sarge and quell the uprising led by The Loyal Nine.

He ordered a drone to destroy Prescott Peninsula. As the Predator was in route, Lau and the Zero Day Gamers discover the threat. After a brief debate, they jumped into action and diverted the drone into the ocean.

The recovery success spread into more states and Sarge's name became synonymous with the effort. At the Constitutional Convention in St. Louis arranged by Sarge, the majority of the states adopted sweeping reforms and the set the country on a new course. The Convention delegates were not able to keep the nation together as the Pacific states left to form their own nation under the leadership of the President.

An election was held in May and Sarge won an overwhelming victory as President. Two weeks later, he married his nine month pregnant love, Julia, in a ceremony at the Morgan estate which was also disrupted by an assassin.

The story closes with Julia giving birth to the Sargent's son, Henry Winthrop Sargent V, nicknamed *Win.* His trusted aide and protector, David Morrell, advised the President that it was time for him to perform another task.

The final excerpt from Choose Freedom …

Sarge paced the floor and circled Elkins, who could only follow Sarge's movements with his eyes. Sarge began to pepper him with questions, despite Elkins's inability to respond.

"*You didn't have to kill my brother. You had no cause to. Did you do it for money? To gain favor?*"

Elkins didn't move or attempt to speak. He sat there, his eyes growing wider as Sarge became more agitated. Sarge became angry. He'd waited so long for this opportunity to confront his brother's murderer.

From all sides, Sarge circled the solitary chair and began screaming at Elkins.

"*You're a traitor! A coward! You betrayed us all!*"

Sarge continued to circle.

"*You killed my brother!*"

Then, as quickly as the anger rose, it subsided. Sarge exhaled as he put his hands in his pockets. He stared at Elkins for another moment, then turned and walked toward the door. He reached for the metal handle and then caught himself.

He looked through the small glass window at his security detail, which waited outside. He shrugged his shoulders and chuckled to himself.

Sarge's family was upstairs—Julia, his loving wife and their newborn baby. He was in the home of his mentor—John Morgan—the man who helped guide him since the death of Sarge's dad.

His brother, Steven, was killed in cold blood by this treacherous murderer.

Sarge unbuttoned his jacket, reached for his shoulder holster, and removed Steven's gun, which he'd retrieved from Katie. As he gripped the handle, Steven's voice swirled through Sarge's mind. *Screw it.*

"*What the hell,*" muttered Sarge as he turned and shot Elkins between the eyes, unceremoniously toppling his dead, worthless soul to the concrete floor.

With that, Henry Winthrop Sargent IV started day one of his presidency.

Patriot's Farewell begins now …

Patriot's Farewell

A Boston Brahmin Novel

PROLOGUE

April 2018
Late Morning
King's Chapel Burying Ground
Boston, Massachusetts

Nobody likes funerals. Yet we plan them to honor our departed loved ones. Sometimes, with a little luck, the dearly departed provides detailed instructions on the type of procession they'd prefer. In other instances, it's up to the family, who often provides elaborate wakes, with multiple orators providing eulogies.

John Morgan succumbed to a heart attack within eighteen months of his life-threatening stroke while the Boston Brahmin sought refuge at Prescott Peninsula. Eighteen months was an eternity under the circumstances, but it was still fresh in his godson's mind.

Sarge, born Henry Winthrop Sargent IV, was not Morgan's son by birth, but he was in all other respects. On that fateful night, Sarge confronted Morgan, his mentor and benefactor, about the heinous cyber attack that brought down the power grid across most of the United States. The nation was thrown into chaos. Many millions died, a foreign army occupied the country's soil, and a battle brewed between a tyrannical president desperately trying to hold onto power and the self-declared protectors of the Constitution, the Loyal Nine and the Boston Brahmin.

The truth surrounding the cyber attack was only known to a few trusted friends of Sarge and certain members of the Boston Brahmin's executive council. The president, who was complicit in the act, was forced to remain silent on the matter for fear of being exposed. Plus, as a politician, he had his future to consider.

When Abigail Morgan, the only surviving daughter of John Morgan, asked Sarge to deliver the eulogy, he reluctantly accepted. She'd told Sarge that several world dignitaries would attend, as well as her father's closest friends, all of whom hinted at an opportunity to speak. But Abbie, who'd known Sarge most of her life, trusted him with the proper words. After all, words were Sarge's forte.

Fittingly, a slight drizzle fell over the beautifully maintained grounds of King's Chapel Burying Ground, the first cemetery in the city of Boston founded in 1630. Adjacent to King's Chapel, completed in 1754, the historic site lay in the shadow of Morgan's top-floor offices at 73 Tremont.

It was within 73 Tremont that Morgan played puppeteer to the world's financial and geopolitical affairs. He had a pulse on everything, especially U.S. politics. If there ever was a kingmaker, it was John Morgan. For what most people suspected but could never prove, an invisible hand of power actually existed over the world's political and financial affairs.

There existed in America a silent, unseen group of patriots, direct descendants of the Founding Fathers and the Sons of Liberty, who were made up of business leaders, politicians, former military officers, and philanthropists. They were everywhere and existed in every aspect of Americans' lives. The average person never saw them or paused to think about their activities, yet they saw the results their hands played in world affairs.

This group—the Boston Brahmin—revered their leader, John Morgan, and his carefully selected replacement, Sarge. For the first time, the world's most powerful group of geopolitical influence sat at the top of the throne through Morgan's godson, Sarge.

The funeral attendees filed out of the chapel building under a canopy of massive oak trees, which provided them some relief from the drizzle. The names were synonymous with New England aristocracy and the founding of our nation—Lowell, Cabot, Lodge, Winthrop, Peabody, Endicott, Bradlee, and Sargent.

Morgan's casket was ready to be lowered into a tomb adjacent to John Winthrop, the first Puritan governor of Massachusetts. Sarge glanced to both sides of the burial plots, wondering if there would be a space for him someday.

A man didn't know his place in history until his dying days when his work was done. Sarge had thought his life was destined to be spent teaching future political and business leaders at Harvard, but fate had other plans for his *back forty*—the term he used for the second half of his life.

To his right stood a solemn, pregnant Julia. She was eight months along with their second child but insisted upon leaving the White House to honor John Morgan—a man whom she had come to love as her father. The birth of their first son, Henry the fifth, as Sarge had quipped before the parents eventually settled on Win, short for Winthrop, came on the day of Sarge's inauguration as President of the United States. It was a joyous day that also had its dark moment.

Sarge had buried his brother, Steven, at sea the year before after he was murdered by a man who sought to endear himself to Governor James O'Brien, the tyrannical monster who used the collapse as a way to advance his power and control. On the first day of his presidency, Sarge ordered the scum to be executed—by Sarge's own hand.

In that moment, he changed. He was a natural born leader despite his humble beginnings as a professor and author. By speaking to the nation from the heart, espousing principles of limited government and freedom that he firmly believed in, Sarge led the nation out of despair.

But after he shot the lowlife who killed his brother, a steely cold resolve came over Sarge. He embraced the tough, sometimes brutal methods used by his brother. This new weapon in his arsenal would serve him well over time.

Abbie squeezed Sarge's hand, indicating it was time to begin. He hadn't prepared a eulogy. His attempts to write one failed him. Draft after draft was crumpled up and thrown in the general direction of the trash can. He could've called upon any of his talented speechwriters within his communications team to create the proper words, but then they wouldn't be his.

He was ready to deliver his remarks, but before he spoke, Sarge recalled the final words spoken by Morgan the evening before his fateful heart attack.

"Henry"—as Morgan always referred to Sarge—"nothing lasts forever. Not power, not wealth, and certainly not life itself. This is why we must make the most of the time we have on this earth. Why would one want to waste their life in creating the perfect epitaph on their gravestone—*fondly remembered* or some such? That's nothing more than sentimental incontinence.

"Face it, young man. Life is a zero-sum game and politics dictates winners and losers. Throughout my life, I've been an active participant in the game and I'm proud of what I've accomplished. Now, it's your turn.

"As you fulfill your dreams, build your family and take over the great responsibilities that I've placed upon you, don't strive for a monumental whimper such as *respected by all who knew him.* It's not respect that motivates a man to follow your lead. It's fear. That's how revolutions begin and empires are built.

"When a man is afraid, you can crush him. Thereafter, you'll gain his respect. Instilling fear in a man is intoxicating and liberating, and always an emotion much stronger than respect. Do not forget this, Henry."

After these final words, John Morgan fell asleep, never to wake again.

Sarge shuddered from the dampness of the rain and the slight breeze that blew over him. He looked into the faces awaiting him to speak. He wasn't sure what their expectations were. Some wanted Sarge to explain Morgan's actions that initiated the collapse. Others wanted him to heap praise upon their associate and friend. He shook off the chill of the weather and the ghosts who surrounded him and began.

"John Morgan belongs to the ages now …"

PART ONE

The Monday before Thanksgiving

Six and a half years later—November 2024

CHAPTER 1

6:00 a.m.
The National Mall
Washington, DC

Sarge jogged through the west gate of the White House grounds with an entourage of Secret Service personnel. Running helped him sleep at night, but it also kept him disciplined. As president, Sarge learned the value of time. His brain never rested, as the burdens of America and the world weighed upon him. The oldest form of exercise known to man became a part of his morning routine the day after the First Family moved into the repaired and renovated White House.

The dark days after the collapse of the power grid had taken its toll on Washington, DC, in more ways than one. Vandals and looters, mad at their politicians and the world in general, took to the streets. Chaos reigned within the beltway for a year before order was restored.

Now, in his final months of an abbreviated two-term presidency, Sarge cherished the opportunity to run through the National Mall, taking in the sights and sounds of a revitalized city. He varied his routes through the historic grassy plaza, which was home to iconic monuments, including the Lincoln Memorial and the Washington Monument.

After the power grid collapsed, madness overtook the population of the District. These tributes to American history were defaced, torn down, and in some cases destroyed entirely. The beautiful cherry trees that had lined the reflecting pool were butchered or uprooted out of maliciousness.

Members of the National Guard had done their best to protect the historical artifacts within the Smithsonian museums before a herculean effort was made to remove them to safety in the mountains of West Virginia.

Fierce battles had raged as dedicated military personnel protected the White House, the Capitol, and the Supreme Court building. Only the establishment of a FEMA regional government and an extraordinary amount of relief supplies calmed the locals down. But eventually, as was the case with the other FEMA regions, the citizens demanded their government back.

Sarge was credited for bringing peace to Washington, DC, and the rest of the nation. He started from the bottom up. He encouraged local and state governments to reestablish their relationships with their constituents. Americans knew their local elected officials on a personal level, which ensured their trust in the efforts taken to restore order. Once trust in government was established, authority over the citizenry was accepted.

Just as the Constitution and the Founding Fathers intended, these local grassroots efforts expanded to the state level. Soon, the regional FEMA officials inserted by the federal government were removed and the nation was on the road to recovery.

Life in the political fishbowl changed after that unusual election following the collapse. The nation came together and party differences were set aside as Sarge guided the nation back onto solid footing. After the scheduled midterm elections of 2018, the honeymoon was over and the struggle for political power began once again.

Sarge learned what a real political campaign was like. Abbie had forewarned him. As the vice presidential candidate prior to the collapse, she'd been through the trenches.

A typical campaign day, Abbie said, was like *Groundhog Day*. "You listen to yourself say the same things over and over until your brain starts to rebel, encouraging you to make random, crazy alterations to your stump speech. While this might amuse you in some way, it would make you appear crazy to the media, and that is unacceptable. Our political candidates are expected to be perfect, not a fallible human being like the rest of the electorate."

There was an upside to campaigning, which he discovered during his quest for re-election. Day after day, for a dozen weeks during the final sprint of the endurance race until Election Day, Sarge bathed in a sea of love. Whether he was addressing the deafening cheers of crowds filling a park in Orlando, Florida, or inside an airplane hangar in Oshkosh, Wisconsin, it had all been the same—hundreds of thousands of ordinary Americans who celebrated the fact that Sarge, one of them, had ascended to the presidency and succeeded.

The love hadn't quite been universal, of course. There were those who criticized his approach to the recovery. Many lamented Sarge using the occasion of the collapse to rewrite several laws, setting the country's social justice agenda back several decades. Sarge was quick to remind them that he didn't invent the phrase *never let a good crisis go to waste*.

Sarge shook off the chill and the memories of the past eight years as he ran along the still waters of the reflecting pool toward the Lincoln Memorial. Yet he couldn't help but recall the quote that was often misattributed to President Lincoln: "America will never be destroyed from the outside. If we falter and lose our freedoms, it will be because we destroyed ourselves."

President Lincoln never delivered this quote precisely as it has been used over time, but the point he made at an educational institution in 1838 was prophetic. America wasn't brought to its knees by a larger, more powerful nation. It was hastened toward an inevitable collapse by the cyber attack that collapsed the grid. But make no mistake, America was a nation in decline socially, morally, and economically. It was just a matter of time because, as Sarge firmly believed, *all empires collapse eventually*.

As Sarge jogged past the large statue of Lincoln, he rehashed the intentions of his mentor, John Morgan, as it related to the *reset*. Morgan, like Sarge, saw the fabric of American society descending into the abyss. The country was destined for societal and economic collapse. Morgan thought a triggering event, the cyber attack, would hasten the collapse, but the nation could then get a fresh start within the principles established by the Founding Fathers.

At the time, his actions seemed reprehensible, but in hindsight, after eight years of Sarge's presidency and leadership, the nation had come back on stronger footing. Sarge was leaving the nation to the new administration in the best fiscal condition in its history. For the most part, the wounds of a divided populace had healed. The recovery effort had brought folks back together. The partisan bickering and sniping prior to the collapse had given way to a spirit of cooperation and a focus on the important things in life.

"Mr. President," interrupted Captain David Morrell, the head of Sarge's security detail. Morrell, a former Marine and part of the protection unit assigned to Prescott Peninsula, had become close friends with Sarge and a constant companion. Despite their friendship, Morrell always referred to Sarge in a manner befitting the president. "Sir, we need to alter your route this morning. Protestors are gathering near the front gate, and with the light traffic on the Mall this morning, you'll be seen."

"Okay, Dave," said Sarge, who glanced at his watch. "This is gonna be a big week and we certainly don't need the aggravation to get it started, do we?"

"No, sir. Let's double back and we'll reenter the White House grounds the way we came. I've already alerted the team."

The shouts began to get louder as Sarge could see the sign-holding protestors gathering along the wrought-iron fence surrounding the White House lawn. The chants and shouts reminded Sarge that not everything was unicorns and rainbows across the fruited plain. It was still, in part, a protestor nation.

CHAPTER 2

7:00 a.m.
The Family Residence
The White House
Washington, DC

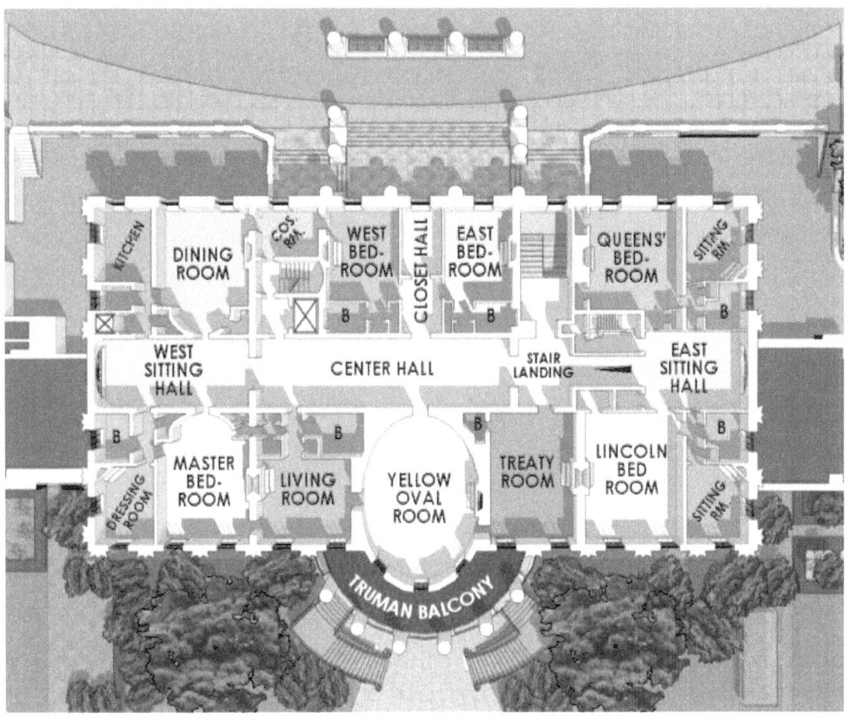

The president's residence is the center structure of the White House Complex, the most famous building in the world. The White House consists of three major parts including the East Wing, the West Wing, and the presidential mansion, or Executive Residence. The second and third floors of the mansion were the private quarters of the First Family and for their guests.

Sarge and Julia's family had expanded with the birth of Win on that first inauguration day. Win was now seven and declared himself to be the *big-brother-in-chief* of his two siblings. Rose was born five years ago following Morgan's funeral, and Francis, who at age three had a mind of his own, was the First Family's youngest. This youngster, who insisted upon being called Frank, was Steven Sargent reincarnated. Basically, he was a walking, talking middle finger without Steven's vocabulary.

The family dynamic was not unlike any other family with three children. Raising three kids was not simply a matter of creating and keeping alive two kids plus one. Four is a tidy number, ask any restaurant with tables that seat four people. A family of four is simple. One parent gets a child, and so does the other one. But who gets the third?

Sarge and Julia made it a point to find time with each child although Sarge admitted having difficulty relating to Rose. She was not a daddy's girl. For Sarge, raising Win was easy. He was his *mini-me.* He could look into little Frank's eyes and see his brother and the future that was in store for the toddler. But with Rose, he stared into his wife's eyes, and Julia, at age three, stared back.

Growing up in the limelight was far from easy. The White House was an office, a museum, a place for gatherings and social events, but many tended to forget it was a home to the First Family.

When President and Mrs. John F. Kennedy moved into the White House, they had young Caroline, who was four, and John-John was a baby. They were the youngest children to live in the White House until President Sargent moved in with Julia and Win. Both Rose and Frank were the first babies to be born in the Executive Residence.

Sarge did the best he could to help raise their children. He kept a strict routine when he was in residence. Following his run, he'd join the family for breakfast and assisted Julia in getting the kids' day started. At night, unless his duties kept him away late, he'd make every effort to tuck the kids in bed, which often included a family bedtime story. Sarge knew his days in public life would come to an end and he didn't intend to lose contact with his children during their formative years.

"Good morning, Rose," said Sarge as he leaned down to plant a kiss on his daughter's cheek. He was still sweating from his run and she quickly let him know about it.

"Daddy!" she squealed. "So yucky! So rude!"

"But," Sarge attempted to protest, "I love you and I missed you during my run." His attempts to tease her fell on deaf ears. She began to swat him with a cloth napkin.

"Yucky!" she shouted again as she tried to pull away from Sarge's smooch.

"Dear," said Julia, coming to the rescue of her distraught five-year-old, "how about a quick shower and then you can join us for breakfast? We've got a busy week ahead of us."

Sarge poured himself a glass of orange juice and took a long drink. Unlike prior presidents, the Sargents insisted on serving themselves breakfast. Julia, under the careful tutelage of Susan Quinn, learned to cook. Not that cooking was a difficult task necessarily, but the menu required to satisfy three young appetites and keep their interest was far different from what adults enjoy. Over time, Julia loosened her grip on the meal preparation and allowed the White House kitchen staff to prepare lunches and dinners, but breakfast was still their family time alone.

"Aren't they always?" said Sarge with an eye roll. "Tell me, *director of all things social* here at the White House, what's the week look like?"

Julia wiped a mess of oatmeal off little Frank's mush and replied, "We don't have that many weeks left, and I know there's a lot going on with you, of course. Anyway, we have the Governor's Ball tonight. The turkey pardon ceremony on Wednesday. Thanksgiving, we're hosting the Boston Brahmin and their families. Not to mention the vote and any schmoozing you'd like me to assist you with. You know I can be quite charming with the senators."

Sarge smiled and attempted to kiss his wife, who also grimaced from his sweatiness. *Like daughter, like mother*, he thought to himself. They would only occupy the White House for another eight weeks, but there were significant social and legislative matters to attend to in a short period of time.

The vote, as Julia called it, related to the one loose end of Sarge's presidency. It was a failure on his part, and by the standards of many pundits. After eight years, the Union was still divided.

Prior to his election as president, Sarge and the Loyal Nine orchestrated a Constitutional Convention in St. Louis to address the issues of rebuilding America, certain changes in the Constitution to make the nation more economically viable and socially conscious, and the matter of the previous president who had overstayed his welcome.

Following the collapse, the president had marshalled federal relief and recovery assets to the states bordering the Pacific Ocean—Hawaii, California, Oregon, and Washington. He'd bought their loyalty and they quickly moved to secede from the United States.

One of Sarge's goals at the Constitutional Convention had been to bring these four states back into the fold, but his attempts fell short. Throughout his presidency, he worked diligently to persuade the state governments to consider the history of the nation first, to set aside their differences, and return to the Union. They refused without their demands being met.

The conditions insisted upon by the four states were both monetary and social in nature. They were at odds with the social values of the majority of the country, and the economic advantages they sought would be unfair to the other states. Moreover, as a condition of reunification, they wanted their specific demands enacted into federal law.

Sarge didn't negotiate with terrorists and these demands felt similar. He imposed a number of methods ranging from sanctions to psychological operations on the citizens of each state to achieve reunification. The methods didn't work and now his hand was being forced.

Congress was prepared to vote on a bill that would be a total capitulation to the conditions requested by the four states. In Sarge's opinion, the Pacific Statehood Act of 2024 was a terrible proposal and would likely result in a political civil war.

"I'll get cleaned up and join you guys," Sarge said, snapping his mind away from the daunting task ahead.

Sarge finished his shower and considered his attire for the day. He didn't always wear a suit during working hours unless he was meeting with foreign dignitaries. Tonight, he'd put on a tux for the Governor's Ball. He glanced out the window and saw a few snow flurries. *Winter is coming early this year.*

Early on in his presidency, Sarge became the brunt of media criticism for his casual dress. One former press secretary wrote, "When you have a dress code in the Supreme Court and a dress code on the floors of the House and Senate, one would think it is appropriate to have an expectation there will be a dress code that respects the office of the president."

Sarge disagreed, to an extent. "When in the people's house," Sarge opined, somewhat mocking the former press secretary, "one should be dressed like the people. However, when one engages other heads of state, one should dress appropriately."

He'd learned not to care what people thought of him. He was his own man. Sarge pulled on a pair of khakis, an LL Bean plaid shirt, and his Sperry Topsiders. Sarge looked very much like the populist president who was elected twice by landslide margins despite the disapproval of some.

CHAPTER 3

8:00 a.m.
The West Wing
The White House
Washington, DC

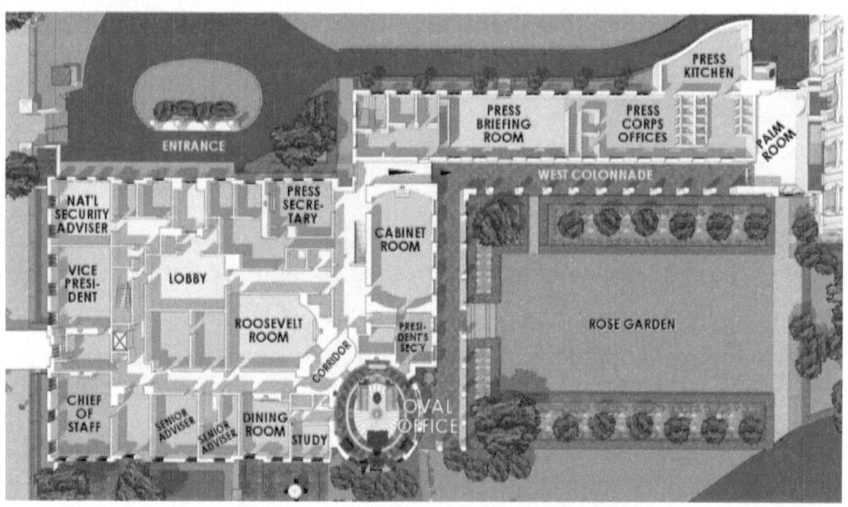

Sarge entered the West Wing from the West Colonnade. Most days, he made this walk alone, gathering his thoughts before he made his way to the heart of the American government.

He passed the windows of the former press corps offices to his right. Now they were used by White House staffers after Sarge ordered the media kicked out of the building. During those initial months in the White House, his presidency was beleaguered by leaks, which were quickly pounced upon by the former president and his loyalists. Some of the leaks were by design, but most were nosy reporters working overtime to eavesdrop on conversations or the comings-and-goings of White House visitors. Soon, reporters' suppositions became fact. The story would grow legs and the White House communications team had to work overtime to dispel rumors and deny conjecture. Sarge recalled asking the question of his team, *how do you disprove a lie?*

When the announcement was made to remove them from the West Wing, naturally the press screamed and threw a fit. In the end, they accepted their fate, and the move was made to the Old Executive Office Building, where there was more room to work. The additional space also allowed for more participants in the daily briefings above the original forty-nine seats in the press briefing room.

For Sarge, it was a welcome relief from the spotlight, which he never sought. The West Wing was no longer crawling with prying reporters. The leaks stopped, except for their own carefully orchestrated releases, and his message was strategically presented to the public. Moreover, for the most part, he was always surrounded by friendly faces. He learned early on, the media was not his friend despite the incredible hurdles he'd overcome in restoring America to its former greatness. Neither were holdovers from the prior administration—career White House staffers who knew the operations of the facility, but who remained loyal to the previous president.

As Sarge approached the West Wing, a member of his security team opened the door and he was immediately surrounded by the normal buzz of activity.

"Good morning, Mr. President," said one staffer nonchalantly as she hustled down the corridor toward the Roosevelt Room.

Sarge returned the greeting to the young woman's back, who was gone in a flash. Sarge took in his surroundings. There seemed to be an added level of tension in the air. A sigh here and a withdrawn look there indicated the White House staff was exhausted. The West Wing crew could only be in a frenzy over one thing, and it wasn't the upcoming Thanksgiving festivities. It was the vote.

It wasn't surprising to Sarge, as there was a renewed sense of urgency within the White House following the election of a new president three weeks ago. Naturally, Sarge, on behalf of the Boston Brahmin, whom he still led, got their candidate elected. The president-elect, Stanford Rawlins, was a Southern democrat governor from South Carolina who had helped bring the coalition of southeastern states into the fold during the Constitutional Convention of 2017. He understood his role and came with the highest recommendations from new allies Sarge had forged over the years. More importantly, he met with the approval of the executive committee of the Boston Brahmin.

Despite his best efforts, he was unable to convince Abbie, his logical successor, to run for the highest office. As vice president, she was hugely popular around the country and had been an integral part of the recovery effort. Although Sarge made a good case for her running, she chose to seek a life with her new husband, Drew Jackson, and their soon-to-be-born baby.

The frantic activity in the White House that Monday morning was a natural result of the change in the political climate in America. Anytime leadership changes, there's sure to be more than enough chaos to go around in the final days. President-elect Rawlins was bought and paid for with Boston Brahmin influence, both cash and in-kind. There was still a transition process, and appearances had to be maintained.

Although the Boston Brahmin were pleased with their new president, it was the change in the makeup of Congress that had Sarge's benefactors concerned, or at least some of them. The hot-button issue in the recently held election was the reunification of the fifty states. After several years of successes, some states were falling back into the old ways that had brought America to the brink of collapse. These states were sending a whole new slate of legislators to Washington who would look favorably upon the Pacific Statehood Act.

Sarge effectively postponed a vote on the act until after the election three weeks ago in order to avoid his like-minded members of Congress from having to vote against a bill that was rapidly gaining steam among the electorate. With the vote coming up during Thanksgiving week, he hoped it wouldn't garner the normal press attention.

Sarge's goal was simple. He thought something of this magnitude should be voted on by all of the states at another Constitutional Convention. It was too big an issue to leave to the political bickering and backroom deals made in Congress. He felt like he could control this Congress and the vote. The next Congress would be another matter.

As he continued down the corridor, Sarge briefly poked his head into his secretary's office to say good morning before he made a beeline to speak with the man who was making sure the vote went their way this week, his Chief of Staff, Donald Quinn.

CHAPTER 4

8:30 a.m.
The West Wing
The White House
Washington, DC

"Mr. President, just a reminder that the morning briefing is in thirty minutes in the Roosevelt Room," said Betty Greer, his secretary of eight years. Betty had been a longtime employee of John Morgan's at 73 Tremont. Completely trustworthy, she was intimately familiar with the business and financial dealings of the Boston Brahmin. Betty and Morgan's aide-de-camp, Malcolm Lowe, had bugged out to Lowe's family home on the Cape during the crisis. Together with members of the Lowell family, the group had found protection from the military units situated at Camp Edwards.

"Thank you, Betty."

Sarge continued down the hallway toward the end of the West Wing, where the Chief of Staff's suite was situated. Donald's team was responsible for everything. They selected and supervised the White House staff. They managed communications and information flow to the media.

Donald carefully guarded access to Sarge, and in the process the Chief of Staff's office became the mouthpiece on most occasions for the White House when negotiating with Congress, executive branch agencies, and external political groups that desired to affect Sarge's agenda.

Several staffers huddled around the doorway to one of Sarge's senior advisors, temporarily blocking his access to the end of the hallway. Because of Sarge's casual attire and lack of an entourage following him, other than Morrell, his ever-present shadow, they didn't acknowledge him in their hurried state of mind.

"Good morning, everyone," said Sarge as he squeezed his way through the group.

Voice recognition kicked in, causing the foursome to fall over themselves to greet the president. Sarge laughed to himself as they reacted. After eight years, it was still difficult for him to accept that he would be treated like a celebrity. Most of the staff in the West Wing had been with him since the move to Washington. He knew them all on a first-name basis. Yet they still seemed giddy with excitement as he greeted them.

All but one of them, anyway. Sarge called her the Gatekeeper. Initially, he'd called her the Crypt Keeper, but Donald cautioned Sarge that she might be insulted if she overheard him. Donald's secretary, Louise McDowell, was a warrior. Now approaching seventy, she had worked in every administration since President Reagan. Donald and Sarge often joked about who was really running things in Washington. The answer always came back the same—*Louise.*

Sarge approached her desk cautiously, being careful not to make any sudden moves. Louise was focused upon a computer printout, firmly and decisively either checking off an item or scratching an item off a list.

"Um, good morning, Louise. Is he in?"

"I'll be glad to check for you," she replied dryly. Without making eye contact, she spun around in an office chair that was nearly as old as her tenure in the government's service, and entered Donald's office. After a moment, she returned to her desk.

"He's available, Mr. President. You may go in now."

Sarge chuckled to himself. He was never able to determine if Louise was miserable in her job, gloomy in general, or simply a no-play, all-work kinda woman. Either way, it would be one of the world's unsolved mysteries.

He poked his head into Donald's office and found his best friend talking on the phone. Donald, who had aged more than any of them in the last eight years, had grown slightly more rotund and was now wearing glasses full time. His receding hairline was kind enough to leave him some salt-and-pepper gray around the sides of his head.

He waved Sarge in and motioned for him to close the door behind him. After a moment, he completed his call and Sarge took a seat in a Queen Anne chair across from his desk.

Sarge pointed a thumb over his shoulder. "She hates me. I'm convinced of it."

"No, she doesn't. She's like that with everybody."

"Yeah, but I'm the president. Shouldn't she at least pretend to like me?"

Donald leaned back in his chair and laughed, causing his belly to shake with each chuckle. "Listen, *Mr. President*," he said sarcastically, "you know what it's like around here. Louise is a better gatekeeper than a six-foot-six sumo wrestler. I wanna remind you of this. If they can't get to me, they can't get to you. Right or wrong?"

Sarge hesitated before responding. He loved Donald Quinn like a brother. After Steven's death, Donald stepped in and became Sarge's right arm, and left arm, for that matter. Donald had navigated them through the Constitutional Convention, Sarge's election, and during those early, difficult days of setting the nation on a course of recovery. After several years, when America reached a sense of normalcy, Donald was a seasoned veteran and a very effective Chief of Staff.

"I suppose." Sarge looked at the four presentation easels that were lined up in front of the windows overlooking the South Lawn. On each easel was a large flip pad with Donald's handwritten list of congressman and senators. His office had been turned into a war room of sorts for the upcoming vote on Pacific statehood. The next three days would be incredibly busy for Donald, and Sarge knew his friend would be stressed.

Sarge stood and approached the easels. He carefully flipped through the pages and studied the names. Those written in black were clearly for the bill; those in red, his allies in Congress, were against it.

Donald joined him to explain the charts. "The red names, as you can probably see, are going to back you in voting against the bill. As of this morning, if everyone holds, the bill will easily die in the House."

"Political alliances aren't as clearly defined as they were before the collapse," said Sarge. "The country became split into four parties, with libertarians and socialists splintering off from the republican and democrat labels."

"That turned out to be a good thing. It got you elected twice."

"Well, it certainly helped me garner traditionally democrat votes. Once the far left of the Democratic Party pulled away into the socialist wing, moderate dems felt comfortable and readily joined libertarians in supporting me. I'm amazed at how quickly the makeup of Congress has swung back to the left."

Donald nodded and returned to his desk. "That's why we need to keep a pulse on this vote. The opinions regarding reunification transcend party lines. Congress is all over the place on this one. Anyway, it's time for the morning brief. Let's not be tardy, Mr. President."

Sarge turned and Donald handed him his iPad Pro contained within a leather-bound BookBook case. The days of ring binders were over. Despite the pitfalls of cyber intrusions in a digital age, the White House was going paperless.

The iPad also contained Donald's checklist, something he'd picked up from studying the history of the Kennedy White House. President Kennedy had devised a daily briefing book that included an eight-by-eight-inch packet, with a dozen matters to be accomplished during the meeting. Each checklist item contained a paragraph summary together with maps, as needed.

Donald created the same thing for Sarge in Apple Pages, a program on the iPad Pro. Sarge could quickly thumb through the topics to be addressed, and if he was interested in further background, there were clickable links to other sections of the document.

Sarge carried it with him throughout the day. The briefing

changed from a once-a-day production-and-brief-engagement report or checklist, to continuous, near-real-time virtual support for the president. The team of staffers assembled in the old press cubicles constantly brought the briefing up to date, providing Sarge a pulse on world and domestic events.

As usual, he had precious little free time as he glanced at his schedule. About the only moments of his day without someone in the Oval Office with him were those few when he read over briefing documents for the next meeting, many of which were planned weeks in advance.

This week, however, was different. Another quick glance at the schedule showed that today and tomorrow allowed for no light moments. There were no World Series champs to host. No Eagle Scouts from Texas. Miss Idaho Potato wasn't coming to the White House for a photo op. No, today and tomorrow would be all about the vote.

CHAPTER 5

9:00 a.m.
The Roosevelt Room
The White House
Washington, DC

The windowless Roosevelt Room served as a daily meeting location for the White House staff and the president's briefings. It had been upgraded over the last several years to include a wall of televisions and a large screen for multimedia presentations. Sarge often used this platform to conduct video conferences with foreign leaders.

Unlike other presidents who enjoyed traveling abroad to conduct summits that were largely for media consumption, Sarge preferred to stay closer to home in the safety of the White House. There had been three attempts to assassinate Sarge.

The first attempt had come when the former president ordered a drone strike to annihilate their bug-out location at the Quabbin Reservoir in central Massachusetts. The second attempt came on his wedding night when Drew Jackson thwarted an assassin. The third was during a rally at a re-election campaign event.

Sarge was popular enough in America to govern effectively. He didn't need to create media shows in so-called swing states to artificially boost his poll numbers.

The two men chatted as they made their way to the Roosevelt Room. Early on, once they had moved into the White House, Donald suggested the daily briefings be divided into two parts for the sake of time efficiency. Every day at 9:00, the Presidential Daily Brief, or PDB for short, took place in the Roosevelt Room and focused on national security issues. The briefing usually lasted around thirty minutes and was attended by key members of the national security team. Afterwards, Donald and Sarge would move to the Oval Office to meet with the communications team to discuss domestic issues.

Producing and presenting the daily brief was the responsibility of the director of National Intelligence, whose office was tasked with fusing intelligence from the Central Intelligence Agency, the Defense Intelligence Agency, the National Security Agency, the Federal Bureau of Investigation and other members of the U.S. intelligence community.

Past administrations preferred to hold this meeting in the Situation Room, but Sarge preferred to have instant access to members of his staff in the event an issue warranted it.

The doors to the Roosevelt Room were open and the national security team was settling into their seats. As Sarge entered, he immediately saw his chairman of the Joint Chiefs—General "Brad" Bradlee, one of the Loyal Nine.

"Hey, Brad! What brings you into the lion's den?" Sarge asked as the two men shook hands.

"Good morning, Mr. President. I wanted to see how my protégé, Frank, was coming along with his training," said Brad, who had been elevated to the rank of general shortly after Sarge's election so that he could assume the position of the president's most trusted military advisor.

Further, Brad was charged with the responsibility of bringing the military together despite the split created by the defection of the four Pacific Coast states. The United States military had a huge presence in Hawaii and on the West Coast. Brad's job was difficult because the military bases were on sovereign U.S. soil and not subject to the claim of any state. There were some very tense moments in that first year during the power struggle between the former president and Sarge's administration. Brad was widely applauded by his military peers and politicians for preventing World War III from occurring between elements of the American military.

Sarge leaned into Brad's ear and whispered, "If Julia hears you talk like that, she'll string us up by the privates. Do you hear me, Marine?"

"Sir, yes, sir!" Brad said with a big grin. "Besides, I'm not sure I'll have time to check in on the little soldier today. We've got a situation brewing that I'll tell you about in a moment. Would you tell Julia that I will be coming on Thursday for dinner?"

"Absolutely, Brad."

Donald checked his watch and urged his friends to take seats. Monday was the busiest briefing day and he wanted to stay focused on the vote.

The director of National Intelligence began the meeting. He covered all of the usual topics, including terrorist activities by ISIS, military maneuvers by the Russians, North Korea's nuclear program, and increased tensions between Iran and Israel.

Sarge shook his head as he listened to the briefing and scrolled through Donald's checklist. After restoring the power and getting the country on its feet, it seemed like geopolitical affairs were quickly back to normal. Terrorism didn't end because America was knocked to its knees. The Russians didn't stop their posturing because they couldn't posture back. The nation most impacted by the cyber attack besides the United States was China.

America was the largest importer of Chinese goods by far. Following the collapse, the demand for consumer goods shrank to nothing for almost two years. As the country regained its footing, lack of income prevented demand for new products. The economic depression that naturally occurred following the collapse of the power grid was felt for several years until just before Sarge's re-election.

As the economy began to mount its recovery, the nation became more focused on the manufacturing and production of consumer goods. Labor laws were rewritten, overly burdensome environmental regulations were discarded, and tort reforms were instituted in the legal system to keep the costs to businesses low. As a result, goods could now compete with foreign manufacturers, namely China.

Under the guise of the recovery process, Sarge effectively manipulated the world economy to become less reliant on Chinese products, which caused their influence on the world stage to diminish. The result was a distinct chill in U.S.-China relations.

"Ambassador James McBride will be making a visit to Taiwan this week to finalize our one-point-five-billion-dollar arms deal with the Taiwan government," said Donald. "He'll be meeting with senior officials of the government, several key business leaders, and will address the Legislative Yuan on Wednesday."

"No doubt the Chinese will be making a statement about the arms deal, which I approved prior to the election," said Sarge. The package included early warning radar, high-speed anti-radiation missiles, torpedoes, and defensive missile components. "I've tried to explain to President Xi Jinping that we're simply supporting Taiwan's ability to maintain a sufficient self-defense capability in the region. I've also asked Ambassador McBride to stress there was no change to our long-standing One China policy, which recognizes Beijing and not Taipei. But as we all know, even the Chinese, it's political BS and has been for decades."

"General Bradlee, do you have something to add?" asked Sarge.

"I do, Mr. President," Brad began. "I've been in contact with my counterpart in the Taiwanese military. He thanks you for your support and he expressed real confidence in Taiwan's ability to maintain the status quo of peace and stability across the Taiwan Strait. But he did caution me on something, which, frankly, I'm surprised the CIA has not brought up today."

Sarge glanced at the deputy director of the CIA, who shifted uncomfortably in her seat. Brad had no use for the CIA, either before or after the collapse. Even with Sarge as president, Brad's distrust for the accuracy of the information presented at these briefings was obvious. Brad had stated his reasons for concern to Sarge many times—the CIA considered themselves a government in and of themselves.

"Go ahead, Brad," Sarge encouraged him to continue.

"Sir, the Taiwan military has seen an increase in political protests in Taipei City. According to my conversations with their military brass, there are elements within the Taiwan government who are tired of what is perceived to be American meddling in its nation's affairs."

"Brad, don't all foreign nations have this inherent belief? For as long as we've been a superpower, we've reached out to assist other countries, or they've come to ask for help. The United States has always been there. Eventually, memories fade and the claws come out. Shall I use Germany as an example? Can anyone doubt that it was largely through American efforts that we saved Germany from Hitler, and after the war, from the Russians? But now look at how they disrespect our country."

"I can't disagree with the premise, Mr. President," said Brad. "All I can do is relay the concerns of my counterparts. There appears to be a boil on the butt of a large part of the Taiwanese people. It might be instigated by the Chinese, or it could be organic."

"Okay, thank you, Brad," said Sarge. "Please keep those channels of communication open, and I'd ask the CIA to look into this further. We still have the greatest intelligence apparatus in the world. I don't need any surprises on this."

CHAPTER 6

9:45 a.m.
The Oval Office
The White House
Washington, DC

The Oval Office had been the sanctuary of eighteen U.S. Presidents since it was built in 1909. Each new occupant was able to stamp his own style on the décor. Three eleven-foot-tall windows overlook the South Lawn and the Oval Office patio. Sarge insisted on bringing his pride and joy—a nineteenth-century partner's desk crafted from oak, with tooled leather inserts and decorated with brass appointments. The desk had been a gift to Winthrop Sargent Gilman when he opened the banking house of Gilman, Son & Co. in New York City around the time the Oval Office was added. It had been passed down through the years to his father, and then to Sarge.

When Sarge entered the Oval Office for the first time, he knew it was by fate and not design. He had never contemplated a life in politics, but the circumstances the nation faced required someone with his unique skills and power. He had entered the most challenging job in the history of the nation since its founding, knowing that he would not always make perfect decisions or say all the right words. His goal was to stay true to his principles. He'd say many times in those early years, when in doubt, *choose freedom.*

Now, eight weeks away from retirement, Sarge sought to leave the country on the best possible footing for his successor. The vote on the Pacific Statehood Act was an important step in bringing the nation together again, but under the right circumstances.

Sarge and Donald were greeted by a chorus of good mornings from his communications team. The White House communications director and the White House press secretary were co-equal in their level of importance and authority. They had a large staff of deputy directors who handled everything, including research, social media, speech writing, and public liaison matters.

When the government made the move from its temporary location in Boston to DC, Sarge brought with him two political novices, but individuals he trusted to speak for him when dealing with the media—Michelle Crepeau and Marcos Ocampo, both former students of his at Harvard.

After the recovery effort allowed for the reopening of Harvard, both of them completed their degrees. Ocampo obtained his Massachusetts law license, and Crepeau immediately began to work as a staffer for Donald. Ocampo and Crepeau got married after he passed the bar and took a job within the administration. Over the years, the two had shown the ability to speak for Sarge without allowing their preconceived notions and political leanings to result in conflicting messages.

The team assembled by Donald soon became known as the *young guns* because of their age compared to prior administrations and their ability to shoot down any dissent to the president's agenda.

Sarge and Donald took their seats in the chairs flanking the fireplace. This briefing was always conducted by Donald, with input from Ocampo and Crepeau. Domestic policy had been their administration's primary focus due to the circumstances. Sarge had been successful in achieving his goals except for the reunification efforts.

"Let's get a few things out of the way before we get to the vote," started Donald. "Do we have the president's speech ready for tonight's Governor's Ball?"

Crepeau, as communications director, handled that one. "Yes, sir. We've incorporated the president's requested modifications and we're uploading the final draft into the checklist as we speak. We can make any further modifications deemed necessary after today's early meeting with select governors."

"Excellent," said Donald. He glanced toward the windows and saw that the snow flurries were continuing to pelt the bulletproof glass. "What's the status of this nor'easter, and does FEMA have its assets in place?"

"Sir, I just got off the phone with the National Weather Service," replied Ocampo. "I plan on leading today's press briefing with a statement. This is going to be a significant weather event impacting the mid-Atlantic states. The extratropical cyclone is going to create heavy winds and pull arctic air from Canada with its counterclockwise rotation. While the DC area will be spared for the most part, states as far south as Kentucky and western Virginia will experience tropical force winds and plunging temperatures. Snowfall across Pennsylvania, New York, and Vermont will be measured in feet, not inches."

Sarge took his mind away from the vote and asked, "Are we prepositioning utility crews to help restore power when the time comes?"

"Yes, Mr. President," replied Crepeau. "FEMA has moved quickly to place assets throughout the region. I'm told that several requests for federal disaster declarations from the states will be made today. If possible, we believe it would be a good idea to sign those in advance of the afternoon press briefing, but certainly before the Governor's Ball."

"Get them to Donald or Betty. I won't hesitate."

"Yes, sir."

Donald scrolled through his iPad to look at the items on the checklist. "I don't see anything else on here that requires the president's immediate attention, so let's take an overview of the week relative to the statehood matter."

Crepeau reviewed her iPad. She leaned back to a member of her team, who hastily excused herself and scrambled out of the Oval Office. She looked up at Donald with trepidation. "Sir, we have a defector."

"Who? A congressman?"

"Yes, sir. Craig Barnes, Arizona four," replied Crepeau.

Donald slapped the arm of the chair. "I knew he was on the fence. His district borders California, stretching from the desert in the south all the way up to the Utah state line. Western Arizona was originally part of the four states that opposed the Constitutional Convention and sided with the former president. Michelle, how do you know this?"

"One of his staffers just sent me a text," she replied. "He plans on making a statement to the press at ten mountain time, noon eastern."

"Donald, should I reach out to him?" asked Sarge.

"Let me look into it first. We can afford a few defections, and Barnes was always a possibility."

"Who else?" asked Sarge.

"Nevada four. Congresswoman Rhimes from Henderson, whose district borders California."

Sarge furrowed his brow. The nature of the presidency was a series of contradictions. The President of the United States was widely considered the most powerful man on the planet, yet his job was to avoid using this power except under the most dire circumstances—which he was expected to avoid rather than engage.

In reality, on the domestic front, Sarge's job was about negotiating, more with Congress than anyone else. It was a team effort that he and Donald learned through trial and error. Most times, Donald conducted the negotiations and would come into the Oval Office to tell Sarge what *his,* meaning the president's, position was on the issue. Sarge likened the process to a lawyer's representation of his client.

A lawyer treated his client that way most of the time—looking after the client's interests while not telling him what those interest were until they were already decided. Donald took the helm and quickly adapted to become the White House consigliere, protecting Sarge from direct negotiations with everyone, especially Congress.

This worked well because Sarge dealt with a relatively tame Congress. Following the collapse, the country came together as they saw the recovery effort come to fruition. All of Washington worked toward this common goal. But after Sarge's re-election, the nation began to slip back into its old, partisan ways. Unfortunately, *political leopards can't change their spots.*

"Same question," Sarge began. "Should I get involved at this point? Donald, you know we need this. The Senate is easily manipulated with cash and promises. We need the House to kill this bill tomorrow so we don't have to sweat it out in the Senate on Wednesday."

"No, sir. Not yet. I'll call in the House Majority Whip and see what the deal is. I've got two hours before Barnes makes his press appearance."

CHAPTER 7

10:30 a.m.
The Oval Office
The White House
Washington, DC

The coalition Sarge had put together over the years to see his legislative agenda passed was a mix between conservatives, libertarians, and moderate democrats who believed in Sarge's plans for the recovery. As the country regained its footing, political parties fell back toward their old, obstructionist ways. In the last midterm election, as more pro-statehood congressmen and senators were elected, Sarge saw his opportunity for a Constitutional Convention shrinking. With the defection of two republican congressmen, his coalition was showing signs of cracking.

For many congressional actions, Sarge found himself holding the hands of key swing voters, providing them constant reassurance in order to push his legislative agenda through. Thus far, he had intentionally avoided the use of executive orders, which had become the norm by presidents on both sides of the aisle. Showing restraint, his well-stated policy vehemently opposed any executive action that made new law. That was the job of Congress.

As the election approached in October, Sarge and Donald carefully watched the polls to determine which way the political winds were blowing regarding the Pacific Statehood Act. Election Day provided him his answer. The new Congress would pass the bill, and America would be facing yet another fundamental transformation forced upon her by the will of a few states. He needed the bill defeated before Congress adjourned for the session before Thanksgiving.

Sarge was pensive as he watched the blowing snow begin to obstruct the view across the South Lawn. Betty quietly entered the room and whispered, "Mr. President, Mr. Quinn has arrived with an entourage. Would you prefer to see them in the Roosevelt Room or here, sir?"

"Here, please, Betty," replied Sarge. "And, Betty, would you mind having them send over a mocha latte. This blowing snow reminds me of Boston, which, oddly, reminds me of mocha lattes." *Comfort food.*

"I will, sir, and I'll advise Mr. Quinn." Betty slipped out as quietly as she had slipped in. Sarge debated whether he wanted to sit in a power position behind his desk or on a personal level at the couches. He opted for the casual arrangement. The vote was tomorrow. Tomorrow, he'd exert muscle if necessary. He'd learned from John Morgan—wield power powerfully, but sparingly.

Sarge stood to greet his guests. Donald led the way and was followed by the House Majority Whip for the Republicans, who held forty-six percent of the seats under the current makeup. However, there were six percent of the members of Congress who were libertarians that caucused with the Republicans in exchange for lucrative committee positions. The fifty-two percent was sufficient to defeat the bill without any support from across the aisle.

Also in attendance was the libertarian leader, a young congressman from Colorado who ran on, in his words, a *pro-pot* platform. He was pushing for the legalization of marijuana nationwide. While he garnered support in parts of Colorado and other Rocky Mountain states, he could never gain enough momentum to bring it to a floor vote.

"Gentlemen, thank you for coming to see me on short notice," started Sarge. "This is a very important vote, and while, as a lame-duck president, I've tried to distance myself from the vote, I've remained attentive nonetheless. Donald, bring us up to speed on the numbers."

"Thank you, Mr. President," said Donald as he handed out a roster of the members of Congress to their guests. "We need two hundred eighteen votes against passage. At the start of the day, with the coalition we've forged in the House, we had two hundred twenty-six votes to kill the bill. I'm now informed that we lost two more this morning."

"Now, Donald," said the Majority Whip, Congressman Billy Trent from Virginia, in his heavy Southern accent, "we've known about Barnes and Rhimes from the beginning. Both have been noncommittal when pressed. Without them, we have two twenty-four, six more votes than we need."

"Six votes is very slim for something this important," interjected Sarge. "If six of them switch to the yea column, the bill passes. Have you three been able to identify any more fence-sitters? I want to know if I need to get more actively involved."

"Sir, we don't think so," replied the congressman from Colorado. "We have several things working in our favor. The Majority Whip can confirm this, but those who are voting against the bill are doing so in large part because the referendums that were held in the four states did not impress anyone, including moderate democrats who are willing to discuss the issue in private."

"What are they saying?" asked Sarge.

Congressman Trent replied, "Mr. President, while the referendum votes were overwhelmingly in favor of pursuing reunification and statehood, turnout by the eligible voters in each of the states was abysmal. Fewer than a quarter of all voters cast ballots. If you couple that with the radical economic and social issue concessions demanded by the four states, the will to pass this legislation just doesn't seem to be there."

"Gentlemen, I need a comfort level here," said Sarge. "Tonight, I host the Governor's Ball, and I plan on making a push for another Constitutional Convention. I'll be meeting with several key, influential governors in the Oval this afternoon. I want to be able to represent to them that the bill will die tomorrow and we can turn our focus toward a convention."

The two congressmen looked at one another and nodded. The Majority Whip answered for them both. "Mr. President, we are unified in opposition to the bill. Where there is unity, there is victory. We'll do what we do best—whip."

There were three stages of *whipping*. The most basic starting point was a simple head count. The Majority Whip instructed his staffers to contact the members of his party's coalition and ask how they're gonna vote.

If the vote appeared to be close, like this one, the whip would move on to the second stage, in which the deputy whips were assigned to approach fence-sitters and hear out their concerns. If the sticking point couldn't be easily addressed, then the negotiations began. Side deals were made and accommodations promised.

The third and final whip occurred the day before a vote, or in the case of an afternoon vote, as was the case in the House version of the Pacific Statehood Act, the whip deputies would approach their particular target in the morning and close the deal.

Whipping could be a delicate business. If you whipped members of your party too early, they might change their mind. If the deputy whips got too heavy-handed, they might alienate a favorable voter.

"Thank you, gentlemen," said Sarge as he indicated the meeting was over. "Crack that whip. No surprises, please."

CHAPTER 8

10:45 a.m.
The Oval Office
The White House
Washington, DC

Donald and Sarge were left alone, and both men stood in silence as they observed the snow fall. Sarge tried not to show concern over the vote, as he'd asked Donald to run point on this and he didn't want to display a lack of confidence in his old friend. But something troubled him and it wasn't just the two expected defections. He'd come to learn that sometimes powerful hands pulled the strings of the puppets on the stage. He'd learned that firsthand. Sarge knew full well he wasn't the only puppetmaster in town.

Sarge took a sip of his coffee drink before addressing Donald. "Whadya think?"

"Look, we've been through this before. You get your ducks in a row and then you get nervous that one of them will lose their way. I know there's a lot riding on this House vote. Like you, I don't want to leave it up to the Senate. There are at least half a dozen backstabbers over there that could upend our agenda."

Sarge slid into his chair and set his drink down on the leather inlay. He suddenly remembered the thousand times Betty had admonished him for leaving rings on his desk and he quickly looked for a folder to use as a coaster. One marked *classified* provided what he needed.

"Stay on top of those two," said Sarge as he nodded toward the door the congressmen used to exit. "I get the sense they're treating this like any other legislation—if it fails, try again later. There won't be another chance. If it passes or gets punted to the next session, we may witness the unraveling of all our accomplishments following the collapse."

"I understand," said Donald, who appeared dejected.

Sarge stood and patted his friend on the back. "Listen, old buddy. Whatever happens, I won't blame you for it. You can't press the nay button for them. I'd just hate to see our work here be defined by our inability to restore the Union. No matter what, I'm proud we've stood on our principles and not capitulated to those who want to go back to the old ways that got us in trouble to begin with."

"Okay." Donald attempted to cheer up, but Sarge sensed his nerves were filling him with negativity.

"Let me ask you something else," started Sarge. "Forget about political parties and past presidents with their social agendas for a minute. Let's look at this from a purely economic perspective."

Sarge grabbed his coffee and joined Donald at the couches. He took another sip of the now chilled brew and then downed it completely.

Donald began speaking while Sarge finished his last sip. "You mean in the sense of who gains from reunification financially? Then if that's the question, we do, um, I mean the Boston Brahmin do. But then again, we gain even if the bill fails. You know I try to cover us financially on all sides."

"I do, and frankly, I don't know how the hell you do it. Chief of Staff is taxing enough, but you've managed to keep an eye on the finances at the same time."

"Well, Malcolm Lowe and 73 Tremont have helped tremendously. You and I had to be careful to avoid even the appearance of impropriety. Thankfully, your real position of power has never been exposed."

"Donald, think for a moment. Who are some of the other players out there who stand to gain politically or financially from reunification under the dictates provided in this bill?"

Donald thought for a moment before responding. "Politically, it's obvious. Those on the left loyal to the former administration who've oppose your agenda will enjoy an instant majority in both chambers when these four states are brought back in. Naturally, you'll be out of office, but the country might head back to its pre-collapse mindset."

"Okay, what about financially?" asked Sarge.

"Wow," replied Donald as he sank onto the couch. "To answer that, we'd have to follow the money. You always consider the usual suspects. Soros comes to mind. He'd find a way to profit and gain political clout to move us towards the European Socialist model."

Sarge leaned forward on the couch and studied his empty coffee cup. "Some of the Bilderbergs could be the answer. I don't know. Something's not right. I can feel it."

"What do you want me to do?" asked Donald.

"Eyes and ears wide open," replied Sarge. "Let's not get lost in the weeds, worrying about which congressman is voting yea or nay. If more defections occur in the House, let's look at the reasons rather than the impact of a lost vote. We'll deal with that when the time comes."

CHAPTER 9

10:45 a.m.
The Lowell Estate
Wellesley, Massachusetts

Lawrence Lowell was the son of a former president of Harvard and a direct descendant of John Lowell, a federal judge in the first United States Continental Congress. As far back as the sixteenth century, the Lowells and Winthrops, part of Sarge's lineage, were allies and friends. When Governor John Winthrop was named the governor of the Massachusetts Bay Colony, he immediately called upon the Lowell family to help settle the New England region.

During the reign of John Morgan as the recognized head of the Boston Brahmin, Lawrence Lowell and Walter Cabot were John Morgan's closest confidants. They were privy to *everything*. As part of the executive council, they were considered to be number two and three in the hierarchy.

Shortly after Morgan's death, Lowell passed away. He'd gained weight after the return to normalcy and it took a toll on his health. He suffered a massive stroke while visiting his grandchildren on Martha's Vineyard that summer and never recovered.

His passing left the Lowell family business interests and their representation in the Boston Brahmin to his widowed wife, Constance. The Boston Brahmin was a men's club and had been since the days of the revolution. Constance, who knew little of their activities prior to her husband's death, would only have the ability to name a suitable family member to the Boston Brahmin. This did not guarantee the new Lowell a seat on the executive committee, as that honor was voted upon by the committee.

As expected, Constance Lowell nominated their oldest son, Gardner Percival Lowell, an international law attorney who split his time between his New York offices and the Vineyard. Lowell's firm specialized in cross-border resolutions—experts in mediating, or litigating, trade and investment disputes between countries. They were also one of the most respected lobbyist firms in America. Lowell kept a pulse on Washington and his thumb on his elected officials.

After Morgan suffered his stroke, he immediately chose Sarge to become the new head of the Boston Brahmin without consulting his associates. The circumstances were such that the members of the executive committee, specifically Morgan's closest friends, Lowell and Walter Cabot, did not object.

But Constance Lowell did. First and foremost, Constance disapproved of Morgan's tactics in initiating the cyber attack. While it was expected that the members of the executive committee were to remain tight-lipped about their activities, Lawrence Lowell was notoriously weak when facing the inquisition of his wife.

Before she left the Lowell estate with Sarge and the Cabots, Constance had been fully informed of Morgan's plan and was none too happy. She voiced her displeasure constantly in those early weeks at Prescott Peninsula and even demanded that she be taken to Gardner's home.

Eventually, her position softened and she came around, but she didn't forget Morgan's choice of Sarge to lead the Boston Brahmin, which she considered to be a slight to her more qualified candidate of choice—Gardner.

"Come, Gardner, sit down for a moment before you leave. You have time for tea, don't you?" asked the eighty-two-year-old matriarch of the Lowell dynasty.

"I do, Mother, but just for a moment. The jet is waiting for me to leave for Egg Harbor."

Gardner's New England accent was strong and sounded very Kennedy-like. It seemed in the northeast, New Yorkers truly enjoyed their dialects, as did those from New Jersey. Jersey always seemed to sound like *joyzee*, and to New Englanders, harbor was pronounced *hahbah*. They spoke the dialect like it was a badge of honor, or *awnah*.

"Gardner, this is a very important time for us and your future," said Constance as she directed her son to sit across from her in their sunroom. The snow flurries were just starting to flutter across Vineyard Sound as the nor'easter made its way toward their east. "This country has proven that it can elect a nonpolitician. Now, it will need one with business savvy and international acumen. Henry Sargent got lucky because of circumstances. In some respects, he has proven himself a capable leader. But in terms of what is best for our business interests and the others among the executive committee who agree with us, it's time to send him back to Boston."

"Mother, I understand the gravity of the situation and I've been working diligently to provide Sarge quite a shock by Wednesday. At Thanksgiving, he'll have to look all of us in the eye. He'll be under a tremendous amount of pressure to respect our wishes."

"Thursday is a long time from now," admonished Constance. "There will be a power struggle within the Brahmin, to be sure, but we have to set the table. Now, have you secured the necessary defections for tomorrow's House vote?"

"I have, and the congressmen involved will absolutely blindside everyone, including their own families. My marks were totally off the radar for Quinn and his staff. I can assure you, Mother, the House vote will make headlines tomorrow evening."

Constance leaned back on the rose tufted settee and clenched her hands together. "Son, tell me about the meeting this afternoon."

"Mother, our friend from New York has pledged his support and will deliver the necessary votes, but symbolically, he cannot vote with us. He is more valuable to us hidden in the shadows. Senator Ellis from Colorado has higher aspirations, and she sees this as an opportunity to endear herself to voters from the Pacific states. She's a libertarian in name only. Her political roots spread into deep blue California, as do two of her fellow libertarians, which she claims she can deliver."

"What's it going to cost us, son?"

"Does it matter?" he quickly replied. After seeing his mother's reaction, he continued. "Well, I'm sorry, Mother, that came out wrong. Yes, as is typical, their demands are high and I will convince them to be more realistic. But as you know, my promises are contingent upon a major upheaval within the Boston Brahmin."

Constance reached out and took his hand. "An upheaval that you're carefully orchestrating, my son. A trap being laid for a political novice who'll never see it coming."

CHAPTER 10

11:00 a.m.
The Jackson Family Home
Muddy Pond, Tennessee

Drew Jackson stood to the side as former Master Sergeant Johnson *King* Dawkins expertly flipped over a dozen burgers and steaks on the charcoal grill outside the barn. The aroma of grilled meat filled the air as the other members of the Aegis Global Response Team razzed their team leader. As he flipped the final burger, something pelted him in the back of the head.

"Hey, what the—?" King shouted as he spun around with the spatula, ready to defend himself against the attacker.

"Sorry, King. I didn't mean to hit you," said Drew's younger brother, Jack. Jack, who'd graduated from the University of Tennessee following the collapse, briefly pursued an opportunity at an NFL football career, but after bouncing around from one team's practice squad to another, he settled back on the Cumberland Plateau as a part-time hunting guide and full-time real estate agent.

"No problem, Jack," said King as he tossed the wayward football back to him. As King returned to the grill, he laid out the buns to toast them.

This was a rare day for the members of the Aegis team. When they weren't on a mission, they'd be back at Fort Bragg, training, far away from the prying eyes of the public or regular forces. Drew had invited them to the farm for some much-needed rest and relaxation. The guys hunted, participated in a traditional turkey shoot, and enjoyed the opportunity to hang out with their families and friends, knowing they could get *the call* at any moment.

Drew's attention was grabbed by a roar of laughter that erupted from one of the picnic tables, undoubtedly a reaction to a joke that couldn't be repeated in polite company, such as their wives and girlfriends, who sat at another table, talking amongst themselves.

"Yup, here we were, rescuing this woman, and as soon as I cut her bindings loose, she kicked me in the balls!"

"No way!"

"I kid you not! I doubled over and then she kneed me in the nose and bolted out the door."

"That explains your warped schnoz!" The guys slapped the table and let out another roar.

"More importantly, did the nuts survive?"

A female voice answered from the other table as she rubbed her pregnant belly. "They survived just fine, thank you very much."

More laughter from all of his guests couldn't bring Drew out of his melancholy mood. Drew's team was unaware that changes might be coming to their dynamic. He had a decision to make that would impact all of them. His mind drifted to Abbie, so he eased away from the group to check on her.

*****

Drew entered the kitchen to find the love of his life helping his mother prepare lunch for the guys. He walked over and kissed Abbie on the neck without saying a word. The smell of baked beans caught his nostrils and he opened the oven door to sneak a peek. The awkward silence began to bug him as he leaned against the counter to observe the two women in his life—Abbie and Drew's mom, Janie Jackson, a retired ER nurse and ruler of the roost in the Jackson home.

"Son, somethin' on your mind?" asked Janie. She kept working on the variety of side dishes, but Abbie looked up and gave her husband a reassuring smile. Abbie was seven months pregnant with a late January due date. She'd cut back on her vice presidential duties but was certainly not a couch potato. She'd carefully managed her weight, exercised regularly, and attempted to avoid stressful situations.

As she and Sarge neared the end of their second administration, they were quite fortunate to have dodged the major international crises that most presidents endure. America was allowed a day of mourning, in a way, to recover from the cyber attack. After the power grid collapsed, a power vacuum was evident in international affairs.

There was some posturing by Russia and China, but for the most part, the world came together to assist the United States in getting back on its feet. Israel, Australia, Japan, and the European nations had led the charge in providing relief supplies, critical electrical grid components, and protection of American military interests abroad.

Drew and Abbie wanted a baby, but both agreed that the ideal timing for their first child would be after she left office. When the calendar permitted, they began to try, and as is often the case with two successful, driven people, positive results came quickly. By their calculations, the new parents would welcome their first child into the world two weeks after the inauguration of the next president.

"Mom, I've been thinking a lot lately," Drew started as he wandered to the breakfast room window to look at his guests, who'd gathered at the picnic tables to exchange stories. The men, all members of the Aegis team he'd worked with since Abbie was assigned a permanent Secret Service detail, had been assigned to Drew for special ops tasks that came directly from the president. "Sarge has suggested I take a leadership role at Aegis in Boston. You know, out of the field, because of the baby and all."

"Drew," interrupted Abbie, "you know how I feel about this. It's a desk job. You'll be miserable."

Janie grabbed a dish towel and wiped her hands. "That doesn't sound like such a terrible idea. I assumed you two would be moving to Boston in January. You could be close to work that way."

Drew continued to stare out the window at the playful banter between his team and their loved ones. King was putting the final touches on the grilled meats and began to remove them onto a platter.

"Janie, deep down, Drew loves what he does and he doesn't want to leave his team. I've told him not to make a rash decision based upon me and our baby. We'll be fine, just as I know he'll be fine when he goes out on a mission."

"Abbie, we can't be so sure," said Drew as he reached out for her hand. "Don't forget, I get shot at sometimes."

"All I know is this," started Abbie in response. "I'll never forget seeing you lying on the ground, getting kicked and beaten that night at Camp Blanding. I thought—no, I just knew you were dead. But you came back to me. And you always will."

Drew hugged her tight and whispered, "I love you."

After a moment, Janie weighed in. "I'm your mother and I vote office job. You've been shot at enough for your country. I think you need to take care of this beautiful girl and your new young'un."

CHAPTER 11

11:30 a.m.
The Hart Senate Office Building
Washington, DC

Under most circumstances, the massive Hart Senate Office Building would be empty. Ordinarily, senators and their congressional counterparts would have scampered off for the safety of their home states several days before Thanksgiving. This year was different, as the vote loomed large.

Snow flurries had turned to flakes and began to stick on the building's windows, casting a faint gray light into the offices and hallways. Staffers scurried in and out of the outer office, which was occupied by his secretary.

Senator Paul Ashley Rutledge, Republican senior senator from Georgia, was a twenty-two-year pillar in the upper chamber of Congress. He'd won re-election by a landslide four years ago and his prospects for a fifth term in two years were good.

As the Senate Majority Leader, Rutledge ruled with a firm hand. Scholarly in appearance, with thick, frameless glasses that hadn't changed since his first term in office, Rutledge led a fairly disciplined life. He'd lost his wife to cancer years ago, which only served to intensify his obsessive tendencies. He demanded promptness, accuracy, and order from his staff. He had fired more than his share of staffers for failing to follow these basic requirements of employment.

His approach to the vote was no different. He relied heavily on the Majority Whip to deliver the votes necessary to deny passage of the Pacific Statehood Act. He was against the bill for many reasons, the least of which was loyalty to the president who'd forged an excellent working relationship with him and the Rutledge family over the last eight years. Leader Rutledge was very pro-Sarge as his agenda was implemented.

Senator Rutledge checked his watch, hoisted himself out of the chair and walked through his secretary's office into his conference room. The room was dedicated to the Majority Leader and was adorned with portraits of past leaders of the Senate—the world's greatest deliberative body. He took a seat at the polished table, clasping his hands across his protruding belly, and waited for his meeting.

Precisely at 11:30 a.m., Congressman Rafael Sánchez entered the room. He was alone. This surprised Rutledge, as the young democrat from Georgia was known for his entourage, which accompanied him throughout Capitol Hill. *This should be interesting*, he thought as he rose to greet his guest. He'd never met Sánchez in person, but like everyone in Washington, he'd seen more than enough of the man on television.

"Senator Rutledge, thank you for seeing me." Sánchez firmly shook Rutledge's hand before taking a seat at the head of the table. *Does he think he belongs at the head of the table?* Rutledge had chosen a neutral chair in the middle of the twelve-seat, nineteenth-century antique.

Sánchez settled into his chair and smoothly unbuttoned his jacket. Crossing his legs, he smiled a bright, white toothy grin and exhaled dramatically. "It's been quite a couple of interesting months, wouldn't you agree, Leader Rutledge?"

Rutledge wasn't going to give the cocky upstart an inch. He'd learned over the years it was better to sit and listen. Instead of answering, he simply nodded at Sánchez.

Sánchez continued. "That election was a barn burner. But I'll say this for President Sargent, he did a magnificent job of keeping the Pacific statehood bill away from a floor vote. Things might have been much different on Election Day if the vote had proceeded in October, wouldn't you agree?"

"Maybe." Again, a noncommittal response from Rutledge. There was silence as Sánchez gathered his thoughts.

Rutledge decided to take the offensive. He leaned forward and crossed his arms on the table. He looked over his glasses like a schoolteacher. "May I call you Rafael?"

"Call me Rafi."

"Fine, Rafi. I don't mean to be inhospitable, but I'm a busy man and have taken the time to meet with you this morning. Maybe we ought to get to the point, young man." Rutledge couldn't resist taking a swipe at the man's youthfulness. It wasn't said condescendingly, rather just the opposite. It was more like a teacher trying to teach a new student how to get with the program.

"You're right, my apologies. Like I said, the last couple of months have been interesting. Your party took it in the teeth on Election Day, including in Congress, where things will be looking up for us next session."

"That's a long time from now."

"To an extent," said Sánchez as he leaned forward in his chair. "Leader Rutledge, change is coming. I know that we're on opposite sides of the aisle, but I think we can agree that one way or the other, this bill will pass this week or next term."

"Maybe."

Sánchez leaned forward and lowered his voice, forcing Rutledge to pay attention. "I am content in the House for now. As you know, Georgia has turned from red to purple in recent elections. There are those who believe it can be turned true blue in the near future. I think they're right."

Rutledge's eyes narrowed. "Why should I care what you think?"

"Because, Leader Rutledge," started Sánchez, "I'm being encouraged by the DNC to run for your seat in two years."

Rutledge began to stand. He'd experienced young bucks coming after him politically in the past and intended to shut this conversation down. "Well, thanks for the heads-up, but don't ever waste my time like this again, *Congressman*." Rutledge intentionally stretched out the word for effect.

Sánchez persisted. "Please, let me finish. I'm here to deliver a message and make a promise to you. Leader Rutledge, I'll bide my time for four years when the junior senator from Georgia runs for re-election. I'll ride the wave of an even larger democratic Congress and take his seat, allowing you a certain re-election in two years."

"Why should I entertain any of this?" asked Senator Rutledge.

"Sir, it's quite simple. We want you to stand down when the vote comes to the Senate floor Wednesday."

"It'll never make it out of the House."

"Yes, sir, it will. And when it comes to a vote on Wednesday, we want you to cut off debate, block any filibusters, and allow a straight up-and-down vote. In exchange, you can retire as the senior senator from Georgia, albeit in the minority."

Rutledge stood and placed his hands palm down on the conference table, a sneer coming across his face. "You've gotta lot of nerve coming in here and threatening me. I'll run the Senate my way, and no snot-nosed kid with a message from the DNC will scare me. As for your running to take my job, you better pack a lunch. You have no idea what hardball politics looks like. Now, get the hell out of my office!"

Sánchez left without saying a word, leaving Rutledge alone in the conference room. He walked to the windows with his hands in his pockets. *The proponents of the Pacific Statehood Act took a big risk by approaching me, what are they doing with others in my party?*

CHAPTER 12

Noon
The President's Dining Room
The White House
Washington, DC

Sarge, Donald, and Brad convened for a working lunch in the President's Dining Room. Located through a small corridor past the president's private study, Sarge often had casual meals with Julia and the kids, as well as working luncheons with Donald. Sarge also had the room equipped with several wall-mounted televisions so that he could keep up with news being reported from around the world.

While they waited for their fourth guest, Brad provided them an update on the situation in Taiwan. "Sarge, the uprising in Taiwan is not that much different from what we're experiencing here over the statehood bill. Taiwanese students feel betrayed by the government's continued friendly relations with China. The recent trade agreements were perceived as hurtful to the Taiwan economy and a slap in the face of recent graduates who are having difficulty finding jobs."

"They're thinking short term," added Donald. "The results of these agreements take time to materialize. You can't just sign a trade agreement and expect instant results."

Sarge nodded and motioned for them to take a seat at the round table, where glasses of tea and water awaited them. "Besides, wouldn't they prefer an air of cooperation with Beijing instead of firing bullets at one another?"

"You'd think so, but that issue has complicated matters," replied Brad. "The arms deal we made has angered the pro-Chinese youth in Taiwan. One side is complaining about the trade pact, and the other side is bemoaning the arms deal. In the end, they're all unhappy."

"I've read Ambassador McBride's address to the Legislative Yuan," said Sarge. "I hope that he can calm the rhetoric and make our position clear. Pulling out of the trade pacts would damage Taiwan's international credibility. The arms sale was absolutely necessary to provide some semblance of military parity in the region. China knows where we stand on both issues. Hopefully, these student protestors will get the message and go back to class."

They settled into their chairs when the door opened from the Oval Office. "Betty escorted me into the Commander-in-Chief's office, so I took the old fool's chair for a spin. You know, I never could find the nuclear football. Good thing, I guess."

Sarge jumped out of his chair and greeted his Secretary of Veteran's Affairs—Dr. John Joseph Warren. "Hello, J.J. We really don't get to see each other enough except in cabinet meetings, and then it's all business."

J.J. was an accomplished Army battalion surgeon who had been deployed to Joint Base Balad as part of the 310th Sustainment Command—located on the former Al-Bakr Air Force base north of Baghdad. J.J. had risen to the rank of major during his decorated career with the Army.

Prior to the cyber attack, he had become close friends with Donald and Susan Quinn. Ultimately, he was introduced to the others and became the armageddon doctor to the Loyal Nine.

Following his retirement from the military, J.J. carried a lot of anger inside. He was disappointed in the lack of appreciation the veterans of the wars in Iraq and Afghanistan received in the media and by politicians. After Sarge was elected, J.J. approached him about a position within Veterans Affairs to help soldiers with PTSD and also to assist returning vets in finding jobs. Sarge surprised everyone by naming him to a cabinet position.

It wasn't unusual for newly elected presidents to surround themselves with close confidants, so Sarge, after consulting with Julia, took advantage of that expectation. Donald was his Chief of Staff with Susan, his wife, still close at hand. J.J. and Brad were both members of the cabinet. Abbie was his vice president and along with husband Drew, who was taken in as Steven's replacement, rounded out the inner circle.

The only member of the Loyal Nine who was not included was Katie. After she successfully tracked down Steven's killer, she accepted a position within Aegis. Sadly, Katie was killed in a terrorist attack in Berlin while running a security detail for an international financier. It was a freak occurrence that was completely unavoidable.

"You better keep your hands off the nukes, old friend," said Donald as he gave J.J. a bro-hug. "I hear you're headed out for a whirlwind tour of the world."

J.J. shook hands with Brad and took the last remaining chair. "I've gotten used to the travel despite my advanced age." He ran his fingers through his thinning gray hair.

"Will this be your last outing?" asked Brad.

"Yeah. I wanted to see our guys during Thanksgiving week. I know Sarge has plans for a surprise visit around Christmas."

Sarge rose to request the food be brought in, and he summoned one of the staff. He turned his attention back to his friends. "It's all tentative right now, but my plans are to visit Guam, Japan, and perhaps South Korea if that little tyrant in the north is behaving himself."

"I'm against the South Korea leg," Brad said with a gruff. "You're too easy a target for that madman. One of these days, somebody is gonna have to take him out."

All of the men stopped speaking as the food was brought in. Everybody was provided a bowl of baked potato soup and a side sandwich. In Sarge's eight years in office, elaborate, gourmet meals were not the norm except when foreign dignitaries were involved.

J.J. continued. "We'll fly out of Andrews tomorrow at oh-six-hundred. I've got the NSA director and the Secretary of the Army coming with me. Our itinerary includes Baghdad and Bagram, with a brief touchdown at Landstuhl Medical in Germany."

Sarge wiped his mouth and patted J.J. on the arm as he finished chewing. "You've done great work these past eight years, my friend. The programs you've implemented will assure that the VA doesn't fall into the same mistakes from the past."

"I guess you could say the collapse made my job easier, but you're right. The natural inclination would be to return to the same failed methodology. We've righted the ship and hopefully the new administration will carry it forward."

Donald raised his hand, as if to make a point before he forgot it. With a mouthful of food, he interrupted. "J.J., we've arranged for Sarge to be patched in via teleconference at each of your stops. He doesn't want to upstage you, but it's his last Thanksgiving in office and he'd like to say a few words."

"Just a few, that's a first," said J.J. laughingly. The group joined in, as Sarge had become known as the long-winded president.

"Give me a break. Sometimes you can't mince words. Donald, will I have prepared remarks? That usually helps."

"Absolutely," he replied.

The four friends finished off their meals after discussing their families and years in the administration. Finally, it was J.J. who spoke up about the issue that they were all acutely aware of, but nobody wanted to speak about.

"Well, are we gonna talk about the elephant in the room—the vote?"

CHAPTER 13

2:00 p.m. ET
The Lowell Summer Cottage
White Cliff Road
Egg Harbor, Wisconsin

The Lowell summer cottage was an outrageously large, sixty-four-hundred-square-foot home with beautiful water views of Green Bay. The home had been featured in multiple issues of *Architectural Digest* prior to the collapse and was the epitome of opulence.

Gardner Lowell was a visionary in many respects, especially in terms of American politics. He saw the trend in national elections to focus on Midwestern states ranging from Wisconsin, through Indiana, and as far east as Pennsylvania. Like John Morgan, who had the ability to look many election cycles in advance, Gardner saw an opportunity to elevate his son, John, into politics through a Midwestern state such as Wisconsin. He purchased the Egg Harbor property to provide John a residence for a future run at Congress, for starters.

In the meantime, it served its purpose as a meeting place far away from New York and Boston. He could meet with his international contacts here, entertain American politicians without being noticed by the media, and engage in the occasional tryst without raising the ire of his wife.

The staff's instructions were to escort the senators to the parlor overlooking the harbor and wait for Lowell's entrance. After offering the two a drink, the staff was to retreat from the room and leave Gardner alone with his guests.

Gardner sat in his study and adjusted the cameras that provided him three angles of the parlor. He carefully adjusted the volume on the microphones hidden within the furniture and lamps. Gardner Lowell had many contacts in Washington, especially in the CIA. His monitoring system in the summer cottage was state of the art and CIA approved.

"Are you sure you wanna go through with it?" asked Senator Ron Billows, the senior senator from New York and the Senate Majority Whip.

The much younger senator, Jemeel Ellis, a rising star within the Democratic Party, was a very attractive black woman from Denver. Her family was well-known in California political circles as big money donors for liberal and social causes. After her move to Colorado to support the pro-marijuana referendums, Senator Ellis positioned herself as a libertarian, leaning left on social issues but right on matters of national security and fiscal responsibility. After she was elected to the Senate four years ago, riding the wave of Sarge's re-election, she began to become more prominent on the national stage.

Senator Ellis took a sip of her drink and quickly responded, "Come on, Ron. Don't doubt my determination to make this happen."

"I just want to make sure," said Senator Billows with a toothy grin. He noticeably surveyed his peer's leggy posture. Senator Ellis was also a former Miss Colorado in the Miss USA pageant. "There will be some very powerful people who are going to be extremely pissed off on Wednesday evening."

She laughed at his statement. "No doubt. Listen, Ron, perhaps I should be asking, are you sure you're up to it?"

Billows stood and walked toward the wall of windows overlooking the water. It was a beautiful, crisp day. "I'm ready for a new challenge. A cause I can believe in. After the collapse, during the recovery, I made a ton of money. I've risen to the leadership position of the libertarians with my sights set on the next level, Senate Majority Leader. When this bill passes, and with the requisite accommodations made, I can possess a tremendous amount of power in the new Congress."

Gardner continued to adjust the cameras and volume to pick up every word. He suspected that Billows would be seeking the Majority Leader post. He could deliver it, but an unexpected forced retirement would be required, something easily arranged.

"Your request doesn't sound unreasonable. Can you deliver the votes?" asked Senator Ellis.

"Enough to tip the balance to even or plus one in favor of the bill."

"What about the vice president? Wouldn't she be there to break the tie?"

Senator Billows laughed. "She's checked out at this point. Abbie is in Tennessee with her new husband and a bun in the oven. I doubt she'll be in Washington this week."

She took another sip of her drink. "So the table's set. I can put everyone's mind at ease with certain assurances. I'll wait until Gardner arrives to discuss what I'm looking for."

Lowell leaned back in his office chair and knew what he had to work with. For Billows, this negotiation was not about money, as the man had become wealthy during his years in the Senate. He sought power, and with the elimination of a single obstacle, the promise could be fulfilled.

Jemeel Ellis had higher aspirations, he could sense it. It was time for her to make her proposal.

Lowell joined them in the parlor and the three shared another drink and exchanged some pleasantries. Senator Billows made his request first and Lowell feigned consternation regarding the ramifications of the senator's request but eventually acquiesced. Pleased with the result, Billows sat back and yielded the floor to Ellis.

She immediately turned on the charm. She slid up in her chair and deftly crossed the legs on her five-foot-ten-inch frame, which drew the immediate attention of both men. Gardner admired her initiative. She exuded sexuality and it had a mesmerizing effect.

"Gardner, I don't need to read my entire résumé to you. But I come from a family of firsts. My grandfather was the first African-American mayor of Los Angeles. My father was just elected the first

African-American governor of California. As a Coloradan, I was the first to win the Miss Colorado title and the first African-American senator."

Gardner nodded and took another sip of his drink. As she'd stated, he knew all of this. Clearly, she wanted to be the first of some other position. "So, Senator, what does your future hold? Where do you see your career headed?"

"Prior to the next presidential election, I'll turn thirty-five. As a libertarian, I want to follow in the footsteps of Abbie Morgan and be named the running mate on the democratic ticket."

Senator Billows spontaneously laughed, drawing a death glare from Senator Ellis. She was serious in her request and Gardner knew it. His mind raced, as he wasn't sure if this was a promise he could keep. A lot depended on the result of this vote and other things that would manifest themselves in the coming days.

Gardner managed a smile without breaking eye contact with Ellis. "Is there anything else?"

"I need a million dollars."

Billows burst out laughing once again. "I sold myself short. Gardner, would you like to sweeten my pot as well? I mean, come on, Jemeel, this is a simple vote. I don't think it's appropriate to shoot for the moon and the stars here."

Ellis ignored her counterpart from New York. Gardner kept eye contact and managed a slight smile. He liked her.

"Ron, I think our business is complete," Gardner said dismissively as he stood to escort Billows out. "Let me show you to the door. Please keep our arrangement confidential, and I want you to provide me constant updates as the vote nears. Rest assured, the Lowells keep their word."

Billows looked perplexed at his sudden departure. He glanced toward Ellis, who continued to ignore him. Stammering, he responded, "Well, okay. Of course, Gardner, I will. Thank you for having me. I'll stay in touch."

After the door was closed behind him, Gardner approached Ellis and extended his hand. She took it and rose to stand dangerously close to him. He leaned and whispered in her ear, "I can give you what you want, and more. But I'll need something else from you in return."

"What might that be, Gardner?" she asked softly.

He leaned closer, his hand on her hip and his whiskey breath on her neck. He whispered his conditions, and she nodded and accepted.

CHAPTER 14

3:15 p.m. ET
The Lowell Summer Cottage
White Cliff Road
Egg Harbor, Wisconsin

The muted buzz of the intercom stirred Gardner out of bed. He glanced over at his companion, Senator Ellis, and then carefully pushed the button to reply, hoping not to wake her.

Gardner's chief butler responded. "Sir, a gentleman has arrived. He has identified himself as Mr. West. He insists upon seeing you."

Gardner took another glance over his shoulder to confirm his bed companion was still sleeping. He slipped on his clothes and quietly left the room. Descending the winding staircase into the foyer, he stared at his guest in disbelief.

"Where have you been?" he asked the man who had identified himself as Mr. West. He was a tall man with impossibly pale skin and neatly combed white hair. His black suit, starched white shirt, and solid black tie gave him the appearance of an undertaker—or a well-dressed grim reaper.

Mr. West didn't bother answering, choosing to put his hands in his pockets instead. Gardner continued. "You'd better not have bad news for me."

Mr. West was opening his mouth to respond when Gardner waved his arm and looked around the ceiling of his foyer. It dawned on him that any of a multitude of government agencies or foreign governments could hack his surveillance system. The CIA spooks he'd hired had probably designed it so they could listen in themselves.

"Never mind, not here." Gardner gestured for the man to follow and led him down a darkened hallway to an opulent sitting room. A myriad of original paintings adorned the walls and a fire in the fireplace warded off the chill from the start of a cold Wisconsin winter. In addition to his study, this was the one room of the Lowell retreat that wasn't bugged.

Mr. West stood in the center of the room, awaiting an offer to sit, but Gardner ignored him and poured himself a drink. He walked toward the fireplace and motioned for Mr. West to help himself to the bar.

"Well, what do you have for me?" asked Gardner.

"I'm sorry, sir. Nothing yet with respect to the congressman from Indiana."

"What do you mean nothing yet?" Gardner bristled. He didn't like loose ends, especially now. Too much was at stake. "This has been going on for weeks. Perhaps, *Mr. West*, I didn't make myself perfectly clear. I tasked you with this and not an underling because failure is not an option."

"Sir, I am assured that the information we seek will be delivered to me in Washington early tomorrow morning. It's only a matter of time, don't worry."

Gardner threw back the rest of his drink and approached the bar for another. "May I assume, *or rest assured*, that the gentlelady from Iowa is on board?"

"Yes, sir. It required an additional contribution to her campaign war chest, but it was not unreasonable."

"Please, sit down," Gardner finally instructed, and the two men sat across from each other. "I don't doubt you, old friend. You've been loyal to my father and now the Lowell family for many years. Do you still enjoy your job with us?"

"Of course, I—"

"After Father died, I could have restructured our business affairs and taken anyone under my wing, but I took you."

"Naturally, sir, I'm grateful for that. I hope I've done my job well for your father and his associates in Boston. Now, you should know where my loyalty lies."

Gardner took another sip of his whiskey and looked at his watch. He wondered if he'd have time for another encounter with the good senator from Colorado. "I have to believe you because I have another job that requires getting your hands dirty."

"No job too big, as they say."

"Good. I've made a promise to an up-and-coming congressman from Georgia who stands to be a vital ally for years to come. There is an obstacle in Washington that needs to be removed."

"Sir, your influence in Washington has grown significantly."

"You bet it has, but I'm just getting started. I want to own every historic tree, every blade of glass, and every rock under which the secrets lie. It's my turn now, and the steps we are taking this week are an integral part of the plan."

Mr. West finished his drink and set it on the table. "What would you like me to do?"

Gardner began to lay out the plan. "After the vote, Congress will adjourn until the new Congress is brought into session in January. In the interim, the House Democrats will meet for the purposes of electing a new Majority Leader, Minority Whip and Speaker of the House."

"I assumed they would elevate their existing team from minority to majority status."

"Ordinarily, yes," started Gardner. "Only, this time, there will be a vacancy in the majority leader slot. I want you to create that vacancy between now and December 11 when the House Democratic Caucus convenes."

"I understand, sir," said Mr. West without showing any emotion.

Gardner stood and walked to a painting of teams competing in the Head of the Charles Regatta event in Boston. "That's good. I want us all in the boat, but most importantly, rowing in the same direction. We just have to take care not to tip it over."

Chapter 15

3:15 p.m. ET
Chief of Staff's Office
The White House
Washington, DC

The legislative process was like sausage making, as the saying goes. The famous German Otto von Bismarck believed that while most people would find the making of sausage repulsive, they'd enjoy the end result.

Prior to the collapse, the process lawmakers followed in Congress was like sausage making, particularly as it related to doling out the pork. Lawmakers' votes and loyalties were bought by assigning federal funds to their districts or pet projects or lobbyist interests.

For example, a transportation bill to repair aging bridges might include millions of dollars to the World Wildlife Federation to study the ecological habitat of the snail darter in the Tellico River. Or, in Nebraska, a retiring senator secured a hundred million dollars for his state's Medicaid program.

At Sarge's first State of the Union address following the reconvening of Congress, he called upon both chambers to adopt the concept of *single-subject bills*, something states like Minnesota and Colorado had adopted many years ago. The rule is simple—any proposed legislation may deal with only one main issue.

In the case of the vote, it was only the granting of statehood to the four states that seceded during the chaos following the collapse. For weeks, the House argued over the ancillary issues raised by the western states, which dealt with gay rights, immigration, legalizing marijuana, and single-payer health care. Many claimed inclusion of their demands on these points violated the spirit and intent of the single-subject concept.

Sarge was one of those. When the House included these specific issues in the final legislation, Sarge undertook a series of legal maneuvers against the bill by seeking an opinion from the attorney general and later a ruling from the DC federal district court. Through appeals and delays, he was able to postpone a vote until after the election, a move that was widely credited in the victory of president-elect Rawlins.

Now, the delay tactics were over. Sarge needed the vote to take place before the new Congress convened. Once the bill was voted down, he'd move quickly to announce a push for a Constitutional Convention. He'd address the nation, create a ground swell of support for the convention, and preempt the new Congress from taking up the matter in January.

Donald studied the charts in his office. The first board showed the balance of power.

CURRENT HOUSE

R-46% D-45% S-3%

NEW HOUSE

D-48% R-47% S-2%

CURRENT SENATE

R-49 D-45 I-6

NEW SENATE

R-48 D-46 I-6

While Donald and Sarge applauded the slight evaporation of two-party rule in Washington, the libertarians and socialists had become wildcards in their voting. Especially the libertarians, who tended to vote conservatively on matters of national security and economics, but with the democrats on social issues.

The Pacific Statehood Act provided incentive for the libertarians to vote on either side of the issue. The social issues regarding gay rights and marijuana legalization had some of these congressmen leaning toward a yea vote. However, they firmly opposed the bill due to the open borders immigration stance and single-payer health care issues. Tactically, proponents of the bill should have left these latter two issues out of the mix, which might have ensured its passage. Instead, they decided to go for the whole enchilada, a level of confidence that concerned Donald.

The Gatekeeper announced to Donald that the House Majority Whip, Congressman Trent, had arrived to discuss the current status of the votes. Sarge had asked Donald to run point on this, and he probably wouldn't sleep until after the House voted against it.

"Good afternoon, Donald," Congressman Trent greeted in his Southern drawl. "I wanted to let you know the final version of the bill has just come out of committee and there are no changes. The vote was dead-locked on removing the four provisions objected to by the president, so it goes to a floor vote as is."

"No surprise there, I guess. Were there any modifications at all?"

"Only a few wording issues as it pertains to effective date. Those in favor of the bill were pushing for immediate enactment upon its being signed by the president. Others insisted on a January 1 effective date so that it made it cleaner for the Treasury Department to identify who was a citizen and who wasn't for tax purposes."

"Why would they insist upon an immediate effective date?" asked Donald.

"I suspect they want a say in the conference leadership and committee appointments next month."

Donald nodded and turned his attention back to the flip charts. "Well, it shouldn't matter, right? What's the latest count?"

The congressman set his briefcase on a chair and retrieved a yellow legal pad with several tattered and torn pages. He approached Donald's flip chart and picked up a permanent marker.

"May I?"

"Sure, but I noticed you picked up the Sharpie. Does that mean the changes you are about to make are irreversible?"

"Yes, I'm afraid so," replied Congressman Trent. He made a few changes, including the two defections they'd discussed this morning. Another libertarian had jumped ship, and he placed all of the socialists into the yea column.

"Whoa," started Donald. "Where does that leave us?"

The congressman didn't reply and traded the marker for a pencil. In an open space, he scribbled *Nay – 222, Yea – 211, Undecided – 2.*

"Still manageable," muttered Donald. He looked to his charts to see if he had the two undecideds identified. One was a republican congressman from Montana and the other was a libertarian from Utah. Donald tapped the flip pad, causing the easel to shake. "I don't understand her indecisiveness at all. Is it because of her daughter?"

"I'll be speaking with her after our meeting, but I am operating under that assumption," replied Congressman Trent. "She was endorsed in her re-election by several LGBT rights organizations because her daughter came out as a lesbian during the campaign and the congresswoman publicly embraced her decision. She feels a debt of gratitude to them and therefore is considering voting for the bill."

"You've got to be kidding me!" exclaimed a frustrated Donald. "This statehood vote is much bigger than a single issue. I applaud her for being principled, but you can't admit four states into the Union as a way of saying thanks for your support!"

"Donald, I know this and I'll speak to her about it."

"Is there anything we can promise her?" asked Donald.

"We'll be in the minority, so committee positions may not carry as much luster as normal. I could offer her a high-ranking position on the rumored House Global Equality committee. The leadership is already having difficulty finding republicans to sit on the committee. We can make her the ranking member."

"Fine, who cares? Just get her vote. Either way, we're still plus six in the nay column. I don't like playing defense, but it's all we got."

"I agree," said Congressman Trent, studying the chart. "We'll hold the line, Donald. At least we can count on our typically solid votes, right?"

CHAPTER 16

3:30 p.m.
The State Dining Room
The White House Residence
Washington, DC

"Okay, kids. I want you to be on your best behavior, and don't get in the way of anybody," admonished Julia as she led her three charges down the staircase toward the State Dining Room. The White House staff was busy making preparations for tonight's Governor's Ball, a perfectly timed event to host the state's executives during the holiday season and to encourage their participation in a Constitutional Convention.

Forty-six governors would be attending, and symbolically, Sarge insisted upon a table in the center of the room be set up with four chairs, one for each of the governors of the Pacific states who would not be in attendance. Traditionally, the ball was hosted by the First Lady, and Julia had received accolades from across the political spectrum for her prior soirées.

This year, the event was postponed until after the election, which was part of Sarge's overall approach to convince the governors to move forward with the convention regarding statehood.

The flower arrangements had just been delivered, a beautiful arrangement of seasonal flowers, including burgundy lilies, orange roses, and orange daisies in fall colors.

Only the table dedicated to the Pacific states was different. Their table included a Thanksgiving-themed cornucopia consisting of festive fruits and vegetables native to each of the four states. The cornucopia, or horn of plenty, was a symbol of abundance and nourishment. Julia wanted to drive the point home that the four states brought something to the table that would enrich the nation.

Julia carried Frank on her hip, and Win held Rose's hand as they wound their way through the State Dining Room to admire the perfectly appointed table settings. Rose, whose curiosity was in high gear, attempted to touch every flower and piece of crystal as they meandered through the tables.

"Where will we sit, Mom?" asked Win.

"Actually, you three won't be joining us this evening," replied Julia with a smile. She patted her son on the head and looked past him and waved to a familiar face. "This is a pretty big event for your dad. However, I do have a surprise I think you'll enjoy. Look who's here."

"Hey," exclaimed Win as he yoked his little sister's arm and began to drag her towards the double doors. "It's Penny and Becca!"

"Yippee!" shouted Rose, who wrenched her hand out of Win's grip and ran through two smiling staff members holding flower arrangements over their heads.

"Princess Rose, it is such a pleasure to see you again," said Becca, using her best Alice in Wonderland imitation. The Quinns' youngest daughter was now fifteen years old. She adored little Rose and jumped at the opportunity to visit the White House and play with her.

"Hi, Susan," greeted Julia, who gave her dear friend a half-hug and a kiss on the cheek. She set her heavy toddler on the floor so he could receive proper hugs and kisses from nineteen-year-old Penny, who was home for Thanksgiving break.

She was attending college back in Boston at Wellesley. Donald had encouraged her to go to school anywhere but Wellesley, which continued to be a bastion of liberal thought, but Penny insisted she was strong enough to withstand the peer pressure. Besides, she quipped, what better way to learn how Martians think than live with them for four years?

"Julia, this is absolutely beautiful once again," started Susan. "I think it was a great idea to reschedule the Governor's Ball for this week if for no other reason than to give the event a new look."

"This is why I love you, Susan. These things have a tendency to wreck my nerves. You gotta be nice to people who've said nasty things about your husband. You have to make small talk with people who look forward to the day you're out of Washington. You know, blah-blah-blah."

"Honey, you'll handle it with grace as always. Besides, no one puts on a party better than you do. The White House will miss you, I'm sure."

"Mom," said Win, tugging on her arm, "can I show Penny and Becca my new PS6?"

"PS6?" asked Penny. "When did that come out?"

"It's not yet," replied Win. "Uncle Brad brought it to me. It is so cool! You'll never believe the graphics. They're in 8K!"

All of the kids looked to Julia for approval, even little Frank, who'd never be allowed near the console as long as Win was running things.

"Well, this is the perfect opportunity for me to bring something up," Julia began to reply. "Susan, how would you and Donald, together with the girls, like to stay with us Wednesday and Thursday nights? These five could have a slumber party on the third floor while you and Donald can take the Lincoln Bedroom. After this week's activities, and the last eight years for that matter, it might be nice for the four of us to have a little time together to look back on things. Whadya think?"

"Absolutely. I know Donald will be ready for a few adult beverages," replied Susan as she turned her attention to her daughters. "Girls, would you like to have a couple of nights upstairs?"

"Heck yeah," replied Becca without hesitation. "Penny will too, right?"

"How can I refuse?"

Win gave Penny a high five and Rose hugged Becca.

"There you have it," said Susan as she bent down to give Frank a kiss on his rosy red cheek. "It appears to be unanimous, right, Francis?"

"Frank says yes."

Julia and Susan began to laugh. "He doesn't like to be called Francis. So he's picked up speaking in third person by referring to himself as Frank."

"I'll stick with Frank. Is that okay, buddy?" asked Susan as she gave him another squeeze. "He's so adorable."

"A-okay," the three-year-old replied.

Julia waved over their nanny and asked her to escort the kids upstairs. When they were on their way, she turned to Susan. "Do you want to help me with the seating arrangements? I'm sure Donald will make some last minute adjustments. He will probably seat certain governors alongside any who might be on the fence."

"Everything has a political angle, doesn't it?" Susan quipped.

"No doubt about it. From the receiving line in the Blue Room during the reception to the seating of the guests, and especially Sarge's toast, it's a complex, orchestrated event to gain a political advantage in some way."

"All of this makes my head hurt," Susan said with a laugh. "How many days until we go back to Boston and slip off into relative obscurity?"

"I wish! Sarge says we'll continue to have a role in national politics after he leaves office. We may always be in the public eye."

"Donald said the same thing. He's already cautioned me that our relationship to the Boston Brahmin will continue to be complicated for years. We've been lucky to avoid the connection so far."

"No kidding. Could you imagine if that got in the media? Fortunately, the only people who know have just as much to lose as we do if it were made public."

Julia's chief of staff arrived with a silver tray of place-card holders, which held the names of their guests. She provided Julia her iPad with her staff's initial seating chart suggestions based upon prior events and political affiliations.

Julia studied the proposed chart. "Okay, Susan. Let's play matchmakers, shall we?"

CHAPTER 17

3:30 p.m. ET
Taiwan Parliament
Legislative Yuan
Taipei City, Taiwan

James McBride, the U.S. ambassador to China, suggested to the Secretary of State that he address the Legislative Yuan in Taiwan as part of finalizing the $1.5-billion arms deal to the Taipei government. The newly elected president of Taiwan was appreciative of the deal, which was substantially smaller than past arms deals made prior to the collapse. Sarge was concerned with the geopolitical impact on China, and he felt the U.S. was not strong enough yet to fend off any serious blowback.

U.S.-Taiwanese relations were complicated by America's acknowledgment of the One China policy from a geopolitical standpoint. By America's actions, Taiwan was treated as its own nation-state. To prevent inflaming hostilities with Beijing, the U.S. did not maintain an embassy in Taiwan, but instead established a nonprofit organization to serve as a functional embassy. The American Institute in Taiwan, or AIT, was designed to advance U.S. business and political interests, but also to protect U.S. citizens who were in Taiwan.

As Ambassador McBride approached the podium to make his remarks, he recalled the scenes outside the building. The protestors on both sides of many contentious issues had ramped up their activities because of his arrival. They had gathered by the thousands in the streets surrounding the Legislative Yuan, attempting to out-yell the other side to make their point. McBride hoped the hostilities wouldn't rise to the level they did in 2014 when the Sunflower Student Movement in Taipei resulted in the Legislative Yuan being occupied by protestors.

His speech was not intended to announce any changes in U.S.-Taiwanese relations, nor was it intended to slight the government in Beijing. If anything, his goal was to reiterate America's long-standing policies and confirm the geostrategic significance of the players.

There were generally two kinds of American ambassadors. High-profile donors were often rewarded with glamorous posts like France, Great Britain, and Japan. Then there were the workhorses—typically career diplomats who were sent to hostile places as a reward for their experience and knowledge. Countries like China and Russia were different. They required skilled politicians who understood the impact words and actions had on their host countries. The ambassadors to these geopolitical foes were required to use finesse, deception, and at times, threats.

Ambassador McBride, the former republican governor of Tennessee, knew the Chinese. Prior to the collapse, Tennessee was the state most reliant on China for imports and exports, to the tune of nine percent of its gross domestic product. He'd held the post of U.S. trade representative at one time and was a logical choice for Sarge to appoint as ambassador to China.

After a few opening remarks, he began his speech. "Today, I wish to speak about the importance of U.S.-Taiwan relations and reaffirm the commitment of Washington to assisting Taiwan in maintaining its defensive capability. As we provide our final approval of the strategic defensive weaponry sales to Taiwan, we are sending a clear message to the region that the Taiwanese people have a right to live in peace, free from threats from its neighbors.

"It is true that the history of our two countries during the last eighty years has not been problem-free, but objectively, there is far more that unites our nations and joins our two peoples than divides us.

"Over time, both of our countries have worked hard to broaden and deepen our communications with one another and include the government in Beijing. The United States and Taiwan share more than military interests. We share economic goals, political values, and the challenge posed by China's increased military modernization.

"As ambassador to China, I will continue to act as a liaison and conduit for open dialogue. In so doing, it is my hope that the two nations can coexist, separately, without the need to force unification upon the proud people of Taiwan."

The members of the Legislative Yuan rose and provided Ambassador McBride a standing ovation as he made this statement. Eighty percent of the country preferred to maintain the status quo in its relationship with China. Only in recent years had the small minority in favor of unification become more vocal. They'd gained the attention of the media by performing outrageous, violent acts, hoping to portray a shift in the will of the people on the issue. Pro-unification demonstrators doused legislators with red paint, blocked them from entering the building, and allegedly engaged in cyber warfare to expose their email communications.

Ambassador McBride knew the tactic was working, hence his desire to make this speech. What the ambassador did not know was that during his remarks, a crowd of nearly six thousand demonstrators gathered outside, demanding a referendum and public hearings on China unification.

Several demonstrators scaled a wall and attempted to storm the building. One young man, dressed in the traditional garb of the samurai, brandished a sword and swung it around his head repeatedly. He was shot by security personnel with rubber bullets, but one struck him in the eyeball. This enraged the demonstrators further.

Protest leaders began to lead the crowd in chants supporting reunification. Chinese flags began to appear throughout the group. The next day, the event would be hailed as the largest pro-unification demonstration on Taiwanese soil since 1979 when President Carter signed the Taiwan Relations Act into law.

What Ambassador McBride and the State Department did not

realize was this was the first step in a multipart plan by China to cross the eighty-mile body of water known as the Taiwan Strait and use its military strength to reestablish One China.

CHAPTER 18

4:00 p.m.
The Oval Office
The White House
Washington, DC

Sarge and Donald prepared for their meeting with four key governors in advance of tonight's event. After the election, the Republican Party maintained a significant thirty-three to thirteen advantage in the legislative chambers. Republicans maintained thirty-one governorships, while the Democrats held fourteen. Two governors identified as independents, and both were libertarians in the Mountain West. If the four Pacific states were thrown into the mix, the Democrat column would increase by four for legislatures and governorships. For purposes of the Constitutional Convention, Sarge needed thirty-one.

The art of politics required looking ahead and reading the tea leaves. Sarge had the requisite number of state legislatures needed to call the convention, but he wanted the governors on board because they played a significant role in the policy making within those same legislatures. If he could gain the support of the governors of the thirty-one states, plus a couple, then he'd be able to push for the Article V convention.

Sarge was on precarious footing with his entire scheme. Ordinarily, states were admitted based upon the vote of Congress. However, the four states included in the Pacific statehood bill made demands beyond just readmission. They wanted their key political issues incorporated into federal law. Allowing this would circumvent the U.S. Constitution, which helped Sarge make his argument that a

Constitutional Convention was necessary to approve the changes.

Getting the governors on board would accomplish two things. It would ensure that the convention would be held, and also, it would send a message that America was committed to the concept of states' rights. Sarge had spent the last eight years decentralizing power from the federal government to the states. This final act of his presidency would put the exclamation point on his agenda.

Donald had a sense for the fence-sitters within the governors' ranks. He didn't bother attempting to sway the clear opponents of the Convention. He sought out the four most likely republican or libertarian governors to break ranks. Two of the governors were women. Currently, there were six women governors, four republican and two democrats—except one of the democrat governors was in Oregon.

The other two republican governors were from Wisconsin and Virginia. Both states were evenly divided politically, and these two were up for re-election in two years. Sarge needed to keep them in the fold with a pep talk.

After some friendly conversation and a brief tour of the Oval Office, Sarge got right to the point. "All compromise is based upon give and take, something all of you have learned as the chief executives of your respective states. But there should be no give and take on your fundamental, core principles. Anytime you compromise your principles, then you're surrendering. You're capitulating. When that happens, you don't have compromise. You have all give and no take."

The female governor of Arkansas spoke first. "Mr. President, I can speak only for myself, but others might agree. We face a difficult decision in supporting a convention. Traditionalists within our state are outraged that these four states seceded to begin with. They are out of their minds at the prospect of allowing them back in, especially with the demands they intend to impose on Washington—demands that necessarily impact each and every one of us. For that reason, we're asking our congressional leaders to vote against the bill before the House."

"That's what we want to hear," started Sarge, "but I also need your support regarding the calling of a convention."

"Mr. President, there are many pitfalls to a convention of the states, as you well know," started the governor of Virginia. He had been present at the convention in St. Louis nearly eight years ago. "You were very successful in St. Louis, but you also had a nation that was desperate for a solution to our problems following the cyber attack. Sadly, the country has settled in and forgotten all about the crisis. I'm not so sure you'd have the consensus you seek."

"I am aware that a convention could become a runaway jury of sorts," said Sarge. "We may go into the convention for a single purpose, but once the delegates get a whiff of the power they hold, things could get out of hand. That is precisely why I need all of our republican and libertarian governors on board. Work with your legislative bodies. Be a big part of the delegate-selection process. Prevent a runaway convention by using due diligence."

Sarge allowed his guests to reflect on what he said, and then he chose to remind them of what they'd accomplished in the last eight years.

"Prior to the collapse, we all knew the federal government did not function as it should. The administrative state was a significant part of the reason why. Nobody was watching over the thousands of administrative agencies created over the years. As a result, the federal government continued to encroach upon the rights of the states to govern themselves.

"We learned that this sad state of affairs was largely the fault of a lazy Congress, one that had weakened its own power over the decades by allowing too many laws to be written by lobbyists and administrative staffers. While in office, I learned there was no simple, administrative cure for what ailed our government. What we were provided as a result of the collapse was a reset, an opportunity to start over with a clean slate.

"I'm committed to bringing the Union back together, but I won't do it with conditions imposed on the federal government that are not consistent with the will of the people in Virginia, Wisconsin,

Arkansas, or Iowa. This is why we must reunify the right way, via a Constitutional Convention that takes up all of these issues, not just statehood."

CHAPTER 19

4:30 p.m.
The Hart Senate Office Building
Washington, DC

Senator Rutledge sat tapping his fingers on the arms of his chair, simulating the ticks of his great-grandfather's clock, one of the few pieces the family had saved when the Union forces led by William Tecumseh Sherman marched through the South and ransacked their family's home south of Atlanta. He hadn't moved in thirty minutes, which was his attempt to carefully weigh the pros and cons of a political decision.

He was slowly digesting the news he'd received from his contact in the House. It didn't look good. Although he couldn't put his finger on the source of the rebellion, the initial signs seemed to justify the confidence shown by Congressman Sánchez.

Senator Rutledge had to tread lightly. Although the upcoming departure of the president from office left him as a political lame duck, Rutledge suspected there were powerful forces behind the president's ascension to power. The president's handpicked team from Boston reflected a loyalty to Washington outsiders with limited or no governmental experiences. Rutledge's own vetting indicated gaping holes in the résumés of some, and evidence of extraordinarily rapid advancement for others. This could only be explained by a more powerful political force behind the Sargent administration.

That, of course, wouldn't surprise him. It had been true of most of the forty-five presidents. But this was different. The revelations of Congressman Sánchez earlier in the day had the potential to destroy much of what President Sargent had worked to build over the last eight years.

Rutledge knew he couldn't get the president on the phone directly. His Chief of Staff, Quinn, kept that door well secured. Besides, Rutledge didn't have anything concrete yet. If he relayed the information to Quinn, it wouldn't give him the kudos worthy of such a magnanimous gesture.

Rutledge stared at the windows in his office as darkening skies crept into Washington. Something sinister was happening and he weighed several options as he decided the fate of his future and that of a president whom he considered to be a friend.

*****

After a lingering kiss, Congressman Sánchez pulled away from the willing intern and got dressed. The intern licked her lips and then presented a pout. "Are you sure you have to leave?"

"I've got work to do," he quickly replied as he checked his text messages. The one he was looking for had not arrived. He was waiting for something, anything from the mysterious Mr. West, confirming that the deal had been struck.

The petite brunette took the hint and made her way to the bathroom. Sánchez took another look at his conquest and then checked his watch. *Maybe I could spare another hour*, but then his phone registered a new text message. Anyone monitoring his congressional phone account would think it was just another message from a constituent, but it wasn't.

Utilizing an agreed-upon coded message system, Congressman Sánchez smiled as he deciphered the message from Mr. West. At some point between Thanksgiving and December 11, the future Majority Leader of the House of Representatives would be out of the picture, and he, Congressman Sánchez, would make a spectacular rise to the top. A leader seeking to give poor and downtrodden Americans a chance to enjoy what the wealthy had claimed for themselves.

He'd been reminded by his new benefactors that politics was a marathon, not a sprint. However, he had his running shoes on and was ready to make his way to the front of the pack. Once he was elected the new House Majority Leader, he'd immediately set his sights on the next rung of the ladder. In the meantime, he leaned to the side to set sights on his favorite intern standing nude in the hotel's bathroom. Perhaps Congressman Sánchez would take a moment to celebrate his anticipated promotion.

CHAPTER 20

5:00 p.m.
PLA Unit 61398
Pudong, Shanghai, China

"The operation is under way," said General Liu Fulian to the premier of China, Wen Peng. General Fulian had been appointed the head of the People's Liberation Army Strategic Support Force. The men sat in a large operations center within PLA Unit 61398, the mysterious division of the Chinese military dedicated to electronic warfare.

"I trust this will go more smoothly than your prior attempts," the premier responded dryly. "The risks attached to this operation are incomparably greater with the addition of the American ambassador in your plan."

"Yes, Premier Peng, I agree. However, his abduction only enhances our deception. We will couple this event with the appearance of a direct threat to Chinese nationals within Taiwan to justify our *rescue effort.*"

"It will act as the perfect false flag, as the Americans say," said the premier with a smile.

The premier of the People's Republic of China was a man known for his steely demeanor, a type of detachment from others around him

"Thus far," the general explained, "we have exposed nothing and we have lost nothing. The troop advancements to our ports at the Taiwan Strait have gone unnoticed by the Americans' NSA. We have carefully monitored their communications and have found no evidence of detection of our plans."

"As I understand it, you rotated troops into the theater, but you never rotated troops out as is our customary practice, am I correct?"

"Yes, Premier. This operation has been many months in the planning and implementation stage. It has been accelerated because of two factors—the presence of the ambassador and the distractions to President Sargent with an important vote on reunification of the four states bordering the Pacific."

"Stupid Americans." Premier Peng chuckled in a rare show of joviality. "I should cable them and offer to take the four states off their hands. We own most of California anyway."

The general allowed himself a laugh and then focused on the mission. "The American ambassador made a speech to the Legislative Yuan, which inflamed the students in Taipei. We quickly mobilized our demonstrators to further incite the crowd. The timing is perfect for our own reunification by asserting our dominion and authority over Taiwan."

Premier Peng grunted in agreement. "The announcement of the arms sale was an insult to Beijing and all of China. The next logical step is a mutual-defense treaty with a singular purpose of placing the American Navy in the Taiwan Strait between us. Perhaps the Americans will negotiate to place a permanent military installation on the island to be built, most likely, with Taiwanese money. This cannot happen, General."

General Fulian's blood pressure rose a few points. For years, he'd warned his fellow military leaders in the PLA that the government's tolerance of Taiwan's independence would result in an increased American military presence in the region. The Beijing leadership stood idly by, acting respectfully, as they allowed United States ambassadors to shuttle back and forth between Beijing and its wayward province across the Taiwan Strait. With every trip and public appearance, the Taipei government was given legitimacy, something obviously not intended by Beijing.

The premier continued. "Even if we wished to crush Taiwan using a single nuclear strike, it would require years and vast amounts of our money to reconstruct the island. There would be no profit in such an attack, and the global political fallout would be far more dangerous than the nuclear fallout from the blast. Our long-range approach has worked, enabling you to undertake this final mission. By growing so successful that Taiwan comes to us with trade proposals, and by carefully inserting our dissidents into their universities and cultural programs, we now have the basis of an uprising."

"An uprising that will appear to be organic and natural as if it were, as they say, a grassroots effort. In reality, it has been part of a carefully orchestrated coup in the making for years."

"A coup that only needs a catalyst to set off a firestorm."

"Very true, Premier, which is why we are here. The collapse of the power grid brought a sea of change to the United States. It will bring the same to Taiwan. Operation Unify begins now."

CHAPTER 21

5:00 p.m.
The Jackson Family Home
Muddy Pond, Tennessee

"Judge, would you be a dear and call everyone in for supper," said Janie Jackson from the kitchen. Drew's father, Wilfred Jackson, who'd been called Judge for more than half his life, put another log on the fire, which caused the split oak to crackle and pop. He tapped the wrought-iron poker against the dog irons and set it to the side. The Jackson home was full of warmth and comradery as the family hosted Drew's associates from Aegis and their significant others.

While the guys were outside playing a touch football game against Jack and some of his friends on the Cumberland Plateau, Judge flipped through the various local news networks. If he didn't know better, he would've thought he'd been teleported back in time to 1860. The local news reported on the attitudes of Southerners toward the Patriot statehood bill. The consensus was indisputable—Southern nationalists were prepared to secede if the bill passed in its current form.

He shook his head in disbelief and walked through the large wooden door onto the porch. The cold, damp air entered his body in an instant. He was getting older, and even the relatively mild Tennessee winters were taking a toll. He'd never let his missus know this, but he sometimes found himself surfing the web in search of Florida winter retreats.

He grabbed the iron rod off a nail acting as a hook on the porch post and rang the dinner bell—a steel rod formed into a triangle, which hung from the eave. "C'mon, y'all. Supper's ready, and Miss

Janie won't tolerate an empty table with cold food!"

"You don't have to tell us twice, Judge!" shouted King. "They're kickin' our tails anyway."

The large group high-fived each other and paired up with their loved ones as they approached the house en masse. This was the largest gathering Janie had entertained in the home, but she'd risen to the challenge. It helped that everyone enjoyed hearty Southern cooking. Tonight, they'd be treated to cornbread with white bean and ham hock soup, one of Janie's specialties. Her recipe varied slightly from most because she smoked the ham hocks first before adding them to the rest of the ingredients. It provided a hearty, meaty taste.

As the group filed in and praised Janie for the wonderful smells that filled the house, the news reports out of Knoxville continued. Before Drew could turn down the volume in preparation for dinner being served, the reporter continued.

"The concept of secession is not an easy argument to win, but it's clear that it's gaining momentum across the South all the way to Texas. For decades, groups have held rallies to achieve what Southerners failed to do in the 1860s. In the past, the groups advocating secession were loosely related to white supremacist groups; they were never taken seriously.

"However, this is much different. The successful abandonment of the Union by the four states seeking reunification showed hard-core Southerners that the South could in fact rise again. Secession speeches are occurring in state houses in every state. Let's take a look at one orator from Jackson, Mississippi."

The reporter stopped his report and allowed the local news network to play a video of a black republican legislator in the Mississippi state house. "Naturally, as a black man, I have no interest in going back and re-creating an un-re-creatable past full of antebellum homes and slavery. Do not allow the national media to mischaracterize our intentions. This is a movement about states' rights and the right to govern ourselves without the federal government imposing its definition of values and morals upon us. If this Pacific statehood bill passes, states like California, who have a wholly different approach to governing, will impose their views upon the rest of the nation. I, for one, reject this bill, and if it passes, I will introduce a bill into the Mississippi legislature advocating secession."

Drew muted the volume and took his seat next to Abbie. His father said the blessing and everyone dug into the beans and cornbread. Some people took up seats on the sofa and comfortable recliners. Others sat at card tables brought into the large open space during mealtimes. The only thing absent after hearing the news report was the usual lighthearted banter between the guests. Everyone seemed to soak in the words of the Mississippi legislator.

Drew's sister, Alexandra, nonchalantly spoke first. "Do y'all think we're headed for a second civil war?"

Judge answered with a question of his own. "Allie, are you being serious?"

"I am, Dad. This whole thing is spinning out of control. That's all they talk about at the state house." Allie was a lobbyist for HCA Healthcare, which was based in Nashville.

Abbie finished her bite of cornbread and politely wiped the crumbs and melted butter off her mouth. "Maybe I should answer that one. Allie, here's the thing. The world is much more complicated than it was in the mid-nineteenth century when the storm clouds were brewing over the country. Our nation is interlocked economically and militarily. We had to deal with the military aspect early on after taking office. Some of our most important military bases are located in Hawaii and California. We couldn't stand for them to be commandeered by a foreign government, which in essence is what the four Pacific states have become."

"Yeah, I was stationed at the Presidio in Monterey when things went south," said one of the Aegis team members. "There was a lot of confusion when the president led the secession movement in the middle of the chaos. I have to tell you, most of us didn't stand to object because we were getting fed and had a roof over our heads. It wasn't until after it happened that the ramifications set in."

"He's right," said Abbie. "Sarge and I worked day and night to establish the legal basis for claiming ownership and control of the military bases, which included the land, the equipment, and the personnel. We treated our installations in those four states just as if they were located in Germany, Japan, or Iraq. With only a few exceptions, the base commanders agreed."

"That's right," interjected King. "When the president was impeached at the Constitutional Convention, paving the way for a presidential election to be held, our guys saw the handwriting on the wall. They upheld their oath to the United States Constitution."

"Which brought about the beginning of the reunification movement," said Abbie. She turned to Drew's younger sister. "Let me finish addressing Allie's question. The lesson learned from this is if a civil war were to break out again, the side leaving the Union would not be able to count on the military installations within their state borders. And even if the military joined them, they'd be woefully outgunned by the rest of our forces."

"Abbie," interrupted Janie, "if that's true, and I suspect you're right, what's to stop the Southern states from seceding if this bill passes?"

"Janie, hopefully cooler heads will prevail. We don't think the bill is going to pass, but if it did and it led to a broader secession movement, it would be up to negotiations and a political solution. An armed conflict between Americans can never happen again."

CHAPTER 22

7:00 p.m.
The Blue Room
The White House Residence
Washington, DC

The Blue Room was in the center of the State Floor of the White House. Over the years, it had become the traditional place for presidents to receive their guests. From entertaining kings to greeting Boy Scouts, the business of the republic and the social graces associated with diplomacy often began in the Blue Room.

Sarge whispered in Julia's ear, "You look breathtaking tonight."

"You're pretty dapper yourself, Mr. President."

"Whadya think about blowing out of this party and slipping upstairs? Do you think anyone would notice?"

"Ha-ha, very funny. Are you kidding? They'd all notice!"

Sarge and Julia continued to greet the governors and their plus-ones. They made small talk about prior get-togethers, visits to the governors' states, and the couple's final weeks in office. As the guests continued through the receiving line, the governor of Alaska was incredibly curious about one aspect of the Blue Room.

Sarge and Julia were positioned in the center of the room nearest the windows overlooking the South Lawn. The governor asked, "Mr. President, is it true that one of these windows is really a working door?"

Julia laughed and squeezed the governor's arm. "Now, Governor Blakely, you've been reading too many Tom Clancy novels."

"But—" he began to stutter.

Sarge laughed and rescued the confused man. "Julia, don't tease our friend. Of course, Governor Blakely, you are correct. Let me show you one of the secret passages of the White House."

"Sarge, um, I mean Mr. President, you can't do that," Julia protested. "You'll let the cold air in."

"Ahh, come on, he's from Alaska. I think he can handle it, right, Governor?"

"I sure can, Mr. President."

Sarge made his way to the center of five windows overlooking the South Lawn. At first glance, it appeared to be merely a window, and the window could be raised and lowered like any other. But the wainscot panels below the windows opened inward like a double Dutch door, allowing access to the porch after the window was raised.

Morrell nodded to a member of the Secret Service, who quickly moved ahead of Sarge toward the jib door. He looked onto the patio and outside into the night to look for any unusual activity.

"Mr. President, if you don't mind, allow me, sir." The agent began to show the governor and Sarge how the door worked when a bright flash of light appeared near the Washington Monument in the distance. The sudden occurrence startled Sarge and he immediately moved against the wall.

"What was that?" asked Sarge.

The flashes of light continued, allowing the Secret Service agent to respond, "It appears to be fireworks in the distance, Mr. President. Perhaps at East Potomac Park. I'll have our team investigate it, sir."

Sarge adjusted his suit and chastised himself for being jumpy. There hadn't been an attempt on his life since his re-election campaign. From the time the former president ordered the drone strike upon Prescott Peninsula, to his wedding night when Drew thwarted the assassin, he knew his life would constantly be in danger. He thought he was over the fear, but apparently it would always reside within him.

"Anyway, Governor, sorry to have to abort the mission. But this is the door you heard about. I look forward to seeing you inside after dinner."

The governor of Alaska walked sheepishly away, appearing guilty at creating the awkward moment. Sarge rejoined Julia, who immediately asked him if he was okay.

"Do you think the memories of those gunshots in New Mexico will ever get out of my head?"

"I hope so, with time," Julia replied. "The nation has come a long way since then. Maybe, under the right circumstances, reunification will heal those wounds."

"Or they might open up some old ones."

CHAPTER 23

8:00 p.m.
The State Dining Room
The White House Residence
Washington, DC

Donald and Sarge completed making the rounds with the key governors whose support they needed to firm up. The guys thanked Julia and Susan for doing a great job of positioning their guests. Donald only had to make a slight adjustment based upon their earlier meeting with the four governors. In politics, the spouse in power typically has someone at home waiting for them at the end of the day. Their loved one has been their confidant longer than any aide or senior advisor. As a result, they get to know the challenges their political spouse faces on a daily basis. As the seating arrangement proved, Julia and Susan had been paying attention.

Despite the weighty subject of the Pacific statehood bill filling the room, the evening was fairly lighthearted. A few jokes were told, and any political rancor seemed to have been set aside.

After dinner, when the mood was at its lightest, Sarge took to the podium to make his pitch. His carefully prepared remarks were designed to speak of unity and reconciliation so he didn't offend the four states seeking reunification. However, he needed to remind everyone that an entire nation couldn't be held hostage by the demands of a few. He planned on doing this by reminding the governors from whence they came prior to the collapse.

"Before the devastating cyber attack on our nation, which resulted in many deaths, societal and economic collapse, we lived in an America where our citizens were increasingly separating themselves into cultural and ideological enclaves distinct from others.

"Prior to the collapse, one lawmaker in Oregon's State House proudly proclaimed at a rally that she didn't have any Republican friends and the crowd roared with approval. States like California were making their own trade pacts with China to the detriment of other states across this great land. In Washington, governmental action took away their citizens' First Amendment rights by imposing harsh penalties upon speakers at universities who incited protestors to riot.

"Our nation was becoming polarized to the point where the only real debate was over the nature of our cultural, political, and religious beliefs. Depending upon where the debate took place, the conversation would be shut down if it wasn't consistent with the politics of the government or institution in control of the conversation.

"We saw this firsthand a decade ago. Citizens were increasingly living separate lives, in separate locations, and relied upon separate media. A conservative would only watch FoxNews or get their news from Drudge and Breitbart. A liberal would only watch MSNBC, CNN, and the major broadcast networks. Neither was interested in the other's point of view because the conversation would invariably turn hostile.

"We faced a tolerance crisis in America prior to the collapse. One side demanded tolerance from the other, but didn't provide it in return. They chose to dominate rather than tolerate. Increasingly, the so-called intolerant side got fed up and began to fight back. As a result, polarization grew.

"And let me add this. The civil-war mentality I'm hearing from many states will not save America, but rather, it will hasten its divorce. Red can't beat blue the same way that blue beat gray nearly two hundred years ago.

"The only way to reunite America and set it on a course that doesn't fall into the polarization of the past is a strict adherence to our Constitution. We simply must protect the privileges and immunities of all American citizens as enumerated in the Bill of

Rights. We must stand by one of the key principles that founded this country—federalism.

"Let California be California. Let Texas be Texas. We must minimize the impact of national politics on everyday citizens' lives. Ideas that worked in Massachusetts shouldn't be crammed down the throats of Tennesseans. What's good for Georgians might not suit New Yorkers.

"Let me repeat, I wholeheartedly endorse bringing California, Hawaii, Oregon, and Washington back into these United States. I wish they'd never left in the first place. But their readmission cannot include demands that the federal government adopt legislation that is inconsistent with the way the governors of Texas, Kentucky, Indiana, or Florida may wish to govern.

"Let me close by reminding everyone of this. The Founding Fathers abhorred the prospect of one political ideology dominating the other. The entirety of our founding documents was based upon the concept of tolerance of one another.

"So there is hope for our quest for tolerance in America. It is our Constitution, a document written to allow our citizens the ability to govern themselves while protecting individual liberties.

"It's built to withstand profound differences without asking our fellow Americans to surrender their strongest convictions. Now is the time for our nation to rediscover our Founders' principles or we may ultimately take a dark and perilous path toward separation.

"Our nation, as currently comprised of the forty-six states, should not capitulate to the demands of a few who wish to fundamentally change our principles. If we are to reunify, then let it be with a clean slate and voted upon by all of the delegates representing your states at a duly called Constitutional Convention."

Part Two

The Tuesday before Thanksgiving

November 2024

CHAPTER 24

6:00 a.m.
The Executive Residence
The White House
Washington, DC

Julia felt around in bed for Sarge, but he was already up for the day. It was still dark, which was not unusual since he'd be headed for his run, except the snow accumulation overnight would have made it too treacherous. Wiping the sleep from her eyes, she wrapped herself in a robe and made her way to the bathroom, where she found him putting the final touches on his tie.

"Looks like you're getting dressed for battle," she whispered in his ear as she hugged him around the waist.

It had only been nine years since the two of them had taken their relationship to the next level. Julia had been enjoying a meteoric rise in her career as the political editor at the *Boston Herald*, and Sarge had been settled into the new freedom he enjoyed as a tenured professor at Harvard's Kennedy School of Government.

Somehow, the stars aligned on that night in December of 2015, which drew them together for dinner *and more*. After that evening, their love grew and their destiny together was etched in stone.

With Sarge's ruggedly handsome face, blue eyes, and muscular six-foot frame, he was attractive by any woman's standards. But it was the man inside who had always drawn Julia to Sarge. In addition to his sense of humor and intelligence, she admired his drive. Sarge was a principled man who lived by one objective—every decision he made for his family, friends, or country must always be couched in terms of whether the result makes us safe and free.

He was not the type of man who lived to climb the corporate ladder of success. Fate bestowed upon him the levels of power he'd achieved as head of the Boston Brahmin and leader of the free world. Those were never on his bucket list.

In a world so often governed by self-interest, being the wife of Henry Sargent made Julia realize what leading a noble life was like. Sarge had well-defined principles and he stood by them despite the peer pressures from others around him. In the face of criticism and condemnation, he always stood for what he believed in, advancing arguments and defenses to his detriment when necessary. Julia feared for Sarge because deep down, she realized the quality she most admired in him might also turn out to one day be his downfall.

Over his time in office, Sarge's desire to do the right thing came into conflict with his duties as the head of the Boston Brahmin. On more than one occasion, he was called before the executive council by Walter Cabot, the elder statesman following the deaths of John Morgan and Lawrence Lowell. He was not-so-subtly reminded, "Henry, presidents come and go, but we've endured for centuries."

There were times when Sarge refused to compromise or bend even a fraction of an inch when it came to his principles. He had been called arrogant behind his back, and Julia understood why. However, she felt people who labeled him as arrogant were missing the point. Sarge believed in himself and the principles that he'd adopted throughout his life. Sure, they might be at odds with certain special interests, but he stood firmly by them.

What's more, he believed in his capability as a consensus builder, as long as the parties remained open-minded. No matter what the risk or how great the danger, Sarge was willing to rise to the occasion when his family, friends, and country needed him. This was one of those times.

"I chose the red tie for today," said Sarge as he kissed Julia on the arm.

"Yeah, aggressive and dominant, big boy," purred Julia. "I like it."

"Down, girl, you're not the one I'm trying to influence today. This will be for the cameras this afternoon after the vote is over. I want the media to see how serious I am about bringing this to a conclusion the right way."

Julia kissed him on the cheek and made her way to the toilet. Sarge adjusted his shirt and slipped on his suit jacket before giving himself one final look in the mirror.

"Can you join us for breakfast?" Julia asked as she washed her hands.

"No, coffee only. I received a text from Brad via Donald. There have been some developments in Taiwan that require my immediate attention."

"Anything serious?"

"I don't know yet. During the ambassador's speech, a mob gathered outside the building and they protested into the night. It became unruly and forced us to lock down the AIT complex."

"Did they storm the embassy? I mean the quasi-embassy?"

"No, but something else happened that might have just been coincidental. Parts of Taiwan began to experience rolling blackouts in their power grid."

"Maybe it was weather related?"

"Maybe," replied Sarge, who turned to Julia and playfully opened her robe. He held himself against her and gave her a proper kiss. "It's just that I've got this thing about power outages, you know?"

"Can't imagine why," she said as she returned his kiss and showed the President of the United States who was really running things.

CHAPTER 25

7:00 a.m.
The Situation Room
Ground Floor, The West Wing
Washington, DC

Snow began to fall against the early morning autumn sky as Brad's car wove through the concrete barricades onto West Executive Drive. The driver slowed, tapping his fingers on the steering wheel impatiently as he waited for the heavy black security gate to open, granting him access to the White House. After crunching through the snow from the night before, they pulled to an abrupt stop in front of the ground-floor entrance to the West Wing.

Brad exited the vehicle without waiting for his aide to open the door. He was not much for the pomp and circumstance afforded men who'd held the position of chairman of the Joint Chiefs. Brad was a Marine, and Marines don't let people open their doors for them.

He made his way under the long white awning that extended from the building to the curb, pausing briefly for Major Charlotte Riley to catch up with him. Major Riley had been tasked with monitoring the Taiwan situation and had alerted Brad to the new developments in the early morning hours. He knew Sarge well enough to realize these events required a personal update. No chairman of the JCS had ever enjoyed this kind of access to the President of the United States in history. Then again, none had ever been through the trenches with one either.

Lieutenant Colonel Francis Crowninshield Bradlee, Brad to his friends, was the consummate military man. In the early, pre-

Revolutionary War days, the Crowninshields were known for their seafaring adventures. But as the War for Independence came to full fruition, as close friends of Thomas Jefferson, the prominent family became the backbone of the United States military for years to come. Descendants of the Crowninshield family held the positions of Secretary of the Navy and Secretary of War under several presidential administrations.

Like so many of the Founding Fathers, the Crowninshield lineage included the surnames Adams, Endicott, Hawthorne, DuPont and Bradlee. Brad's father was the editor of the *Washington Post* before his death, and his mother was a highly respected, influential journalist. While the Bradlee branch of the Crowninshield family tree generally abhorred the military, Brad lived for it. He attended the Naval Academy and during his second class year he chose Leatherneck for his summer training. He received praise from his mentors and surpassed all of the academic and physical standards required to graduate as one of a few dozen Marine Selects.

His career was stellar, and after three years as a major, he earned the rank of lieutenant colonel. Under his command were 750 infantry designated service members comprising the 25th Marine Regiment of 1st Battalion. At age forty, he had fast-tracked his career to battalion commander. Now, at fifty, he'd been elevated to the highest military rank and honor in the nation.

Brad had met Steven Sargent at the Naval Academy, and the two became good friends despite their several-year age difference. Brad encouraged Steven to become a Marine, but the younger Sargent was hell-bent on becoming a SEAL via the Navy rather than through the BUDS training option offered by the Marines. Either way, Brad admired Steven for becoming one heck of a warrior, and the two stayed close friends over the years. They also realized they had common interests, which they immediately pursued.

As one of the Loyal Nine, Brad had worked closely with Sarge as they managed the events following the collapse. Together, they defended Prescott Peninsula and later went on the offensive by driving the UN Security Forces out of Boston, together with their ringleader, FEMA Governor O'Brien. Brad's reputation became more prominent within the military around the country, and using Sarge's guidance and the power of consensus building, Brad held the massive armed forces apparatus together. He'd earned his stars.

Brad gave the snow-filled sky one last look, and with Major Riley in tow, the two entered through the double doors, where two uniformed officers were posted. He started down the deserted hallway of the ground floor of the West Wing, which served primarily as offices for support staff as well as the cafeteria.

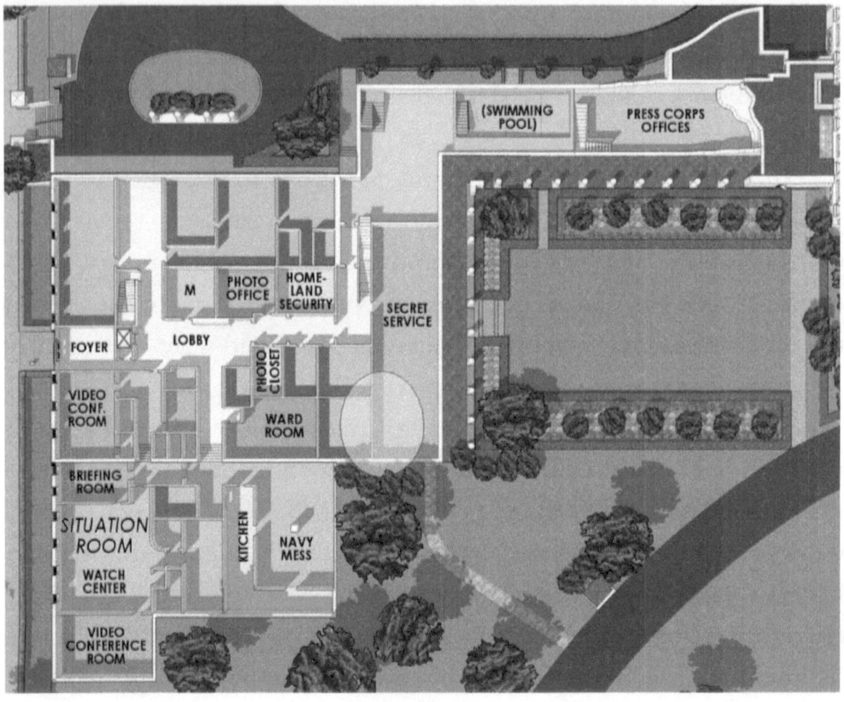

The president's office was located above them, but Brad needed the benefit of the audio-visual equipment contained within the Situation Room to provide Sarge and Donald images of the activities taking place in Taiwan. The time in Taiwan was just after 7:00 p.m. and darkness had set in a couple of hours ago. The unrest had escalated after dark.

Down the hallway on the right, the watch officer, a lieutenant commander in the United States Navy, stood by the door to the Situation Room in a sharply pressed black uniform. He greeted Brad professionally and gestured toward the door. "Good morning, General. The president and Chief of Staff just arrived, sir."

"Thank you, Lieutenant Commander Bowlin," said Brad as he glanced at the watch officer's nametape. Brad approached the secure door with a camera mounted above it. A black-and-gold plaque with the words *White House Situation Room: Restricted Access* warned visitors of the room's importance.

The White House Situation Room was a five-thousand-square-foot complex of rooms located on the ground floor of the West Wing. It was commonly referred to as the *Woodshed.*

The Situation Room was born out of frustration on the part of President John Kennedy after the Bay of Pigs debacle in Cuba. President Kennedy felt betrayed by the conflicting advice and information coming in to him from the various agencies that comprised the nation's defense departments. Kennedy ordered the bowling alley built during the Truman presidency removed and replaced with the Situation Room.

Initially, before the age of electronics, President Kennedy required at least one Central Intelligence analyst remain in the Situation Room at all times. The analyst would work a twenty-hour shift and sleep on a cot during the night.

Other presidents, like Nixon and Ford, never used the Situation Room. In most cases, a visit from the president was a formal undertaking, happening only on rare occasions. President George H.W. Bush, a former CIA head, would frequently call and ask if he could stop by and say hello.

When there had been a foreign policy failure, such as when the shoe bomber boarded a flight on Christmas Day in 2009, the Situation Room became a forum for a tongue-lashing directed at top-level intelligence and national security personnel. Sarge had never issued a tongue-lashing because Brad ran a tight ship. Fortunately, this administration had not experienced foreign policy failures like its predecessor. Brad didn't like surprises, nor did Sarge. They had also learned not to ignore odd coincidences, hence the need for this hastily called meeting.

CHAPTER 26

7:00 a.m.
The Situation Room
Ground Floor, The West Wing
Washington, DC

The lock on the door buzzed and Brad entered the main conference room. Updated in 2006, the room now had six flat-screen monitors for secure video conferences, and the technology linked them to world leaders around the globe. The beautiful mahogany walls installed during the early years had been removed in favor of the new, more sound-friendly, whisper walls.

During the renovation, the room was modified to include a bank of curved computer terminals, allowing National Security team watch officers to monitor events in real time, make instant contact with military personnel in the theater of engagement, and create graphics or produce maps to help the president in his decision making.

After greeting one another, several of the attendees filled their coffee cups and got settled in to listen to Brad and Major Riley provide their update. "If everyone will be seated, we can get started. Major Riley, please bring up the first of the images from outside the Legislative Yuan during the ambassador's speech."

A map of Taipei City appeared with arrows pointing toward key points of interest, including the Legislative Yuan and the AIT complex. Then satellite images appeared, which were portrayed in a time-stamped slide show depicting the systematic occupation of the surrounding grounds by Taiwanese students.

"Were they gathering before or after the ambassador's speech?" asked Donald.

"Major," said Brad, indicating that Major Riley should take the floor.

"Sir, based upon these time stamps, the students appeared from all directions throughout the city. At first, maybe a hundred or so mainly peaceful protestors carried signs and occasionally shouted toward legislators as they arrived. As the session continued, more than a thousand had arrived from various directions."

"I assume that at some point the demonstrations escalated to a point of violence?" asked Sarge.

"Yes, Mr. President, they did," replied Major Riley. "Let me add three additional images in the sequences. You will note that the time stamps coincide with the conclusion of the ambassador's remarks."

The new satellite images were added and what they represented was obvious. A large mob of people began to approach the Legislative Yuan from the south. They marched deliberately toward the complex and bulled their way through the other demonstrators until they reached the entrance to the building.

"Wow!" Donald exclaimed. "It looks like a tsunami pushing its way through the streets of a coastal city. These new demonstrators appeared to be on a mission."

"They were, sir. Based upon our intelligence, this group of late arriving students and young people were primarily Chinese nationals who were advancing their One China demands."

"This is different from the previous slides," said Sarge. "The other protestors arrived sporadically, as if drawn to a spectacle. This group appears orchestrated, similar to an astroturf political uprising here. It's not unusual for political parties to pay people to pretend to be supportive. The faux support often takes the form of creating a phony demonstration to raise public awareness by grabbing media attention."

Major Riley nodded and walked back to the street map of the area surrounding the Legislative Yuan. "Yes, Mr. President. But there's more. Let me bring everyone's attention back to the map. This large group of demonstrators began to gather earlier in the day here, at Chiang Kai-Shek Memorial Hall and its surrounding grounds. As everyone knows, he was the president of the Republic of China, during which time he fought a civil war with the forces of the Chinese Communist Party led by Chairman Mao Zedong. Chiang Kai-Shek retreated to Taiwan, where he ran the Chinese government until his death in 1975."

"He is widely considered a symbol of the One China policy espoused by Beijing," added Sarge, who took pride in his historical knowledge.

"Are you saying this large group, which joined the fray late, were organized throughout the day at the memorial?" asked Donald.

"Yes, sir," replied Major Riley. "We also believe there was direct Chinese involvement."

"Please explain," said Sarge.

Major Riley returned to the map. "This building down the street is China's Ministry of Foreign Affairs. The CIA keeps eyes on it at all times. There were several yet-to-be-identified individuals who traversed the grounds between the memorial and the ministry throughout the hours leading up to Ambassador McBride's remarks. Our satellite imagery, unfortunately, is blurred, but let me show you these images."

Major Riley returned to her iPad and began to bring up images on the monitors one by one. She continued. "As you can see, it's impossible to identify these three individuals, but they are wearing similar attire."

"They all look like samurais," interrupted Donald.

"Imperial Chinese warriors, actually," said Brad. "Samurais are Japanese. Similar concept although the samurais were an elevated class within Japanese culture, whereas the imperial warriors were exceptional soldiers."

Sarge rose out of his chair and walked up to the monitor, where he pointed at the men. "Are those swords?"

"Yes, Mr. President. One of these individuals breached the security of the Legislative Yuan, swinging a sword. He was subdued but not before stabbing one of the military guards. The man, identified as a Chinese national, was carrying a Taiwan flag in his backpack at the time. We believe his carrying of the flag was a ruse."

"Are we able to interrogate him? Is it even necessary?" asked Sarge.

Brad took that question. "The Taiwanese authorities claim to have the situation in hand. Sending in the CIA at this point might escalate this to something bigger than it needs to be."

"Sir, if I might add," continued Major Riley. "According to the briefing our people received, the man is an unemployed engineer who claims to have taken the sword from a nearby military museum to protect himself during the demonstration. He claims he wanted to express his political views against the One China policy."

"Yet we believe he was part of the late-arriving demonstrators who came from the direction of the memorial and China's Ministry of Foreign Affairs," interrupted Donald. "The actions and the words don't mesh."

The room fell silent as Donald's words soaked in.

Sarge shook his head and his brow furrowed. He stared at Brad and leaned forward. "Brad, I take it there's more."

"Yes, Mr. President," said Brad. "There have been a series of rolling blackouts across the country, which, according to the official government's statements, occurred because of human error at Taiwan's largest gas-fired power plant."

"This has happened before, has it not?" asked Sarge.

"Yes, Mr. President," replied Major Riley. "Taiwan's current administration is adamantly against the use of nuclear power. President Tsai Ing-wen has definitively stated that opening a fourth nuclear power plant is not an option."

"She's playing to her antinuclear base," interrupted Donald. "Business leaders have put pressure on her to resolve the current electricity shortages, but she's firmly against it. Taiwan is barely able to supply sufficient electricity to residential and business users."

"The official statement is an accident?" asked Sarge.

"Yes, however," began Brad in response, "the management team at the power plant in question initially issued a statement that they experienced unusual technical difficulties within their computer operations systems. They had to switch to a backup system in order to get power restored."

"Sounds familiar," mumbled Donald.

"Yes, it does," continued Brad.

"How did they shift from that initial statement to human error?" asked Sarge.

Major Riley responded, "According to the government spokesman, the island's generation capacity was diminished when workers accidentally shut off the natural gas supply to the plant."

"Come on," said Donald. "That's as lame as blaming the squirrels for the massive Vegas outage that spring before the cyber attack."

"Brad, bottom line it for me." Sarge shifted uncomfortably in his seat. "Are the Chinese behind this?"

"It certainly has their fingerprints all over it, Mr. President. At this time, however, it's impossible to state affirmatively whether this is just political shenanigans or part of a larger goal to destabilize Taiwan."

"Then let me ask another obvious question. Is there any evidence of military preparations across the Taiwan Strait that warrants our sending the U.S. Navy closer to the region?"

"Mr. President, it is rare for our naval vessels to enter the Taiwan Strait. As we've discussed in the past, such a move carries a high degree of military and political significance."

Sarge looked at his watch. It was approaching 8:00 a.m. "Determine what we have in the region and let me know our options during the daily briefing in an hour. We'll take this up again in the Roosevelt Room."

CHAPTER 27

9:00 a.m.
The Roosevelt Room
The White House
Washington, DC

Sarge scrolled through the day's schedule before he entered the Roosevelt Room for the daily briefing. He saw that Julia had added a thirty-minute window for him to take photographs with the family as part of the presidential historian's duties. He would have to be more actively involved as they wound down their days in the White House.

Otherwise, the schedule was almost completely dedicated to the vote in the House this afternoon. In addition, the new revelations regarding Taiwan weighed heavily on his mind.

"Good morning, Mr. President," greeted several of the attendees as they rose out of their seats to show respect.

"Yes, good morning to you all," he replied. Sarge removed his jacket and handed it to his secretary, Betty. He whispered in her ear, "Betty, I need you to contact 73 Tremont immediately. I need to speak with Malcolm the moment I come out of this briefing."

"Yes, Mr. President." Betty nodded, excused herself, and exited the room while closing the door behind her.

Before Sarge sat in his chair, he bypassed the customary protocols and spoke. "Let's get right to it. Brad, do you have an update for me from this morning's briefing?"

"Yes, sir, I do. In addition, I've asked Darla Walton, the Assistant Secretary of State for East Asian and Pacific Affairs, to join us. She can provide background as needed."

"Welcome, Ms. Walton," said Sarge with a smile.

"Thank you, Mr. President."

Sarge looked around the room and said, "Who's here from the CIA?"

"I am, sir," replied a CIA analyst. "My name is Max Chen."

Brad continued the introduction. "Mr. President, Chen is an accomplished field agent with extensive experience working on mainland China as well as in Taiwan. I'm told he's also a savant of sorts at intelligence analysis. He has the ability to see through noise created by large volumes of data that inundate the CIA, and pick and choose only that which is relevant."

"Good," said Sarge. "Now where are we? Are we any closer to knowing what really happened yesterday in Taipei?"

"Mr. President, Chen has something to add to this morning's briefing. Go ahead, Chen," replied Brad.

"Mr. President," started Chen without a hint of an Asian accent. He was born in California but was a master of various Chinese languages and dialects. "My contacts in Taipei tell me the power outage was most likely a cyber attack. They have an excellent cyber forensics team working on the situation as we speak, but early indications point to the PLA cyber-terror division—PLA Unit 61398."

"When will they have definitive evidence?" asked Sarge.

"Honestly, sir, probably never. It's near impossible to attribute a cyber attack to any one organization, whether state sponsored through PLA Unit 61398 or through their patriot hackers who act extra-governmental. They've become the world's superpower in cyber warfare for a reason. The hackers rejected by the PLA could be considered the elite in any other nation-state, including Russia and the United States."

Sarge thought for a moment and then asked, "Is there any other group or organization that would initiate a cyber attack at this time? What would they stand to gain?"

"May I take that one?" asked Ms. Walton from State.

"Please," said Sarge, gesturing with both hands.

"Taiwan's president has been under continuous pressure from

business leaders to ramp up their nuclear power program. It is possible that a consortium of her political opponents used the occasion of Ambassador McBride's visit to sabotage the grid to bring the issue to the forefront. Illuminating the shortage of electricity, if you'll pardon the pun, during the ambassador's visit would cause us to take notice. Clearly, the United States has geostrategic interests in Taiwan to protect. An unreliable power grid would threaten our interests, thus forcing us to put additional political pressure on their president."

Donald nodded. "That makes sense as well. In fact, the issue really should be addressed by the next administration anyway. I'll alert the transition team."

"Okay, so it appears the cyber attack is the real culprit for the rolling blackouts, but as is typical, it's near impossible to accurately point the finger of blame," said Sarge. "Obviously, there is no connection between the grid failure and the protests yesterday."

"Correct," replied Brad. "Mr. President, I've also reviewed our military options. I can deploy an Arleigh Burke-class destroyer to the region to monitor the Chinese. Together with a Taiwanese warship escort, we'll send a message to the Chinese."

"Brad, are you suggesting we sail into the Strait?" asked Donald.

"No, just hover nearby. I've got the newly commissioned USS *Frank E. Petersen Jr.* guided-missile destroyer two days' sail away in the Sea of Japan."

Sarge stifled a smile, as he knew the ship well. It had been built under a contract with Huntington-Ingalls Industries, a prized acquisition by Walter Cabot and his financial partner, the Boston Brahmin.

"Do it," instructed Sarge without hesitation. "Make sure they have adequate support as well. I'll deal with the fallout from Beijing. We have U.S. nationals in Taiwan who may need to be evacuated in light of the recent unrest."

"They'll claim that using a destroyer to evacuate citizens is overkill," said Donald.

"Let them cry about it," Sarge shot back. "I want them to know we're paying attention."

"Yes, sir, Mr. President," said Brad as he quickly sent a message to his aides. "But, sir, if this is the start of something bigger, the destroyer won't be enough to fend off an assault by the PLA."

"Understood. We'll see what type of response this maneuver elicits," said Sarge, who then turned his attention back to their new attendees. "While she's here, and we have the benefit of Mr. Chen as well, I'd like to get a little background on our past dealings with China when they threaten Taiwan. Ms. Walton, and Brad too, can China invade Taiwan? Has it ever come close?"

Ms. Walton looked to Brad, who gestured for her to go first. "Mr. President, despite our continued defense of Taiwan, in the past, China has demonstrated a willingness to apply military pressure when it can. China's ongoing military modernization has greatly enhanced the PLA's capabilities, but our models are unclear as to whether they could both seize and occupy Taiwan militarily."

"I recall that twenty years ago China proved they could scare Taiwan," interjected Sarge. "They strategically fired missiles, effectively bracketing the island. My recollection regarding those missile threats is that they had several unintended consequences. First, it proved that Taiwan would stand firm. Second, it caused the Clinton administration to bolster its monitoring of the region and defense of Taiwan. Third, the Chinese proved they could punish Taiwan using missile and air strikes in a way that could inflict a lot of damage. But they may have realized without political views on the island changing, they could never effectively control the Taiwanese."

"May I add something?" asked Chen.

"Please," Sarge replied.

"The 1996 event that you describe was not coupled with any other strategies. In the current situation, you have an interesting combination of unrest among the people plus the added complication of the power grid potentially collapsing. It's straight out of Moscow's playbook."

"Georgia, Estonia, and Ukraine," interjected Sarge.

"Exactly, Mr. President," said Chen. "The only difference thus far is the military component. In each of the incidents you mentioned, the Russians had amassed troops at the borders of the target countries. To my knowledge, thus far, the Chinese haven't made any hostile military overtures. Am I correct?"

All eyes in the room looked in Brad's direction. "That's correct. The Chinese haven't even announced any maneuvers or war games. All appears quiet on their side of the Taiwan Strait."

"Brad, what assets do we have in the Asia Pacific theater besides the *Petersen*?"

"Within the Navy's 7th fleet area of operations, we currently have three carrier strike groups operating in the Pacific. The nuclear-powered aircraft carrier USS *Nimitz* deployed there last summer. The strike group consists of three additional Arleigh Burke-class guided-missile destroyers and the Ticonderoga-class cruiser USS *Princeton*."

"I assume the *Ronald Reagan* carrier strike group could be redeployed if necessary?" asked Sarge.

"Yes, Mr. President," replied Brad. "It's our only forward-deployed carrier strike group in the South China Sea. It's currently on a four-day port visit to Singapore."

"Damn," muttered Donald. "That's two thousand miles away."

"Yes, unfortunate timing," added Brad. "This was a planned maneuver from many months ago to what amounts to the farthest reaches of the galaxy for the *Ronald Reagan* from its home port in Japan."

Sarge immediately made eye contact with Donald and shook his head. He didn't like this added coincidence to the mix.

"Brad, what's the status of the *Petersen* strike group?"

"It's currently in the Sea of Japan, keeping an eye on rocket man in North Korea. It's nine hundred miles away."

"How long would it take to redeploy them to the Taiwan Strait?" asked Sarge.

"Sir, the whole fleet?" asked Brad.

"Yes."

"The *Petersen* can easily cruise at thirty knots without leaving its support ships in the strike group behind. That's twenty-eight miles per hour. If it were able to sail alone, we can have them redeployed to be within striking distance within eighteen hours."

"How long until we can fill the East China Sea with a real show of force?"

"Thirty-six to forty-eight hours if we push the entire carrier strike group balls to the wall."

"Mr. President, moving the *Petersen* strike group that close to the mainland may be seen as an act of war, especially if it isn't part of pre-declared maneuvers," added Ms. Walton from the State Department.

"Not to mention the fact that we are leaving a large hole between North Korea and Japan's defense," added Brad. "The fat kid keeps his fingers within reach of the nuclear button at all times. He might take a shot if we pull out of the Sea of Japan."

Sarge grimaced and nodded. "All good points and duly noted. That'll be all for now." Sarge stood and indicated that the briefing was over.

He went for the door and Donald opened it for him. Donald leaned in to whisper in Sarge's ear, "We need to discuss this further, don't you think?"

"Absolutely. Get Brad and meet me in the Oval. I've got a phone call to make."

CHAPTER 28

9:40 a.m.
The Oval Office
The White House
Washington, DC

Sarge left Donald in the doorway to the Roosevelt Room, and he dashed to Betty's office as if he were one of Teddy's Rough Riders. He found her speaking with the presidential historian and the White House photographer regarding Sarge's schedule.

"Good morning, Mr. President," said the historian as he entered the office.

Hurried, Sarge quickly greeted both men. "Hello, good morning to you both. Betty, may I have a word, please?"

"Yes, sir."

Sarge led her into the Oval Office and whispered to her, "Did you get in touch with Malcolm?"

"I did, and he said he knew why you were calling. China, correct?"

Sarge smiled and shook his head from side to side. "This is why he's so important to us. Get him on the secure line and patch him through as soon as possible. I'll also have Brad and Donald with me, and we're not to be disturbed."

"Yes, Mr. President," Betty said as she turned to leave.

"Oh, Betty, one more thing. I don't need those two hovering around here today. Too much can be overheard. Send them over to the East Wing. Tell them, um, tell them how important the East Wing has been to the First Family during their years at the White House. Play up the theater, garden room, et cetera. I don't care. Just get rid of them."

"With pleasure. Shall I inform the First Lady?"

"No, I did promise a brief photo shoot later. I'll explain it to her then. Now, get me Malcolm."

Betty left and closed the door behind her, but it was immediately opened by Donald and Brad, who entered together.

"Hang on, guys, let me speak to Malcolm first," said Sarge.

"I knew you'd employ our other intelligence assets," said Donald.

Sarge nodded as the phone rang. He settled into his chair and answered.

"Malcolm, I gather you've seen the news out of Taiwan. What have you heard from our back-channel sources?"

Sarge listened intently as Malcolm Lowe provided him the information he'd learned in the last hour. Occasionally, Sarge would break in with a question, but for the most part, he absorbed the intelligence and then thanked Malcolm for his help before he spoke up.

"They're a wily bunch," quipped Sarge as he exhaled, allowing some stress to leave his body. He rolled his head around his neck, allowing several audible pops and cracks to be heard.

"What has Malcolm learned?" asked Donald.

"Drawing on his own State Department experience, he agrees with us that the China-Taiwan relationship is structurally unstable and potentially explosive. When Taiwan's president recently stated she would avoid formally declaring their independence from the PRC, she added it was only on the grounds that such an announcement was unnecessary given that Taiwan was already a sovereign nation in her eyes."

"How is that different from their previously stated positions?" asked Brad.

"It's not, really," Sarge started to reply, "except in this respect. Taiwan's Democratic Progressive Party is the closest thing the PRC has seen to its own Communist rule in many decades. They considered her election to be an opening to bring Taiwan into the fold. By that statement, and the agreement to accept the arms deal from us, Beijing sees their window of opportunity closing."

"Do you think they're making a move? Is that what this is all about?" asked Donald.

"We can't rule it out," said Sarge. "Brad, could you imagine any worse timing to send the *Reagan* to Singapore?"

"We only did it because the *Petersen* would be there to fill the void," said Brad defensively.

"No, don't get me wrong. I'm not questioning the decision. I'm simply pointing out three seemingly unrelated events that are starting to coalesce into subterfuge. With our carrier groups spread out, we couldn't react quickly enough to a military incursion by the Chinese. We have to make up between a thousand and two thousand miles to mount the necessary defense. Their military bases are a hundred miles across the strait."

"But there's no indication of a military buildup on their part," interrupted Brad.

"That's the puzzling aspect of all of this. Malcolm will explore this issue further, but he raised another point. A military incursion is unnecessary if they use their nukes."

With that suggestion, both Brad and Donald rose out of the seats they'd just taken moments ago.

"They wouldn't dare!" asserted Donald.

"The world would condemn it and we'd immediately respond in kind," argued Brad.

"Maybe, but perhaps they're underestimating my resolve because I'm a lame-duck president. Besides, I don't necessarily agree with Malcolm."

"Why not?" asked Donald.

"I believe they finally got smart over there and realized that military force alone is not always the solution to regime change, or in this case, reunification in keeping with their One China policy."

Donald began to laugh. "Where do you think they got that idea? You, Sarge. Your approach to the Pacific statehood or restoring the Union was different from the likes of Lincoln or Putin. You're using political means."

"Exactly!" exclaimed Brad.

"Consider what we learned in the two briefings today," said Sarge. "You have a demonstration that got out of control because China assembled a bunch of thugs that look like students to cause violence at the Legislative Yuan. In the meantime, Taiwanese citizens who are pro-nuclear power will rise up against their president because she won't fix their power grid problems with a fourth nuclear plant. Taiwanese businesses already stand in opposition to her, which negatively impacts their economy."

Brad slammed his right fist into his left palm. "The PLA initiates cyber attacks to disrupt their electricity, effectively fanning the flames of those two groups. Now, nobody is happy with the government."

"Which has the effect of destabilizing Taiwan," concluded Sarge.

"Why now?" asked Donald.

Brad answered in part. "Militarily, it's a chess match. They've caught us with one naval strike group out of range. Our other option is to pull a strike group out of the Sea of Japan, which will piss off the Japanese and possibly open the door for the DPRK to make a move against South Korea, Japan, or both. After the collapse and the recovery effort, we simply aren't prepared militarily to fight wars on multiple fronts."

The DPRK was an acronym for the Democratic People's Republic of Korea despite the fact there was nothing democratic nor *of the people* about the hermit kingdom. North Korea ranked as one of the world's most brutal dictatorships.

"They have the advantage of speed and proximity," added Sarge. "If my hunch is correct, they're setting up the geopolitical foundation for justifying an invasion. Without the use of military force at their disposal, they could collapse Taiwan from within. Under the guise of protesting our arms deal, the Chinese could institute a blockade. Using their quick reaction assets, they could divert Taiwan-bound ships to mainland China ports for inspection."

Brad paced from one side of the room to the other. "If we didn't tolerate that, they could attempt a potential alternative—a de facto blockade."

"What are you thinking?" asked Sarge.

"The PLA could attempt the equivalent of a blockade by declaring military exercises or missile-closure areas in the typical approaches to their ports. In essence, by conducting announced military drills, they could choke off the island while having their military assets at the ready for an invasion. Further, it would be intended to deter us from crossing through their military exercises to plant our happy asses in the Taiwan Strait."

Sarge ran his fingers through his hair. "The blockade combined with the asymmetric warfare could undermine the fabric of Taiwanese society. If the nation's economic infrastructure fails as a result of the combination of the two, they'll effectuate regime change without firing a bullet."

"Wouldn't they still need to involve the military?" asked Donald.

"Yes, but to what degree depends on conditions on the ground," replied Brad. "Listen, Chinese military strategists have published numerous texts analyzing the various scenarios and realities of an amphibious landing on Taiwan's beaches. Recently, I read one titled the Joint Island Landing Campaign, which lays out a complex operation utilizing coordinated, interlocking campaigns for logistics, air, and naval support. Cyber warfare was an added component to the strategy, which hadn't been discussed often in prior strategies."

"Like we said, they're learning from the Russians and us," Sarge said with a sigh.

"That still leaves the question of how would they take physical control of Taiwan if their other measures are successful?" asked Donald.

Sarge thought for a moment and then replied, "They'd do the same thing we're doing—move into Taiwan in the name of protecting their citizens on the island."

CHAPTER 29

10:00 a.m.
Stafford Regional Airport
Stafford, Virginia

Gardner Lowell chose the Stafford Regional Airport approximately forty miles outside Washington for his arrival. There were three regional airports capable of handling his Embraer Lineage 1000E, including Baltimore Washington International, the busiest, and Washington Executive in Prince Georges County, Maryland, the choice of frequent business visitors to DC.

Stafford suited Gardner's tastes. The facility offered limousine services, catering with luxurious conference rooms, concierge services, but most importantly, privacy from the media. Despite his arrival in the ostentatious Lineage 1000 aircraft, he could enter Metro DC unnoticed because Stafford prevented media onlookers from catching a glimpse of the airport's clientele. He could travel into the Capital Beltway and go directly to his suite at the Trump Hotel on Pennsylvania Avenue without raising an eyebrow.

He chuckled to himself at the irony of staying at the Trump Hotel. Donald Trump was the one candidate, besides Sarge, who couldn't be bought by men like Gardner Lowell. He shuddered to think what a Trump presidency would be like—completely unpredictable, wild, and unruly, but likely effective in a way that would stump all of the experts.

He retrieved his iPhone from his briefcase and checked his messages. There was a text marked urgent from his inside man in the House leadership. The final two names were provided to him. He'd think through an approach to these two on his commute into the city. First, he'd call and touch base with his mother.

After several rings, one of the staff answered the phone and passed the call on to Constance. They discussed his progress with the senators from Colorado and New York. The Senate vote would be close and required keeping a pulse on every one of their yea votes. Swaying them would also require the most political capital. She insisted upon being present for the final vote on Wednesday, so Gardner promised to send the jet to pick her up.

Following the call, Gardner turned his attention to the final two names on his list, both congressmen from Florida. Over the years, South Florida had turned increasingly blue in its politics. The snowbirds from typically left-leaning states like New York, Connecticut, and New Jersey either became permanent residents in Florida, or they established residency there because of favorable tax laws.

Unlike the heavy tax burden imposed upon property, income, and estates in their native states back East, they enjoyed a favorable tax climate in the Sunshine State, enabling them to keep more of their money and pass the majority of their estates to their family. There was, however, a disconnect for these new residents between their political leanings and the burdensome tax environment they were fleeing. The majority of these transplants were unable to see the correlation between their votes and the politicians who created the high tax structure from which they fled.

Due to this migration into South Florida, several congressional districts had turned purple, meaning the votes could sway either left or right depending upon turnout. Gardner knew the two congressmen well. In Florida-26, which encompassed the Everglades down to Key West, a Republican held the seat that had voted Democrat in the last six presidential elections. Likewise, another Republican in the adjacent district, Florida-27, which included Kendall and downtown Miami, won her seat by riding Sarge's coattails four years ago.

Both of the congressmen won re-election three weeks ago by the slimmest of margins. With reunification, whether by the passage of the Pacific Statehood Act or a Constitutional Convention, their seats would be put at risk in the upcoming midterms.

The text message was one of many that had come to Gardner over the last week, which provided him low-hanging fruit from the tree in opposition to the bill. He was assured the congressmen presented to him could be swayed, for a price, of course. Thus far, he hadn't been misled.

Gardner's next call was to the number one mover-and-shaker on Capitol Hill, daughter of the former vice president of the United States, Barbara Victory with Victory Consulting Group. Victory was known on the Hill for getting things done. In addition to their extensive lobbyist division, Victory Consulting also specialized in fundraising in the post-Citizens United era in which corporations could donate massive amounts of cash into the nonprofit political organizations where Federal Election Commission disclosures were not required.

Gardner had used Victory Consulting for years to funnel dollars into campaign coffers for the purpose of buying influence. When he needed to set up an impromptu, private meeting with an official of the United States government, Barbara Victory would make it happen. In the last several days, she'd been invaluable in arranging hastily requested phone calls or meetings. She would be rewarded handsomely for her efforts, as would her favorite legislators, with a more prominent seat at the table.

CHAPTER 30

10:30 a.m. ET
The American Institute in Taiwan
Taipei City, Taiwan

Every nation practiced unofficial diplomacy—nongovernmental relations with nation-states that appear to be your enemies on the surface, but require open channels of communications nonetheless. The relationship with Taiwan was different. For the first time in its history, the U.S. maintained full diplomatic relations with a foreign entity through a private, nonprofit corporation rather than the traditional embassy format.

Yet despite its officially unofficial status, AIT's website was incorporated in the Secretary of State's list of U.S. embassies and the director of AIT, Kim Moy, was included in the biographies of the State Department's diplomatic personnel, as were the two most important of the nine section chiefs who operated AIT. Chuck Miller, the Political section chief, and the section chief for Public Diplomacy, Marilyn Taylor, were both CIA agents.

Ambassador McBride received a phone call just after 10:00 p.m. that evening after he'd returned to the upscale Mandarin Oriental Hotel. He'd finished dinner and drinks with the managing directors of DuPont Taiwan, 3M, and Corning, all of which maintained manufacturing facilities on the island. The urgent call from Chuck Miller advised him to gather his belongings and wait in his room until a security detail arrived to escort him to AIT.

His dinner with the corporate executives had taken place inside the hotel's dining facilities, so he was unaware of the second consecutive night of demonstrations escalating in the area of the

Official Residence of the president, Taiwan's equivalent of the White House. The Taiwanese military had been called in to provide additional security and to quell the uprising.

The complex sits in the heart of Taipei City and is made up of several interconnected buildings. A total staff of four hundred and fifty maintain the facility and conduct the day-to-day operations of AIT as if it were any other American embassy.

Ambassador McBride rode without any conversation in the back of the Lincoln Town Car from the hotel until it cleared the perimeter walls and security gate onto the property, which contained a complete city block. The complex's main features included two guards posted at both the front and rear entrances, the director's residence, a large office building, and several smaller structures for vehicles, maintenance equipment, and dedicated generators to overcome the power outages plaguing the island.

Within the building, personnel were mostly diplomatic level although the basement floor was devoted to CIA and NSA activities. Miller, publically known as the Political section chief for AIT, also doubled as the CIA base chief. His deputy station chief and right arm was Taylor.

The CIA's command center, nicknamed the dugout, contained the most secure intelligence area, the Sensitive Compartmented Information Facility, or SCIF, which was accessible only through a blast-proof steel door with a cipher lock.

The dugout was constructed after the facility was completed in the seventies, so-named to honor the Taiwanese love of baseball and the construction process itself. Still in the midst of the Cold War, the Carter Administration thoughtfully created a facility that could withstand a Chinese nuclear attack. Within the dugout, there was a medical area, two bedrooms, and a secure room where AIT security staffers watched video feeds from the cameras mounted throughout the complex and around Taipei.

Ambassador McBride was led to a conference room where Deputy Moy awaited. Also present was the chief of security for the complex, a Taiwanese national named Lee Matsu.

"Mr. Ambassador, I must apologize for the unusual circumstances, but this evening's events required us to take these extraordinary measures," said Deputy Moy. "May I offer you something to drink, some water perhaps?"

"No, I'm fine," replied Ambassador McBride. "Am I in some kind of danger? Has there been a credible threat to my life?"

Miller responded to his question. "No, Mr. Ambassador, but with the escalation of violence by the demonstrators, out of an abundance of caution, we felt you'd be safer here in a secured facility."

"Has it gotten that bad?" asked Ambassador McBride. "Worse than last night?" Visions of the annex at Benghazi, Libya, flashed through his mind. In his opinion, Ambassador Chris Stevens and the rest of the personnel had been abandoned by the administration. He had no intention of being burned alive or beheaded by some samurai wannabe. President Sargent had taken extraordinary moves to protect diplomatic personnel abroad, and from what he knew of the AIT operations, he felt like he was in good hands.

"I'm afraid so," replied Deputy Moy. "Dissidents have stormed the Official Residence and are clashing with the military. Matters got worse in the last hour after the security personnel deployed sonic cannons to disperse the crowd."

Law enforcement in Taiwan, like many foreign nations, liberally used long-range acoustic devices, or LRADs, to issue shrill warning tones that could be heard as much as sixteen hundred feet away. The devices could blast a maximum sound of one hundred fifty decibels, the equivalent of hearing a loud gunshot within three feet away.

The use of an LRAD over one hundred twenty decibels was noticeably painful, and any use above one hundred fifty decibels could damage the small hair cells in the inner ear that convert sound energy into electrical signals comprehended by the brain. Misuse of the LRAD could cause hearing loss and concussions.

Matsu, the chief of security, added, "The Russians have developed a new generation of sonic weapons that span frequencies far above the LRAD devices used by law enforcement. The high-powered, low-frequency sonic weapons cause long-term psychological damage—

including panic attacks, depression, fear, and anxiety—on top of the concussive effect."

Deputy Moy continued. "As word spread via social media that the LRADs had been deployed, angry citizens from all walks of life descended upon the Official Residence to demand the president bring a halt to their use. We felt the situation might escalate further and we thought it best to pull you in."

Ambassador McBride exhaled and sighed. "Well, I certainly appreciate that. Is the president safe under these circumstances? Have you been in contact with her?"

"We have, and she was safely removed to an undisclosed location. Her staff assures us that the protests will cease as the evening progresses, and tomorrow afternoon's signing of the arms-sale documents will go on as planned."

Ambassador McBride finally relaxed in his chair and looked at his watch. It was approaching midnight in Taipei, but it was only noon in Washington. Under the circumstances, he thought it was a good idea to touch base with State. He was sure the information was based upon what was being provided by the CIA team here in Taipei. But it wouldn't hurt to confirm it. "Can you provide me a quiet place to make a secured phone call to the Secretary of State?"

"Yes, sir," replied Miller. "They're expecting your call."

CHAPTER 31

Noon
The Palm Restaurant
Washington, DC

Washington, DC, was known for its big events. Every day, something was being celebrated or memorialized. Somebody was being honored or laid to rest. Those-in-the-know knew when something big was going down on Capitol Hill, The Palm Restaurant would be packed.

While administrations come and go, and the power in Congress teeters between political parties, one thing remains constant in the lives of Washington's elite—the power lunch. Between noon and two, brokers meet to clinch deals with the emphasis more on the power than the palate.

Fifty years ago, Tommy Jacomo moved to Washington with his brother and built The Palm brick by brick with his bare hands. During the aftermath of the collapse when DC became a dystopian war zone, the brothers took an unusual approach to protect their famed eatery in Dupont Circle—they looted it themselves.

Acting quickly and decisively, they worked with their staff to empty the restaurant and remove its most prized fixtures and accessories to the Jacomo home on Corcoran Street. Tommy surmised immediately the cyber attack was far-reaching and that the power grid would be down for an extensive period of time. By removing the most valuable fixtures and giving the restaurant the appearance of being looted, he hoped it would avoid the onslaught that would eventually overtake the DC metro area.

His decision proved to be prudent, and the iconic restaurant survived relatively unscathed. Within a year after Sarge's election and subsequent move into the White House, Tommy Jacomo had The Palm open for business as the nation's capital's most famous power spot. He was once again the *keeper of the keys*, as everyone knew him.

Tommy seated his old friend from Savannah, a longtime patron and the matriarch of the Rutledge family. As power brokers go, Sarah Rutledge played the game quite differently. Her mere presence in Washington sent the rest of the diners into whispering fits of gossip, all speculating as to what dog did the Rutledge family have in the fight.

"Thank you, Tommy," said the aristocratic woman dressed as if she'd just walked out of a *Gone with the Wind* showing at The Avalon on Connecticut Avenue. She removed her coat and Tommy immediately helped her with it.

"You're very welcome, Sarah. Will the senator be joining you today?"

"Yes, Tommy. Would you be a dear and have someone bring me an Apple Blossom? I'm parched after my flight."

"Of course. Right away. Enjoy lunch with your son."

Within a minute, a sharply dressed waiter delivered Sarah Rutledge's favorite libation when she visited The Palm—an Apple Blossom cocktail made with Buffalo Trace Bourbon, St. Germain liqueur, and apple juice, served chilled in a martini glass. It was a power drink befitting a power lunch.

Sarah Rutledge was a descendant of Edward Rutledge, the first of the South Carolina delegation to affix his name to the Declaration of Independence. His brother, John Rutledge, possessed all of the qualities that a man born to win and command required. His branch of the family owned plantations stretching from Charleston to Savannah. After the Civil War, the Rutledges astutely made alliances with the Union Army to spare their homes and businesses in exchange for lucrative deals for cotton. The Rutledges had a nose for the changes in the political winds and were always carefully positioned on the right side of any bluster.

Sarah was the first woman in the Rutledge lineage to make a name for herself in the world of finance and politics. She was the managing partner in the private equity firm of Windfall Inc., which had a net worth of $2.3 billion. Her late husband, Richard Windfall, founded the firm in the late eighties but could never take it to the next level. Sarah Rutledge took the firm from stagnation to Wall Street stardom.

Her accomplishments earned her a place as one of the first female members of the Augusta National Golf Club along with Condoleezza Rice. She's always been one of the most powerful women in American business, but she carried considerable influence in national politics as well. She was instrumental in getting President-elect Stanford Rawlins into office. Equally important, she was a big admirer and supporter of President Henry Sargent.

"Hello, Mom," said Senator Rutledge as he bent over and provided his mother a peck on the cheek. He pointed to the half-empty cocktail. "I see you've started without me."

"Good afternoon, Paul. You and I have turned more than a few heads in the last minute or so."

"I can only imagine. I'm sure messages are flying from cell phone to cell phone at a record pace. How was your flight?"

"Fine, dear. I don't like to make this trip in the wintertime, particularly with snow on the ground before Thanksgiving. One of these days, perhaps they'll consider moving the capital to Atlanta."

Senator Rutledge laughed as a waiter began to approach their table. He leaned in and whispered to his mother, "The way this vote is looking, that time might come sooner than you think."

Sarah's mouth opened wide and a look of surprise crossed her face. She was about to speak when the waiter interrupted them and took their lunch orders. After he was dismissed, the conversation continued.

"Do tell," she whispered across the table, suddenly aware that several sets of eyes were darting in their direction. Her son, as Senate Majority Leader, was one of the most powerful men in Washington and was likely to draw attention anytime he went to lunch. Their choice of The Palm for today's lunch was clearly sending a political message—the power behind the nay votes was in town too.

"In the last few days, it has become apparent to me that there are powerful forces at work pushing passage of the Pacific Statehood Act. They've been so bold as to send one of their minions to subtly threaten me to stand down as they make their backroom deals."

"Really?" asked Sarah with a tone of incredulity. "Who on earth thinks they could defeat you in Georgia?"

"That attention whore—Congressman Rafael Sánchez."

"He's a twerp, son. And he's not even a Georgian. The good people of our state won't elect a transplant from El Paso to statewide office, much less the sitting Senate Majority Leader's seat."

"He's from New Mexico, Mom."

"Whatever," she said, brushing her hand in front of her as if she were sweeping a bread crumb off the white tablecloth. "Where did he get the gumption to challenge you?"

Senator Rutledge leaned back while their lunch was served. He was about to reply when a reporter from the *Washington Post* walked behind him.

"There goes the enemy," he mumbled as he took in a spoonful of lobster bisque.

"Aren't they all?"

He smiled and nodded before continuing. "I think he's been promised the moon by the DNC, but I've seen this kind of thing before. This was not some type of bluff. This guy was too ballsy, excuse my French, Mom. The smug, arrogant little you-know-what was certain he could back up his demands."

"What exactly does he want?" she asked.

"He's certain the House will pass the bill this afternoon."

"No way. I'll be back on a plane to Savannah before dinner."

"Mom, I'm not so sure. As you know, I try to stay out of the House's affairs unless directly approached by their leadership. We have an understanding—they deliver their votes and I deliver ours."

Sarah finished her coconut-crusted sea scallops beautifully garnished with a watermelon jelly and asked, "What's your gut telling you?"

Senator Rutledge wiped his mouth and pushed his plate into the center of the table. "Two things. First, our friend in the Oval Office has a problem and he doesn't know it."

"Should we warn him?"

"That's why we needed to have this discussion. I don't think we can control or change this afternoon's vote at this late hour anyway. Perhaps we should just wait and see the results."

"I can't disagree with that. What is the second aspect of all of this to consider?"

"Mom, I've been thinking. What is the worst-case scenario if the House passes the bill?"

Sarah shrugged. "It goes to the Senate, where Pacific statehood goes down in flames."

"But what if it doesn't? By that I mean, what if we were to get blindsided tomorrow and the Senate passes the bill as well?"

"The four states come back in and force their political ideologies upon all of us," she replied.

Senator Rutledge nodded his head and his mouth formed into a devious grin. "And then the Southern states, the eleven within the original confederacy minus Virginia, led by this family, would band together and plan their exit strategy."

The matriarch of the family who made lucrative deals with the federal government in order to survive the end of the Civil War began to smile as well. "The president would never stand for it, especially since we agreed to help fund the Constitutional Convention."

"I love Sarge, but he's a lame duck. I'm thinking about down the road, next term."

Sarah reached across the table and held her son's hand. Her wrinkled, bony hands were still capable of holding a firm grip in many ways. "If it's secession you want, the next president is our guy. He'll never stand in the way. Heck, he might even pave the exit ramp for us!"

Chapter 32

Noon
The Green Room
The White House
Washington, DC

Julia bent down to adjust Win's tie, which had already been yoked out of shape courtesy of her little angel—Rose the Barbarian. She had arrived in the Green Room early so Sarge wouldn't be delayed. Originally used as a guest room before being turned into a dining room by Thomas Jefferson, the Green Room was used for small receptions and predinner cocktails for guests at state dinners. Julia thought it would provide a quiet setting away from the extraordinarily busy day within the White House.

The West Wing was full of frantic staffers in preparation for the vote, and the Executive Residence was being prepared for their upcoming Thanksgiving dinner to be held in the adjacent Blue Room.

"Mom, are they going to do a painting of us like they did of Dad?" asked Win.

"I don't think so, son. Portraits are for the president. Pictures are for the First Family."

"Didn't they already do a First Family picture? It's hanging upstairs."

Julia laughed. "They did, Win, but you were just a toddler, and since they took that picture, we've had a couple of additions to the family."

Rose and Frank were holding hands, skipping between the red Duncan Phyfe side chairs and around a table that had been in place for nearly two hundred years. "Frankie, Miss Rose, you two need to sit down. Your father will be here any minute."

Jon Madison, former editor of *Time* magazine and a well-known historian, was coordinating the effort to chronicle the Sargents' final days in the White House. In addition to the official White House photographer, Madison always had a videographer alongside him. A hardcover book suitable for tabletop display would be produced from his efforts, as well as a documentary found exclusively on Netflix.

Sarge had laughed when Julia had informed him of the Netflix appearance. "Great," he'd said with a laugh. "They'll be able to compare me with President Frank Underwood on *House of Cards*. I wonder who viewers will like more, Henry or Francis?"

Her response was classic Julia humor. "Neither, it'll be a battle between Claire and me, of course, for best-dressed First Lady."

"Good afternoon, everyone," announced Madison as he and his team entered the Green Room and began setting up. He looked around the room for Sarge. "Will the president be able to join us?"

"He'll be here according to—" Julia started to respond before she was interrupted.

"Daddddy!" Rose squealed with delight as Sarge entered from the Blue Room entrance. "You made it!"

"Come here, my darling princess," Sarge said as he stooped to one knee to prepare for the impact of the hard-charging Rose. He grunted as she flew into his arms full force. "Ugh."

She quickly pulled away and struck a pose. "Look at my new dress. Mom and Abbie picked it out for me just for this picture. What do you think?"

Sarge began to laugh and looked at a beaming Julia. His daughter had grown so much. Life in the White House suited her just fine, especially being in the constant presence of adults other than her parents. She learned manners and respect. Further, she was treated like an adult in many respects, which made her more sociable. Rose did have a bit of an independent streak, but Sarge and Julia didn't think that was unusual considering she was a middle child. She didn't want to do the things her older brother, Win, could do. She wanted to make her own mark on the universe, at age five.

Frank marched proudly toward his father in a three-year-old toy-soldier kind of way. As the youngest Sargent, Francis Steven Sargent was on a mission to prove that his bigger, faster, and smarter siblings were not necessarily the cat's meow. He'd developed a rebellious streak, an *I'll show 'em* persona that had turned him into somewhat of a monster.

"Hello, sir," said young Frank as he presented the Commander-in-Chief with a snappy salute.

Sarge laughed and stood, proudly returning the salute to his young soldier. "Frank, you look very much like a naval commander. Very impressive, son."

"Thank you, sir."

The room erupted in laughter at Frank's formality. Sarge leaned down and whispered into Frank's ear, "You can call me Daddy, you know."

Frank whispered back, "I know, but only at home, okay?"

"Okay, Frank. I understand."

Sarge shook hands with Madison and then walked over to give Julia a kiss. Win stood dutifully by his mom.

"Nice tie, Win."

"Thanks, Dad," Win said proudly. "Mom calls it a power tie. You know, I think it suits me."

Sarge burst out in laughter. "You think so?"

"Yes, sir. It works for you."

Sarge, who continued to laugh, caught Julia's eye, who was beaming at the family they had raised. "If your mom says so, then it is so, right?"

"Right," said Win, looking up at Julia for approval. She placed her arm around Win's shoulder and pulled him tight against her. "Let's get started, shall we? I think your dad's pretty busy today."

Sarge looked around the room and determined they were setting up for a photograph of the family under the painting of Independence Hall in Philadelphia at the time the Constitution was signed.

The striped settee was large enough for the five of them, although Madison wanted to position Frank on Julia's lap and Rose on Sarge's, with Win in the middle. After some jaw-jousting and near-nuclear negotiation between the two youngest kids, Rose landed on Julia, and Frank sat proudly on his father's leg. Win, mature beyond his years at seven, sat steadfastly in the middle while an agreement was reached.

The entire thirty-minute session was filmed, creating one of the more comical behind-the-scenes looks at President Sargent and the First Family. During the photo session, the business of Washington continued, and there wasn't anything humorous in DC at the moment.

CHAPTER 33

11:30 a.m.
The Oval Office
The White House
Washington, DC

Sarge returned to the Oval Office and was greeted by his communications team and Donald. They'd been discussing messaging for the White House press briefing, which Ocampo would lead in an hour. Crepeau was coordinating the post-vote remarks to be made by Sarge. Also, it was agreed they wouldn't waste any time trotting out pro convention governors in front of the cameras in key swing states.

"Anything new?" asked Sarge as he entered the room and removed his jacket. Ocampo politely took the president's jacket and draped it over a side chair next to the bust of George Washington. His question wasn't unusual despite only a thirty-minute absence. When you're President of the United States, world events can transpire in the blink of an eye.

"I have Congressman Trent coming in for one last head count before the vote," replied Donald, who scrolled through his roster of congressmen on his iPad.

"Does he think it's necessary to get together again?" asked Sarge.

"No, but I do. I'm leaving nothing to chance here. The morning after the election, I sat down with Trent and looked at every one of the four hundred thirty-five members of the House. We identified those who were retiring and lame ducks who just lost re-election. That group was quickly identified as wild cards. Then we separated from the pack the votes that were absolute yeas and nays. This enabled us to focus on the four dozen or so potential fence-sitters."

"I take it Billy has been on top of those fence-sitters."

"He has, and thus far with the exception of a few defectors, the rest have held true to their word," said Donald.

"Well, let's wrap it up quickly because I need to make a decision on Taiwan."

"I agree," said Donald. "I want Congressman Trent back in the trenches to make sure we don't get blindsided. At noon, I'm conferencing into a meeting at the Pentagon led by Brad. They are going to agree upon and adopt a final proposed military solution to stymie the Chinese in any effort to invade Taiwan. Keep in mind, this operation is not designed to put us on a war footing. We're simply going to show sufficient force to make them think twice about crossing the Taiwan Strait."

"Mr. President, if I might add," started Crepeau. "My counterpart at State informed me a few minutes ago that out of an abundance of precaution, they evacuated Ambassador McBride from his hotel to AIT. Neither the Secretary of State, nor Ambassador McBride, I'm told, is interested in a repeat of Benghazi."

"What about tomorrow's ceremony with the president?" asked Sarge. "This is just a dog-and-pony show anyway. They don't need a media presentation for something that's already been approved by both sides."

"That's true, sir," said Ocampo, who was particularly astute in international relations. He was the grandson of the former United Nations Under-Secretary of Economic and Social Affairs. "However, the Taiwanese relish the opportunity to flaunt their relationship with the U.S. any chance they get. They're very much like Kim Jong-un in that respect. They get immense pleasure in poking at the nation that could annihilate them."

Donald started to laugh. "Sometimes, you can needlessly anger or annoy your adversary. It's kinda like road rage. You never know when the act of flipping someone off or blaring your horn at another driver out of anger might send them over the edge. The next thing you know, you're fighting for your life with an enraged maniac."

"What are you saying, Donald? Should we cancel tomorrow's signing?" asked Sarge.

"No, I don't think we need to go that far, but it's a lesson the Taiwanese and North Koreans need to learn," Donald replied. "Sometimes it's better to lie low. When you poke the hornet's nest, you better make sure you kill 'em all. If you don't, you might get bit."

"Hey, I like that," said Crepeau. "I might use that in a press statement."

"Yeah, it's a great adage. I read it in a book once."

Sarge laughed and took a seat behind his desk. He unconsciously rubbed the palms of both hands to caress the leather inlay. This desk had been a source of inspiration for him prior to the collapse, and since then, it had given him confidence and strength.

"Do we have anything else for the dynamic duo?" he asked, waving his fingers at the husband and wife communications team. Sarge was extremely proud of his former students, and himself, for giving them extraordinary access to the president, considering they had no experience in Washington. They had a great future ahead of them.

"Just two things," responded Donald. "If they ask whether the president will be making a statement this afternoon, tell them that hasn't been determined yet. I don't want to commit to anything in advance that we'd be locked into."

"What about the Taiwan situation?" asked Ocampo.

"I imagine they'll be focused on the vote," replied Donald. "But if it comes up, tell them the Pentagon—no, the State Department will be issuing its own statement later this evening after daylight in Taipei."

"Why not let the Pentagon handle it?" asked Crepeau.

"We don't want the media to suspect the military would need to be involved at this point," replied Donald.

"And," started Sarge, "we never communicate or hint to our allies about our military strategies. Too often, prior administrations told the enemy what our plans were, giving them more than sufficient time to make adjustments. That has never happened in this administration."

A light knock at the door preceded Betty, who slowly opened the door and poked her head into the Oval Office. "Congressman Trent has arrived."

"That's our cue to leave," said Crepeau.

"Thank you both," said Sarge as he rose to greet the House Majority Whip.

"Good afternoon, Mr. President, Donald." Congressman Trent shook hands with both men. He had a spiral notebook and a legal pad tucked under his arm. His tie was loosened and he appeared generally disheveled and tired.

"Billy, have you slept?" asked Sarge.

The hefty man chuckled and replied, "Tonight, Mr. President, when I'm safely tucked in bed back at the farm in Salem." Congressman Trent had served fourteen terms in the House and had never faced a serious challenge for his seat. Roanoke County and the rest of southwestern Virginia was very conservative.

"Billy, we'll be brief," started Sarge. "You've been a tremendous asset and a good friend to this administration during my two terms in office. I want you to know we don't doubt your abilities on this. As you know, when I feel strongly about something, I'm like a dog with a bone. This vote's in a few hours and I would be remiss if I didn't touch base with you one last time. Please take a few minutes to update Donald and myself."

"Yeah, Billy, humor us." Donald took a seat on the sofa and he was quickly joined by the Majority Whip and Sarge. Like an eager child ready to hear a story, Donald scooted up to the edge of his seat, iPad at the ready.

"Well, first off, thank you, Mr. President. I'd like to think that I've attempted everything you've asked of me. Things didn't change much after the collapse. The Senate remained the world's most deliberative body and the House will always be, well—Congress is strange, gentlemen. A man can stand up to address the House and say absolutely nothing. Furthermore, nobody listens. But despite this, everybody disagrees. The same can be said of the Pacific statehood bill. There's something in there for everyone to dislike."

"Then voting nay should be easy, right?" asked Donald, wanting to stick to the subject.

"I wish it were that simple," replied Congressman Trent. "But that said, based upon the reports from my deputy whips, we've held onto the same number of nay votes as yesterday afternoon when we met."

"Plus six?" asked Sarge.

"Well, not quite, Mr. President. We've been focusing on the same forty-nine members since after the election results were in three weeks ago. Our deputy whips have done their jobs well except for the three that we know about. The two undecided members have publicly announced they'll vote for the bill. In any event, we're now looking at two twenty-two to two thirteen."

"Is this your final tally?" asked Donald.

"I believe so. Technically, that puts us at plus five. However, if five switch to yeas, the bill passes."

"Too close, but not razor thin," said Sarge. "Billy, I'm gonna ask the same question I've asked for days. Do I need to make an appearance on the Hill or bring any members of the House in here to speak with them? I'll make the time even though this thing is scheduled this afternoon."

Congressman Trent thumbed through his notes as he made an effort to identify prospects for the president. Without making eye contact, he replied, "No, Mr. President. I believe it is what it is at this point."

Donald and Sarge exchanged glances and Donald shrugged. Sarge had to rely upon House leadership to keep him abreast of attitudes on Capitol Hill. It wasn't typically the province of the president to interfere in their activities. He provides gentle nudging from time to time, but rarely does he apply muscle. That was the job of men like Majority Whip Billy Trent and Donald Quinn.

"Okay, then," said Sarge as he stood to dismiss the congressman. "Billy, as always, thank you for your efforts. I look forward to placing that phone call to you this afternoon with hearty congratulations."

"Likewise, Mr. President." Congressman Trent shook hands with Sarge and Donald without another word spoken between them.

After Congressman Trent left, Sarge wandered through the Oval Office and glanced out the window as the snow began to lessen. A chill came over his body as he turned to Donald.

"Thoughts?"

"We've done all we can short of dragging every one of the SOBs in here to bend a knee, as they say."

"Billy said it best—it is what it is."

CHAPTER 34

Noon
Joint Chiefs of Staff Conference Room
The Pentagon
Washington, DC

Officially, it was known as the JCS conference room, the sanctum sanctorum of America's most brilliant military minds. Unofficially, it was called the Gold Room after the color of its carpeting and drapes. But for those who worked within the Pentagon, their meeting place was simply called the Tank.

Its moniker, the Tank, was a coinage from the Second World War when, in 1942, the newly formed American Joint Chiefs met with their British wartime counterparts in a basement room of the Public Health Services building on Constitution Avenue. To enter the room, the Joint Chiefs and their staff had to pass through an ornate archway that resembled, to some of the former members of the Armor Branch, the turret hatch of a tank.

The nation's senior military leaders met routinely to wrestle with the country's security challenges in order to formulate an appropriate response. The decisions reached here were then presented to the president who, as Commander-in-Chief, made the final decision on military strategy.

It was customary for the chairman of the JCS, in this case Brad, to sit in the place of honor midway down the table. He was always flanked on the left by the vice chairman, with the director of the staff to his right. On the weekly occasions that the Secretary of Defense joined the briefings, the director of staff sat to the Secretary's right. The United States military respected the protocols they'd adopted over the years, and the formality adopted by the JCS was strictly adhered to.

Visitors were rarely afforded a glimpse inside the Tank, but typically their reaction was one of surprise. The room didn't have the mysterious quality depicted in Hollywood, but rather, looked like an ordinary corporate boardroom, with lots of flags.

The meetings were normally scheduled for 2:00 p.m., but Brad moved today's briefing up to noon because the matter was time sensitive. Based upon the scenarios presented to him by his staff, the president would need to make a decision soon about the redeployment of the USS *Frank E. Petersen Jr.* strike force from the Sea of Japan to the Taiwan Strait and East China Sea.

Donald had been brought into the briefing by teleconference and remained mostly silent while Rear Admiral David Faulkner explained their options. Admiral Faulkner presented maps to each of the attendees and to Donald via email. He also had a PowerPoint-style presentation, which he stood next to with a pointer. These maps laid out ship positioning for both the *Petersen* and the Chinese Navy in the region.

"For two decades, the world has been focused on the test of wills between us and Beijing in the South China Sea," started Admiral Faulkner. "China began asserting their territorial claims long before their building of the network of artificial islands that now operate largely as military bases and outposts for them. They stepped up their program during the two years that we recovered from the cyber attack, basically unchecked, because we had to tend to the defense of our own shores."

Admiral Faulkner switched the slide from the South China Sea, which lay between the Taiwan Strait and the Strait of Malacca at Singapore, to the East China Sea.

"While our focus on the South China Sea was necessary, a thousand-plus miles to the north, in the East China Sea, tensions have quietly and steadily mounted into a potentially dangerous cocktail of disputed islands and a well-armed adversary. In the last year, China has begun sailing bigger ships, older naval vessels that were repainted and reflagged as their equivalent of the Coast Guard. Make no mistake, these ships are every bit as battle capable as their Navy."

Brad interrupted. "Let me add for the Chief of Staff's benefit, that it was these same *Coast Guard* vessels that carried out aggressive and provocative maneuvers near Japan last spring. We roundly condemned their activities and publically supported Tokyo with the promise to honor our treaty obligations and come to their rescue if requested."

"Yes, thank you, General," said Donald, respecting the formality of the briefing. "These activities were an ancillary reason for the deployment of the *Petersen* to the Sea of Japan."

Brad nodded at Admiral Faulkner. "Please, continue."

"The Chinese have strategically deployed Coast Guard vessels that are much faster and could easily outmaneuver our carrier strike force. As soon as the *Petersen* cleared the narrow strait between Japan and South Korea, the Chinese Coast Guard would swiftly move to block our progress."

"Undoubtedly," said Brad. "What are our options?"

Admiral Falkner walked away from the screen and turned to his notes. "The first option would place the *Petersen* strike group close to Taipei within thirty-six hours of redeployment. It is also the riskiest option."

"Please explain," said Brad.

"We would need the cooperation of the Japanese, sir, but what I propose is that the Japanese deploy a Takanami-class destroyer together with two small frigates into the Yellow Sea between South Korea and the Chinese coast. They would be reminded to remain in international waters. Further, Tokyo should make a casual announcement that these ships are performing routine maneuvers."

"They'll still draw the ire of Beijing," interrupted Brad.

"That is true, General. However, the Takanami-class destroyers are not armed with guided missiles, so they are less aggressive than their Atago- and Kongo-class counterparts. Also, the suggested frigates, most likely Asagiri-class, are considered defensive in nature and, therefore, less threatening."

"I see," said Brad. "Regardless of their offensive capabilities, the destroyer and her escorts would draw the attention of the Chinese Coast Guard into the Yellow Sea."

"And out of the way of the USS *Petersen*, sir," added Admiral Faulkner, finishing Brad's sentence.

Brad turned toward the camera. "Mr. Quinn, this would necessarily involve a quickly arranged conversation between us and the Japanese, most likely at the highest levels. We're approaching a situation where hours matter."

"I understand, General," said Donald. "Admiral Faulkner, you mentioned a second option."

He looked over to Brad, who nodded his acquiescence to continue. "Option two would require a longer sail for the fleet but would not involve the Japanese Maritime Self-Defense force except with one respect, which applies under both scenarios. As we pull out, the JMSDF will have to fill the void we leave between Japan and the DPRK."

"We'll make that clear to the prime minister," interjected Donald.

Admiral Faulkner continued. "Currently, more than half of the *Petersen*'s escorts are located to the north end of the Sea of Japan, off the coast of Fukushima. The Japanese consider the nuclear plant there to be a primary target for the DPRK's missiles. Accordingly, once the order to redeploy is given, we can sail the destroyers and escort vessels through the Tsugaru Straits, which separates Northern Japan from the south. The USS *Petersen*, with its superior cruising ability, would catch up with the fleet by the time it reached the southern tip of Japan, here." Admiral Faulkner pointed to the rendezvous point on the map.

"Will the Japanese have an issue with our sailing the nuclear-powered *Petersen* that close to their shores?" asked Donald, before adding, "They have a prohibition against nukes within their borders."

"You're correct, sir," replied Admiral Faulkner. "However, Japan's territorial waters only extend to three nautical miles into the Tsugaru Straits instead of the usual twelve, which allows our nuclear-armed warships and submarines to transit the strait without violating Japan's prohibition against nuclear weapons in its territory."

Faulkner pointed to a map of the region to provide the deployment some context.

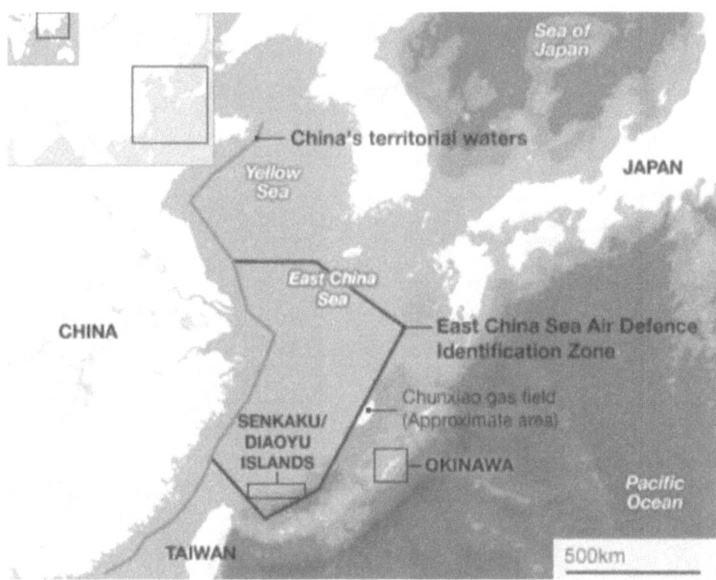

"The USS *Petersen* would regroup with the destroyers and support vessels near Okinawa, well outside the East China Sea Air Defense Zone identified by Beijing. At that point, we'd be three hundred miles from the Taiwan Strait, well within striking distance of any military installation within the Chinese mainland."

"Yet clearly in international waters," added Donald through the speakers. "I like it. But what about the remaining vessels within the *Petersen*'s strike force. Won't they be cut off from the rest of the fleet?"

"Yes, sir," replied Admiral Faulkner. "The only way to include them is to sail directly to the south and along the edge of the Air Defense Zone. If we do that, it's likely the Chinese Coast Guard will move quickly to intercept. It's not likely they'll move into the disputed Senkaku Islands, which would be a direct affront to Tokyo."

"What if hostilities escalate?" asked Donald. "Can the USS *Petersen*, with only half its fleet, effectively fight off a Chinese invasion of Taiwan?"

"Mr. Quinn," replied Brad dryly, "that depends upon how big a fight the Chinese want. Every asset at our disposal in the region will be carefully watching what they do. You can assure the president we'll be prepared to bring the house down with pleasure."

CHAPTER 35

1:00 p.m.
The Trump Townhouse
Trump International Hotel
Washington, DC

Gardner Lowell could afford the most luxurious accommodations that Washington had to offer. When you were born into the kind of wealth the Lowell family had amassed over the years, it was easy to lose touch with what some considered ridiculously overpriced and ostentatious. Lowell could never say this out loud for fear of rebuke, but at his level of wealth, paying twenty-five hundred dollars a night for a hotel room was a speck of sand in his bank account.

As a result, he never thought twice about reserving the bi-level, sixty-three-hundred-square-foot Trump Townhouse, which featured a private entrance on Pennsylvania Avenue, a dedicated conference room, its own gym, and a dining room that could seat two dozen.

Gardner liked the private entrance as the most useful feature to the townhouse. He could easily meet with K Street lobbyists without being detected by the media or his political adversaries. These hired guns who populated K Street derived their power from grassroots organizing to control of various trade associations to the corporations who paid top dollar in order to influence the nation's lawmakers.

Most of the K Street lobbying firms catered to a niche market. For example, S-3 Group focused on the appropriations committees. Eris was approached for their financial services clientele from hedge funds to payday lenders.

Beyond K Street, working in the shadows, were the so-called espionage firms known for creating dirty dossiers and digging up dirt on politicians both in office and those seeking office. Fusion GPS was one such opposition research firm. Apolitical by design, these secretive groups were hired by private companies and political campaigns all across the Washington spectrum.

Run by three former *Wall Street Journal* reporters, they'd uncovered dirt on Mitt Romney's top donors during the 2012 presidential campaign. They'd also been adept at creating juicy innuendo out of thin air, delivering it to friendly alternative media sources, and promoted the fake news behind the scenes until it grew legs within the mainstream media. Oftentimes, it took a politician many months to debunk the reports, but by that point, the rumors had become fact and the reputation of their target was destroyed.

When Gardner was contacted by Fusion GPS with allegedly damaging information about two Republican congressmen learned during a trade junket to Phuket, Thailand, Gardner immediately demanded to know if the information they had was true or a manufactured rumor. As a show of good faith, the incriminating images of the two congressmen with several underage Thai girls were delivered to him by email. After his own team authenticated their attendance in Phuket at the time, he agreed to a meeting with Fusion GPS.

After an hour-long meeting, an accord was reached and Gardner paid Fusion GPS handsomely for their efforts. Then he made an unusual request. He demanded that neither the pictures, nor the circumstances, ever saw the light of day.

Gardner Lowell only destroyed careers and lives when necessary. He lived in a world of power and influence. While it was impossible to exert your will over a dead man, one whose career had been destroyed by their sexual indiscretions was of no use in Washington.

The doorbell to the Trump Townhouse chimed and the Lowells' butler moved efficiently to provide their guests entry. Constance Lowell, who'd arrived early that morning, pushed herself off the white-tufted sofa.

"You'll have to excuse me, dear," she said to Gardner. "I have no desire to meet with these vermin. Make them do as we say while I retire to the bedroom to freshen up. I do, however, want to meet with our next guest. He deserves my personal thanks."

Gardner stood and escorted his mother across the spacious living area to the walnut door leading to the master suite. He'd just shut the door as the two congressmen entered the room. He turned to greet the men.

"Gentlemen, please come take a seat. I don't intend to keep you long on this occasion."

"Mr. Lowell, it's a pleasure to meet you," said the young congressman from Louisiana's third congressional district. He was a charismatic young man of Cajun descent who spoke with a distinctive accent. He'd been elected three times by twenty-plus percent margins and was widely considered a staunch ally of the Sargent administration.

Likewise, his companion, a former governor of Louisiana who chose to run for Congress after the collapse, was from a solid red district, which included Baton Rouge. He'd run virtually unopposed in the last two re-election campaigns.

The two men sat in wing chairs across from the sofa. Gardner, however, remained standing.

"Sir," said the former governor, who carried a heavy Southern accent. "As you must surely be aware, there is an important vote in the House shortly that requires our attention. We are here because the leadership of our caucus said it was absolutely necessary. Perhaps you'd do us the honor of telling us what this is all about."

Smug bastard, Gardner thought to himself. *I'll show you what this is all about.*

He picked the folder up off the glass coffee table and began to spin eight-by-ten photographs of the two men into the air. Some landed on the table. Others slammed into the chests of his guests.

The images depicted the two degenerates in various states of undress with the nude young girls. The younger of the congressmen was photographed snorting two lines of cocaine off the buttocks of one of the girls. The former governor was seen in one image, fully naked, diving into the water off the side of a boat dock, holding the hands of two nude consorts. Both were shown engaging in sexual acts with the girls.

"What's the meaning of this?" demanded the former governor.

"Well, Congressman, I think the meaning of this is pretty clear," said Gardner as he continued to send the images at the man like he was tossing Frisbees.

"Enough, Mr. Lowell, you've made your point," said the young ragin' Cajun. In response, Gardner grabbed the rest of the photos and threw them in the man's lap.

"Now I've made my point!" he shouted. The outburst caused his mother's butler to stick his head around the corner from the dining room.

"What do you want?" asked the former governor, resigned to an expected fate of endless apologies and probably a divorce.

"Not what you think, Congressman. Each of these images and, I might add, the ages of these young girls will remain forever locked in my vault alongside similar dossiers of those you rub elbows with every day."

The two men looked at one another, sensing a glimmer of hope that their careers and lives would survive their indiscretions.

"Provided," Gardner said with emphasis, "you do as I say when I say. It's very simple, actually. When Gardner Lowell or my designate calls, you jump. But rest assured, this will not necessarily be a one-way relationship. You will gain a powerful, wealthy ally, which can allow you to remain in your House seats for years to come."

"What is it that you expect from us?" asked the younger of the two after he removed his balls from his throat.

"Just remember, do as I say," replied Gardner with a growl.

"Absolutely, Mr. Lowell," said the young Cajun congressman. He began to rise off the sofa, eager to get out of the Trump Townhouse. His fellow congressman didn't, or couldn't say a word, but gathered himself to follow the young man's lead.

"Sit down, gentlemen," Lowell barked. "I'm not finished."

The two men looked at one another and lowered themselves back into their seats.

Gardner continued. "In an hour, you will vote for the Pacific Statehood Act."

"But, Mr. Lowell, nobody would believe it," protested the former governor. "I've voted in lockstep with every initiative proposed by President Sargent. They'd think I was drunk or off my medication and simply pushed the yea button by mistake. Nobody will buy it."

Lowell slammed the rest of the file on the table. "Oh, Congressman, you'll do it and they'll buy it! I don't care what you two pedophiles tell the media, your constituents, your wives, or your God. Remember rule number one, which governs our new relationship. You two will always do as I say! Got it?"

The younger man dropped his chin to his chest and shook his head. The former governor glared at Gardner and then nodded. It was the look of conquest and defeat. He took his young charge by the arm.

"Come along, young man. We'll give the man what he wants. Mr. Lowell, we'll find our way out."

Gardner shoved his hands in his pockets and nodded toward the door. *That's two more. Now, let's see where we are.*

CHAPTER 36

1:30 p.m.
The Trump Townhouse
Trump International Hotel
Washington, DC

"That sounded like the conversation went well." Constance chuckled as she emerged from the bedroom. Her butler was busy picking up the dozens of photographs that had landed throughout the plush living area.

"Indeed," responded Gardner. "They're scum, and at some point I'll cut them loose. Is it too early for a cocktail?"

"Not from where I'm standing." Constance stood at the windows and watched the sun begin to peek through the clouds. Pennsylvania was bustling with activity.

"I agree. I'll pour. The usual?"

"Of course, dear. What time does the next congressman enter your lair?" she asked with a giggle. Her late husband, Lawrence, had always excluded her from this aspect of the family's business affairs. It wasn't until after his death that she inserted herself more and more into the affairs of the Boston Brahmin. Historically, the executive committee of the Brahmin was a boys' club, and Constance found herself uncomfortable during their meetings. She also sensed they'd prefer she not hold a seat at the table, which made it easier for her to elevate Gardner into her place. It was what she wanted all along.

Gardner delivered his mother a dirty martini cocktail, which was heavy on the gin and light on the vermouth. He had his customary Tanqueray and tonic. They clinked glasses, provided each other a silent toast by way of a smile, and took their first sip when the doorbell rang once again.

The butler attended to the door and their guest entered the room empty-handed. Dispensing with the preliminaries, having kissed the rings of the Lowells already, the gentleman spoke first.

"I trust your meeting with the gentlemen from Louisiana went well?"

"Yes, very well," Gardner replied. "You can count on two more votes for passage. Where does that leave us?"

"I called in a chit on the final three we need. I hope you don't mind an additional contribution to a few war chests."

"Not under the circumstances. How about their loyalty in the future?" asked Gardner.

"These three are squeaky clean. For them, it'll be all about money and committee positions in the future. More importantly, they were never on anyone's radar as possible defectors from the party line. Accordingly, they cannot be traced to anyone within the House leadership, or you, naturally."

Gardner sipped his drink and glanced at his mother, who had studied their guest from the moment he walked in. After an awkward silence, he responded, "That's good, and you can let them know their new benefactors can accommodate their needs, political or otherwise, in the future."

"Good, then it appears we have the votes secured. This will send shock waves through the White House, which will make your task all the more difficult in the Senate tomorrow."

Gardner set his empty glass on the glass table and slipped a piece of paper out of his pocket onto the corner next to it.

"One step at a time," he said quietly and extended his hand to shake the congressman's firm grip. "Thank you for your help, Congressman. I look forward to a long and prosperous future for us both."

"And I as well, Mr. Lowell," the man replied as he picked up the paper. "Mrs. Lowell, it was a pleasure seeing you again. I'll be going now."

With that, Congressman Billy Trent from Virginia, House Majority Whip and longtime ally of President Sargent, turned for the door with a smile on his face and a check payable to his political action committee for two million dollars.

CHAPTER 37

2:00 p.m.
The Oval Office
The White House
Washington, DC

Sarge pored over the maps and charts provided by the Pentagon. Brad had just delivered a new intelligence report, which indicated an increase in troop movement and equipment activity in the Nanjing Military Region directly across the Taiwan Strait. After Sarge had reviewed the documentation, Brad provided him a summary.

"For a nonmilitary guy, you've got pretty good gut instincts, Mr. Commander-in-Chief," said Brad as he patted Sarge on the shoulder.

"Very funny, General," Sarge said with a laugh. "I did a pretty good job back in Boston. Besides, I've learned a thing or two about subterfuge in the last eight years. Give us the details of what the spooks have learned."

Brad pushed some of the maps out of the way and found the one that identified the Chinese military bases under suspicion. "These images are based upon the NSA's most recent flyovers, as well as CIA operatives reporting from on the ground. This area outlined in red is designated as their Nanjing Military Region, one of seven scattered across Mainland China. It stretches from Hong Kong in the south to Shanghai in the north."

Sarge slid another aerial reconnaissance image next to the one referred to by Brad. "This appears to be a close-up of an area closest to Taiwan."

"Correct. We've isolated Fujian province and the PLA's 31st Group Army, which was based here."

"How do you pronounce this?" asked Sarge, pointing to the city of Xiamen.

"Jow-min," replied Brad. "Do we need to call Julia down to interpret?"

"Smart-ass." Sarge laughed. "She's got bigger problems on her platter, like Thanksgiving dinner."

"And hosting the Boston Brahmin," added Donald. "She'll have to muster all of her diplomatic skills to keep the peace."

"No doubt," said Sarge with a chuckle as he turned his attention back to the images. "Brad, I don't want to split hairs, but you said *was based* here with an emphasis on *was*. This looks like an active military base to me."

"That's the thing. In late 2017, Beijing announced it was redeploying its motorized infantry divisions and the 3rd Artillery Brigade to the North Korean border to prevent an influx of Korean refugees in the event a war broke out there. Reportedly, all they left behind were four elements—an amphibious assault group, an air defense brigade, an aviation regiment, but most importantly, their renowned Flying Dragon Special Ops unit."

"I've heard of them," interrupted Donald.

"They're legendary," said Brad. "The PLA handpicked them to conduct rapid reaction combat in a limited regional war scenario."

"Like the invasion of Taiwan," interjected Sarge.

"Exactly," said Brad. "The PLA strategists know that a ground invasion isn't going to bring Taiwan back into the fold. It'll take commando operations, intelligence gathering, and cyber warfare. That's why Beijing was confident to move its traditional infantry units to the north and leave them there."

"An invasion would not look like the beaches of Normandy," said Donald.

"That's right," said Brad. "Our concern needs to be the Flying Dragons."

Sarge studied the activity on the images again. "Brad, what's their troop strength?"

"The analysts estimate between seven and fourteen thousand. My hunch is that many of them are already in Taiwan, waiting to be activated."

Sarge pulled out the CIA report just received from their operatives on the mainland. "These numbers suggest a far bigger presence on this base than your estimate."

"They do, but they're also preliminary. If they're correct, then I have a theory."

"Let's hear it," said Donald as he looked at a text message that just came through.

"The 31st Group has participated in war games with other special forces units in Nanjing. I've studied the recon photos provided by our analysts. They participated in the maneuvers, but never left to return to their bases. The build-up of troop levels, especially within the Flying Dragons, was done over time and barely noticeable by our people unless they were specifically looking for it."

Sarge sat in his chair and stroked his chin. "Are you saying they've been building up for this operation for some time?"

"In a way, for years. But, with respect to the escalated troop buildup, for at least eight months."

"Which leads me to the question, why act now?" asked Sarge.

Brad set the maps and images down on Sarge's desk. "This operation has probably been on the drawing board for years. I suspect they hoped for an opening during the switch in administrations. Lame-duck presidents don't usually make big moves militarily."

Sarge reflected on the information he'd been provided the last two days. If he was going to back the Chinese down, he'd need to exhibit a show of force. That was all that bullies understand.

"Brad, implement option B. Redeploy the USS *Petersen* strike group around the east side of Japan and send them toward Okinawa. Raise our alert levels in the theater and call back the USS *Ronald Reagan* from Singapore. Donald, contact the State Department. Have them issue a travel advisory to Taiwan based upon the political unrest. Further, issue an alert to American nationals on the island to shelter in place during the evening hours."

"What about tomorrow's ceremony with Ambassador McBride?" asked Donald.

"Let the schedule stand, but I want Jimmy on that plane back to Beijing as soon as it's over. We can't afford for the Chinese to advance on Taiwan before our ships are in position. As for Jimmy, tell him to be ready to call on President Xi Jinping as soon as he returns to the embassy in Beijing."

"I agree, Sarge," said Brad. "Let me get started. Good luck with the vote today."

Sarge laughed nervously. "Oh yeah, you mean the vote that starts in about an hour? I'd rather do battle with the Chinese."

Brad said his good-byes, leaving Donald and Sarge alone in the Oval Office. "Sarge, I should probably bring the president-elect's transition team up to speed on this."

"How is that going?" asked Sarge.

"Not as difficult as it was for us," quipped Donald. "We had to start from scratch. First, we had to decide where to house the government while we restored order in Washington. Then we had to see who was still alive to work within said government. Finally, we had to determine who would be loyal to the Constitution and us, as opposed to the tyrant who ran off to Hawaii."

"You don't have to remind me. Now that it's business as usual, what does it look like?"

"They have to fill almost two thousand positions, over two thousand less than transition teams prior to the collapse since you eliminated agencies like the Environmental Protection Agency, the Department of Education, the Interior Department and sixty-two other bloated bureaucracies that expanded the federal budget.

"The idea, of course, is to ensure a smooth transfer of power. But we also need them to stay up to speed on geopolitical events. They don't get to insert their opinions, but they are entitled to an update."

Sarge walked toward Betty's office. "Donald, you've got enough on your plate. I'll have Betty get Stanford on the phone. I haven't spoken with him for a week or so. I'll use the occasion to wish him and his wife happy Thanksgiving and let him know that we're about to go to war with China."

Donald started laughing. "Yeah, it's like, *good luck with your future endeavors, Stan.* See ya in the funny papers!"

Sarge continued toward the door to his secretary's office, laughing along with Donald. "Exactly. We'll drop a hot war with China, a cold war with California, and a nuclear war with Congress right in his lap. I hope you enjoy your new job!"

CHAPTER 38

2:30 p.m.
The Hart Senate Office Building
Washington, DC

It had been a little over twenty-four hours since the meeting with that arrogant Congressman Sánchez had concluded. He'd cancelled dinner plans last night with his wife, citing the worsening weather. In reality, Senator Rutledge had too much on his mind. The luncheon with his mother earlier didn't help his cluttered mind as he tried to sort things out.

While it was true that Congressman Sánchez was arrogant on most days, his hunger for media attention was a testament to that. No, this was different. The young man was extremely confident in his assertions

The Civil War-era clock ticked methodically on the corner of his desk as the veteran politician replayed the conversation with Congressman Sánchez over and over. Then he weighed the options before him.

At first, his mother scoffed at the idea of intentionally setting the stage for the secession of the Southern block of states, repeating the events of the 1860s. But as the evidence began to mount regarding the fate of the House vote, Senator Rutledge had to consider all contingencies. If the House could be swayed, so could his domain—the United States Senate.

He called upon his trusted chief of staff to make some inquiries. Before he took his next step, Senator Rutledge decided to get the final update on today's vote count. He called his aide into his office.

"The House starts voting in thirty minutes. What's your opinion?" asked Senator Rutledge.

"I've looked into this from all angles, Senator. Trust me when I tell you that the bill is going to pass. I've never seen such smug self-assuredness on the part of the minority leadership."

"Do you have any specifics on how the vote shifted so suddenly?"

"Here's what I'm told by my girlfriend," said the much younger man, who was sleeping with a member of the enemy's camp. "They've plucked off a few Republicans who were never on anyone's radar."

"Are they disgruntled?"

"No, she didn't say that. It was just typical give-and-take. You know, if you've got the money to give, I'll take it. Quite simply, they've sold their votes."

"And you think they've swayed enough members over to the yea column to pass the bill?"

"Yes, sir. I do."

Senator Rutledge contemplated his next move while his chief of staff stood motionless in front of him. He still had time to decide whether allowing the bill to pass and pushing for secession would be the best option or to work overtime to prevent its passage in the Senate.

He reached a decision, albeit a temporary, politically expedient one. "Get me Donald Quinn on the phone. Thanks."

Senator Rutledge never wanted to be president and therefore never threw his hat into the ring. He preferred to work behind the scenes to influence the nation in the direction he envisioned. When Sarge took office, he was amazed that the New Englander's dedication to the Constitution and the visions of the Founding Fathers would so closely mesh with his own. Sarge was a Yankee version of himself.

In those early days, he'd showered his new president with wisdom and insight into the ways of Washington politics. Now, his friend and ally was in trouble. Sarge's desire to restore the Union was about to be thrown a sharp curve ball, and Rutledge would feel terribly guilty if he didn't give them a heads-up.

He sat in his darkened office as clouds continued to engulf DC during this early winter storm. The Civil War clock continued to tick toward 3:00 p.m., the start of the vote, when the phone rang. They had Donald on the line for him.

"Good afternoon, Donald. I'll be brief. My mother and I need to meet with you and the president tomorrow morning. It's urgent."

Donald questioned Senator Rutledge as to the purpose and he was assured of the important nature of the gathering.

"Okay, before the daily briefing. Yes, 8:00 a.m. is fine."

Donald then asked Senator Rutledge specifically about his opinion on the House vote. *Now was not the time to equivocate. Now was the time for brutal honesty.*

"Donald, I believe the bill will pass."

He was asked by Donald how that was possible. He was assured the votes were there to defeat it.

"It's too late to do anything now, I'm afraid. Suffice it to say, it's not what you think."

Donald protested, reassuring Senator Rutledge that they'd kept a pulse on any potential members of their coalition who might stray.

"Did you check your own backyard?" Rutledge asked of Donald.

"What?" he asked.

"Sometimes, your friends at the party are the first ones to screw you over. We'll talk more in the morning."

There. Conscience cleared, for now.

CHAPTER 39

3:00 p.m.
The President's Study
The White House
Washington, DC

Immediately off the Oval Office, across from the president's private bathroom and a small kitchenette, was a very small room used in many administrations as the president's private study. The room contained four chairs, together with a desk and two wall-mounted televisions. The monitors were tuned to C-Span and CNN as the communications team joined Sarge and Donald to watch the House cast its final vote on the Pacific Statehood Act.

The room was tense as both Sarge and Donald nervously paced from the president's study to the Oval Office, discussing the revelations provided by Senator Rutledge and the ramifications of the House turning on them. As the votes slowly appeared on the screen, both men convinced each other that the fight would not be lost in the House alone. The Senate vote was still looking favorable although they'd not focused on it. Until now, their confidence level had been running high.

Betty joined them eventually, as did two of Sarge's political strategists and his speechwriter. The clock had trickled down to zero with thirteen votes remaining uncast. It was deadlocked at two hundred eleven votes each.

Betty asked if the thirteen votes would be nullified because of the time stamp. Donald walked back and forth with his cell phone pressed to his ear. He held up a hand, asking for quiet in the room.

"They extended voting for five more minutes," he announced.

"Mr. President, more votes are being tallied."

Sarge spun around and headed back into the study, followed close on his heels by Donald. Two more nay votes were recorded, the screen remained unchanged, and then the yea side ticked up.

212, 213, 214, 215

"That's more than they were supposed to get," commented Crepeau.

"Five votes left, all republicans," muttered Sarge.

The tally registered three more votes against the bill, leaving the total nays at two hundred seventeen.

"Come on, baby," shouted Donald over Sarge's shoulder. "Just gimme one more vote. Come on!"

The yea side ticked up again.

216, 217

"Last one," said Ocampo.

The next thirty seconds seemed like an eternity. Even the members of the House stopped, staring down at their smart phones and computer tablets. Everyone waited.

And then it was tallied. The final vote—for passage of the bill. The CNN screen said it all. Amidst the jubilation of those manning the news desk, the graphic read The Pacific Statehood Act moves on to the Senate.

Sarge spun out of the room and shoved his way past Donald into the Oval Office. He was livid. Behind him, his senior staff debated what happened while Donald frantically attempted to reach House leadership in search of answers.

The entourage eventually made their way into the Oval Office, still chattering about the devastating results. Sarge remained quiet as he stared out at the snow-filled skies, which obscured his view of the Washington Monument.

His team peppered him with questions.

"Mr. President, do you want me to prepare a statement?"

"Do you still plan on addressing the media, sir?"

"What would you like us to do next?"

They were all chirping in his ear at once.

"What I want," he replied calmly but assertively, "is fifteen minutes of peace and quiet so I can think."

The room immediately became silent and Donald hung up on the caller. "Okay, everyone. Please, give us the room. Ocampo, Crepeau, prepare a statement and have it in my office in thirty minutes. The rest of you, shut down any leaks regarding our opinion of the outcome. Why? Because we haven't formulated it yet. Now, go on. Get to work."

Once the Oval Office had emptied, Sarge sat in his chair and leaned back, closed his eyes, and massaged his forehead with the heels of his hand. His oath of office called upon him to preserve, protect, and defend the Constitution. He'd lived by those words throughout his time in office.

He reminded himself of the first State of the Union address by newly elected President George Washington at Federal Hall in New York. With the recently founded nation in its infancy, President Washington focused on the very concept of the Union itself and the incredible accomplishment of establishing it. In this first State of the Union, he also spoke at length about the importance of maintaining it.

How the hell had things come to this? Sarge was not a particularly religious man, but he closed his eyes and prayed to God for guidance. The decisions he'd make in the next twenty-four hours would determine the fate of millions of Americans and the nation in which they lived.

CHAPTER 40

4:00 p.m.
The Oval Office
The White House
Washington, DC

Donald walked over to a two-drawer console that had rarely been used in the two-term presidency of his best friend. He swung open the door and retrieved the bottle of Glenlivet Scotch whisky together with a couple of crystal glasses. He poured two fingers for himself and the same for the president.

Sarge raised his glass and, without a formal toast, slammed the scotch to the back of his throat, causing him to wince. Donald followed his lead. Without having to ask, Donald poured another round, half full this time, which the men took to the couches and set on the side tables under the lamps.

Donald broke the silence. "Well, should we drink and hope that it goes away, or do we hitch up our panties and fight another day?"

"I say hitch 'em up!" replied Sarge with a hearty laugh. The first shot of Glenlivet seemed to change his spirits. He leaned forward and took a smaller, more controlled sip.

"Sarge, here's the thing," started Donald. "If Rutledge is right, then we know someone is applying an incredible amount of pressure and influence over the vote. You can get away with that in the House, where there are four hundred and thirty-five members. I don't know who defected yet, but I will find out. But it doesn't matter. We need to look toward tomorrow and try to keep from getting blindsided again."

"This is why I need you, Donald. After Steven's death, I found myself assuming more of his persona. I made decisions, initiated actions, and, hell, pulled the trigger myself in ways I never imagined. My initial inclination was to track down every congressman who screwed us and tear them a new one. But what would that accomplish at this point?"

"Nothing," Donald replied. "It probably wouldn't make you feel any better. The betrayal of a friend is bad enough. But confronting the defectors would just exacerbate your ill feelings toward them and the anger you're holding inside."

Sarge laughed as he took another sip of his drink. "Steven would say *just shoot 'em*. That may have worked back in Boston during the early days following the collapse, but I can't get away with that anymore."

"I totally agree. So let's talk about tomorrow."

"First off, in light of the fact the vote was destined to be tight in the Senate, and even more so now, I think I should recall Abbie to Washington. We may need her as a tiebreaker."

"Definitely," started Donald. "Plus, she's admired by everyone in the Senate Chamber. She knows these people better than we do. If something's brewing, she'll be able to sniff it out."

"Good. I'll call her in a minute. Let me throw something else out to consider."

Donald finished off his drink and looked at Sarge over the top of his glass. "Okay, I'm listening."

"If we think the Senate vote will be a problem, we could use this Taiwan crisis to postpone the vote," started Sarge.

"As Senator Majority Leader, Rutledge could postpone the vote," interrupted Donald.

"Exactly. We could have Paul arrange an emergency meeting of the Senate Armed Services Committee regarding this Taiwan matter. We could postpone the vote until next week, which will give us time to ferret out who's behind this late push to pass the bill."

"That's a possibility, but naturally the Senate would be incensed. They're tired after a long campaign. They've pushed a lot of legislation through since the election—which was mostly at our behest. Plus, we've been the driving force behind the timing of the vote."

Sarge leaned back into the plush couch and pulled a pillow under his right arm to prop it up. His shoulder had never been the same since the assassination attempt. On cold, damp days like this one, it tended to get stiff and sore.

"Yeah, that's all true. I'm just looking at options."

"Why don't we run it by Paul in the morning?" asked Donald.

"Deal. In that regard, do you find it odd that he has Sarah tagging along?"

Donald laughed. "Sometimes, I wonder if it's the other way around. The first few times we met with the good senator, it was his mother who walked through the door first."

"She's certainly enjoyed her access to the White House," said Sarge.

"And benefitted from it greatly," added Donald.

Sarge continued. "My guess is that she wants to see the vote go down in flames every bit as much as we do, but for different reasons. We want the four states brought back into the Union because it's the right thing to do. I think Sarah Rutledge would like to avoid a proverbial civil war if they come in and fundamentally change the social fabric of this nation in the process."

"Let's stay the course, meet with Paul, and touch base ourselves with key senators tomorrow. We approached the House in a hands-off manner. Let's be more involved on the Senate side."

"Agreed," said Sarge. He looked at his watch and saw that it was nearly six. "I'm gonna call Abbie and then try to have a rare dinner with my family. Why don't you head out as well?"

Donald chuckled. "With all that's going on, it seems to be the opposite of what I *should* do. However, you're the boss, so who am I to argue. I'll see ya in the morning."

CHAPTER 41

6:00 p.m.
The Jackson Family Home
Muddy Pond, Tennessee

Abbie emerged from the bedroom, where she had spoken with Sarge for thirty minutes. After watching the news regarding the vote, she knew her presence in Washington was needed. In the event the Senate deadlocked on the vote, she would cast the tiebreaking vote to defeat the measure. It wasn't just the brief conversation regarding the Pacific Statehood Act that concerned her. It was also the revelations from Sarge about the situation in Taiwan. It was more grave than the news reports of demonstrations and protests depicted. The nation might be moving towards a military conflict with one of its most potent adversaries—China.

"How did it go, Madame Vice President?" asked Drew as he approached his wife and gave her a kiss on the cheek. He gently placed his hands on her belly, which carried their first child together.

Inside the Jackson home, Drew's family and his extended family, the Aegis team, were milling about, discussing the news of the day while sniffing around the kitchen at Janie Jackson's cooking. A playful dialogue between King Dawkins and Drew's mother could be heard. King kept wanting to grab a taste of her Muddy Pond delicacy—roast hog from the spit. Janie threatened to beat the big man with a wooden spoon if he dared enter the kitchen one more time. The back-and-forth between the two caused an uproar of laughter in the family room as the six-foot-five former Delta operative cowered under the spoon waving near his head.

Abbie laughed as she watched the exchange take place. "It seems your mother is enjoying a house full of kids again."

"Yeah." Drew chuckled with her. "King is the bratty son she never had. If I knew how much she enjoyed attempting to discipline the big guy, I would have been more unruly myself."

Abbie squeezed Drew's chiseled face with her right hand. "I take it you were the perfect son, never causing your parents any grief."

"Now, I never said that. But I sure knew to stay out of Janie Jackson's kitchen."

Abbie smiled and then a look of dread came over her face. "I don't know how I'm gonna break it to her, Drew. Sarge needs me back in Washington. I've got to be present for the Senate vote tomorrow in case there's a tie."

"Honey, don't worry about it. Mom understands that stuff. She was just commenting to me this morning while I helped her clean up after breakfast that this was the first time she's had me at the house for four days in a row without being called away. Listen, she's learned to take what she can get as her kids became adults."

Abbie sighed. "I know, but I still feel bad. Let's tell her tonight after everyone kinda clears out for bed."

"Okay," said Drew as he looked into Abbie's eyes.

She tried to avert his probing, but he was a master at reading people, both in a situation like this and when he was torturing them for information. Abbie finally looked back at him. She didn't want to be tortured.

"There's more, isn't there? There's always more."

The room burst into laughter again as King ducked a biscuit, which sailed over his head. The Judge entered the fray, his voice of warning directed at King. "Careful, young man, Janie's got a gun." More laughter emerged at the vague reference to the song lyric.

Abbie pulled Drew closer to him and whispered into his ear, "I don't want to put a damper on the evening. The situation in Taiwan is worse than what the media knows."

"I wondered," said Drew. "What did Sarge say?"

"The protests are largely organic, but when the demonstrations turn violent, they're instigated by Chinese nationals controlled by their Ministry of Foreign Affairs."

"Why are they trying to cause trouble?"

"That's still undetermined. There's more. The country is experiencing rolling power outages. The CIA seems to have confirmed cyber attacks are causing their power plants' operations to fail. The likely source is the PLA's Unit 61398."

"They're top cyber-espionage arm. They've got a whole army of hackers that do everything from stealing military secrets to spying on U.S. companies. Does Brad have an opinion as to whether they're following the Russian's playbook?"

Abbie looked around to make sure she wasn't being overheard. The information she was providing was highly classified. Drew, as her spouse, and Julia, as First Lady, weren't necessarily given a security clearance, but information was shared with them anyway. Spouses of high-level politicians are known to receive classified data as part of the proverbial pillow talk between loved ones. Julia and Drew, as members of the Loyal Nine, would be kept abreast of these matters anyway, the law notwithstanding.

"There appears to be a buildup of a special forces unit on a military facility directly across from Taiwan," started Abbie.

"The Flying Dragons," interjected Drew. "They are some badass dudes."

"Yeah, that's what I gather. Nothing has happened so far other than the unrest within Taiwan. But this Flying Dragons outfit is poised to strike because of their close proximity across the Taiwan Strait."

"What are we doing in response, anything?"

Abbie raised her eybrows and grimaced. "Sarge has redeployed half of the USS *Petersen*'s strike force out of the Sea of Japan and into the East China Sea."

"Dang it, Abbie. The ChiComms will flip out."

Abbie nodded. "Sarge wants to provide a show of force in addition to having a carrier group in position to repel any ambhipious or air invasion."

"Where is the *Ronald Reagan*?" asked Drew. He made it his job to keep abreast of the general location of the nation's primary military assets and any hot spots related to their positioning. His mind was always on his team's next potential assignment.

"They're in Singapore, but they're leaving port and heading toward Taiwan."

"Wow, Abbie. This is moving fast."

"It is, which is all the more reason I need to get back to Washington."

Drew was about to respond when his mother interrupted their conversation. "Everyone get settled and come to dinner. We've got plenty tonight thanks to some pretty fine shootin' from you folks. I reckon they trained y'all well."

Abbie and Drew began to join the group when he suddenly grabbed her arm and stopped her. "Abbie, what about the ambassador? Jimmy McBride is an old friend of the Judge's. Is he still in Taipei?"

"Yes, at least for another few hours. He has an afternoon event with their president and then he's been instructed to head straight for Beijing to confront the Chinese about all of this."

"Does he have adequate security?" asked Drew.

Abbie smiled reassuringly. "The CIA security team at the AIT facility brought him into the compound. He'll be escorted everywhere by a Taiwanese military security team."

"Good, let's eat. I'm hungrier than King!"

CHAPTER 42

8:15 p.m.
The Executive Residence
The White House
Washington, DC

The Sargents lovingly prepared Frank and Rose for bed. Sarge wasn't always able to be around for the eight o'clock hour when the two youngest children were tucked in. Tonight, he read each of them a story until their eyelids succumbed to the influence of the sandman. The two of them stared at their children and exchanged comments about how adorable and peaceful they looked.

Win was seven and a half years old, which allowed him a 9:00 bedtime. He'd lost interest in bedtime stories a year ago and now preferred to read age-appropriate books. His love of reading and the encouragement the Sargents provided him advanced him to a ten- or eleven-year-old's reading level.

At the moment, Win was immersed in the Harry Potter novels. Next on his TBR list were The Hunger Games novels, a box set that his parents continued to delay by suggesting other works.

Sarge and Julia wondered if Win had experienced too much of the post-apocalyptic world while in Julia's womb. Studies showed unborn children absorbed and reacted to external stimuli, so pregnant mothers played classical music to them during pregnancy. Win had the pleasure of experiencing the collapse of society and the battle to restore America to a functioning nation.

Sarge entered his room alone while Julia attended to Rose, who had stirred back awake. "Hey, buddy. How's Harry and the rest of the Hogwarts crew coming along?"

"Pretty good, Dad. It's a really good story."

"That's good, son. Are you looking forward to the Quinns visiting with us over Thanksgiving?"

"Yes, sir. Becca is really good at the games I like and she shows me a lot of tricks. Penny is older and she'll probably spend her time talking to her friends on the phone."

Sarge smiled as he thought of the life of teens before and after the collapse. It was amazing how quickly they picked up where they left off. Win propped himself up in bed and leaned against the headboard. A serious look came over his face.

"Win, you seem to have something on your mind. Is there anything you want to talk about?"

"Dad, something came up in school Friday."

Sarge scooted Win's legs over so he could sit on the side of his son's bed. "What happened?"

"It was no big deal," started Win. "Some of the kids were talking about California. They said you don't like California."

Sarge, before responding to the statement, decided to probe further to see what else Win had been told. "Why would they say something like that? Did you hear more?"

"Well, only that they said you don't like California because they're not like you. They said you only want a country that thinks the way you think."

"Hmmm," said Sarge as he pursed his lips and nodded. "Anything else?"

"No, sir. They were older kids and a girl walked by, which made them talk about her."

Sarge laughed. "Girls can be a distraction sometimes."

Win simply shrugged and then looked sheepishly into his lap.

Sarge got serious and tried to address his son's concerns. "I'm not sure I understand what they're talking about because I happen to love California—Oregon, Washington, and Hawaii, too. Did you know that I've been to all of those states in my life?"

"You have?"

"I have and I enjoyed them all," he replied. He took a deep breath and continued. "Son, here's the thing. We live in a big country with a lot of different kinds of people in it. We will never completely agree on everything. That would be pretty boring, wouldn't it?"

Win shrugged again, not completely convinced at the *difference in opinion* concept. He mumbled, "Nobody would argue anymore."

"That might be true, but throughout the history of the world, people have been at odds with each other. It's a part of human nature that we can't change. As president, I have to deal with it every day."

"Are people in California not like us?"

"Yes, they are exactly like us, and believe it or not, they want the same thing for America that we do. Some of them have a different way of going about things than we do."

"They think different?"

"No, not all the time. But on some issues, they do. My job as president is to try to bring all sides together for a common goal of rebuilding America and making it a great place to live. Now, I have certain principles that have been a part of my way of thinking since I was a young boy like you. I've never changed my mind regarding these principles because they were formed by my studying American history and the Bible."

"Like me?" asked Win.

"Yes, Win, just like you. Even at seven, you are deciding right from wrong. You are also deciding how you interact with friends and strangers. As you get older, you will form principles that will guide you, just like I did."

Win smiled as he began to comprehend what his dad was saying. "What if we disagree?"

"That'll be fine too because I will always love you as my son."

"What if I hear people saying the wrong things about you? Lies, like those kids were saying."

Sarge glanced over his shoulder and saw Julia leaning against the doorway, listening to the conversation. Sarge noticed it was nine o'clock, so he assisted Win in sliding under the covers.

"The Founding Fathers, our ancestors from my family and your mom's, fought hard to give everyone in America the freedom to express themselves and to speak their minds. Their words may be lies, hateful, and the opposite of what you believe. But it's their right to speak them because we live in a free country."

"That's in the Bill of Rights, right, Dad?"

"That's right, Win," replied Sarge as he tucked the covers up to the young man's chin. "Every time you hear a conversation like that, let me remind you of an old rhyme, you know, the one about sticks and stones."

Win recited the rhyme. "Sticks and stones may break my bones, but words can never hurt me."

Sarge smiled and rubbed his hand on his son's head. "Here's the lesson from that children's rhyme. If more people would live by these words, the world would get along better. Don't let words hurt you. Brush them off and go about your day. The people who allow another's words to consume their feelings and make themselves angry are the ones who are inflicting pain—upon themselves."

"Okay, Dad. I'll try extra hard not to let their words bother me."

"That's my boy. Just let 'em stew in their own madness."

"What's that mean, Dad?"

"Yeah, let's leave that discussion for another night. I love you, Win." Sarge gave his son a kiss on the forehead.

"I love you too, Dad."

PART THREE

The day before Thanksgiving

November 2024

CHAPTER 43

4:00 a.m. ET
Undisclosed Location
Taipei City, Taiwan

Hell began precisely at four o'clock in the afternoon following Ambassador Jimmy McBride's departure from the Presidential Palace in Taipei City. It all happened so fast—suddenly, but with little violence. After a night of unrest in which the demonstrations intensified, the sunrise brought a new day, and business as usual once again returned to Taipei City.

His event with the Taiwanese president followed the schedule laid out for him by their diplomatic corps. The media was present, recording every interaction between Ambassador McBride and the officials of the Taiwan government.

Following the ceremony, he was escorted out of the building by palace security and handed over to his own detail. These appeared to be the same members of the Taiwan military detail assigned to AIT, although one face seemed unfamiliar to him. He would rack his brain in the hours to come as he wondered whether his instincts were correct about the new face.

November was one of the best times of the year to visit Taiwan with mostly sunny and pleasant weather. But in the windowless cell—no, steel box in which he was held, the subtropical sun seemed to be directly overhead, beating mercilessly down upon him.

The steel box provided him little or no air. A smattering of air holes the size of a pencil eraser provided him sufficient oxygen to keep him alive. They afforded him little or no opportunity to view his outside surroundings. The steel door was bolted shut, providing no means of escape.

Nor could he escape the insects that seemed to thrive on the interior heat of the steel box and the profuse, salty sweat that poured out of him. He wondered how many bugs had joined him through the tiny portholes to the outside. All he knew was the insects who accompanied him made it their mission to do everything they could to hurt or offend him, which, in his mind, was as concise a definition of hell as anything he'd learned from the Mount Zion Baptist Church in Nashville.

Ambassador McBride had been trained for possible capture, although it was many years ago in a time long before his life in politics began in Middle Tennessee. He'd been through the survival, evasion, resistance, and escape course—the SERE school. It was something you had to do if you flew airplanes for a living, and it was intentionally the most demanding thing in the military because it did things to otherwise pampered Naval and Air Force officers that even Marine drill instructors would find cringeworthy.

The experience in SERE school for Ambassador McBride, as for most others, had been one he would never willingly repeat, or forget. Yet here he was, captured by an unknown enemy in a well-executed kidnapping. He was repeating SERE school, but not of his own volition.

He knew he was alone here. He'd tried shouting, hoping to attract the attention of someone friendly. There was no response. He made every attempt to listen for his captors. All he could discern were muffled voices and shuffling feet. For a while, he tried to keep track of time by watching the sun, then darkness came and the sun never returned.

Ambassador McBride then turned to his faith. He was afraid to pray for death, a thought that he was unable to admit aloud, even to himself. In a way, it would be an internal admission that he'd given up on God, something he would not allow as long as he was breathing. Besides, if he prayed for deliverence to Heaven, and it didn't come, then his faith would be shattered even more and he might start to die inside. And with that, his soul would be lost.

For Ambassador McBride, that was how despair began to set in as he contemplated his fate. It was a slow realization at first; then it came at him in a rush, not with a few thoughts, but with his unwillingness to ask God for a solution that might not come.

CHAPTER 44

4:50 a.m.
The Quinn Residence
Washington, DC

Donald's phone was ringing, he was sure of it. But in his dream, he was fishing off the banks of Prescott Peninsula with Susan and the girls. Cell phones weren't working after the grid collapsed. So he disregarded its incessant ring-buzz cacophony and focused on casting another line. Then his beloved shoved him, not because he was snoring and needed to roll over. She heard the ringing and wanted it to stop.

"Dammit!" he grumbled.

He forced his left eye open and studied the clock. *Oh dark thirty.* His brain began to function. *Not good.* Yet his need for sleep forced his mind to debate whether or not to answer his phone. He knew he had to—his job required that it not go unanswered.

The ringing stopped. Donald breathed a sigh of relief and closed his eyes, hoping to return to that time at Prescott Peninsula when cell phones didn't exist and there was downtime, allowing him to fish with his girls.

When he was asked by Sarge to be his Chief of Staff, he hadn't realized how much work there'd be. And neither had Susan. Early on, she'd tolerated it better than he'd hoped. As the years passed and Sarge's administration was challenged by a variety of tests, Donald was summoned to adapt new approaches to problem-solving. The proverbial 3:00 a.m. phone call had not occurred until now.

A second ring! This time he pounced on the phone.

"Quinn," he barked into the phone.

"Sir, please hold for the watch commander."

"Yes, of course."

The overnight watch commander for the Situation Room came on the line. "Sir, I've been instructed to contact you by the State Department. Ambassador McBride has gone missing in Taipei City, sir. He had completed his diplomatic engagement with the president at the Presidential Palace and entered his vehicle with the Taiwanese security team. They never arrived at the AIT, sir."

"Has the president been notified?" asked Donald, knowing that the protocol was to call the Chief of Staff first.

"No, sir. We have notified the chairman of the JCS. He is en route. Sir, we are sending a driver and an escort for you per the Secret Service's instructions."

"Um, okay. I will contact the president and advise him of the situation. Thank you."

Just as Donald disconnected the call, Susan turned on a bedside lamp. "That didn't sound good," she mumbled as she wiped the sleep out of her eyes.

Donald sat there for a moment and slowly digested the information he'd just received. "No, well, we don't know for certain yet. It appears Ambassador McBride has disappeared."

"Kidnapped?"

"The watch commander didn't use that word. I'm sure I'll learn more shortly."

Donald swung out of bed and headed immediately for the bathroom and started the shower. He was a morning person by nature, but a shower helped him wake up further.

Susan started some coffee and warmed a sausage biscuit for him to get something in his stomach. While she readied this light breakfast, two Lincoln Navigators arrived outside their home, and several men in dark suits emerged to prepare for Donald's trip into the White House.

He appeared and hugged Susan around the waist. "Don't be alarmed, dear. It's just protocol. You never know when an isolated event is part of a bigger operation by people who don't like us very much."

She grabbed both of his hands, turned and gave him a loving kiss. "I know. Over the years, I've grown accustomed to the unusual aspects of our life. Most soccer moms would be envious of the drama we get to live."

Donald laughed and poured a cup of coffee into a spill-proof tumbler. "Circle January 20th on your calendar. It'll be over then."

"I already have," she said with a smile. "This has been an interesting eight years, but I'm ready to slip into a life of our own, aren't you?"

Donald didn't reply because he honestly didn't know how he felt about that. The hectic days didn't allow him to consider *what's next.* Donald kissed his wife again and set out the front door with a purpose, managing an *I love you* as he strode down the sidewalk toward the Secret Service team.

CHAPTER 45

6:00 a.m.
The Situation Room
The White House
Washington, DC

Sarge's National Security team greeted him with a mixture of cautious apprehension and an edginess he hadn't felt in prior sessions. Even Donald appeared to be on edge, having received the urgent wake-up call at the ungodly hour.

"Everyone, please take a seat so we can get started," said Sarge as he took his place at the head of the table. He was fully dressed for the day. The matters unfolding in Taiwan were just part of a day that would test his presidential mettle. "Do we have any new intel on the location of our ambassador?"

"No, Mr. President," offered Brad. "As you know, the demonstrations in Taipei City have escalated each evening for the past several days. The demonstration started peacefully in the middle of the day with protestors carrying printed signs that read Taiwan is not China. Matters escalated when activists in opposition to the One China policy beheaded the statue of Chiang Kai-shek and drenched it in red paint."

"Let me get my bearings straight," interrupted Sarge. "If you would, when briefing me on specific events, advise me of the local time in Taiwan when they occurred."

"Of course, Mr. President. Currently it is 6:00 in the evening in Taipei City. It's been dark for about an hour."

"Okay, now when did these initial protests begin?"

Brad continued. "The protestors arrived at China's Ministry of Economic Affairs at 1:00 local time while Ambassador McBride was at a State luncheon with the president. Soon, the Ministry was surrounded and they began to engage the Chinese military personnel guarding the complex. That was when things got interesting."

Brad paused and Sarge asked him to continue. "Go ahead."

"I would like the CIA to describe the events, if I may, sir. Max Chen can provide the details."

"Fine. Mr. Chen, what was unusual about these protests?"

"Sir, over the last two days, we have assigned more CIA field operatives to conduct surveillance on Chinese government facilities and housing units in Taipei. We were trying to determine where the large contingent of pro-China demonstrators lived and how they could be mobilized so quickly."

Sarge was growing impatient. He wanted to make a decision based upon the facts on the ground, but he was tempted to dispense with the preliminaries.

Chen continued. "The Chinese military appeared to allow the demonstrators to overrun the compound without allowing them full access to the building. By 4:00 p.m. local time, the facility was overrun and the military had retreated. The demonstrators began to deface statues and symbols of Chinese heritage throughout the grounds."

Sarge asked, "At this point, where was our ambassador?"

"He had just completed his visit at the Presidential Palace. About the same time he was departing the palace, a group of several hundred Chinese nationals descended upon the Ministry and engaged the demonstrators. The two groups fought in what can best be described as brutal hand-to-hand combat. According to my most recent intel, after the fighting had waned, many dozens had been killed."

"How does this relate to the disappearance of Ambassador McBride?" asked Sarge.

"Sir, the actions of the Chinese security forces and the sudden appearance, yet again, of Chinese nationals to counter-demonstrate leads us to believe that the distraction was used as an opportunity to abduct the ambassador."

Donald had remained silent until now. "Who would abduct an American ambassador and for what purpose?"

"We still cannot provide you an answer to those questions. The situation is very fluid."

"Come on," said Donald, who was becoming annoyed, and rightfully so, thought Sarge. The CIA's budget was enormous because they were tasked with anticipating these types of events and having answers, or at least plausible explanations, when the president asked.

Chen turned his attention to Sarge. "Mr. President, Langley's working theory is that Beijing has set into motion a series of operations intended to destabilize—" Chen stopped midsentence as a text message crossed his phone.

"What is it?" asked Sarge.

Chen read the message aloud. "This is from news reports in Taiwan. The electricity supply to Taipei City has failed. The outages are limited to the northern provinces and as far south as Nantou province. The government has not issued a formal statement."

"It's starting," mumbled Sarge. "Brad, where's the *Petersen* strike group?"

"An eternity away if this thing blows up further today. They'll regroup near Okinawa in just over twenty-four hours."

"The *Ronald Reagan*?" asked Sarge.

"They'll be in the immediate theater around the same time, although both strike forces can engage with air support as needed before then."

Sarge leaned onto the table and stood. He walked around the room. On this day, pacing had to substitute for his normal morning run to clear his head.

"Mr. Chen, is the CIA prepared to suggest that the Chinese government actually orchestrated the confrontation at the ministry as cover for an American ambassador's abduction?"

"Mr. President, we have no concrete proof of that, but—"

"Well, what do you have?"

"Sir, I have an opinion, but it's not the official position of Langley," started Chen.

"I wanna hear it," barked Sarge.

"Sir, over the last few days, there has been virtually no conversations between the Chinese Ministry and Beijing. We monitor everything they transmit through official channels. Ordinarily, with unrest taking place near their facility, especially coupled with the attendance of the American ambassador for an occasion as momentous as this one, the control freaks within the PLA would be calling for constant updates. To the contrary, they're doing nothing."

Sarge stopped dead in his tracks and caught the eye of both Brad and Donald.

"Sneaky bastards," he mumbled. "Chen, you mentioned official channels. Do we monitor unofficial channels?"

"Yes, Mr. President, of course. But the point is the official channels would be buzzing. There would be no need to utilize unofficial means of communications unless—"

Sarge completed the young analyst's statement. "Unless they're orchestrating everything to avoid our detection. Back to Donald's question. Why would they abduct the ambassador?"

"There are three possibilities, Mr. President," replied Brad. "One, based upon the proximity of the Presidential Palace to the ministry to the AIT complex, the security team may have avoided the area and taken the ambassador to another safe house."

"Wouldn't we have heard from them by now?" asked Donald.

"Not necessarily," replied Brad. "If they suspected a connection, the security team is focusing on the ambassador's safety first and then finding a secure form of communications second."

"Brad, what are the other possibilities?" asked Sarge.

"Second, pro-Taiwan, anti-American activists may have seen this as an opportunity to make a statement by snatching the most recognizable symbol of America available at the moment—McBride."

"Third?"

"Third, Mr. President, if our suspicions are correct, and this is part of a larger operation to invade Taiwan, would it be out of the realm of possibility that the PLA would abduct McBride and use him as a pawn?"

"What kind of pawn?" asked Donald.

Sarge dropped into his chair and responded, "The kind they kill if we don't mind our own business."

CHAPTER 46

7:00 a.m. ET
The Jackson Family Home
Muddy Pond, Tennessee

Drew finished his conversation with Brad and then passed the phone back to Abbie, who exchanged a few more words with Sarge. After a minute, she disconnected the call and placed her right arm under her protruding belly before she sat on the edge of the bed. Downstairs, the hustle and bustle of their family and guests could be heard as the large group lined up for a breakfast of oatmeal with apples.

"This is nuts, Abbie."

"No doubt about it. I know the Chinese, and they wouldn't pull a stunt like this without careful planning and placement of the proper personnel. This may have been months in the planning."

Drew sat down next to her and placed his hand on her belly. He needed to tell her how he felt about his involvement with Aegis.

"Abbie, we've discussed this before, but now I've been deployed to an extremely unpredictable, hostile environment. It'll be as bad as any locale in the Middle East. I've made my decision."

Abbie shook her head and took his face in her hands. "No, you haven't, so don't say another word. I love you and I trust your abilities. Just as importantly, I trust those men downstairs with your life. They are your brothers, which makes them my brothers too."

"But, Abbie, this will be dangerous. I have you and the baby to think about."

"Drew, before I became pregnant, did you hesitate to serve your country in whatever mission Sarge requested of you?"

Drew hesitated. She was outmaneuvering him. "Um, no. But it's different now. We're having a baby."

"Yeah, so? Did you lose your skills or your desire to fight for our freedoms?"

"Of course not," he said sheepishly.

"Then get to work. King has kids. In fact, most of your team does. I've talked to their wives and looked at their kids' pictures. You know what they all told me when I asked how they do it?"

"What?"

"They said you guys are warriors. It's what you love and you're great at it. I know this already because we went through it in Boston together, right?"

"Yeah, Abbie. I understand. But the guys don't need me to do this."

"You're wrong, Drew. They do. I've seen how they look at you. They respect you. You're their leader. I'm not sure they could retrieve Ambassador McBride without you."

"Maybe, but—"

"Besides, are you gonna tell the Judge and Janie Jackson that you've decided to sit this one out while their longtime friend Ambassador McBride is missing? You're gonna be safer dodging bullets in the streets of Taipei."

Drew began laughing. "Okay, okay. Jeez, you're relentless. I gotta tell Mom and Pop what's going on."

Abbie rose off the bed and hugged her husband. She whispered into his ear, "We'll do it together. Just so you know, your mom supports me on this. It's been *discussed*."

"Whoa, hold up!" he protested. "You had a family discussion without me?"

"Sure did, and it was settled because I knew a situation would arise sooner rather than later. You know what, there will be other missions and you will conduct them with one hundred percent of my love and support. Got it?"

"Dang, where are those Guard transports? It's gettin' hot in here."

Drew and Abbie made their way to the kitchen and pulled his

parents aside. As Abbie represented, after the mission was laid out for them, both the Judge and Janie gave him the full support he needed to go to Taiwan.

Abbie continued her conversation in the kitchen and extended her regrets for abandoning them before Thanksgiving. Drew made his way into the large family room, where most of the guys were finishing up their coffee and watching CNN's coverage of the unrest in Taiwan. Thus far, news of the ambassador going missing hadn't reached the media.

"Hey, guys, I need y'all to listen up."

The conversation started to die down, but the elevated volume of the television became a distraction.

"King, can you turn that down, please, sir?" asked Drew.

"What's up, Drew? You're lookin' pretty dang serious."

"It is, King. Guys, I'm afraid we've got to cut the week short. We've been called back to Andrews."

"Where to?" asked one of his men.

Drew simply pointed to the television. "The ambo's gone missin'. We need to get our collective asses to Taiwan immediately to help cover our diplomats and find Jimmy McBride."

"When do we pull out?" asked King.

Before Drew could respond, the massive tandem rotors of the Tennessee Air Guard's Chinook CH-47 could be heard arriving from their east.

"Now. Let's pack it up. We'll hitch a ride with Abbie to Andrews and then deploy from there."

CHAPTER 47

8:30 a.m.
The Roosevelt Room
The White House
Washington, DC

Prior to the daily briefing, Sarge huddled with Donald and the White House communications team just outside the Roosevelt Room. Donald was studying the announced schedule for the president's activities. This was supposed to be an easy day. The House vote should have put an end to the Pacific statehood bill and no international crisis would be consuming their minds. The most challenging matter on the schedule had been the traditional pardoning of the turkey followed by some early afternoon cocktails as Sarge wished his staff happy Thanksgiving and sent them home for a well-earned day off.

"I take it Sarah and Paul were agreeable to postponing their meeting until after the PDB?" asked Sarge. Senator Rutledge, unaware of the disappearance of the ambassador, was a bit perturbed with Donald at the delay. He reiterated the importance of their meeting, and the delay placed them within hours of the start of Senate proceedings on the vote.

"Yeah, sort of," replied Donald without elaborating. He returned to his iPad. "All public events after the turkey pardon are cancelled or rescheduled. With the Senate vote this afternoon, the media wouldn't be surprised at a few minor appearances and meetings being put off. The turkey pardon is typically picked up by the networks for dissemination to their local affiliates. We've got to keep that in place."

"Also, I don't want to cancel my address to the troops for Thanksgiving. That's very important to me."

"Yes, Mr. President," said Donald.

"Will we have time to get together before the White House press briefing, which will begin just before the Senate gets started this afternoon?" asked Ocampo.

"No, but don't disappear on me," said Donald. "If something breaks on the Taiwan situation, we'll need to be in a position to respond. At this point, we're saying nothing until we can locate the ambassador."

"Mr. President, we had prepared remarks to be delivered following the House vote," started Crepeau. "I believe they still apply for today, unless, of course, the vote doesn't go our way."

"I understand," said Sarge. "Let's see how the vote goes and we can modify them on the fly. Now, we better get inside. Thank you both."

Sarge made his way toward the Roosevelt Room and Donald hustled to catch up with him. Before they entered, Sarge stopped and whispered back to Donald, "Message the attorney general. Make sure she doesn't go anywhere this afternoon. I might need her."

"Will do," replied Donald.

Before Sarge sat down, he told the attendees to take a seat and looked directly to Brad. "Have we located Ambassador McBride?"

"No, Mr. President, but we have analysts poring over NSA imagery and local security camera footage. There's been an additional development in that regard."

"What's happened?"

"It's almost nine o'clock in the evening in Taipei, with darkness settling in about three and a half hours ago. The protests began, as has been the case for the last several days, except now they are much larger. Based upon the opinion of State, who is represented by Mrs. Walton again, these demonstrators are more organic."

"Mrs. Walton, what leads you to believe that?" asked Sarge.

"The sheer size of the crowd, Mr. President. Taiwan has a large population, but it would be difficult to find five to seven thousand

Chinese nationals in Taipei City. The protests, which are occurring as we speak, are well in excess of ten thousand on multiple fronts. Security at the Legislative Yuan has been breached and the facility is now occupied by young militants advocating the One China policy. The Presidential Palace is surrounded by thousands of protestors as well."

"What are they doing to get the matter under control?" asked Sarge.

"Once again, they've called in the military, which has resulted in several violent clashes."

"Are they shooting at one another? I mean, is this another Benghazi situation?"

"Not yet, sir. The military is using traditional crowd-control measures, including water cannons, rubber bullets, tear gas, and the LRAD sound devices."

"What about our embassy, um, I mean the AIT compound? Has it been threatened?"

Walton looked to Chen, the CIA analyst, who had remained in constant contact with CIA personnel within the AIT facility. "Mr. President, at this time our people believe the compound is well secured. There are a lot of people milling about outside the building, but there haven't been any threatening movements yet. It appears the brunt of the hostilities are directed toward the Taiwanese government."

"General," said Sarge as he directed his attention toward Brad, "bring us up to speed on our immediate military response."

"Mr. President, the Pentagon is primarily interested in the protection of American citizens within the country. I'm informed that our diplomatic personnel have sought the protection of the AIT complex. However, there are over ten thousand Americans who currently reside in Taiwan, most of whom are long-term residents. It's impossible for us to account for all of the tourists or short-term visitors, but the State Department did issue the travel advisories, and reportedly, Americans cut their trips short and returned home."

"I don't want to get ahead of ourselves here," began Sarge. "But if this thing escalates into a full-blown military conflict, we need to look at an evacuation of Americans. Do we have a plan for that?"

"We do, Mr. President. Our evacuation protocols involve the use of a military airbase at Hualien County on the east coast of Taiwan. Our assumptions have always been that an evac would be necessary because of a Chinese amphibious invasion along the west coast. Hualien is centrally located and farthest away from anticipated points of attack, should it come to that."

"What about the diplomatic personnel at AIT?" asked Sarge.

Chen took that question. "Mr. President, the facility is well equipped to repel most attacks, including those initiated by a rioting mob, with our existing group of private contractors. If Taiwan is invaded by the Chinese, however, we'd be at a huge disadvantage because there is no manner of escape if the complex is surrounded. The buildings there are not suitable for helicopter extractions."

"Under the present circumstances in which large mobs are gathering at these various locations, how would we evacuate the AIT?"

"We'd have to clear a path, sir," replied Chen. "In other words, we'd have to bull our way out."

"Brad, what's that look like?" asked Sarge.

"Mr. President, our Global Response Team has already been deployed out of Andrews Air Force Base a short time ago. They will be augmented with additional personnel and all the tools they need to secure our facility and extract personnel, if necessary."

"How do you do that without choppers?" asked Sarge.

"Brute force, Mr. President. May I also add that the GRT will also be tasked with locating our ambassador. By the time they're on final approach to Taipei City, I'm confident our eyes in the sky will have traced his route and point of abduction, if that has actually happened."

Sarge let out a deep sigh and checked his watch. It was late in Beijing and the opportunity to reach the Chinese president was ten hours away. The current level of conflict didn't warrant a call at this hour.

"We're not in a position to conduct a regionalized skirmish with the Chinese at this point, much less a full-scale war. Our first goals are to protect our citizens, evacuate them as necessary, and secure our ambassador's safety. Secondly, we'll continue to push our naval strike groups into position to force the Chinese to stand down. However, we need to prepare for the worst-case scenario. Brad, I'll need to be briefed on this later in the day. I want to know exactly how China would invade Taiwan and what we can do to stop it."

CHAPTER 48

10:00 a.m.
The Oval Office
The White House
Washington, DC

"Sarah, it's so nice to see you again." Sarge greeted his guests. Shortly after his first inauguration, he was contacted by Sarah Rutledge to express her congratulations. He knew of the Rutledge family through his conversations with John Morgan and Prescott Peninsula. When Sarge devised a plan to bring relief supplies, generators, and replacement parts for the power grid components, Morgan suggested that he locate Sarah. Her family was highly respected in the South and she had considerable sway over the man appointed FEMA governor in Atlanta. Her influence helped pave the way for the Sunbelt states to join him at the Constitutional Convention. He also made a powerful, wealthy ally in the process.

"Sarge, it has been such a long time," said Sarah. "I'd hoped to visit before the change of administrations."

Sarge chuckled and leaned down to whisper in her ear, "You could spend the night in the Lincoln Bedroom on the evening of the nineteenth and wake up the afternoon of the twentieth. You'd feel right at home on both days."

She playfully slapped his shoulder and laughed. "I wholeheartedly support continuity of government, as long as it's my government."

Sarge gave her a friendly hug and then turned to shake Senator Rutledge's hand. Despite enjoying the moment with his old friend, Senator Rutledge, and the U. S. Senate he led, was the reason for the meeting.

"Paul, we got blindsided yesterday," Sarge began as he led the group to the seating area by the fireplace. The sun brought slightly warmer temperatures, which began to melt the snow delivered by the nor'easter. The fire provided a sense of coziness to the Oval Office. If it were up to Sarge, there'd be a fire burning there daily.

Senator Rutledge began to recount the day's events. "Yes, Mr. President, and I'm sorry for that. I wasn't certain of the result, but my gut instinct told me we had a problem, which prompted my call to Donald late yesterday."

"Well, thank you for that heads-up although it didn't lessen the sting of defeat," said Sarge.

"Or the betrayal," added Donald, unable to contain himself.

"Yes, the betrayal," said Senator Rutledge. "What I observed yesterday, taken alone as isolated events, would've appeared to be politics as usual in Washington. In hindsight, especially in light of the result, it's become clear to me that someone is working behind the scenes to push this legislation through."

"Someone powerful, Sarge," interjected Sarah.

"Do you have an opinion before we move on to today's vote?" asked Sarge.

"I do, but Paul doesn't want to believe me," replied Sarah. "I will find out who it is eventually, although at that point, the vote will be history and we'll have to deal with the aftermath."

"I still want to know," said Donald, who was still fuming at the outcome in the House. Despite the situation in Taiwan, Sarge was aware that Donald would be seeking revenge for the betrayal. He'd also be focused on the vote this afternoon above all other White House functions.

Senator Rutledge turned his attention to Sarge. "As you know, the Senate is evenly divided. Because we have forty-eight senators and three of the independents caucus with us, we control a slim fifty-one to forty-nine majority."

"We can only lose one," mumbled Donald.

"Is the vice president available to cast a tiebreaker?" asked Senator Rutledge.

"Yes, she just returned to Andrews and will stop by her residence before making her way to Capitol Hill. She advised that her chief of staff will be contacting your office to offer assistance. Paul, if there are any senators who need encouragement on this vote, let Abbie speak to them. Hell, send them to me. I stayed away from yesterday's vote. I won't make that mistake again."

Senator Rutledge nodded and then glanced at Donald. Rutledge knew that Donald was spearheading the vote from the administration's perspective and that he took the defeat personally.

"Mr. President, with all sincerity, you could have talked to each of the members and it wouldn't have mattered. I've reviewed the roll call provided by the House Tally Clerks under the supervision of the Clerk of the House. They were valid, and the defectors, if you will, could not have been on anybody's radar."

Donald spoke up on the issue. "We relied heavily upon a list compiled with the assistance of the Majority Whip. Admittedly, we took quite a few votes for granted based upon past relationships. As it turns out, those who switched sides were beyond reproach."

"Today, we need fifty-one votes," said Sarge. "Paul, will you take an active role with the Majority Whip? You're the only person I trust on the Hill right now."

"Sarge, that's why I'm here as well," said Sarah. "My donations run deep into the Senate. I'll look every darn one of the rascals in the eye until I get the truth."

"I can't imagine you'd do it any other way," said Sarge with a laugh. "I remember the first time we met. Your eyes probed my brain the whole conversation."

"I was studying you to determine your sincerity and commitment. Sarge, I knew immediately you were the right man to lead this country. It's a shame they instituted those awful term limits."

Sarge let out a boisterous laugh. "Don't even think about it, Lady Rutledge. I plan on bidding farewell on January 20. I verily believe that my wife, and my Chief of Staff, would tie me up and drag me through the front door if I proposed otherwise."

CHAPTER 49

10:30 a.m.
Somewhere over the American Southwest

Phase one of Operation Golden Retriever had begun twenty-four hours prior with the redeployment of the two carrier strike groups toward Taiwan. The carrier USS *Frank E. Petersen Jr.* reversed its southerly course through the Sea of Japan with the transmission of a single code word. Two cruisers and six destroyers led the nation's newest aircraft carrier and shot through the Tsugaru Strait, which divides Japan, leading the way toward a rendezvous within striking distance of the narrow body of water between China and Taiwan.

The abrupt maneuver coupled with the Japanese Navy's unnecessary, but certainly appreciated, incursions into the Yellow Sea between South Korea and China confused North Korea while catching the Chinese off guard.

Phase two of the operation was under way as air transports were being sent from various U.S. military installations in the Western Pacific, bound for the Hualien Airport along Taiwan's east coast. The State Department had issued communiques to Taipei City and Beijing that the transports were being made available to American citizens who were concerned for their safety due to the recent uprising. Because of the unrest, the Taiwan government could not assure Americans of safe passage out of the country from its major commercial airports.

Phase three of Operation Golden Retriever boarded a Xi'an Y-20 military transport at Andrews AFB for the direct flight to Guam. The irony of boarding the *Chubby Girl*, the nickname given by the aviation industry to the Y-20 because of its wide fuselage, was not lost on Drew. Placed into service ten years ago during a period when U.S.-Chinese relations were agreeable, the government had purchased six of the strategic airlifters for missions like this one, which involved long-range deployments and required a sense of urgency. With its eight-thousand-mile range and cruising speed of nearly six hundred miles per hour, the Y-20 was the perfect aircraft to place the Aegis team in position to do battle with the people who built it.

While most of the guys were catching up on some sleep, Drew thought back upon his career and the men he led into these special operations. Over time, U.S. government agencies began increasing their reliance on special ops veterans willing to provide security to Americans in the world's hot spots.

When Steven Sargent had brought Drew on board, the Aegis Team performed work almost exclusively for the interests of John Morgan and the Boston Brahmin although none of the operators were made aware of this.

After Steven was killed, Drew earned his way into the Aegis operations by way of his outstanding security work for Abbie, Morgan's daughter, and his efforts on behalf of the Loyal Nine. He was honored when Sarge invited him to join the Loyal Nine to fill the incredible void left by Steven's death.

After the election, Abbie and Drew were married, and it was agreed that he was too emotionally involved with the new vice president to remain the head of her security detail. Sarge had bigger plans for Drew, which involved his taking the reins of an elite team of operators working for Aegis, but called upon exclusively by Sarge.

Drew led special ops missions for the government and the interests of the Boston Brahmin although the requests for the latter had changed over the years. Gone were the days of assassinations and the use of so-called enhanced interrogation techniques. Sarge's requests were far different than the heavy-handed approach used by his predecessor, John Morgan.

Sarge provided Drew a vision for the use of Aegis during his years in office. He wanted the team to be made up of accomplished former operators from all branches of the armed services. They needed to be talented without blemishes on their service records. Sarge could not afford to go outside the U.S. military to achieve certain objectives if he had men prone to going off the reservation or who had a record of insubordination, which could come out in the media if a mission was exposed.

Drew discussed Sarge's criteria and they both agreed money was a big part of the recruiting inducements available to potential operators. Drew put out feelers throughout the ranks of former SEALs, Army Rangers, and Delta Force operators, offering guaranteed six-figure salaries, top-of-the-line equipment, and most importantly, the opportunity to return to the camaraderie and the purpose they loved as elite operatives within the armed forces.

He also understood something else because it applied to him as well. It was something he'd never admitted to Abbie for fear it might frighten her. If comradery and money were the yin, the thrill of danger was the yang in the equation. One thing each of the operators would admit to one another, in private, was they loved to hunt and kill, knowing that someone was returning the favor.

Drew, King, and many other special operators balanced the risk and rewards, then chose to join Aegis. Drew and King assessed their guys and eventually settled on eight elite operatives to make up the Global Response Team. This group, which named themselves the Elite Eight, had performed admirably when called upon.

They'd saved lives. They'd deterred military coups. They'd foiled assassination attempts. Next, as phase three of Operation Golden Retriever, they'd lead the charge into Taipei City to secure the AIT compound and rescue a beloved ambassador who also happened to be a family friend. Drew knew his guys were up for the challenge.

CHAPTER 50

11:00 a.m.
The Trump Townhouse
Trump International Hotel
Washington, DC

"I'm not one for sports analogies, Mother, but as our dear friend Robert Kraft once said, let's push this one over the goal line," said Gardner Lowell as he and his mother, Constance, reviewed a chart of one hundred senators just emailed to him by the mysterious Mr. West. The chart, obtained off the laptop of the Senate Majority Whip, was the blueprint the Whip was using to deliver the fifty-one nay votes in the Senate this afternoon. The anticipated tally was fifty-one nays.

"Gardner, I don't know what that means, however, if it helps you win the day, then I wholeheartedly agree with Bob."

Gardner continued to review the names on the roster. A wicked grin came across his face. "I'm pleased to see that my new friend, the young beauty queen from Colorado, is still showing up in the nay column. They will continue to put subtle pressure on her, but she will not bend. She's had a taste of what wealth and power can deliver for her, and I'm certain she liked it."

"You still need one more vote to overcome John's daughter exercising the tiebreaker."

"There are two likely candidates for defection to the yea column, both of which could backfire on me if they remain loyal to Sarge. Handled improperly, they could very well go public or, at the very least, expose my activities to the White House."

Constance returned to her seat on the sofa and summoned her butler to bring her a cup of peppermint tea. She'd eaten something disagreeable to her stomach and it was providing her some indigestion.

"Am I familiar with these senators?" asked Constance.

"One is from Vermont, an often overlooked senator who took the seat of Bernie Sanders following his death. He had labeled himself an independent like his predecessor, but his loyalties lie on the democrat side of the aisle. He was late in making his decision because he wanted to poll his constituents for direction on his vote."

"That's a coward's way out," quipped Constance as she daintily took another sip of tea. "Once elected, you do things your way but provide the illusion to your constituents that your politics mesh perfectly with theirs. You know this, Gardner. Make them believe you're speaking directly to them when you look into the camera."

"He isn't my primary target," continued Gardner. "This vote is quite different from normal lawmaking in Washington. Regardless of whether the Pacific Statehood Act passes in its current form or the Constitutional Convention brings the states back into the Union without condition, the electoral dynamics will change for years to come. Most members of Congress are astute enough to sense the winds of change."

"Son, you are quite the match for that cerebral Henry Sargent."

Gardner laughed and walked over to his mother, kissing her cheek. "Perhaps so, on a cerebral level. However, I have one major advantage that our friend Henry Sargent doesn't have."

"What's that, dear?"

"A moral compass. He has one. I don't, which is why I will always win."

CHAPTER 51

Noon
The Rose Garden
The White House
Washington, DC

Throughout America's history, the nation's citizens adopted certain traditions that enabled them to display their patriotism. Patriotism was this country's way of showing commitment to their home, the values upon which their nation was built, and the principles of their Founding Fathers. Whether it was America's children reciting the Pledge of Allegiance before school each day, or red-blooded Americans standing in reverence to the flag during the playing of the National Anthem during a sporting event, American patriots were unabashedly supportive of these traditions.

Over the years, the White House adopted certain traditions that, by comparison, did not carry the patriotic importance of the National Anthem, but reflected the history and reverence for what made this country great.

The National Thanksgiving Turkey Presentation, and the ceremonial pardoning of the prize bird, dated back to the 1940s when America was in the midst of the Second World War and our young men were fighting for our freedoms.

History reflects that as early as 1873, a Rhode Island turkey farmer would provide the president a turkey every year as a gift at Thanksgiving. The tradition continued unto the farmer's death in 1913, when other turkey farmers picked up the practice.

From the 1940s until the presidency of Ronald Reagan, the turkeys were not pardoned, although a couple of presidents elected to spare the bird from its certain demise and delivery to the White House Thanksgiving table.

President Ronald Reagan started the concept of pardoning the turkey in 1987. Charlie, sent to him from a petting zoo, was given an official presidential pardon largely as a snarky response to criticism from the media that President Reagan received for considering a pardon for Lieutenant Colonel Oliver North. The practice carried forward and continued under Sarge's administration.

In typical fashion, something that became a playful tradition in the White House was often mocked by comedians and ultimately politicized as harmful to the birds by animal rights activists. Sarge never understood this line of thinking in light of the fact that forty years ago the prized turkeys ended up on the dinner table.

Sarge bundled up in a herringbone trench coat and made his way to the Rose Garden ceremony to say a few words and provide the official pardon. Despite the significant events surrounding him on this day, it was important for him to adhere to events like this one.

Americans looked up to him for guidance and strength in times of trouble. Whether it be a potential war brewing in East Asia, or a political conflict on Capitol Hill, Americans wanted to be proud of their institutions, and the annual turkey pardon was one of them.

"I want to thank everyone for braving this unusually cold day before Thanksgiving. The sun is out, the snow is melting, and our friend Lenny, this beautiful turkey from West Virginia, has come all the way to the White House to seek a pardon from me. Now, before I get started, let me mention this unknown fact. Lenny stayed in the Watergate Hotel last night."

The crowd began laughing, certain that Sarge was pulling their leg.

"Please, don't doubt me on this," he continued as Lenny's handlers laughed and nodded their heads in unison. "Yesterday afternoon, at two hundred twenty-nine dollars per night, Lenny was afforded luxury accommodations within the Watergate Hotel. I'm told they positioned two six-foot folding tables to create a containment area for Lenny. They used cardboard to keep him from pecking holes in the sheetrock walls. You never know, there are probably a lot of unusual wires running through the walls of the Watergate."

Everyone laughed again at Sarge's not-so-subtle reference to the Watergate scandal during the Nixon years.

"I'm told by Mr. Willard, standing to my right, that the floor was lined with heavy brown paper and taped into place. They tell me it was lined with pine shavings from Lenny's home near Beckley, which made the task of, you know, scoopin' the poop much easier."

Sarge was on a roll. The attendees would have no idea the enormous pressure he was under. Julia knew and stood within Sarge's field of vision. She beamed with pride and provided him an occasional wink of encouragement.

"You know, this is the eighth and last time I'll be providing a pardon of the turkey. I must say that something just dawned on me this morning. Lenny hasn't been accused of nor committed any crimes that require a pardon. I spoke with the attorney general about this and asked her to provide me a legal opinion on the whole process. She basically opined that I don't have any judicial jurisdiction over Lenny."

A few in the crowd chuckled while a few more gasped at the prospect of abandoning the tradition. Sarge, however, did not disappoint.

"So, this morning, in a separate ceremony, I drafted Lenny into the Air Force, although I'm told he doesn't fly very well because he's too stuffed. I'm going to pardon him and deploy him to the Washington Zoo to stand guard over our country's finest critters."

A smattering of applause was provided by the guests. Out of the corner of his eye, Sarge saw Donald emerge from the West Wing onto the Colonnade. His trusted friend wouldn't come looking for him if it wasn't important.

"Without further ado, I, Henry Winthrop Sargent the Fourth, President of the United States, pursuant to the pardon power conferred upon me by Article II, Section 2, of the Constitution, hereby grant a full pardon to Lenny the Turkey from Beckley, West Virginia."

As if prompted to do so, Lenny stood on his legs and flapped his wings, creating quite a ruckus in appreciation. Sarge, after taking a moment to kiss his wife and hug his children, joined Donald to deal with another kind of ruckus.

CHAPTER 52

12:30 p.m.
Russell Senate Office Building
Washington, DC

Gardner made his way to Capitol Hill to have a personal conversation with his final vote—his ace in the hole, a senator who owed his family a favor from many years ago. The woman didn't have skeletons in the closet. She wasn't in financial trouble although everyone needs more money. No, this was personal, much more so than every form of pressure Gardner had ever exerted on a member of Congress. The conversation would be brief, it needed to occur at the last minute before the senator entered the Senate Chamber for deliberations, and the senator's response would have to be unequivocal.

He was scrolling through the news of the day on the Drudge Report app when he received a text message from Mr. West.

W: Veep returned. On the hill now.

G.L.: Specific meetings?

W: No. Retail politicking.

G.L.: Stand by.

Gardner considered this information for a moment. He wasn't surprised that Sarge would pull out all the stops after yesterday's fiasco. Reportedly, the president was involved in a national security matter that hadn't been revealed to the media, or Gardner's sources. The only international news at the moment was the unrest in Taiwan, but that hardly qualified as a matter of utmost importance to distract Sarge from the vote.

If Sarge was distracted, he didn't show it. He was still making phone calls to key senators to firm up the vote. Gardner's newest conquest, the great senator from Colorado, had reported the context of her phone call with Sarge an hour ago. She did not tell him how she planned on voting, although a reasonable person could surmise that she was a vote against passage. Technically, she explained to her new lover, it was a lie of omission. In Washington, lies of omission were passed around as casually as a good morning.

Gardner's original intention was to camp out in the hallway near the Senate Chamber entrance, grab the attention of his target senator, and make his play. The presence of Abbie on the Hill wouldn't deter him, in fact, it encouraged him to set the tone for what would happen after the vote.

He decided to make a bold move to expedite the passing of the torch. It was a subtle maneuver, but someone as astute as the president would figure it out soon enough. Gardner returned to his phone.

G.P.: VP location?

W: Russell. 4th floor

Gardner chuckled to himself. *Naturally, starting at the top and working her way down.*

G.P.: Shadow her. I'm headed your way.

"Driver," he instructed using the limousine's intercom button above his head, "change of plans. Take me to the Russell Senate Office Building."

The Russell Building was the oldest of the three office buildings housing the U.S. senators and their staffs. It occupied a site north of the Capitol. The building was an ornate structure combining marble and stained glass to provide a smaller compliment to the Capitol itself. Like other buildings that provided offices for Congress, the Russell Building was connected to the Capitol by underground passages.

The limousine arrived and Gardner jumped out of the back without waiting for the driver to open his door. "Don't go far," he instructed. What he planned on doing was simple—be seen.

He sent a text to Mr. West as he was waiting to go through security.

G.P.: Location?

W: Third floor. LaRocco—Wyoming.

Senator LaRocco! No! Gardner was shouting in his head as he unconsciously pressed against a woman in line before him. She gave him a nasty look before proceeding through the security scanner.

Senator Louise LaRocco, junior senator from Wyoming, had been an attorney in Boston many years ago. She was new to politics at the time and was starting her first run for statewide office when her young daughter became ill with a rare disease.

Constance Lowell heard of the family's plight and reached out to LaRocco to offer financial assistance—no strings attached, which was a rare gesture from the Lowell family but not unusual for Mrs. Lowell decades ago.

The Lowells provided the child the finest in medical care and their efforts were widely praised as an unselfish gesture that saved the child's life.

For a while, Louise LaRocco and Constance remained in touch, especially as the young child grew up to have a normal life. But her husband took an executive position with an oil company in Wyoming, and Senator LaRocco, a Republican, decided to pursue her political career in a state more accepting of her conservative leanings.

It had been years since Gardner's mother had spoken to Senator LaRocco, although the generous donations to her campaign war chest were always recognized with a handwritten thank-you.

On this day, Gardner planned on calling in a marker. A chit that was never agreed upon but, in his mind, one that was owed by Senator LaRocco nonetheless. Of course, he'd sweeten the pot with promises of funding, positions of power within the new Congress, and all of that. But his primary tack was to tug on the heartstrings, an emotional ploy used against a mother far more effective than money and power.

The first thing Gardner had to do was get Abbie out of her office. He passed through security and entered the center rotunda of the building. Surrounded by eighteen Corinthian columns, he took in the beauty of the design. He decided to skip the elevator and chose one of the twin marble staircases leading to the upper floors. Running up the stairs two at a time, he reached the landing of the third floor slightly out of breath.

Standing against the wall, he searched through the busy hallway for his political operative dressed like an undertaker. Staffers scurried about in preparation for the vote. A smattering of reporters would stop a high-ranking senior official from time-to-time for an anonymous quote.

"Hello, sir," said Mr. West from behind Gardner, startling the younger man.

"Dammit, West."

"Sorry, sir. It's best you not turn around at this moment. The veep just emerged from Senator LaRocco's office. Her next stop is Hoeven from North Dakota, but she is signing autographs outside his office door."

"Autographs?"

"She's a rock star on the Hill, sir. Highly respected and, I might add, influential."

Gardner bristled at the comment. "Let me tell you something about influence. You want to know something? I can walk up and down this hallway for fifteen minutes. I won't smile or shake hands or sign any damn autographs. I won't even be recognized by ninety-five percent of these people. But you know what? I can influence every one of these senators, not just the ones I make idle chitchat with."

"She went into Hoeven's office, sir."

"Good, now I plan on giving her something to chat about. Help me find Senator Lee's office."

"Will he switch his vote?"

Gardner chuckled. "No, it's not about that. I want the vice president to get the impression that I'm working on it. I plan on milling about until she sees me, and then feign a look of guilt as I disappear into a senator's office."

"You want her to bust you up here?"

"Indeed, I do. And I hope it sends shock waves all the way to 1600 Pennsylvania Avenue."

CHAPTER 53

1:00 p.m. ET
800 Miles Southeast of Hawaii
The Pacific Ocean

The Aegis team rested and were now going over the latest intelligence reports received from the Pentagon and the CIA. With respect to the overall mission, they were impressed with the repositioning of the two carrier strike groups ordered by the president. Aerial photos showed the Chinese Coast Guard being duped, leaving the *Petersen*'s strike group safe passage on its way to Okinawa. Thus far, the *Ronald Reagan* had not drawn the attention of the military presence on the newly created islands in the South China Sea.

The conversation turned to their potential adversaries, although none of the intel reports indicated direct involvement by them in the uprising in Taipei.

"Anybody have direct experience with the Flying Dragons?" asked Drew as the men passed around the satellite imagery.

"Nah, but Pete knows those flying pink elephants pretty good," bellowed King.

"Yeah, buddy. Those were the good old days. Good drugs. Good whiskey. Good women." Peter Parker, whose name was the same as the character in the Spiderman comic series, was a tall, lanky operative from East Texas. Despite the obvious correlation, Parker's nickname was Spidey for his ability to scale walls, climb trees, and his borderline-suicidal lack of fear of heights.

Chris St. Nicholas, nicknamed Santa, a former SEAL who trained with Drew, added some serious context. "They're the best of the best within the PLA. Their military treats them like royalty. They're also a proud bunch. When a Chinese street gang took up their name as part of their criminal operations in New York's Chinatown, several of the Flying Dragon's operatives veered off the reservation a decade ago and began murdering the gangbangers. Their success was so great that the Flying Dragons gang in Hong Kong, the FDS, was almost eradicated by the military operatives' assassinations."

"Well, doesn't that make them a bunch of vigilante good guys," said King.

"It did in China," replied Santa, a valuable member of the team because he was fluent in Modern Standard Arabic, or *fusha;* Korean; and Mandarin Chinese, which is spoken in Beijing.

Turning back to the satellite photos, Drew set a side-by-side comparison of the AIT facility this evening next to the image from the night before.

"The crowd surrounding AIT has doubled since last night," said Drew. "But, according to the reports, none of the protestors have made a move on our facility."

"What are the gun laws in Taiwan?" asked Spidey.

King, a vocal proponent of the Second Amendment, was always researching the correlation between violence and a nation's gun laws. "They're allowed shotguns, rifles, and handguns, but not assault rifles."

"You mean like the mighty AR-15," said Spidey, drawing laughter from the group.

"No, you dope," said King jokingly. He grabbed an M-16 off the weapons rack behind him. "This is an assault rifle. An AR-15 packs less punch than most hunting rifles. It just looks all badass to make the preppers think they're warriors and to put the fear of God in the snowflakes."

Drew spoke up. "Spidey's question raises an interesting point. Based upon what I've read, there haven't been any shots fired during these protests other than the rubber bullets used at the Chinese Ministry."

"Yeah, well, this ain't Beirut or Fallujah or Helmand Province, where they shoot their weapons in the air to celebrate Ramadan or some such," added King.

"I get that, but I wonder if that's part of the overall plan by the PLA. They're creating this unrest, which naturally draws a police response in the form of crowd control."

Santa began nodding his head and finished Drew's thought. "But they're keeping the streets from flowing with blood in order to prevent a military escalation. It's like a low-key coup d'etat."

"More like a roper dope," Spidey chimed in.

"You mean rope-a-dope, dopey," said King with a laugh. "It was Muhammad Ali's famed boxing style, which lured his opponent in under the false impression he was winning the skirmish. Then, *BOOM*, the Greatest would knock the other fighter out."

"Whatever," said Drew dryly, wishing the guys would focus. He had no doubt they would once on the ground, but they were certainly loose beforehand. "Let's turn to the missing ambo."

"We need to study this video footage, Slash," Santa said to Drew. The operative brought up the .mp4 video file on the MacBook and mirrored it on a monitor adjacent to the cockpit. "They've done a great job of isolating the ambo's vehicle and following it through Taipei. Watch what happens at the three-minute mark on the footage."

The operatives watched the video, periodically pointing at the vehicle travelling at a high rate of speed through Taipei City.

"Why the hell-fire emergency?" asked King.

Drew summarized what was shown on the video. "They left the Presidential Palace without a sense of urgency. Then, within a mile of the AIT complex, they turned toward the south on this freeway and took off."

"Yeah, that's when it gets weird," interrupted Santa. "Watch this maneuver."

The vehicle, marked with a circle by the NSA analysts, jammed on the brakes in the fast lane of the busy freeway and darted between two concrete barriers into the oncoming traffic. As the approaching vehicles slid to a stop to allow the ambassador's vehicle to correct itself, several cars crashed into each other in the process.

"The ambo's vehicle was on the move again," said King.

"Clearly, it's an evasion maneuver," said Santa. "I have to tell ya, I've watched the tape six times and I don't see anything that looks like a tail."

"Skittish driver, maybe?" asked Drew.

"Maybe, but then how do you explain this?" asked Santa.

The vehicle continued to carry the ambassador on the freeway until it exited into a residential neighborhood, where it pulled into a walled residence with two four-car garages. The vehicle drove under an overhang of trees and entered the garage.

"I'm confused," started Spidey. "Maybe this is one of the CIA's safe houses? The driver knew exactly where he was going."

"Who cares if it's CIA? We know where the ambo is, why haven't we sent a team on station to fetch him out of there?"

"There are two reasons," replied Santa. "Remember, this is not drone footage, so there is a time delay in it being relayed to DC. Secondly, watch the end of this footage."

All eyes returned to the monitor. Santa approached the screen and pointed to the location of the two garages. Everything was still until suddenly, from underneath the canopy of trees obscuring the view of the garage, six white delivery vans poured out of the garages and through the compound's iron gate. They turned in different directions on the street and then made additional haphazard turns, resulting in the six vans seeking different parts of Taipei City.

"Now, doesn't this look like a Jason Bourne movie," said King. "These guys don't mess around. Whadya think?"

"Well planned and perfectly orchestrated," replied Drew. "Whoever pulled this off knew our satellites would be watching. In fact, they probably expect that we'll find the ambassador at some point. They just want to make it difficult and time-consuming for us."

"Why? Ransom?" asked Spidey.

"No," replied Drew. "I think politics are behind this. All of these events are connected. The intel shows Chinese nationals are behind the escalation of the protests. Now, the CIA tells us the Flying Dragons have tripled their personnel along the coast across from Taiwan. But in the end, it doesn't matter. We've got a job to do and that's find Ambassador McBride."

CHAPTER 54

2:00 p.m.
North Wing of the Capitol
The Senate Chamber
Washington, DC

Some sociologists claimed humans were naturally self-absorbed. In order to function and survive as a species, evolution taught us to think short-term—remaining focused on our individual survival. A perceived crisis demanded our immediate attention while somewhere far away, another of our fellow man reasonably feared a certain death. The threat of death to one clearly outweighed the possible crisis perceived by another, yet we all go about our business, focusing on our own shit. Or at least we should, anyway.

Gardner Lowell was self-absorbed, just like the rest of us, but he constantly was mindful that his actions would have a direct impact on his family and closest associates. He had a plan that he considered to be good for the country and for his family. While it was true his position of power within the Boston Brahmin would be advanced, in the end, all of his family would benefit from his schemes for generations to come.

Since 1859, the United States Senate Chamber was located in a room in the north wing of the U.S. Capitol. A rectangular room with one hundred individual desks for each senator, the multileveled main floor was overlooked on all sides by a gallery on the second floor.

As planned, Gardner found Senator LaRocco just as she entered the Senate Chamber. The two had never met, but when he introduced himself as Gardner Lowell, son of Lawrence and Constance, a look of trepidation engulfed the senator's demeanor.

She appeared genuinely frightened at meeting the man whose reputation for brutal dealings with his adversaries preceded him.

In a single minute, Gardner reminded the mother of her beautiful child who'd cheated death and grew up with a Wellesley education courtesy of the Lowell family. In the next minute, Gardner got to the point. His request was simple.

"Senator, once, our family set aside our priorities to save your daughter and provide her a remarkable future. Nothing was asked of you in return. Now, my family needs your help. A simple gesture—one which will cost you nothing except the casting of a vote in favor of this bill."

"Mr. Lowell, it would require me to vote against my party, my president, and my conscience," Senator LaRocco protested. "Of course, I am grateful to your family for saving my daughter, but surely there is some other way I can repay you."

"No, Senator, this is it. This is the time to show your gratitude. There will be some fallout, to be sure. With my guidance, you will receive a multitude of benefits in addition to the one you hold most dear."

Senator LaRocco looked around the grand hallway just outside the Senate Chamber. For the most part, her private conversation with the well-dressed man had gone unnoticed.

Abbie entered the hallway with an entourage, which presented an immediate problem for Gardner. The success of this vote hinged upon his pressure of Senator LaRocco. He needed her commitment before he shoved her into the Senate, figuratively, to do her duty to the Lowell family.

"Senator," he pressed her for an answer, "do not deny me this request. It will be fine, I assure you."

She glanced down, and Gardner moved slightly to her left to shield him from Abbie's view. Then she acquiesced. Her body language said it all. Her shoulders drooped, her knees buckled slightly and her chin hit her chest.

"I'll do it. But please, just leave us alone. I'll deal with the consequences on my own."

She turned to leave when Gardner gently touched her arm. "Thank you, Senator. This means a lot to my family."

Gardner disappeared into the shadows of the stairwell leading up to the gallery surrounding the Senate proceedings. He'd instructed Mr. West to save a seat for him in the front row overlooking the central rostrum in the front of the room. From his seat he could look into the eyes of the senators whose arms had been twisted, and they could see him.

During the vote, he'd watched these proceedings often enough to know that the C-SPAN cameras would pan the gallery, which would reveal his face to those in the White House hoping for the bill's defeat. Like an arsonist watching a blaze he'd just set, Gardner would smile for the camera, reveling in a victory that would set in motion the downfall of his nemesis—Sarge.

CHAPTER 55

2:00 p.m.
The Oval Office
Washington, DC

Sarge completed the half-dozen phone calls to specific service members and their families, thanking them for their sacrifices for America and wishing them happy Thanksgiving. Next, a videographer set up the camera and lighting for him to make a live address to Camp Casey, which would also be recorded for distribution to other military facilities around the world.

Addressing the troops for Thanksgiving was a welcome distraction for Sarge. The new information regarding the ambassador's now confirmed abduction was troubling because it was planned well in advance and U.S. intelligence agencies missed it. The sudden uprisings were also related, and his working theory remained the events of the last few days had been orchestrated by Beijing.

Plus, there was the vote. In between calls to service members, he encouraged senators to stick with him on the concept of a Constitutional Convention and vote against the Pacific Statehood Act. As a lame duck, Sarge didn't have much political capital left, but he did have years of relationships to call upon for loyalty, if nothing else.

Sarge put partisan politics out of his mind as he was given the final countdown to address J.J. and the troops at Camp Casey. Located forty miles north of Seoul, South Korea, Camp Casey was one of several U.S. Army bases near the Korean Demilitarized Zone, or DMZ. Along with Camps Hovey, Castle, and Mobile, Camp Casey held the main armor and mechanized infantry elements of the 2nd Infantry Division. A field artillery brigade was also added to Camp Casey recently, as the North Koreans continued to demand economic sanctions be lifted.

A standing-room-only crowd had gathered in the USO facility at Camp Casey. The troops were treated to complimentary donuts and coffee from Krispy Kreme, which was located within the AAFES building operated by the Army & Air Force Exchange Services.

Sarge began with his prepared remarks. "As Americans, we have so much to be thankful for. We give thanks for all our men and women in uniform. We also thank their families, some of whom I've just spoken with by phone. They miss you very much and I want all of them to know we're grateful for their sacrifice too.

"Too often, we, as Americans, lose sight of your mission. There are some who've forgotten why we have a military. You serve your country not to promote war, but, rather, as a member of our armed forces, you are there to insure we can live in peace. Every American should be grateful for what you, and all those before you, have done to protect our shores and defeat those enemies who challenge our freedoms.

"When you deploy to faraway lands, your mothers see a young child dragging an overstuffed rucksack almost as big as you are. God bless every mother who raised her sons and daughters to want to make the sacrifices you make for our country. We will forever be indebted to your mothers and fathers, and all of you who've made the commitment to give your lives so that we may live in peace and freedom.

"My commitment in return is that we will always stand with you, and with our country, to acknowledge your sacrifice, which allows us to live in a free land, the greatest country on earth, these United States of America. Thank you, God bless you and your families, and God bless America."

CHAPTER 56

3:00 p.m.
The Oval Office
Washington, DC

"I just received a text message from J.J.," started Donald as Brad entered the Oval Office to join him and Sarge. "He said the troops were very appreciative of your remarks and especially the emphasis on their families. He said you've got a lot of fans over there."

"I don't know if I'd call them fans—rock stars have fans," Sarge said as he walked toward Betty's office. "Their job is a heckuva lot tougher than mine. They're heroes and I'm merely the people's humble servant."

Sarge opened the door and summoned Betty.

"Yes, Mr. President?"

"Betty, would you mind letting the First Lady know that Donald and I can make it for dinner around seven? The Quinns will be staying in the Residence with us for a couple of nights."

"I will, thank you, Mr. President."

"Hey, Abbie!" Sarge exclaimed as she entered Betty's office. He immediately moved to give his vice president a hug. They hadn't seen each other in thirteen days due to her travels abroad and time with Drew's family in Tennessee.

"Hello, Mr. President. Fancy meeting you here." Abbie laughed as she returned the hug. She looked over Sarge's shoulder to Betty and winked. The two had become close over the years, with Betty given carte blanche authority to dole out motherly advice to the mother-to-be.

Sarge escorted Abbie into the Oval Office and shut the door

behind them. Four of the most powerful and influential public servants in the United States, for a moment behind closed doors, became the old friends and comrades from those days at Prescott Peninsula following the collapse.

They made small talk, namely about Abbie's due date, which was just after the inauguration of the new administration. They had an honest conversation about Drew's continued involvement in dangerous Aegis operations. Sarge threatened to assert his executive authority over his friend and tie him to a desk in Boston, but Abbie said he'd likely escape.

"You don't want Slash as your enemy, Sarge. I wouldn't piss him off. Listen, guys, he loves what he does and he's very good at it. I know that he'll never take unnecessary risks, but by the same token, I want us all to support him because he doesn't need to be out there thinking about what's waiting at home for him. He needs to remain focused on his mission."

"I totally agree, Abbie," said Brad. "For so long as he's going to do his job, he can't be wondering if he's making a mistake. He's got to keep his head in the game."

Abbie turned to Donald. "Donald, would you mind keeping me abreast of his team's progress? For example, where are they at this point?"

Donald pulled up his iPad, logged into the NSA secured server and studied the notes. "They are about to land in Guam where they'll quickly finalize their gear and switch transportation for the trip to Taiwan. Throughout their long ride, they've been continuously updated with satellite imagery and intel from all of our resources on the ground and in space."

"Drew won't be walking into the unknown, Abbie," said Sarge reassuringly. "He'll have the benefit of his team and our eyes in the sky."

"Okay, thanks, guys. I do worry about him, of course, but I'll never let him know it. When the time comes to hang it up, I'll trust him to tell me."

Donald opened the door to the Presidential Study and found his communications team watching the pre-vote deliberations. "Hey, guys, why don't you get us set up in the Roosevelt Room to watch the vote. Is CNN's little countdown clock accurate? Is the vote set for thirty minutes from now?"

"Yes," replied Ocampo. "I just received a text from an aide to Senator Rutledge, confirming the timing."

"Okay, I'll get the Veep on her way. Please get us set up, and I don't want anyone in there except the three of us and you guys. The president avoided giving the media comments on this yesterday. Today will be a different story, so we'll have to formulate a response either way."

"Yes, sir," replied Crepeau. "I've created a draft to work from regardless of outcome."

Donald returned to the Oval Office and interrupted their conversation about Taiwan. "Abbie, the vote will be in less than thirty minutes. We better get you on your way."

"Thanks, Donald. This brings me to the reason I took the time to see you in person. I caught a glimpse of Gardner Lowell on Capitol Hill earlier. I don't know if he was aware that I saw him, but it struck me as odd that he'd be sniffing around senators today."

"Yeah, it sure is," said Sarge. "I haven't spoken with him in months. Back in the summer, he expressed his support for the reunification effort, but we never discussed the mechanics of bringing the states back in. He's never struck me as a Constitutionalist, so I can't assume he's advocating against the bill."

"There could be something else to consider," interjected Donald. "The House vote flipped suddenly. I'm telling you, guys, we thought we had a handle on it until the end. Is it possible someone, perhaps Gardner Lowell, is behind all of this?"

"If he is, he should have come to me first," started Sarge angrily. He looked around the Oval Office to make sure none of the doors were open. He lowered his voice as he spoke. "If he's acting on behalf of the executive committee of the Brahmin, then we've got a bigger problem than this vote. It means I've been cut out of the loop."

"Can they do that?" asked Donald. "I mean, for years, you've maintained your position as the accepted chairman, if you will, of the executive committee. All of the members, including Gardner, acquiesced in the way things would be handled. Frankly, I think we've done a great job of looking after their interests while running this administration."

"I agree, Donald," started Sarge. "But go back to those early days after we bugged out to Prescott Peninsula. Constance Lowell was none too happy about it all. She only accepted John Morgan's decision to unilaterally elevate me to my position for a short while because we kept her alive. After I came into office, she became distant."

"And Gardner became more vocal about things," said Donald. He turned his attention to Abbie because it was time for her to leave for the Senate Chamber in case she needed to cast a tie vote. "Abbie, did you see him speaking to any senators in particular?"

Abbie provided Donald a few names and then she said, "If any of these were to vote yea, I'd be shocked. Donald, see what you can find out, and I'll hit the Senate floor."

"Talk to Rutledge," said Sarge. "He's kept tabs on the vulnerable senators."

"Okay, gotta go. Let's stay positive, guys. I'll touch base after the vote."

Abbie gave each of them a hug and left.

"I'm headed for my office to make some calls. I've set up the Roosevelt Room to watch the vote. I'll catch up with you in there."

Donald bolted out the other door toward his office, shouting for Ocampo and Crepeau as he went.

Sarge rubbed his temples and stared out of the windows onto the South Lawn. "Brad, how do you really feel about this Taiwan situation? Am I overreacting by redirecting the carrier strike groups to the region. I'm really provoking the Chinese by doing this."

"That's part of the problem of being Commander-in-Chief," he quickly replied. "You have to make decisions regarding national security without all of the information. It's not always black-and-white. I know this, if we didn't move decisively, we'd be skewered around the world for being weak."

"They'd hold me responsible for Taiwan falling into Beijing's control."

"Moving the carriers was the right thing to do. Better to ask for forgiveness than permission. Besides, we haven't made an overt threat toward China or their interests. We've just *shifted our assets* around a little." Brad used his fingers to create air quotes around the phrase.

"Yeah, if they'd *shifted their assets* to surround Hawaii, we'd be out-of-our-minds apoplectic. We'll see what happens in the next twenty-four hours. But first, let's go watch the war games in the Senate."

CHAPTER 57

3:00 p.m. ET
Andersen Air Force Base
The Pacific Ocean
Guam

Major Carl Beckett, operations officer of the Ready Reaction Force, a platoon-sized unit in the U.S. Army, took to the podium in the hangar at Andersen Air Force Base in Guam. AFB was host to the 36th Wing of the Air Force. On the surface, it was primarily an operations and maintenance group, providing support to more than nine thousand military personal on Guam and nearby military installations. On this day, it would act as the base of operations for the mission in Taiwan. Major Beckett was accompanied by two aides and Lieutenant Colonel Gerald Sherman, commander of Delta's Operational Detachment, the ground operations of the force.

Following Benghazi, Sarge tasked Brad with creating more of these Ready Reaction Forces wherever their military bases were throughout the world. Each RRF was designed to quickly intervene as a spearhead to gain control of an unfolding combat situation or one that involved protection of Americans abroad.

Protocols were put into place to quickly identify low-intensity conflicts such as civil unrest that necessitated the defense of strategic and tactical locations of importance, or to repel attacks on American interests around the world.

The RRFs were expected to maintain a split-second level of readiness in their personnel and equipment. During a high-intensity conflict where lives had been taken or Americans had been fired upon, the RRF was expected to be at the ready with their motors running.

Operation Golden Retriever started slower than other conflicts because of the added complexity of carrier movement. While the low-intensity threat existed in Taipei City, a bigger conflict loomed on the horizon in the form of a Chinese military incursion onto the island. Deployment of the RRF to Taiwan would raise more red flags in Beijing, which would inhibit the *Ronald Reagan* and the *Petersen* from advancing into effective striking positions.

Drew's eight operatives were the only non-active-duty participants in the briefing. They stood out because of their lack of military uniforms. Drew's team wore khakis with cargo pockets and black or tan tee shirts.

"Okay, let's get started. Members of the Ready Reaction Force have been assigned to assist existing security personnel at the AIT and prepare the four-hundred or so diplomatic personnel for evacuation. Several others have been assigned to perform security detail at the Hualien Airport along Taiwan's east coast. At this point, the locals believe we are readying transports for the evacuation of American nationals who feel their safety is at risk due to the demonstrations. So officially those of you within the RRF have been assigned to the visible protection of Americans."

Major Beckett took another draw on his cigar and studied his men. "I've assigned six of you to work with these gentlemen behind you. If you've been so designated, please remain here for now. The rest of you are to report immediately to the air transports waiting outside."

The RRF unit shuffled out of the hangar, leaving Major Beckett, Lieutenant Colonel Sherman, and Drew's newly expanded team behind.

Major Beckett shoved the cigar butt into the corner of his mouth and took a seat in the center of the folding tables set up next to the podium. "Folks, gather around and let's take a look at the latest from the birds in the sky."

His aides spread out the reconnaissance photos and maps along the tables and secured their corners with masking tape.

Beckett picked up a simple wooden stick pointer and looked from one end of the table to the other. "Okay, for the benefit of my people, this operation, code-named Golden Retriever, is classified top secret and is compartmented on a strict need-to-know basis. I've chosen each of you because of your security clearances, language skills, and your familiarity with Taipei.

"Our specific mission is to locate Ambassador McBride, secure his safety and, if possible, interrogate his abductors to find out who they work for. The CIA has its suspicions, and without prejudicing your efforts, it's likely these are Chinese operatives from their Flying Dragons unit or some other element of the PLA. With that said, these guys will be pros. This is not some snatch-for-ransom situation. There has been no request for payment, or any contact for that matter."

"Sir, have the intelligence people updated the whereabouts of the six vans that left the compound together?" asked Drew.

"They have," he replied as he stood up with the pointer. "We have six ultimate destinations for the white vans." He pointed at six different maps. They ranged from parking garages to small businesses to other residential locations.

Drew studied the maps. "How current are these?"

"Three hours ago, but our eyes in the sky are about to give us glasses," interjected Lieutenant Colonel Sherman. "The Navy has assisted us with the new MQ-4C Triton Drone in Taipei. The drone is on its way from Hawaii and will be providing us live feeds by the time you touch down."

"That's a big bird, sir," said King. "It won't go unnoticed by the PLA."

Lieutenant Colonel Sherman nodded. "That's true, but it's the best we've got at the moment. Besides, we're hours away from everyone showing their cards anyway."

"The real-time video will be a huge help," mumbled Drew.

"Gentlemen, you've got six destinations to investigate and the potential for eight teams. I will send these most recent images with you aboard the newest air transport in the Corps. Jackson, my guys are your guys now. Use them as you see fit."

"Thank you, Major," said Drew. "Let's saddle up, y'all. Time's a-wastin'."

CHAPTER 58

3:30 p.m.
The Roosevelt Room
The White House
Washington, DC

Sarge paced the floor as he waited for the vote to begin. A roll call vote in the Senate occurs when each senator votes yea or nay as their name is called by the clerk, who records the votes on a simple tally sheet. The procedural aspects of today's vote on the Pacific Statehood Act, such as determining a quorum and invoking cloture, which was the procedure for ending debate on the bill, had been completed. Opportunities to filibuster had passed.

The presiding officer, Vice President Abbie Morgan Jackson, as was customary, conducted a voice vote. "On the passage of the Pacific Statehood Act of 2024, all in favor say aye!"

"Aye!" shouted half the Senate.

"All opposed say nay!"

"Nay!" replied the other half.

Abbie slapped the gavel down several times and announced that a voice vote would be forthcoming. She welcomed a motion for a recorded vote, which was promptly seconded.

For several minutes, Abbie conferred with the Clerk of the Senate while the appropriate paperwork was being assembled for her.

"Good Lord," Donald moaned. "This is ridiculous. C'mon, Abbie, get on with it already."

Brad began to laugh at his friend. "Donald, do we need to fix you a cocktail?"

"No, not yet. Depending on how it goes, I might need a bottle."

The C-SPAN cameras had been focused on Abbie but began to pan the Senate floor and then the gallery.

"Wait!" shouted Sarge. "Where's the remote?"

"Here, sir," replied Ocampo.

"Pause and rewind the C-SPAN feed," instructed Sarge. Ocampo hit the rewind button and the images were shown in reverse. "Slowly. Keep going. There. Stop. Stop there!"

"Sarge," interrupted Donald, "is that—?"

"Yeah, I see the smug bastard. Gardner Lowell is in the front row of the gallery, right over Abbie's head."

Sarge reached into his jacket pocket and removed his phone. He frantically typed a text message to Senator Rutledge.

POTUS: Gardner Lowell. Gallery, first row, center. Do you see?

Rutledge: Pompous fool. I see him.

POTUS: Who did he get to?

Rutledge: IDK.I spoke to every one of them pre-vote.

Abbie began to call the roll, which brought Sarge's attention back to the monitors. Donald had his iPad ready to check off the votes as they were announced. Ocampo had retrieved the easel with the senator's names on the flip pad to display the votes for Sarge and Brad.

One by one, Abbie called out the states in alphabetical order. Alabama. Alaska. Arizona. Arkansas. The senators from each of these states cast their votes by declaring yea or nay.

"So far, we have no surprises," muttered Donald as the process continued.

"Colorado, Senior Senator Higgenbottom," said Abbie.

"Nay!" Donald recorded the vote, as did Ocampo.

"Colorado, Junior Senator Ellis," said Abbie.

"Yea!"

Donald stared at his iPad and then at Ocampo's handwritten tally on the easel. "Yea?" he asked.

"Yes, sir. She flipped."

"You've got to be kidding," said Sarge. "I would have never thought she'd change sides."

Abbie seemed to recognize the betrayal as well because she hesitated in continuing while she stared at Senator Ellis from her elevated position.

Sarge received a text message from the Senate Majority Leader.

Rutledge: I confirmed her this morning. No doubt. Now this!

"We can't lose any more," said Donald.

"Gardner Lowell wouldn't be in the gallery if he wasn't sure of himself," said Sarge. "Donald, go through your list again. Who are we missing? We can still text them."

"Not necessarily, Mr. President," said Crepeau. "Senate rules prohibit the use of cell phones during voice votes."

"What about Paul? He's texting me."

Crepeau shrugged. "He made the rules, sir. I imagine they don't apply to him."

Abbie continued. "Missouri, Senior Senator Taggett."

"Yea!" came the reply.

Donald continued to frantically scroll through his iPad. Sarge studied the names for the remaining states. They were halfway through.

"Can we get Senator Rutledge to confirm Sanders from Nevada? I'm grasping here, but Nevada borders Cali and Colorado."

Sarge didn't bother with a reply. Abbie was calling Montana now.

POTUS: Confirm Sanders, Nevada.

Rutledge: On it.

CNN was showing a long-range view of the Senate chamber. The group in the Roosevelt Room watched as Senator Rutledge ambled over to where Senator Sanders was seated. He put his hands on the man's shoulders and whispered into his ear. The senator from Reno, Nevada, nodded and patted Rutledge on the hand, who smiled and returned the gesture.

Rutledge made his way back to his seat and sent a text.

Rutledge: Confirmed nay.

POTUS: TY. We saw.

"Donald, who else?" asked Sarge.

"Sarge, I'm grasping here," replied Donald, his voice trailing off.

Sarge studied the flip board, focusing on the names to determine who could be bought off. As Abbie recorded the votes from Pennsylvania, he focused on the last dozen states. Abbie must have read his mind with some form of extrasensory perception because she purposefully stalled before she called Rhode Island.

"She's thinking also," said Sarge aloud without realizing he'd done so.

"Yes, our girl smells trouble," said Brad, the military man weighing in on the proceedings for the first time. "I'll bet she saw Rutledge approach the Nevada guy."

Sarge got excited. "Yes, you're right, Brad. She's trying to help us. Donald, come on, buddy."

"Sarge, I mean Mr.—damn, whatever. The rest of these votes are solid yeas or nays."

"There he is again," exclaimed Ocampo, pointing at the monitor that showed Gardner in the front row, leaning on the edge of his seat, staring intently onto the Senate floor.

Abbie began the roll call again, now up to Texas.

"Ocampo, hurry, go back," ordered Sarge. "Where is he looking?"

"It appears he's looking toward the left, sir."

"The Republican side of the chamber," said Sarge and then yelled at the television, "Slow down, Abbie!"

"Come on, Donald, who can Gardner buy from Virginia, West Virginia, Wisconsin, or Wyoming."

Donald replied, "The House Minority Whip was from Virginia. What if he was double-dealing?"

"Then Gardner may have bought Adams from Virginia!" replied Ocampo.

Sarge didn't hesitate. He sent another frantic text, misspelling the junior female senator's name in the process.

POTUS: Admas VA!!!

The group immediately turned their attention to the screen and watched Senator Rutledge jump out of his chair, drawing the attention of several members of the Senate. He pushed his way past a conversation and made his way to where Virginia's junior senator was seated.

Abbie announced Vermont, whose senators placed both of their votes in the yea column. She continued, but her attention was noticeably on the Majority Leader.

"Virginia, Senior Senator Campbell."

"Yea!"

Senator Rutledge approached Senator Adams from Virginia while Abbie hesitated, allowing him to speak with her. She appeared to pull away from him, causing a visibly dejected Senator Rutledge to flop into the vacant seat next to her, which belonged to Senator LaRocco from Wyoming.

Abbie continued. "Virginia, Junior Senator Adams."

The senator glanced back over to Senator Rutledge and then announced her vote. "Nay!"

Ocampo and Crepeau exchanged high fives. "Excellent," shouted the young woman, who had been Sarge's prized student at Harvard.

Abbie moved on to West Virginia and Wisconsin, bypassing Washington state, which had left the Union.

"It's gonna come down to a tie," said Donald. "I think he got to her just in time."

Sarge didn't comment as he received another text message from Senator Rutledge.

Rutledge: It wasn't her. Never was. Always solid.

Abbie came to the final state. "Wyoming, Senior Senator Wyatt."

"Nay!"

The tension was thick in the Roosevelt Room as everyone was standing in front of the three monitors. The final vote was about to be cast.

"Wyoming, Junior Senator LaRocco."

The Senate Chamber fell deathly silent as the C-SPAN camera moved to focus on Senator LaRocco's customary seat in the chamber, which she'd vacated during the latter part of the vote. She was no longer there, but her seat was still occupied by Senator Rutledge.

Abbie repeated the call. "Wyoming, Junior Senator LaRocco."

The other senators appeared to be confused and then concerned as she didn't respond. People began looking around the chamber for her.

"Where did she go?" asked Donald. "It's fifty to forty-nine in favor. We need her vote to create the tie."

"What if she abstains?" asked Sarge.

Donald replied, "She has to give a reason. But where is she?"

Abbie covered her hand over the microphone and leaned over to the clerk, who immediately summoned the sergeant-at-arms. By this point, the mumbling among the members of the Senate rose to a crescendo, forcing Abbie to call the Senate to order.

The Rules of the Senate were forcing her to make a decision. She had to continue with the vote. She repeated the roll call, causing the senators to stop their chatter.

"Wyoming, Junior Senator LaRocco."

"We're screwed," said Sarge. "She's been co-opted by Gardner, or something has happened to her. Either way, it's over. Abbie is going to have to call it or half the Senate will riot."

"Final call. Wyoming Senator LaRocco, are you in the chamber?"

A long pause followed before the members of the Senate in favor of the Pacific Statehood Act began to embrace each other and celebrate.

"The clerk of the Senate shall read the final tally."

"On passage of the Pacific Statehood Act of 2024, there are fifty for and forty-nine against. The ayes have it and the House version of the bill is passed."

Sarge slumped in the first available chair while Donald paced the floor, his face enraged. The communications team didn't wait for their instructions to leave. Brad led them to the door and closed it behind them.

"Thanks, Brad," said Sarge. "There'll be plenty of time to prepare a statement for the press. Donald, sit down, old friend. I don't need you strokin' out on me. The girls have a slumber party scheduled for tonight and we've got wounds to lick."

"Guys, I'm sorry about this. I'd love to throw down a bottle of booze with ya, but I need to get back to the Pentagon. Things are about to get hot in Taiwan."

Sarge stood and shook his friend's hand. "Go ahead, Brad. Thanks for hanging with us for moral support. Please keep me informed as things develop."

"Of course," said Brad as he turned to the dejected Chief of Staff. "Donald, hang in there. I'll see you tomorrow at dinner, hopefully."

"Dinner?" asked Donald, who was somewhat oblivious to the conversation.

"Yeah, buddy," said Sarge, who patted his friend on the back. "Thanksgiving dinner, tomorrow."

Sarge followed Brad out and poked his head into Betty's office.

She frowned and looked up from her work and offered her condolences. "I'm truly sorry, Mr. President."

"Yeah, me too, Betty, on many levels. Would you please get the attorney general on the phone? Tell him I need to see him on an urgent matter. Also, let the Gatekeeper know that Donald will be indisposed for a little while. I think he needs to decompress."

"I will, sir. Will you be in the Oval?"

Sarge laughed. "I may have to wheel my Chief of Staff in there from across the hall, but that's where I'll see the AG."

Sarge smiled at several staffers in the hallway, who looked like they'd all lost their best friend. He didn't make any small talk, focusing on his next steps, which had ramifications far beyond today's vote.

He walked back into the Roosevelt Room, where Donald seemed close to tears. Sarge always admired his good friend for not being afraid to show his emotions. Sarge closed the door behind him.

"We've got lots to discuss, Donald, and then we need to turn our attention to saving our ambassador."

"I know, but let me ask this first. Will Gardner Percival Lowell be at Thanksgiving dinner tomorrow?"

"I think he's on the list. I'll check with Julia."

"Is it too late to uninvite him?" asked Donald.

"You mean disinvite?"

"What's the difference?" asked Donald.

"Disinvite means you're no longer welcome. It's a little more mean-spirited."

"Yeah, disinvite him. Can we do it?"

Sarge laughed and grabbed Donald by the shoulders and gave him a playful shake. "I wanna remind you of something. There was a night when the two of us were standing up on the widow's walk at 1PP. You started to tease me by suggesting I run for President of the United States. Do you remember that?"

"Yeah, I remember. You threatened to throw me off the roof," replied Donald.

"That's right."

"You should have thrown me off the roof and saved us the aggravation."

"Well, I'm glad I didn't. Donald, the Founding Fathers would have been proud of what we've accomplished in the White House. So would John Morgan. Today was a setback, to be sure. But it's not the end of the world as we know it. We know what that looks like."

"What about Gardner?" asked Donald.

"Listen, there is a conversation that will most likely take place tomorrow that is long overdue. We need to clear our heads, get our ducks in a row, because a new battle is brewing that won't involve weapons of war or wrangling of votes. Now, are you with me?"

"Hell yeah!"

CHAPTER 59

5:00 p.m.
The Trump Townhouse
Trump International Hotel
Washington, DC

Gardner Lowell returned to the Trump Townhouse a triumphant man. In the past seventy-two hours, he'd accomplished three very important political achievements. First, he'd proven that he could manipulate the nation's influential lawmakers just as well as his predecessors on the Boston Brahmin executive council by securing several diverse allies in the halls of Congress who'd do his bidding in the future. Second, he'd set the stage for the reunification of the nation, which would expand the balance sheets of his family and his associates. But finally, and most importantly to his ego, he'd stuck it to the president—Henry Sargent, who'd been appointed to his position of power without merit, in Gardner's humble opinion.

"Mother, may I propose a toast to you, Father, and the Lowell family, whose name is once again synonymous with power in this town?"

"Absolutely, Gardner. Cheers!" Constance stood and lifted her glass in the air to touch Gardner's.

His grin widened as the alcohol fueled his euphoria. "Mother, the exhilaration of manipulating these people is beyond description. I undertook to change the course of our nation's history these last few days, and by using the cunning Father taught me, I pulled off a tremendous turn of events that surprised everyone."

"You have, son. Now, I must ask. Do you believe our illustrious president has any clue you were behind this?"

"I must assume so, Mother. In fact, I hope so."

"Why?"

"It's a gambit, Mother. As you know, the executive council was for this bill as proposed. Only Sarge, Arthur Peabody and Paul Winthrop opposed it."

"Pshaw," said Constance with an aristocratic swipe of her free hand. "Winthrop is older than I am and only supports Sarge because he's distant family. Peabody is a do-gooder who believes every word of the Constitution. Naturally, so do we, but the document needs to evolve with the times and be flexible to deal with unusual situations like this one."

"I agree, Mother. All I know is this, the elder statesman of the organization my father participated in for nearly five decades, Walter Cabot, is one hundred percent behind me. He phoned me and offered congratulations. He also vowed to support me when we confront Sarge about signing the bill."

"How does that work?"

"I expect him to veto the legislation when it hits his desk," replied Gardner.

"Son, that means all of your work was for naught."

Gardner moved to the bar and refilled their drinks. He received a text message of congratulations from Phillip Endicott, son of Henry Endicott, who was suffering from dementia. Phillip had proven to be a loyal supporter of Gardner's.

"Not necessarily, Mother, if you look at the big picture. When the new Congress convenes, we will have our man in the White House and several new members of Congress, who will give us a veto-proof majority in both houses to pass another version of the bill. Sarge hopes to rally the states to bring a Constitutional Convention before the new bill gets through the process."

"Can he accomplish that?" asked Constance.

"Possibly. He's very popular with the nation's governors. But I don't think it will come to that."

"Why not?" asked the aging Lowell matriarch.

"Consider this. Setting aside the ancillary victories achieved through expanding our base of loyalists on the Hill, I've set Sarge up to make a decision that will run contrary to the will of the Boston Brahmin executive council. You see, Cabot will approach Sarge tomorrow and demand he commit to signing the bill. If Sarge compromises his *oh-so-honorable* principles, he'll sign it for the good of the Boston Brahmin. If he chooses to veto the bill, I'll covertly suggest his complete ouster from the executive council."

"And, my son, you will ascend to the top where you belong."

"Yes, Mother, and Walter Cabot has promised to lead the call to make a change."

Constance raised her dirty martini for another toast. "To a memorable Thanksgiving!"

"Hear, hear!"

CHAPTER 60

5:00 p.m.
The Oval Office
The White House
Washington, DC

Sometimes, despite the hundreds of people that Sarge interacted with on a daily basis, the presidency seemed to be a lonely job. He'd learned there were only a handful of close friends he could trust who weren't attempting to manipulate him for their own selfish purposes. Over time, sound advice might be discarded because a level of paranoia set in. When this happened, Sarge chose to shut out the world, consider what he'd learned from history, and then acted accordingly.

He would be under tremendous pressure from the media and others within the government to declare his intentions regarding signing the Pacific Statehood Act. He drew upon his knowledge of American history, in particular a similar conundrum that faced President Andrew Johnson following the Civil War.

With the assassination of Abraham Lincoln, Vice President Johnson, an old-fashioned Southern Jacksonian democrat from Tennessee, became the seventeenth President of the United States.

During the secession of the Southern states, which included Tennessee, then Senator Johnson, a staunch proponent of states' rights, remained in the United States Senate, much to the delight of Lincoln's Republicans in the North. The decision earned him the label *traitor* in the eyes of most Southerners.

In 1864, the Republicans, contending they were the party of all Americans, nominated Johnson, a senator and a Southern Democrat,

Heaven forbid, as President Lincoln's running mate. After Lincoln's death, President Johnson began the process of Reconstruction.

President Johnson faced the challenge of opposing political views in reconstituting the Union. He, like most Democrats and some Republicans, preferred a gentler approach to readmitting Southern states and creating several new ones.

He simply wanted to get the Southern states back in the Union and figure out the tough questions at a later time. However, most Republicans, emboldened by their Civil War victory, wanted strong language and fundamental changes enforced by federal law such as loyalty oaths; reparations and suffrage for freed slaves; and ratification of the Fourteenth Amendment, which specified that *no state should deprive any person of life, liberty, or property, without due process of law.*

The Republicans controlled Congress at the time, and the first test came when Nebraska was proposed as a new state. Nebraska came to the table with a state constitution that extended suffrage only to white males, which was contrary to President Johnson's platform.

Congress passed a law allowing Nebraska into the Union with their whites-only suffrage law intact. Congress preferred to correct the issue by separate legislation. Instead, President Johnson elected to exercise a simple *pocket veto*, which allowed the president to let the bill lapse without signing it. When a new Congress was seated in 1867, they tried again, this time adding an amendment to the Nebraska Statehood Act, which stated if a state is applying to join the Union, it's with the understanding that blacks can vote, whether your state Constitution says so or not.

President Johnson, a strict Constitutionalist, objected to this language as a violation of the Constitution because it forced a law upon Nebraska that the state's legislature never adopted. Although he agreed with the action of Congress in principle, he vetoed the bill because it was unconstitutional. Nevertheless, Congress overrode the veto and Nebraska became a state later that spring.

"Mr. President, Attorney General Stein is here for you," said Betty as she cracked the door to the Oval Office.

"Send her in, please."

Attorney General Rachel Stein, a Cleveland, Ohio native, was an acclaimed federal court litigator in the area of constitutional law. She'd learned to navigate the myriad of federal regulations to assist business in the hyper-regulatory environment created by Sarge's predecessors.

One of his goals as president was to reduce the burden on business, a platform that was sure to meet a flurry of litigation from various rights and social justice groups. She was also the nation's top cop charged with the responsibility of enforcing the laws. Today, Sarge had issues to discuss in both contexts.

"Hi, Rachel. Thank you for sticking around before the holiday break."

"You're welcome, Mr. President. You can expect my bill will reflect the overtime."

The two shared a few words concerning their families and the attorney general's plans after this administration came to an end. Sarge appreciated the conversation, but he could visualize people milling about outside Donald's office, waiting for a statement.

"Rachel, I need your opinion on my veto options."

She nodded and got down to business. "Naturally, you could formally veto the bill when it hits your desk, likely next week some time. This would require the House and Senate to reconvene and override your veto by a two-thirds majority."

"That's straightforward. I've vetoed bills before, but they've never tried to override one. I doubt they'd try here either. A two-thirds majority is unattainable."

"Another option is to ignore the bill, essentially refusing to sign it. The net effect of that inaction could create a veto."

"You said *could*. What do you mean?"

"It depends on whether Congress is in session," replied the attorney general. "If Congress remains in session and you sit on it for ten days, the bill becomes law as if you had signed it."

"I'd have to confirm this, but I believe the House adjourned yesterday and the members headed for their home districts. I'm fairly certain the Senate adjourned after the vote today."

AG Stein scooted to the edge of the couch and continued. "If Congress is adjourned during the ten-day period when the president has the bill on his desk for signature, and you refuse to sign it, the bill doesn't become law. In historical terms, this is known as a *pocket veto* because the president puts the bill in his pocket, waits out Congress, and nothing happens. The bill dies from stagnation, in essence."

Sarge relaxed. *I bet the bastard didn't think of this.*

"Great. Now, next topic."

Sarge paused for a long time before moving forward. What he was about to do would be considered traitorous, but not in the eyes of Americans. He was about to betray the unspoken understandings and oaths taken among his fellow Boston Brahmin.

Sarge began. "I'm going to bring something to your attention that is out of the ordinary. What you do with this information will be up to you although I think it warrants an investigation."

"Is this related to a possible criminal matter? If so, I should bring others from the Justice Department into the loop."

"I understand. I am simply suggesting you look into a possible bribery situation."

"Okay, I think I understand your meaning, Mr. President. We've worked together for a long time and you've never approached me for anything. I have to believe you are sincere in your suggestions."

Sarge decided to spit it out. "You might look into any recent large dollar financial transactions or deposits of House Majority Whip Billy Trent."

"Isn't this something more appropriate for the House Oversight Committee?"

Sarge had to tread carefully because he didn't want to mislead his attorney general with false information. He was operating strictly on a hunch.

"It's possible the financial transaction was initiated through a foreign government or business entity."

The Lowell financial empire had tentacles stretching into many parts of the world. Their foreign holdings would not be subject to the same scrutiny as their American business interests. If Gardner bribed Congressman Trent, he would use untraceable funds from overseas. This would start the investigation at a much higher level than an oversight matter.

"Well, that certainly puts it within my jurisdiction. I'll get this anonymous tip in front of the right people at the bureau. I'll keep you abreast of their findings. Mr. President, you know these types of investigations can take time, right?"

"I understand. It may be that I'm out of office before the matter gets the full attention of the FBI and the Justice Department. I know the players involved, and the events of the last few days reek of manipulation, if you know what I mean."

"I understand, Mr. President. Is there anything else I can help you with today?"

"No. Thank you very much for helping me on this issue as well as your sound advice. I can make a prudent decision now."

Sarge stood to dismiss Attorney General Stein. *Yes, Rachel, these investigations do take time and can be drawn out for years. However, it only takes a few hours to make the news of an investigation spread through the media like wildfire.*

They really shouldn't underestimate me.

CHAPTER 61

8:00 p.m. ET
Ruifang District
Northeastern Taiwan

Drew and his team prepared to land at a CIA compound in Keelung City, thirty miles northeast of Taipei, which lent the outward appearance of a day care center. The rotors of the newly commissioned Bell-Boeing V-26 Osprey started their slow drooping turn into the center of the three-block buildings. Within a minute, the tiltrotor aircraft put into use for its first mission was spinning level with the ground, its rotor wash buffeting the earth, throwing dust and debris in all directions.

Several locals who handled security for the compound scrambled around to remove picnic tables and children's playground equipment to make room for the turboprop aircraft turned helicopter. They were unaware of the increased size of the V-26 over its predecessor, the V-22.

Inside the V-26, the fourteen members of the covert ops force checked their weapons. The trip took a little over four hours, in which time Drew's team of eight paired up with the six Delta guys. One Aegis member joined one Delta guy to track down each of the white vans that had scattered throughout the city. Once the vans were located, they'd make every effort to get eyes on Ambassador McBride. Once identified, the other teams would converge on that location to lend assistance.

The plan allowed for Drew and King to *roam*, as Drew called it. By circling the suspected location of each van, using the most up-to-date

NSA recon images, Drew took a map and marked a straight line to the last known, confirmed location of the ambassador—the compound in south-central Taipei.

On a hunch, Drew elected to conduct surveillance on the compound. It would allow him to reach his other teams quickly while looking for clues as to Ambassador McBride's whereabouts. As the V-26 made its final touchdown, his mind wandered to concern for the ambassador.

The fact that there had been no contact from his captors was of great concern. The men who comprised his security detail were Taiwanese military. They could have been compromised by the Chinese, or might have been a sleeper cell for the Flying Dragons, operating under the CIA's nose all along.

If their purpose in snatching America's top diplomat in China was ideological rather than strategic, Ambassador McBride might be subjected to any manner of torture. Back home, the government would be outraged. The ambassador's family would emotionally suffer for the pain inflicted upon their loved one. The State Department would issue its strongest possible condemnation on the floor of the United Nations.

Yet he, Drew Jackson, was trained as and continued to work as a modern-day assassin who was provided the title *operative* so as not to offend the sensibilities of the intellectually enlightened people who sat at the centers of power in DC.

If those people knew what his Aegis team did for the benefit of the United States, they would fly off the handle into an indignant rage and spill their cosmopolitan cocktails on the floor of a penthouse party on New York's Fifth Avenue. The actions of Drew and his team were necessary to keep America free. Assassinations and torture were part of the job.

But there was a red line that Drew refused to cross, although he came dangerously close one time when he tortured a German banker who had sexually assaulted innocent boys forced into prostitution. Drew's job was to influence the man's way of thinking that night in Frankfurt, but he had approached his job with a little too much zeal, resulting in the man's death from a heart attack.

His past experience and the information relayed to him about the Flying Dragons led him to this apprehension. They had no red line and certainly had no moral obligation toward the treatment of Americans. These devils would torture Ambassador McBride for sport.

He checked his weapon one more time and adjusted his kit, which carried the customary backup ammunition and communications gear. They were going into a war zone and would be prepared for all contingencies. The sun was up in Taipei, but the streets were not empty of protestors.

As the Osprey hit the ground, he looked his men in the eyes. Each was more than capable of finding the ambassador and taking out his captors. There was a reason why professional killers came from Special Forces outfits. They were desensitized to violence. Operators looked at killing as a way to achieve their mission. The formula for success was no more complicated than confronting violence with greater levels of violence. In order for the group to operate as a cohesive unit, they could have no doubt that their partners would become killing machines, as they were.

The doors opened and the team hit the ground running for the covered porches at the rear of the buildings. They were greeted by the deputy chief of station for Taipei who headed up this annex.

"Let's get you boys inside," said Madeline Wu, a Chinese-American career diplomat born in San Francisco. "We don't have a lot of time."

The fourteen operatives filed into the room, which was a large open space filled with folding tables and chairs. Around the walls were whiteboards with notes scribbled on them, as well as maps of Taiwan. Wu was fully prepared for their arrival.

"Thank you, ma'am," said Drew as he tipped his camouflage hat with a U.S. flag patch attached to the front with Velcro. "My name is Jackson. We understand that the demonstrations have intensified through the night here and continue around the city."

"That's correct," she said, pointing to a television monitor displaying TTV, Taiwan's primary television station, which had been recently privatized. "Our sources tell us the president is going to declare martial law to get the city under control. When that happens, your ability to travel will be severely hampered, especially in light of the way you entered the country."

As she made this statement, the V-26 Osprey lifted off the ground to return to Guam. With its size, it would be noticeable to any Chinese satellite reconnaissance, as well as other prying eyes in this part of Ruifang District.

"Tell us what you can before we head out," said Drew.

"First and foremost, let me discuss your rally points for extraction. This is one location. In the next twelve to fifteen hours, the USS *Petersen* will be in position on the eastern side of Okinawa. They will have choppers on standby to pick you up from this point. If we are compromised, or if you are unable to travel northeast out of Taipei, then the more rural escape route will be toward Hualien Airport, where the rest of the Guam units landed earlier today."

"Did they have any difficulty reaching the AIT?" asked Drew.

"Delays but no meaningful, hostile resistance," she replied. "I have to tell you, the biggest challenge you're going to face is getting through the throngs of people filling the streets. It appears that half of Taipei's three million residents are wandering about, complaining about one thing or another."

King Dawson wandered closer to Wu and asked, "What kind of vehicles do you have for us?"

"We have ten undistinguished Veryca vans made by, ironically, the Chinese Motor Corporation. The CMCs have been modified by International Armoring to be fully bulletproof. In addition, the rear cargo has secure lockers for additional weapons, ammo, medical supplies, and communications gear."

"We broke into teams of two on our way from Guam," Drew said as he studied the maps pinned to the walls.

"Before you go, we can spend a few minutes going over each location with your teams, providing you the benefit of our local knowledge," said Wu. "Jackson, I understand you and a partner will take the original location of Ambassador McBride following the abduction."

"That's correct."

"Who is your partner?"

"Me, ma'am," said King in his booming, baritone voice.

"Do either of you speak Mandarin or know the city?" she asked.

"Only what we've studied during the long trip out here, ma'am," replied Drew.

"I have one of my most trusted people on station to assist you. He also happens to be my son-in-law, Tai Shi Liu."

"Ma'am, this is going to be dangerous. I'm not sure I want the responsibility of your—"

"Let me assure you, Mr. Jackson, Tai is more than capable of keeping you and King alive. He is an extremely rare tenth-degree black belt. Further, he is also a past champion in Filipino martial arts."

Drew nodded his head with approval. He was unaware of the relative degrees of martial arts, but he was sure he'd never encountered a tenth degree. Filipino martial arts caught his attention. As a boy, Drew practiced tirelessly using his knife both defensively and offensively. He began to study the techniques of the Filipinos, which he quickly admired because they were a blade culture. The number of targets he'd eliminated with the lightning-quick, deadly accurate throw of his blade were numerous. If Wu was offering this asset for his use, he'd be foolish to turn her down, family or not.

"Absolutely, Tai is more than welcome. Let's get started on this briefing so we can find the ambo."

CHAPTER 62

8:00 p.m.
The Yellow Oval Room in the Executive Residence
The White House
Washington, DC

The Yellow Oval Room was located in the center of the Executive Residence and was used to privately host important guests. The yellow-dominated décor was introduced to the room by Dolly Madison in the early nineteenth century, but its first real makeover came courtesy of President Harry Truman, who added a large balcony under the roof of the South Portico. The addition provided incredible outdoor views of the South Lawn and the Washington Monument.

The Sargent children, along with Penny and Becca Quinn, were happily settled on the third floor above them. Becca, always the organized one, had a schedule that carried them until well after their normal bedtime. The two sets of parents acquiesced to the late night soiree under one condition—*none of you are allowed to come downstairs.*

The Sargents and Quinns needed some adult time to calm down from an eventful three days. In addition, Donald and Sargent would only be allowed the next eight hours to relax before they might be summoned to the Situation Room because of Operation Golden Retriever.

"You know what's funny about this room," started Donald. "You just don't feel like you can kick your shoes off and throw your smelly feet on the coffee table."

"Watch me." The group began to laugh as Sarge kicked off his Topsiders and propped his feet on the antique table.

Julia took a sip of her wine and set it on the table next to Sarge's feet. Then she thought better of it and stretched to place it on an end table. "The White House photographer took pictures of this room for *Architectural Digest* this morning. It made me realize how far our country has come since all hell broke loose."

"Yeah, there was a time that I thought we'd be living in the bungalows at Prescott Peninsula for years to come," added Susan. "I don't ever want to take this moment for granted."

Sarge lifted his glass and said, "Cheers to that!"

"Are you guys gonna miss all of this?" asked Susan.

Sarge showed a devilish grin as he sipped his Glenlivet. "We won't miss it as much as Donald."

"Screw you, Mr. President," Donald snapped back. "Don't start with me after the last crappy couple of days."

"C'mon, Donald, you know you've loved it," teased Sarge. "Besides, what are we gonna do when this is over? My days running the affairs of the Boston Brahmin may be numbered."

"Honey, do you think it'll come to that?" asked Julia.

"I don't know, maybe. Probably. It could be for the best. Gardner Lowell played me like a fiddle on this one."

"It's my fault," interjected Donald, his dejection over the events consuming him through dinner.

"No, Donald, it's mine. I've relied upon you so much that I didn't take a more active role in watching over those scoundrels on Capitol Hill. I don't blame Gardner too much. His betrayal was a long time coming. I blame the members of Congress I thought I could count on."

"Well, it's done now, right, guys?" asked Susan.

Sarge didn't want to burst Susan's bubble, but in many ways, the real battle was just beginning. The vote was the equivalent to the shot heard around the world. The real shooting would begin tomorrow.

"Yeah, over and done," said Donald.

Sarge was starting to feel sorry for his dear friend, and he needed to snap him out of the doldrums. *Time to get him riled up.*

"Hey, enough serious shoptalk. Let's refill our cocktails and play an adult game."

Sarge jumped off the couch and moseyed over to the small bar wheeled in by the White House staff. He refilled everyone's drinks as they waited for what he had in mind.

"We're a little too old for strip poker, don't you think, Henry?" quipped Julia.

"Agreed. How about *would you rather—after the White House edition.*"

"Forget it," objected Donald.

"Come on, Donald. Let's talk about it. We'll be moving back to Boston before we know it. What will our life look like?"

"Okay, Sarge," started Donald. "Would you rather sign on for a third term or run the Boston Brahmin?"

Sarge almost choked on his scotch. "Fortunately, I don't really have to make that choice, thanks to the Twenty-Second Amendment. But you know, I don't have the drive to run the Brahmin interests the way they need to be run. If it were possible, I think I'd do another four-year tour of duty."

"Interesting," said Julia. "I thought you'd had enough."

"After today, I think I have, right, Donald?" asked Sarge.

"Yeah, for sure."

"Quid pro quo, Donald. Would you rather work by my side in the

Oval for another four years, or run things from your perch at 73 Tremont?"

"I'd rather jump off the Truman Balcony behind me and go screaming into the night!"

"I vote Boston. What about you, Susan?" asked Julia.

"Boston."

"Guys?" asked Susan.

"Boston, without a doubt," replied Donald.

Sarge furrowed his brow and stared into space. An odd sense of foreboding came over him as he heard Julia repeatedly trying to draw him out of his trance.

Sarge, Sarge.

CHAPTER 63

11:00 p.m. ET
New Taipei City
Taiwan

Tai took a circuitous route in his approach to the southern part of the Taipei metropolis where the original vehicle carrying Ambassador McBride had pulled into a residential compound. The direct options through the city were bogged down by protestors and military vehicles attempting to cordon off the city.

Drew was notified by Control at Aegis that martial law would in fact be announced before nightfall. The teams would have less than six hours to find their locations and, hopefully, the ambassador. Depending on the location of the ambassador, in order to regroup, the rest of the teams might have to travel across the area known as New Taipei City after dark and through the obstacles established by the Taiwan military.

As they approached the southernmost point of New Taipei City, Drew came to the realization that each team might be on their own without support for hours. Once the ambassador was located, they might have to move on their own. He didn't like the odds, especially being located in a foreign country surrounded by angry mobs.

"This is Xindian District," announced Tai, carefully pronouncing the word *shin-din* for his American companions. Slowing to take a large banked curve, he turned up the same six-lane freeway used by the abductors. The traffic began to slow as they got closer to the central part of the city. "Another mile and we will enter the residential neighborhood where the compound is located. This part of the city was originally under Japanese rule in the 1920s. It was primarily farmland until the eighties when this highway was built. After that, the town exploded with development, but it remains home to Taiwan's largest population of Japanese descendants."

As Tai narrated, Drew and King studied every available photograph of the compound from the sky. Once they left the vehicle and made their approach, they wouldn't have the luxury of pulling out pictures, notes, or maps.

Suddenly, Tai jammed on the brakes as the vehicle approached a slight incline. Traffic had slowed to a crawl. Bumper-to-bumper traffic continued to block their advance for twenty minutes.

"C'mon, man. This is ridiculous," complained King. He grabbed the map and handed it to Drew and Tai in the front seat. "How far is it from here?"

Tai studied the map and pointed to their location on the freeway. "We're half a mile from the exit and another mile or so from the compound."

"C'mon, Drew. Let's hoof it," said King.

"You're out of your mind, right? You and me, in full kits, strolling down the streets of Taipei. *That* won't attract attention."

"We gotta do something 'cause we're goin' nowhere fast."

Tai continued to inch the van forward while Drew contemplated their options. "We could get a head start. There are other people walking along the highway. We could ditch the kits, go to sidearms only, and follow the crowd. It might take us thirty minutes to get there, but at least we could start our recon."

"Yeah, we won't engage until Tai catches up with us, right?"

Drew nodded as he looked out the passenger window. "That's what I'm thinkin'."

"Gentlemen," interjected Tai, "even without your gear, you two will stand out. Mr. Dawkins, I'm willing to bet you are the only six-foot-five black man in all of Taiwan at the moment."

"Yeah," said King with a bellowing laugh. "Maybe they'll get out of my way as I plow down the road."

"I understand what you're saying, Tai, but I'm willing to risk it. It may take you an hour or more to catch up with us. We can get the lay of the land while we wait."

"Let's do this, Slash," said King.

"Slash?" asked Tai.

"Yeah, it's a nickname I've carried since I was a kid. I'm pretty good with a blade myself."

"Have you practiced the arts?"

Drew began to laugh as he got his gear ready. "I don't know if you would call it art. But I could stick a wild pig in the woods faster than my buddies could shoot it."

"Hands-on training," mumbled Tai.

Drew and King were ready to leave the van when Drew hesitated for a moment. "Tai?"

"Yes."

"Have you ever killed anyone?" asked Drew.

"I have been trained to the highest level of physical and Filipino martial arts, so—"

Drew cut him off. "Tai, I need to know. Have you ever killed anyone?"

"Um, no. I have not."

"Good to know. Meet us at the compound, but, Tai, under no circumstances are you to leave this van. Are we clear?"

"Clear. I understand."

"Text me your progress. Let's go, King."

PART FOUR

Thanksgiving Day

November 2024

CHAPTER 64

5:00 a.m. ET
Xindian District
New Taipei City

Drew mentally ticked off a list of possible hazards before he and King entered the compound—overwhelming defenses, snipers, and tripwires with improvised explosive devices. Their surveillance of the residential area didn't reveal anything out of the norm. Vehicular traffic was brisk, but no one had entered or exited the compound since they'd arrived. As nightfall set in, it was time to make their move.

"Alpha One, you're a go." Drew received his green light from Aegis Control. From this point forward, he and his team of eight were ghosts. Officially, the United States government handed them off to the private contractor, Aegis. Control, however, would have full access to the real-time imagery supplied by the NSA drone flying overhead.

"Roger that." Drew nodded to King before the two darted between parked cars and underneath the fronds of palm trees that lined the sidewalk and gave a modicum of coverage.

The residential compound took up a city block of approximately two and a half acres. As they had circled the perimeter during the daylight, they identified the two four-car garages under a stand of trees. There was a large swimming pool with an adjacent pool house on the back side of the garages. A two-story main house was placed near the center of the compound together with a guest house containing its own entrance off the street.

The top of the ten-foot wall was rounded but otherwise

unprotected by any form of deterrent like wire. Earlier, they'd identified their breach point—an area between two palm trees that was marked no parking.

Drew whispered into his comms, "All teams, we're a go." At the six locations across the city where the vans were last seen, each team was given the green light to search the likely location where the ambassador was being held.

"Alpha Two, let's roll," said Drew into the radio, advising Tai to get into position.

"Roger, Alpha One," replied Tai, who had remained with the vehicle. His job was to drive to the breach point, quickly back into the void between the two palms, thus creating a ladder of sorts, allowing Drew and King to crawl up on the van and drop quickly into the compound.

Tai slowly turned the corner and approached the opening. Traffic in both directions prevented him from stopping and backing in to the compound's wall. After a moment of waiting for a break in the traffic, Tai took off and rounded the block.

Drew was concerned this might draw attention, so he radioed Tai. He turned to King. "If I hoist you onto the wall, I'll need you to pull me up."

"Piece of cake for these guns. What are you? One eighty-five soaking wet?"

"Two hundred plus, big guy," replied Drew. "Tai will never be able to stop and back in. He's gonna have to go hood first, which will make it a bigger leap to the top of the wall. You'll be exposed while you pull me to the top."

"No problem, let's do it."

Drew raised Tai on the radio. "After you circle the block, don't try to back in. Just pull onto the sidewalk nose first. We'll make it work."

"Roger."

Five minutes later, the men had scaled the wall and dropped onto the ground within the compound. This was their first real look at the layout. They scrambled along the wall until they found an overgrown bougainvillea bush.

"That's a hundred yards of lawn to cross with no cover," said King. "If we hug the wall and head to our right, one of us can cross toward the side of the house with fewer windows."

"I'll go first," volunteered the smaller, quicker Drew. "Moving."

Using the bounding overwatch buddy system of providing suppressive fire if necessary while your partner moved through an open area, Drew darted toward a darkened part of the compound and found protection behind a short grouping of palms.

"Move," Drew said, instructing King to follow him along the wall to the slight cover of the sago palm cluster.

"Moving." King, who was fairly agile for his size, lumbered along the wall in a short crouch.

The men carefully made their way across the lawn and approached the rear of the two-story home. Drew easily gained access to a utility room by picking the lock on a rear door.

Methodically, they cleared the home and found no evidence that anyone had been there. The kitchen was neat and tidy. The living spaces were immaculate and well kept.

"Drew, have we wasted our time surveilling an empty house?" asked King.

"It appears so," he replied. "We need to check out the guest garage and the other two buildings. Then we'll check in with the rest of the teams to see where we can assist."

Once again, the men checked their gear and worked their way to the guest house, which was also empty and immaculately kept. The pool house adjacent to the garage was next.

Drew was unable to pick the lock, which required them to break through the set of patio doors, which opened inward. "On my go," said Drew. They each trained their silenced weapons on the hinges of the double doors.

"Go!" Both men fired repeatedly, shredding the wood around the hinges, causing the doors to barely hang in place. With a swift kick, King put his boot into the area just below the door handle, causing the patio doors to crash into the room. Drew entered first, swinging his rifle from side to side, prepared to take out any threats, but none presented themselves.

The large room contained a bar, some furniture, and a passageway to the rear leading to a bathroom and a storage room. King took the storage room first, slowly turning the handle on the door while Drew provided cover. It was empty.

The bathroom was next. The door was ajar, so King slowly pushed it open. Drew entered slowly and then flipped his Mag-Tac flashlight on.

"Whoa, they're getting ripe already," he moaned as he pulled his shemagh over his nose and mouth. The shemagh scarf had been given to him during a tour of duty in Iraq by a Kurdish man whose life Drew had saved. The man had said the scarf had been worn by his father during his battles against Saddam Hussein's Republican Guard.

Drew flipped on the light and found four dead men lined up in the walk-in shower of the pool house. He approached them cautiously to make sure they weren't connected to any type of explosive device.

"We're still clear on the perimeter," announced King after doing a quick check of the pool area and compound's grounds.

Drew started with the dead man on the right. The lifeless eyes, the dime-sized bullet hole between them, and the trickle of blood down his face were all expected. One bullet, clean kill, just the way he'd done it so many times before.

The next two uniformed soldiers from Taiwan looked the same, including the red holes in the center of their eyebrows. The three men were bound, gagged, and expertly executed. The fourth man, however, was different.

He'd been shot through the back of the head. Half his face was an irregularly shaped crater of mangled flesh, bone, and blood. The exit wound revealed the man had been shot by a caliber more powerful than the suppressed .22 that was probably used on the other three. This shot came from a 9mm or larger.

"King, whadya think? .45 cal?"

"No doubt," replied King as he pulled the man's hair and twisted the remains of his skull to get a better view. "They wanted this one good and dead. A .45 round is gonna pancake and tumble around the man's head for maximum damage."

"You gotta wonder why," started Drew. "Best I can tell, he's Asian like the rest of the detail. Also, he's in a suit, not military fatigues like these other guys."

"All executed, but why the difference?" asked King, also puzzled by the executions.

Drew was troubled by this as well. He and King had easily breached the perimeter security. There were no cameras, motion sensors, security personnel, or traps. Whoever was responsible for kidnapping the ambassador had carefully orchestrated the entire operation, but surely had to know these bodies would be discovered.

"Where do you want to start?" asked King.

"Here's what I think," replied Drew. "Crater face here is the odd man out. Based on the video footage, the ambo was picked up by his four uniformed security personnel. We had eyes on the vehicle until the moment it pulled into the garage behind us. Six cars later pulled away, which meant there were six drivers already here waiting for their part of the mission. Of the four guards, only three are here."

"The three uniformed guys," added King. "Who's the fourth—crater face, as you call him?"

Drew focused on the man he'd dubbed crater face. He carefully checked his suit pockets for any form of clue, knowing he'd find nothing.

"My guess is he's part of this, but the killer didn't want his identity readily discovered. Let's upload photos of their faces and fingerprints to Control."

"I'm on it," said King.

Drew turned the man's body so he could determine if there were any facial features left to help identify him. "I'm gonna clear the garage and then get Tai in here. I wanna know if this guy is Taiwanese or Chinese."

"What are you saying—they all look alike?" said King, a black man who was not afraid to joke about his race, as he feigned moral outrage.

Drew knew his buddy well. "Can you tell them apart?"

"Nope, they all look alike to me," King replied with a laugh as he began to snap the photos.

"That's what I thought. I'll check the garage and then let in Tai. Tell Control to focus on crater face. I want to know everything there is to know about him—especially his family. Does he live in Taipei? Is he related to the Chinese government, or some kind of sympathizer? Anything they can find."

"What about the other three? Do you think they were compromised somehow by the Chinese?"

"Maybe, but I doubt it. I think they were following orders. The other uniformed escort may hold the answers. He might be a superior officer."

"Drew, how in the hell are we gonna find him?"

"At this point, if the other teams come up empty and the six vans were just a diversion, I'm not sure." Drew began to suspect their chances for success were remote, but they had to start somewhere. He continued. "I think the answers lie with this guy," he said as he knelt down next to the dead man in the suit. Then he pointed to the other three. "Or the guy who started out with these three and is now gone."

Drew took pictures of the three dead security personnel. There was still one missing from the detail and he possibly held the answers to all of this. Drew prepared a text message with the images of the three dead men and sent them to the CIA station chief at the AIT facility. Maybe the CIA could shed some more light on the detail they'd entrusted to protect Ambassador McBride.

CHAPTER 65

6:00 a.m.
The National Mall
Washington, DC

On Thanksgiving, Sarge woke up before his alarm sounded, and the first thing he did after kissing his wife was look outside to see if running was an option. The clear morning sky and lack of snow on the ground lifted his spirits. The weather had cleared and the protestors had returned home, most likely convinced it was their screaming through the fence with signs held high that made the difference.

For the beginning of the run with his constant companion, Captain Dave Morrell, Sarge was quiet as he reflected on the last two months of his presidency. Coming into this Thanksgiving week, he knew the vote would loom large over the White House, but the explosive situation in Taiwan was completely unforeseen.

It showed him that despite having the best intelligence apparatus in the world, the United States still did not possess a crystal ball. Hot spots could emerge at any given moment, and the president needed to be prepared to act, making the tough decisions that would be judged under the prism of twenty-twenty hindsight.

Sarge had made a commitment to himself when he'd begun this endeavor, long before the Constitutional Convention of eight years ago in St. Louis. He'd never shy away from a fight or a challenge. As president, he was never accused of cowering in the Executive Residence or behind a White House spokesman. While he might not have sought out the spotlight by campaign-style appearances, he certainly wasn't shy about addressing the White House press corps when appropriate, or the nation from the Oval Office as necessary.

Today would be a difficult day. Over the evening hours, news broke that Ambassador McBride was missing. Sarge knew this was inevitable, but it didn't appear to impact the way Drew and his team approached their mission. The breaking news would turn an otherwise uneventful Thanksgiving celebration to a full-blown media firestorm. The traditional NFL games shown on the networks would be interrupted by scenes of chaos in the streets of Taipei.

Sarge's first stop upon returning from his run would be the Situation Room. For now, he wanted to talk with his old friend to change the subject.

"Dave, what time will Shelby and baby BAM be arriving at the White House this morning?" BAM was the nickname Sarge had bestowed upon the Morrell's daughter after she was born based upon the initials in her full name. Morrell and his wife had met during Sarge's campaign the first go-around. She began to assist in the campaign and the two got married while Sarge made a stump speech in Las Vegas. When a shooter attempted to assassinate Sarge during his re-election campaign, it was Morrell who caught a glimpse of the shooter's rifle peeking through a window. Morrell quickly shoved him to the ground, but Sarge took a bullet in the back of his right shoulder. He was in serious condition for several days but recovered except for some loss of mobility, which prevented him from throwing out the first pitch at any Washington Nationals game.

When the sniper took his second shot, Morrell was hit. The powerful round barely missed his protective vest and lodged in Morrell's upper arm—the one wrapped around Sarge's neck. Morrell's instincts and quick reflexes saved Sarge's life.

"I told them to come around eleven," replied Morrell. "Brie's excited about playing with Rose. I've warned her not to touch anything though."

Sarge laughed as they made the loop near the Lincoln Memorial. "Julia has instructed the staff to clear the Blue Room of any antiques or breakables. We can let them run around wild Indians and the two of us will sneak outside for a cigar."

"Count me in."

Sarge had not broached the subject of his friend's future. He thought it might be a good time to do so.

"Dave, we'll be done here in eight weeks. I don't want to be presumptuous, but do you have anything planned for after we get the hell out of Washington?"

"I have thought about it. Shelby has family in upstate New York, and my people alternate between Florida and Canada. I guess I should settle somewhere in between, you know, like Boston. I hear they have pretty good golf courses."

Sarge laughed and grabbed his buddy around the neck. The two were more than president and Secret Service protection, they'd become like brothers. Morrell had fought to protect the Loyal Nine at Prescott Peninsula and had taken a bullet for the president. He'd earned his way into Sarge's inner circle.

"Then, my friend, you and I will see what the world has in store for us after political life. Some of my old friends will be at dinner today and we'll be having a come-to-Jesus meeting at some point. I'll need you to stay close by. This bunch may want to string me up when I'm done with them."

"You got it, Sarge. We'll ride or die, brother. Just like always."

"Yeah, ride or die."

CHAPTER 66

7:00 a.m.
The Situation Room
The White House
Washington, DC

Sarge entered the Situation Room, which was already in full swing. Donald was poring over some satellite images with Brad, who was pointing out the differences between the current activity on the Chinese side of the Taiwan Strait and the relative calm the day before.

"It's a striking difference," remarked Donald.

"It can lead to only one conclusion—they're amassing their troops for an amphibious assault," said Brad.

Sarge was finally noticed by those in the room, and the group snapped to attention.

"Please, carry on," said Sarge. "It felt good to be a fly on the wall for an albeit brief moment. Brad, this appears to be a significant buildup."

"It is, Mr. President," said Brad. "Let me bring these up on the monitor and produce a side-by-side image so you can get the full picture."

Brad instructed his aide to mirror the satellite imagery onto the wall monitor. The picture, which was blurred, depicted several amphibious vehicles loading onto barges while others seemed to be getting into position on the beaches.

Brad continued. "Sir, these are elements of the PLA Marine Corps. For amphibious assaults, they use a variety of vehicles, including this ZBD2000."

"It looks like a small tank," said Sarge.

"It's that and more. This amphibious fighting vehicle, or AFB, is propelled by two water jets with a hydraulic bow that allows it to skim across the water. The operator activates the bow and transom flaps to form a planing surface with the bottom of the hull. This reduces drag and provides it a top speed of twenty-eight miles per hour."

"Incredible. Do we have something like this?"

"No, sir. Our version, the expeditionary fighting vehicle, developed by General Dynamics for use by the Corps, was cancelled by the prior administration due to budget cutbacks."

"How do we, and Taiwan, counter something like this?"

"Air strikes, sir. But that leads me to the next satellite image." Brad nodded to his aide, who brought up more NSA photos of airfields on the Chinese mainland.

He continued. "These are the newest fighter jets in the PLAAF—the Xian JH-7B, which NATO has dubbed Flounder."

"Why's that?" asked Donald.

"I have no idea because this beast is anything but a flounder. The Chinese have upgraded this jet with the latest in advanced avionics, a more powerful engine than anything we've deployed, and an advanced weapons package, which includes the YJ-12 supersonic antiship cruise missile."

"Undoubtedly designed with the aid and benefit of cyber intrusions into our defense department or military contractor servers," added Sarge.

"Yes, sir. The JH-7Bs would serve a dual purpose. First, they'd protect this armada of what appears to be eighty AFBs ready for deployment. Second, they'd easily back off Taiwan's standing fleet of F-16s."

"What about the air defense measures we assisted Taiwan with years ago?" asked Sarge.

"A2/AD, sir?" asked Brad.

"Yeah, that. Didn't we push back against Beijing when they began flying their fighter jets along Taiwan's west coast as a show of force?"

"We did. A2/AD, short for anti-access area denial, was part of the overall strategy we adopted for Air-Sea Battles. The Air Force and the Navy have carefully coordinated defensive plans to deal with China's air superiority in the theater."

Sarge began to wander around the room, using pacing to allow him to think. "These cruise missiles, the YJ-12s. Aren't they a threat to our carrier strike groups?"

"Yes, sir. But if they're gonna engage the *Petersen* or the *Ronald Reagan*, they'd better get ready for a fight. Our pilots are the best in the business aboard those carriers."

Sarge sat at the head of the table and removed his Harvard sweatshirt. "This really raises a much larger issue that needs to be answered. Can America still defend Taiwan?"

Brad took a moment to gather his thoughts and then responded, "We have some history in the region, which supports the contention that we can. In the mid-nineties, in defense of Taiwan's right to elect a pro-independence candidate, we sailed two aircraft carriers into position as a warning to China—hands off!"

Sarge interrupted. "I remember that. The elections went off without a hitch, but they were furious across the Taiwan Straits. They didn't appreciate our show of muscle for something like an election."

"You're right, Mr. President. They learned from that moment and marshaled a significant amount of money and resources into military upgrades to counter our action. They developed a whole new suite of weapons designed to kill any encroaching American fleet using asymmetric warfare."

"Like what?" asked Donald.

"The carrier killer, for one. Their new DF-21D antiship ballistic missile can be launched from over a thousand miles away, drop slowly from space, and blast one of our carriers even if it's taking a defensive, zigzagging course."

"Great," mumbled Donald sarcastically.

"The PLA has also added a hypersonic glide vehicle. It can achieve speeds of Mach 10 and higher. Its maneuverability makes it nearly impossible to track. The DF-ZF can be used for nuclear weapons delivery but also to perform precision-strike conventional missions with these new next-gen antiship ballistic missiles."

"Brad, can they penetrate the layered air defenses of our carrier strike groups?"

"Most likely, yes, Mr. President."

Suddenly, Sarge became extremely uncomfortable with his earlier decision. "You mean I've sent these carrier strike groups into the region and they're sitting ducks?"

"Mr. President, this new development certainly makes our decision to position the *Petersen* and *Ronald Reagan* in the region to appear risky, but there is a solution."

"Let's hear it, because by my recollection, these carrier strike groups will converge on Taiwan in about six hours or so."

"That's correct, sir," said Brad. He took a deep breath and whispered to his aide. She pulled up a screen of the Pacific Ocean with eleven flashing red triangle symbols.

"What are those?" asked Sarge.

"Mr. President, these are the present locations of our Virginia-class submarines in the region. As you know, these nuclear-powered fast-attack subs can be a tremendous asset in a situation like this."

"How do they help us defend Taiwan and our carrier fleets?" asked Sarge.

"If you'll allow me to point out the strategic deployment of these subs, then I'll show you how they can assist," started Brad. He approached a map that had been displayed on the largest monitor at the end of the room. "This map depicts the deployment of our eleven Virginia-class submarines at the moment."

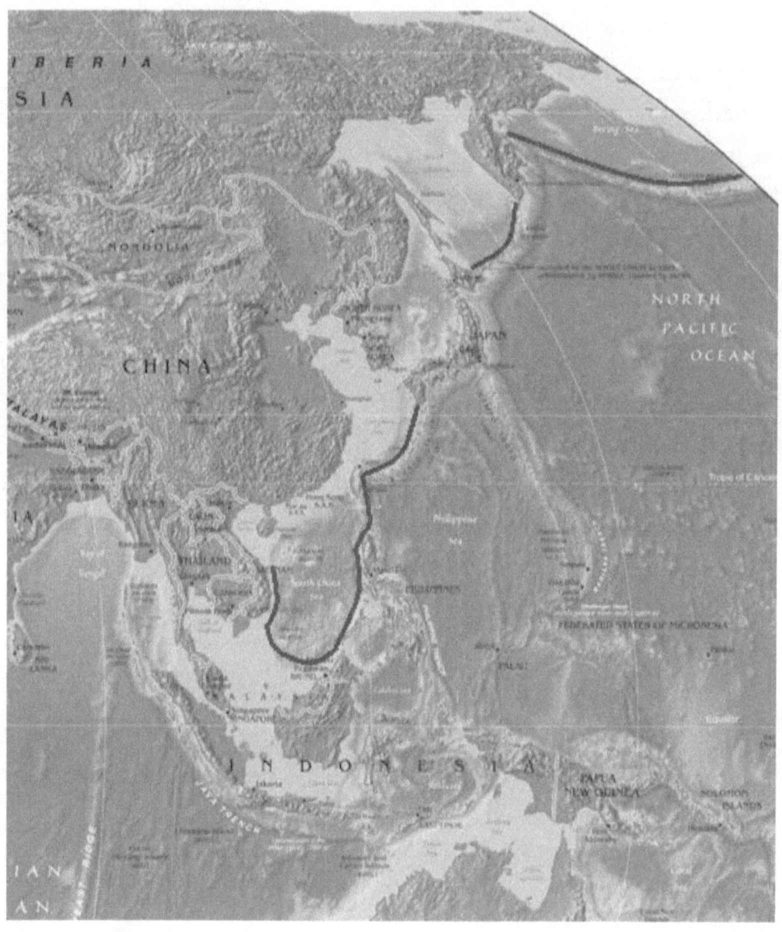

Brad continued. "The areas marked in red represent the first island chain—the major archipelagos bordering the Chinese mainland from the Malay Peninsula to Japan. We have submarines spread throughout the areas marked in red."

"Do the Chinese know this?"

"I'm sure they suspect them, but would never be able to pinpoint our exact locations," replied Brad. "There are a lot of folks at the Pentagon that think a crisis like this may be best fought with the Virginia-class sub rather than the flattops we deployed, but our goal was different. We wanted to send a message, and I'm still one hundred percent behind the decision."

"How do the subs help us now?" asked Sarge.

"We up the ante."

"You mean escalate?"

"Meet power with power," replied Brad.

"Has the State Department reached out to Beijing since their increased activity and positioning of the amphibs?" asked Sarge.

"They have with no response," replied Donald.

"What are they saying in Taiwan's military?" Sarge directed this question to Brad.

"Taiwan's all-out defense strategy calls for mobilizing the entire country, gearing up every able-bodied man and woman in support of anti-invasion operations."

"You're kidding, right?" quipped Donald.

"No. Listen, despite what you've seen on the TV screen the last few days, the vast majority of Taiwanese relish their independence from China. They'll fight with sticks and stones to defend their nation."

Sarge wondered if the American people would do the same in the face of a more powerful invader.

"Okay," said Sarge. "Donald, whoever is in the office at State, tell them to meet me in the Oval at nine. Also, advise everyone we'll have an abbreviated PDB at the same time. I need the communications team there as well."

"Yes, Mr. President," said Donald.

"Brad, if we deploy two of our subs to the Taiwan Straits, can we make their appearance known to the Chinese?"

"Oh, absolutely, Mr. President. It'll be the most choreographed event in naval history. I'll have them break the surface in unison to stare the ChiComms down."

"Give the order."

CHAPTER 67

8:45 a.m.
The Oval Office
The White House
Washington, DC

Sarge, Abbie, Donald, and Brad met in the Oval Office prior to the scheduled PDB at nine. The decisions Sarge made in the next few hours could result in a major conflict with the Chinese and could also explode into an international crisis.

Brad provided an update. "Mr. President, two Virginia-class submarines will be in position by noon, awaiting our orders. I've placed the carrier strike groups on high alert to provide air support. We've also elevated our armed forces to DEFCON 3 until further notice."

DEFCON 3 was an increase in overall force readiness above that required for normal defense readiness. The Air Force would be prepared to mobilize within fifteen minutes. Air support was critical to the defense of the two carrier strike groups and to the defense of Taiwan.

"I have to ask an obvious question, and I apologize if this was discussed in the Situation Room earlier," started Abbie. "Could Beijing be responding to our diversion of these two carrier groups to Taiwan?"

Sarge replied, "The timing would certainly suggest it."

"That's true," added Brad. "Except the military assets being prepared by the PLA are not defensive in nature. Their maneuvers have a definite offensive intention."

Abbie continued. "How does the increased activity by this invading force, assuming that's what it is, affect the mission to find and recover Ambassador McBride?"

"That's part of the reason I wanted us to convene prior to the daily briefing. If I force their hand and reveal our two attack subs right off their shore, this thing could blow. However, it may be the only way to defend Taiwan and prevent an international crisis."

"If a hot war breaks out," added Brad, "we would have to abandon Operation Golden Retriever and get the team out of there."

"How long do we have to make a decision?" asked Abbie.

"We've given Drew the green light to advance on the hostage positions without confirmation of McBride being held there," replied Brad. He took a deep breath and continued. "Waiting for confirmation would've made it more dangerous for our team. We also had to green light them to use deadly force if warranted in any location where the ambassador was not found."

"There will be political fallout for that," said Donald.

Sarge looked onto the South Lawn. It was so peaceful on this quiet day in Washington, relatively speaking.

"I gave them the green light," said Sarge. "I'm not going to risk the lives of our guys because the Chinese got the jump on us. If lives are lost on their side, we'll disavow all knowledge anyway. In the scheme of things, time is of the essence. Brad, I want constant reports."

"We'll be operating the mission from the Situation Room," said Brad. "I'll keep you posted by text and pull you downstairs if need be. We'll be monitoring all activity with the unit's communications and video gear. Further, we now have a drone overhead providing real-time visuals on the ground."

Sarge walked up to Abbie. He'd just ordered her husband into battle. "Are you still okay with this?"

"Totally. Let's get back McBride and tell the Chinese to shove it!"

CHAPTER 68

9:00 a.m.
The Oval Office
The White House
Washington, DC

Brad left for the Situation Room, and the White House communications team entered to start the Presidential Daily Briefing. They were joined by an Under Secretary of State and Mr. Chen from the CIA. Sarge was making small talk with the attendees when he was pulled aside by Donald. Sarge excused himself and walked to the side of the desk with his friend.

"Walter Cabot claims he's been trying to reach you," started Donald. "You don't have your phone, do you?"

Sarge, who was still in his running clothes, planned on getting dressed for Thanksgiving dinner after the briefing. "Nah, crap. It's still in the residence. What does he want?"

"He wants to meet."

"I'm going to see him at dinner in a couple of hours. Can't it wait? Or is it about yesterday's vote?"

Donald looked at his phone, searching for answers. "He really didn't say and it didn't sound urgent. I suppose he can wait until dinner."

"Let's make him wait," said Sarge. "I need to get my head straight before I do battle with the Brahmin. Plus, I've still gotta bake cookies."

"What?" asked Donald.

"You know, my contribution to our potluck-style Thanksgiving. Every year, I provide the cookies."

Donald started laughing, drawing the attention of the rest of the people in the room. "All of these years, I thought Julia did it, or one of the bakers downstairs."

"Nope. It's all me. As a matter of fact, let's address that right now."

Sarge made his way toward the couches while Donald informed Walter Cabot that the president was handling a crisis at the moment but would see him in a couple of hours.

"Before we get started, I want the comms team to hear this story. As you all know, every president has his own theme at Thanksgiving. After what this country went through following the collapse, I didn't think it was appropriate to conduct elaborate, expensive dinners when we should be giving thanks for what we've been blessed with. So I elected to have a potluck theme. Each Thanksgiving, I've asked everyone to bring their own specialty dish, hopefully one which is in keeping with our roots dating back to the Revolution."

"You always bring a dessert, don't you, sir?" asked Crepeau.

"That's correct, and I try to choose a recipe from Colonial days. This year, I've chosen gingersnaps."

"Do you mean like gingerbread cookies?" asked Ocampo.

"Sort of," replied Sarge. "For thousands of years, spices derived from the ginger root were used in cooking and bread-making. The Greeks used it as far back as 2400 BC. The Germans made it well known with their creations of intricate gingerbread houses.

"Gingerbread arrived in the New World with the English colonists. The spice was hard to come by, so the cookies became a delicacy. There are stories of gingerbread man cookies being used in Virginia to sway voters to favor one candidate over another."

"I wish it had been that easy for us," Donald said with a chuckle.

"Me too. Anyway, because of their rarity, they were only enjoyed by the wealthier colonists, much to the dismay of the regular folks. But all was not lost. The bakers who made these wonderful gingerbread men would cut the strips to mold the shapes and have small bits of dough leftover. They would bake these leftover pieces and create small gingerbread snaps, as they were called."

"Why were they called gingersnaps?" asked Crepeau.

"They were baked very thin and crispy, which caused a snapping sound when eaten. Gingersnaps were passed out of the back doors of many homes to children and adults, who'd often dip them into rum or whiskey for extra flavor. It became known as the cookie of the common man during colonial times."

"Wow, that's really cool," remarked Ocampo. "Are you making gingerbread men today?"

"Nope, I think for this final Thanksgiving, I'll make the cookie of the common man—gingersnaps. Now, let's talk about what's going on in the world."

CHAPTER 69

9:00 a.m. ET
Xindian District
New Taipei City

"Control, are you absolutely sure?" Drew had asked two hours ago as he walked around the swimming pool, looking into the clear sky where the MQ-4C Triton drone was filming from nearly five miles above him.

The identities of the three men were confirmed by the CIA Taipei station chief as being assigned to protect the ambassador. Absent from the trio and presumably still alive was Lee Matsu, the Taiwanese national who was also the chief of security at the AIT complex.

This sent the intelligence apparatus into a mad scramble. They immediately expected the AIT complex to come under attack because Matsu had detailed knowledge of its security measures and the presence of the CIA team in the bunker.

Over the last two hours, one by one, Drew's team reported they'd found no trace of the ambassador. Out of precaution, the Delta Force operators were redirected to the AIT while the drivers supplied by the CIA were returned to their compound in Keelung City.

Santa and Spidey were dropped off at the compound with Drew. The other four members of his Elite Eight immediately took up perimeter security around them. Drew continued his pacing around the compound, studying every aspect of his surroundings hopefully for a sign of some kind.

As he walked past the garage doors for the third time, he widened his arc to hug the protective concrete walls enclosing the compound.

This time, he noticed a gate exiting the north side of the property, on the opposite side of where he and King had entered. The gate had a typical wrought-iron latch mechanism to close it together with a hole to slip a padlock through.

He tried the gate and it easily swung open into the street. He took a step onto the narrow sidewalk and immediately raised his hands when a red laser light illuminated his chest, barely dancing as a steady hand guided its path.

"Alpha One, Charlie One. Over."

"Yeah, that's me, Charlie One."

The light immediately left his chest and Drew studied his surroundings. He looked to the sky and saw that the trees covered him from the drone's view.

He ducked back into the compound and turned on his flashlight. He began searching through the tall grass that surrounded the gate. He shuffled his feet, looking for the missing lock to confirm his suspicions. He kicked through the grass until his toe met something solid.

Between his legs lay a standard combination lock with a long shackle. It was left open. Drew walked back into the street.

"Control, Alpha One."

"Go ahead, Alpha One."

"Did you run a property records check on this compound? Over."

"Affirmative. The owner is a Taiwanese businessman reportedly out of the country. We've confirmed that he is not the dead man in the suit."

"Roger that. Run a check on his other property holdings in the area, especially this neighborhood. The analysts may need to check his company's holdings as well as family members."

"Will do, Alpha One."

"Control, one more thing," started Drew.

"Go ahead, Alpha One."

"Did we maintain aerial surveillance on this compound following the departure of the six vehicles? If so, for how long and what size perimeter?"

"That would be continuous, Alpha One. We maintained a quarter-mile visual."

"Send that to me. Over."

"Roger, Alpha One. Control out."

Drew ran back to the house, where King, Spidey, and Santa continued to search every inch of the house, looking for clues. "Santa, I need your eyes."

"Sure thing, boss," the younger man replied as he deftly hopped over a leather couch and joined Drew at the laptop.

"Control has just sent us footage for the hours after the abduction. I need you to go through this in 2X or 3X speed and focus on this area of the compound."

Drew pointed to the monitor where the trees obscured the satellite imagery of the gate and the street outside it. He continued. "Watch for any pedestrian activity that seems out of sorts, especially if one or more people emerge from the trees that didn't enter from the other side."

"Do you think they left on foot?"

"Possibly, or they may have entered another vehicle that was hidden under the canopy. These people are very calculating. The six vehicles left here in an obviously choreographed move. It was designed to have us chasing our tails in search of an empty van and zero leads."

"That part of the master plan was effective," said Santa.

"Further, they had to know we'd find the bodies after our search of the compound. Everything was fed to us on a silver platter except crater face. My guess is that he'll turn out to be an unrelated diversion. Control is stymied in their attempts to identify the man. His prints turn up nothing and facial recognition software is still searching. They've got a forensics team trying to do a computer reconstruction of the guy."

"Okay, I'll let you know if I find anything. What are you gonna do?"

"Spidey and I are going to take a romantic stroll through the neighborhood," said Drew with a laugh.

"C'mon, man, not me again," complained Spidey, who was always being teased about his handsome, model-like qualities. "Take King this time, would ya?"

"He's not my type," said Drew with a chuckle. "Besides, I might need you to perform some of your circus acts. Now, drop your kit. Sidearms and sticks only." Drew was referring to the USMC-issued KA-BAR knives the guys preferred to have strapped to their legs and the .45 caliber 1911s strapped to their waists.

"Fine, but we're not holding hands," squalled Spidey.

CHAPTER 70

10:00 a.m. ET
Xindian District
New Taipei City

Drew and Spidey exited the compound. They turned eastward away from the major freeway and deeper into Xindian District. When they emerged from the stand of trees, he contacted Control.

"Control, Alpha One. Over."

"Go ahead, Alpha One."

"Exiting compound on north side street. Do you have us? Over."

"Roger that, Alpha One. We'll widen our perimeter visuals as necessary. Over."

A strong gust of wind struck them in the face as they crossed the street and continued on their eastward path. Drew had no particular destination in mind. He just had a sense that the ambassador was right under his nose.

Once again, he pulled his shemagh over his face as a wall of dust and trash blew past them, bits of dirt peppering the upper half of his face as they moved forward.

"What are we looking for, Drew?" asked Spidey.

"Brother, truthfully, I'm not sure. Somebody left that compound in a hurry. They didn't bother to secure the lock from the outside, which left the compound open to any passersby. The fact it was under the tree canopy makes me think we missed something when we studied the video footage earlier."

"It's possible," said Spidey. "Santa was focused on following the vehicles. I don't think it crossed his mind to study the foot traffic around the residence."

"Alpha One, Control. Over."

"Go ahead, Control."

"We've got the property records search back. The owner of the home has another property about three clicks to your north. Sending aerial and ground-level images to you now. Over."

Drew waited for the images to load on his phone. It was another residential compound, although much smaller than the one the ambassador was originally taken to. The ground-level view revealed a wrought-iron gate leading into the property. Once again, trees obscured the driveway entrance toward the garage from any prying eyes above.

"Roger, Control. We're en route. Over."

"Alpha One, we've designated a team to study activity in both properties following the abduction. Will advise."

"Roger that. Over and out."

Drew summoned Tai to pick them up. He updated Santa on what to look for in his surveillance tapes. He also forwarded the images to him.

Tai emerged from around the corner and Drew jumped into the passenger's seat. They got closer to the smaller compound and immediately noticed the difference from the other location. This looked more like a prison camp than a residence.

The compound was surrounded by a ten-foot block wall topped by barbed wire. At each of the four corners, an elevated platform must've existed, because an armed guard stood where he could see over the top of the wall. Inside the compound, large halogen lights illuminated the yard.

"This place is lit up like a shopping mall on Christmas Eve," said Drew as Tai pulled to a stop a block away. "These guys are dressed like gardeners in their green coveralls, but those Chinese QBZ-95s are a dead giveaway." The QBZ-95 and its updated variant was a Chinese-made version of the American M4. Its standard rounds were NATO 5.56.

"Flying Dragons?" asked Spidey.

"Damn straight," replied Drew. "Look at the guy closest to us.

He's leaning on the wall, smoking a cigarette, looking toward the compound."

"He's bored, maybe?" asked Tai.

"Yeah, or he's got a false sense of security that they wouldn't be located," replied Drew. "It's almost as if he's more concerned with what's happening inside the compound than he is outside those walls."

"Big mistake," quipped Spidey.

"I agree, bud."

Drew's earpiece came to life with Santa's voice. "Alpha One, got something for you."

"Go ahead."

"Eighteen hours after the abduction, a man emerged from under the group of trees onto the sidewalk. He seemed to come out of nowhere. He walked down the street and got into a mid-size sedan. As he drove down the street to make a U-ey, another guy shows up on the sidewalk, helping someone walk. It looked like the third guy was drunk or something. They got in the car and headed north in your direction."

"Did they come here?" asked Drew.

"Can't tell 'cause they were outside the bird's peripheral vision."

Drew paused for a moment. He wanted to study their surroundings before they conducted an assault on the compound. From the lackadaisical approach of the guards, there didn't appear to be a sense of urgency other than daylight would be coming and he wanted to secure Ambassador McBride's safety before then.

He turned to Spidey and Tai. "Let's get back to the other compound and put an assault plan together. If these guys want to chill and smoke a cigarette while on duty, then I have no problem puttin' them on ice so we can get our ambassador back."

CHAPTER 71

11:00 a.m.
The Blue Room
The White House
Washington, DC

General Thankſgiving.

BY THE PRESIDENT
OF THE UNITED STATES of AMERICA.
A PROCLAMATION.

WHEREAS it is the duty of all nations to acknowledge the Providence of Almighty God---to obey his will---to be grateful for his benefits---and humbly to implore his protection and favour: And whereas both Houſes have, by their joint committee, requeſted me "to recommend to the people of the United States, a DAY of PUBLICK THANKSGIVING and PRAYER, to be obſerved by acknowledging with grateful hearts the many and ſignal favours of Almighty God, eſpecially by affording them an opportunity peaceably to eſtabliſh a form of government for their ſafety and happineſs :"

The first colonists fled England seeking religious freedom. Few sailed into the unknown out of a sense of adventure. They sought a better life that would allow them freedom of expression without fear of government retribution, and the ability to worship God in the manner they sought appropriate for their family.

In the early settlements, it was part of their everyday life to set aside days of thanksgiving, prayer, and fasting in response to significant events. While American history traditionally recognizes the first Thanksgiving as having taken place at Plymouth colony in the fall of 1621, it wasn't until 1789 that President George Washington issued a formal proclamation designating November 26 as a national day of Thanksgiving to recognize the nation's accomplishments in creating the new United States and the Constitution.

During the American Revolution, Thanksgiving was declared at various times in the fall to recognize military victories. But the war brought alterations to the traditional menu. Raisins were unavailable, *not for love or money*, as they said back in the day. Beef had been completely absent from the colonists' tables since the beginning of the war, as one historian from the time wrote—*it all must go to the Army & too little they get, poor fellows.*

But the Thanksgiving tables were heavily laden nonetheless. The tradition of the colonists was to invite friends and family over for a Thanksgiving celebration, which included storytelling for the children, prayers of thanks, and potluck dishes contributed by each of the guests to the meal.

Venison, pork roasts, turkey and goose were accompanied by great amounts of vegetables from the harvests particular to the colony's locale. Desserts included pumpkin pies, apple tarts, and a variety of cookies.

During Sarge's first year in office, he was asked about the theme he'd like to adopt for Thanksgiving. He was not interested in flaunting an extravagant menu at the White House when so many Americans were suffering just fifteen months after the collapse. Instead, holding true to his revolutionary roots, Sarge declared during his years as president, the White House would celebrate as the Founding Fathers did, with a potluck-style Thanksgiving meal.

The guests were encouraged to bring dishes served during the American Revolution. Beginning with the Sargents' first Thanksgiving in the White House, their guests, which included the

Loyal Nine, the Boston Brahmin and their families, brought dishes such as venison, pork, baked beans and Johnnycakes, french beans, potato soup, molasses graham bread, and Indian pudding. Sarge always committed to making some form of dessert, and this year, he baked gingersnaps.

The size of their annual Thanksgiving dinner at the White House grew over the years with the additions of two new children to Sarge and Julia, as well as grandchildren born into the Boston Brahmin families.

The Blue Room, which doubled as a diplomatic reception room, was used for the Thanksgiving dinners. It was perfectly suited for smaller gatherings than the State Room warranted, and its proximity to the South Portico lent incredible views across the South Lawn for attendees.

As their guests arrived, Sarge and Julia greeted each one of them. Their names were synonymous with New England gentry and would be familiar to anyone who had studied American history in high school—Cabot, Lowell, Hancock, Tudor, Bradlee, Crowninshield, Winthrop, Endicott, Peabody, Adams, Sargent, and Morgan.

Sarge greeted them all heartily and with genuine respect. They were more than his wealthy, powerful friends and associates. They were members of an exclusive group of patriotic Americans dating back to the War for Independence. The members of these families were lineal descendants of the Sons of Liberty—the Founding Fathers.

They were the Boston Brahmin, and as they entered the White House with their families, Sarge could sense the walls saying *Welcome Home!*

CHAPTER 72

11:30 a.m.
The Blue Room
The White House
Washington, DC

The group had settled into the Blue Room and the adjacent Red Room with Estelle Peabody, Julia's aunt. As befitting the literary heritage of the Peabodys and Hawthornes, Aunt Stella was holding court around the fire, telling the children a story.

"Today is Thanksgiving and I want to tell you a story about some wonderful family gatherings over two hundred fifty years ago. That's a long time, isn't it?"

"Yeah!" they replied in unison.

"Rose, dear, how old are you?"

"Five."

"So, if you're five, and we're going to tell a story from two hundred fifty years ago, how many Roses does that make?"

"Fifty times five. Fifty Roses!" proclaimed Win.

"That's right, Win. That's a long time. Now, I want you all to gather close by and close your eyes."

The kids scooted along the floor in front of the fire.

"Close your eyes and feel the warm fire on your faces. I'm going to start telling the story of our Founding Fathers and their Thanksgiving dinners. When you open your eyes, all of us will be watching them enjoy their dinner, okay?"

"Okay!" they replied gleefully as they formed a tight-knit group around Aunt Stella.

Julia joined Sarge's side and wrapped her arms through his. They enjoyed a moment of quiet solitude as Aunt Stella told the story, which was made up as she continued. The children's faces were locked on her words, enjoying the tale she told.

Sarge spoke to Julia in a low tone of voice so he didn't disrupt the story. "I remember the day I met Art and Stella at their home. I was there to pick them up and bring them back to safety at 100 Beacon. They treated me like family from the moment we met. It was as if Aunt Stella knew you and I were destined to be together."

"I believe in fate," said Julia. "The Hawthornes and Peabodys have been intertwined in their lineage for a couple of centuries. As it turns out, there was a Sargent in the mix back in the early nineteenth century."

"Shhh," Sarge playfully admonished Julia. "We might be kissin' cousins. Think of the scandal!"

"Oh yes, people will most certainly talk," said Julia with a laugh. She turned her head to notice Walter Cabot hovering nearby. "Speaking of *talk*, Mr. Cabot has followed you around since he arrived. It's as if he's waiting for his opportunity to pounce on you."

"I know. I've avoided him since yesterday. Well, for a couple of weeks, really. He wants to address this statehood issue, and to be honest, my mind is in Taiwan. Retrieving our ambassador and keeping Drew out of harm's way is tantamount to the pressure Walter and the Boston Brahmin want to place on my shoulders."

"Well, he's headed your way, my darling Mr. President, and I see that Abbie just arrived. Good luck."

Julia kissed him on the cheek and darted back into the Blue Room. Sarge stood and watched Stella continue with the story, pretending to be oblivious of Cabot's advance.

"Happy Thanksgiving, Mr. President," started Cabot with a jovial tone. *Maybe this wasn't going to be a difficult conversation after all.* "May I have a moment to speak with you?"

"Happy Thanksgiving to you as well, Walter. You're looking good."

"Thank you, Henry, if I may be informal?" Cabot, like his dearly departed friends Lawrence Lowell and John Morgan, always referred to Sarge as Henry. The three eldest members of the Boston Brahmin, whom Sarge had known most of his life, were friends of his father and had known Sarge by his given name—Henry.

"Of course, Walter," said Sarge. Let's step over here by the window and talk for a moment."

"Henry, you've been difficult to speak with lately. Other than the usual trials and tribulations of the presidency, is there anything else wrong?"

"No, Walter, I'm fine. I have been preoccupied as my administration winds down. I have a lot to accomplish in these last two months. Now, I have this crisis in Taiwan to deal with."

"Completely unexpected, I take it," interrupted Cabot. "Any word on the missing ambassador?"

"Not yet, but I expect something will surface today."

Cabot abruptly shifted gears to discussing the election. Sarge could sense he was leading up to something and this small talk was intended to set the table for a long-overdue conversation with the oldest member of the Boston Brahmin's executive council.

"We were very pleased with the election results, as always," he began. "Our track record with electing presidents has been quite incredible, wouldn't you agree?"

"Of course," replied Sarge. *Here's the part where Walter reminds me of how I got into office.*

"I must say, installing one of our own to the highest office in the land was a great accomplishment."

Sarge hesitated, choosing his words carefully. "Yes, Walter, and naturally, I appreciate everyone's support."

Cabot continued. "The process of electing candidates to any level of office can be excruciating. Placing a candidate into the White House is elegant as hell, but there's no elegance in modern politics, only hell."

Sarge nodded and looked past Cabot into the Blue Room, where his guests seemed to be making their way toward their seats. Aunt Stella had finished up her story and the children were being escorted to the Red Room, where the Quinn daughters, the oldest of the children in attendance, were hosting a children's version of Thanksgiving, which included traditional favorites like chicken nuggets with mac-and-cheese.

"I was fortunate that the people certainly approved of my candidacy and the platform I ran on," said Sarge as he chose to subtly remind Cabot that he could've won his two election campaigns on his own merit without the usual Boston Brahmin manipulations.

"The new man, Rawling, shares your passion for bringing the *wayward four*, as I like to call the secessionists, back into the fold. Undoubtedly, he would support the bill just passed by—"

The White House butler had entered the room and announced that dinner was served, cutting off Cabot in mid-sentence.

Saved by the bell.

"I'm sorry, Walter. Why don't we take up our conversation after dinner? Perhaps cigars in the Sunroom upstairs would be a good idea."

Cabot frowned as he'd been stymied by the timing of dinner. "I suppose that would be best."

"Good. Let's join the others. I understand they have located an extraordinary treat for this final Thanksgiving in office."

CHAPTER 73

Noon
The Blue Room
The White House
Washington, DC

Everyone took a seat around the elegantly set table in the Blue Room. After everyone was seated, Sarge said a few words before leading them in prayer.

"Happy Thanksgiving to everyone and thank you for joining us in our final Thanksgiving dinner at the White House.

"This special day invites us to reflect on the blessings we enjoy and the freedoms we cherish. As we gather with family and friends to take part in this uniquely American celebration, we give thanks for the extraordinary opportunities we have in a nation of limitless possibilities, and we pay tribute to all those who defend America as members of our armed forces.

"This holiday reminds us to show compassion and concern for people we've never met and deep gratitude toward those who have sacrificed to help build the most prosperous nation on earth. Our traditions honor the rich history of our country and hold us together as one American family.

"Nearly four hundred years ago, a group of Pilgrims left their homeland and sailed across an ocean in pursuit of liberty and prosperity. With the friendship and kindness of the Indians who lived here, they learned to harvest the rich bounty of a new world. Together, they shared a successful crop, celebrating bonds of community during a time of great hardship. During the American Revolution, days of thanksgiving drew Americans together in prayer and in the spirit that guides us to better days, and in each year since, America has paused to show our gratitude for our families, communities, and country.

"With God's grace, we carry forward the legacy of our forebearers. In the company of our loved ones, we give thanks for the people we care about and the joy we share, and we remember those who are less fortunate. During the aftermath of the collapse, after a brief period of tribulation, Americans gave meaning to the simple truth that binds us together—we are our brother's and our sister's keepers. Today, let's remember how a determined people set out for a better world, how through faith and the charity of others, they forged a new life built on freedom and opportunity and made us into the great, caring nation we are today.

"The spirit of Thanksgiving is universal. It is found in small moments between strangers, reunions shared with friends and loved ones, and in quiet prayers for others. This Thanksgiving, let us recall the values that unite our country, and let us promise to strengthen these lasting ties."

Sarge paused and smiled to his guests. "I'd like us to pray together, so please bow your heads." The entire room of twenty-four adults took each other's hands and bowed their heads in reverence.

"Our Heavenly Father, every year at Thanksgiving, we bow our heads to offer thanks for the blessings you've bestowed upon us. My family thanks you for providing us health and well-being. As our friends and their families gather around, we ask that you look kindly upon us and receive our heartfelt gratitude in this time of giving thanks.

"Thank you for all the graces and blessings of food, shelter, health and the love we have for one another, our family and friends. Dear Father, in Your infinite generosity, please grant us, your humble servants, continued graces and blessing throughout the coming year.

"We ask that you pray for our men and women overseas who have devoted their lives, precious lives which they risk daily, to protect our great nation and the freedoms to which we've grown accustomed.

"Father, we ask that you protect Ambassador McBride, as he has been placed in danger in a foreign land, far away from his family, who love and cherish him. We ask that you protect our brave men who seek to secure his safety and that you'll show those responsible for stealing him from his family the error of their ways.

"This we ask in the name of your son, Christ Jesus, Amen."

The room responded *amen* and then provided Sarge accolades for his prayer. Julia squeezed his hand and gave him a congratulatory smile. Then she stood to address the group, clasping her hands in front of her.

"I would just like to add and say thanks to all of you who've joined us each year while we've been in the White House. This has been an incredible journey for our family, which will soon come to an end. We couldn't think of a better way to say a formal farewell to the White House than to share it with all of you."

"Thank you, Julia, and you, Mr. President!" said Art Peabody.

"Now, I'm extremely excited to start our special meal with a surprise. Recently, historians were in the process of renovating the Liberty Hall Museum, and the team found three cases of Madeira wine dating back to the eighteenth century. At the time, it was the most popular wine in America, as it was consumed by sailors traveling to the new land from Europe. As part of their renovation efforts, they also located forty-two casks of the vintage red, and one was proudly donated to the White House just for this special occasion."

Several of the White House staff began to go around the long, rectangular table and poured the red wine into the guests' glasses. When everyone had been served, Sarge stood to propose a toast.

"Ben Franklin once said, 'Wine makes daily living easier, less hurried, with fewer tensions and more tolerance.' I believe these are words to live by and are indicative of how our Founding Fathers established this great nation. My toast is a simple one. Please join me in raising your glasses."

Everyone raised their glasses into the air. Sarge looked around the room, attempting to make eye contact with each of his guests before he made the toast. All of them were fully attentive, except one—Gardner Lowell. Sarge shook off the slight and continued.

"Borrowing from the words of the immortal Daniel Webster, it is my heartfelt sentiment to you all, and by the blessing of God it shall be my dying sentiment, that in all things, I will choose freedom now and I will choose freedom forever!"

"Choose freedom!" shouted the guests as they joined in the toast and clinked glasses with their closest neighbors at the table. Everyone took a sip of the wine.

There are not many foods or drinks that last more than two hundred fifty days, let alone two hundred fifty years, but Madeira wine, made in Portugal specifically on the Madeira islands, aged and lasted indefinately like the port wines of the era. Because Madeira was a standard port of call for ships starting for the New World, the sweet wine was commonplace throughout the colonies. This particular cask had aged well and drew smiles from all who partook.

The food began to be served and the chatter commenced. Sarge, despite always being the model of humility, was the frequent target of questions and conversations.

"What are your plans, Mr. President, after you leave office?" asked Henry Endicott's wife, Emily. The former general had turned the Endicott family fortune into a company building the most advanced, modern weaponry available to the nation's armed forces. Emily, his much younger wife, had found her place among the Brahmin wives at Prescott Peninsula during those trying times. She was now considered an equal.

"You know, Emily, I'd love to provide some magnaminous answer like I intend to write a book or focus on my presidential library, but the truth is I'm just excited to go back to private life where I can play with Julia and the kids without being under a microscope. Or I might start a foundation." Several of the Boston Brahmin laughed at the inside joke.

Art Peabody fired off the next question. "What do you consider your greatest achievement in the last eight years?"

Sarge laughed. "Staying alive, for one."

Julia slugged him because the close call in which her husband was almost assassinated was an indelible memory in her mind.

"Okay, just kidding. Naturally, raising our beautiful family was a major accomplishment. It's not easy growing up a kid in the White House. I must say, all of the credit goes to the First Lady." Sarge raised a glass to Julia, who blushed the color of the wine.

"Hear, hear!" said Abbie, who encouraged everyone to raise their glasses in Julia's honor.

Sarge toasted his wife and then kissed her. He added a few more words. "The White House has served as the backdrop to the tough decisions and trying times that often characterize the presidency, but it's also been home, where Julia and I have watched our children grow into the extraordinary youngsters they are today."

More glasses were raised as the group continued to eat. Sarge continued to survey the room and caught Donald's eye. Donald tilted his head down the table and furrowed his brow. The two men had known each other long enough to read one another's thoughts.

Sarge's eyes scanned the table until he reached Gardner. The man's dour, sullen look spoke volumes. Gardner Lowell wasn't happy to be there and certainly didn't approve of the host being heaped with praise and admiration.

Sarge was enjoying himself and refused to allow Gardner's surly expressions to ruin his mood. But it did make the President of the United States and chair of the Boston Brahmin's executive council take notice.

And it pissed him off.

CHAPTER 74

12:15 p.m. ET
Xindian District
Taipei

It was just after midnight in Taipei and everything was proceeding as planned. Drew and his team had to sit and wait to allow the last of the AIT diplomatic personnel to get safely to their transports at Hualien Airport. His team and Control agreed that the retrieval of the ambassador would necessarily require a firefight. While they wanted to proceed under cover of darkness, Drew suggested the team stand down until the diplomats were safe and the AIT facility was properly secured. Knowing the events of the next hour could trigger a war with the Chinese, he was agreeable to waiting while the big guns got into place.

His mind wandered to Abbie and Thanksgiving dinner. In his service to the country, and now with Aegis as the head of a black-ops team, Drew had missed many holidays and birthday celebrations. Once again, doubt crossed his mind as to whether he should be on this mission or back in Washington with his pregnant wife. He continued to wrestle with the decision of his future.

He didn't have to work another day in his life if he didn't want to. Abbie, as the sole heir to John Morgan's fortune, was wealthy beyond imagination. The two of them could raise a family, travel, and spend their days together out of the limelight that politics had thrust upon them.

Drew looked at his watch again. He hated the downtime when he was on a mission. It required his adrenaline levels to rise and fall abruptly, which eventually tired any person. Some of the guys could zone out and daydream of exotic locales or girls back home. Drew's default place of respite was with Abbie. Thoughts of her invariably led him to their unborn baby and the risks his job entailed.

He purposefully shook himself to bring his mind back to the task at hand. King, who'd taken over the wheel, looked over at Drew.

"Are you cold, honey?" he asked.

"Screw you." Drew snapped back to life. "I was just falling asleep. You guys are boring as hell."

"You told us to stay quiet," Santa shot back. "If you want some chatter, I've got a few things on my mind."

"Hell naw," moaned King. "Please don't let him get started."

Control interrupted the back-and-forth. "Alpha One, Control. Over."

"Go ahead, Control."

"Green light, Alpha One."

"Roger that, Alpha One out," said Drew. "All right, guys. Showtime."

Drew, Santa, and Spidey exited the van and took up their positions across from the entrance gate to the compound. Drew checked in with each of his operatives to make sure they were in position.

There was no way to enter the compound covertly. In addition to the four sentries at each corner of the four walls surrounding the property, at least two guards covered the gate. The first step was to take the sentries out of play.

The other four members of the Elite Eight were assigned a guard. On Drew's signal, Tai was to fire a flare into the sky to draw the guards' attention. When they showed their heads above the wall, the team would take each of them out with their silenced M4s.

While the distraction was taking place, King Dawkins would crash through the gate, enabling Drew and his comrades to enter and provide King cover. The unknown variable was the number of reinforcements that would come scrambling out of the residence to back up their security team. Drew and the guys would have to be quick and efficient in dispatching the threats. More importantly,

Drew and Spidey had to find their way into the house to locate the ambassador.

Drew leaned against the stucco wall, closed his eyes and focused on his breathing. In his mind, he kissed his wife as he headed out to an imaginary desk job in an imaginary office. He walked the plan through in his mind. Flare. Sentries taken down. Gate breached. Gate guards eliminated. Threats from residence appear through front door, maybe side entrances.

He visualized each step, including how many men were inside to assist the others. When he was ready, he gave Spidey and Santa the thumbs-up and started the operation.

"Alpha Two, you're a go," instructed Drew.

"Roger, Alpha One."

Seconds later, Tai shot a bright red flare, which soared into the sky, arching its way from one side of the residence to the other.

As predicted, this grabbed the complacent guards' attention, who began to shout to one another. In the relative quiet of the sleepy neighborhood, the spits of the suppressed weapons could be heard followed by the tumbling of the bodies down the platforms until they landed with thumps.

Drew hugged the stucco wall as he led his team closer to the gate. The sound of the van roaring down the road drew the attention of the guards at the gate, who immediately opened fire on King. The windshield shattered as the van broke through the wrought-iron gates, shoving them inward and knocking the guards to the concrete driveway.

King brought the van to a stop, but not before he crushed the shooters beneath the tires. Drew ran through the opening and placed an insurance bullet into the heads of the men writhing underneath the van.

"Are you good?" he asked King.

"Yeah, man," he replied with his deep voice. "I lay down on the seat after I got her pointed in the right direction. I ate some glass, though."

"Your belly can handle it." Drew laughed as the four men fanned out and took cover behind parked vehicles in the driveway.

"We've got multiple tangos coming out!" shouted Santa, who immediately engaged them. The Chinese weapons were not suppressed, and the otherwise quiet neighborhood in Xindian District erupted into a war zone.

Their adversaries had the benefit of a small retaining wall formed into a planter that lined the front of the house. Their men took up positions behind the wall, and soon the front windows were broken out, producing more barrels pointed in the Aegis team's direction.

The second flare was airborne as planned when the remainder of the team had taken up their positions on top of vehicles parked against the compound's wall. It wasn't the best of vantage points, but the crossfire enabled the enemy to be distracted rather than focusing all of their efforts on the front gate.

The sound of gunfire and brass hitting the pavement filled the air. Drew and Santa leaned with their backs against the front of the vehicle, using the engine block as additional cover.

Drew pulled up the aerial feed from the drone onto his phone. The left side of the house had been cleared by his team. The rear of the home was now being heavily defended by four men. His only hope of entry was through a set of patio doors that had been left open when the backup security guards emerged a few minutes earlier.

"What's the plan?" asked Santa.

Drew studied the images again and replied, "If we can't take these guys out quickly, at some point they'll bring the ambassador out as a human shield. Then we're screwed."

"Agreed," said Santa.

"We gotta hit 'em while they're reactive. We just gotta bust in on 'em."

"Lead the way," said Santa dryly. "I'll be with you."

Drew looked his comrade in the eyes and nodded. He slapped the side of the car to get King's attention. Using hand signals, he indicated his intention to lead Santa around the side of the house. He needed King and Spidey to lay down cover fire to keep the guards behind the retaining wall occupied. Then he contacted the two members of his team on the left side of the house to pick off any shooters who emerged while they made their entry.

"Let's do this!" shouted Drew as he rose out of his crouch.

Simultaneously, King and Spidey opened fire on the four men guarding the front of the house. Glass shattered and wood window frames were splintered. The brick retaining wall was the only thing preventing the guards from being torn to ribbons. But as the two operatives rained hellfire upon the front of the house, Drew and Santa darted across the front lawn and reached the open patio doors.

The two men nodded to one another and entered the house, their weapons leading the way.

CHAPTER 75

1:15 p.m.
The Blue Room
The White House
Washington, DC

"Donald, they've been circling me like vultures since dinner was over," Sarge whispered as they casually walked toward the doorway leading to the Entrance Hall of the Executive Residence. "I expect this conversation will get contentious, so I plan on taking them upstairs to the Solarium. I'll couch it in terms of a tour of the Solarium, but actually it'll be a *come-to-Jesus meeting* for all of us."

"Things are about to heat up in Taipei," Donald added. "Do you still want me to pull you away if the situation warrants?"

"Yes, absolutely. I'll have David with me," Sarge said with a chuckle. "I'll probably need his protection."

"I'm going down to the Situation Room to get an update. Brad slipped away earlier."

Sarge gestured behind him toward the activity and loud conversation within the Blue Room. "Brad doesn't like this stuff anyway. He didn't even try my gingersnaps."

"Ungrateful bastard." Donald laughed. "All right, buddy, good luck with those buzzards. When things get hot, I'll send for you."

Sarge patted Donald on the back and sent him on his way. He took a deep breath and whispered to Morrell, "I'm gonna need you to go with me to the Solarium. Shelby and BAM can stay if they want."

"Thank you, sir, but they've said their good-byes. I hope I wasn't out of place, but I let Brie tell Rose we're moving back to Boston.

Those two have a lot of fun together."

"Dave, no problem at all. You guys are like family. Let me go round up a few people I need to speak with and we'll take the elevator."

Sarge made his way through the crowd toward Walter Cabot when there was an uproar in the Red Room.

"He is not!"

"Is so!"

"Is not!"

"Yes, he is! My grandpa said—"

"Boys, stop yelling." Julia raced into the room and interrupted the fracas just as Win was charging toward his adversary. Sarge made his way toward the opening between the two rooms to assist.

Julia quizzed the young men. "Why are you two yelling at each other?"

"He said Dad was weak," started Win. His face was red with anger.

Young Gardner Percival Lowell II, grandson of Gardner Lowell, stood defiantly in the face of questioning by Julia. His father, John Stewart Lowell, entered the room right after Julia.

"Is that true, son?" asked John Lowell.

"Dad, Grandpa said Win's dad is a weak president."

"Well, neither your grandfather, nor you, should speak of the president this way. Until you've walked in his shoes, you don't know how difficult his job is. Now, I want you to apologize to Win."

"But, Dad, I believe Grandpa. Why should I apologize?"

"Because you're nine years old and you're too young to know what you believe, that's why. Tell Win you're sorry. Go ahead."

The youngster provided a halfhearted, insincere apology. As Sarge listened to the exchange, he thought of the phrase *out of the mouths of babes.* Originally a proverb from Psalms in the Bible, the modern usage meant something a child has just said that is clever, interesting, or truthful.

Sarge scanned the room to gauge the reaction of the guests who overheard the argument. To his rear stood Gardner Lowell, arms crossed, the dour look unchanged throughout dinner, staring directly at Sarge.

Julia continued to mediate the dispute and the guests gradually left her alone with the boys and John Lowell to sort things out.

The exchange caused Sarge to bristle. He stood a little taller, set his jaw, and found Walter Cabot. He asked Cabot to gather the Boston Brahmin in the Cross Hall outside the Blue Room. "It's time we talk."

CHAPTER 76

1:30 p.m.
The Solarium
The White House
Washington, DC

The top floor of the Executive Residence was designed as a place of relaxation. Over the years, the rooms were used as a billiards parlor, a fitness center, and a music room. It was originally used as a *sleeping porch*, as designated by President William Howard Taft. Before the days of air-conditioning in the White House, the First Family used the Solarium as a cool place to sleep on hot nights. During the Truman reconstruction of the White House, it was expanded again and now included a kitchenette and bar.

During the nineties, President Clinton, who was extremely fond of cigars, used to slip away for some solitude from time to time to smoke a stogie and relax. The Solarium became a place of respite for him. There was a period of time when his wife became angry with President Clinton, in particular with his cigar habits, and banned all kinds of smoking within the White House.

The First Lady ordered all ashtrays to be removed and they were never again placed on tables for official dinners. Her press secretary stated the First Lady's target with the new policy was cigarettes, yet the effect of her decision took dead aim at her husband's affinity for a good cigar.

Sarge believed in the freedom to enjoy a good cigar. Following in the tradition of statesman from Winston Churchill to John F. Kennedy, he revised the Hillary Clinton policy of banning cigar smoking, at least in the Solarium.

The executive council of the Boston Brahmin used the elevator to arrive on the third floor of the Executive Residence, where Sarge joined them. He asked Morrell to wait in the hallway and he closed the door. He trusted Morrell with his life and could probably make him privy to the history of the Boston Brahmin, but for his own safety, Sarge kept him out of the loop regarding the true nature of his relationship to the group.

Sarge poured everyone a brandy and unlocked the cigar humidor for his guests to make their selection. After everyone lit their cigars and exchanged clinks of their glasses, Sarge began.

"Gentlemen, once again, I want to thank all of you for joining me in this final Thanksgiving celebration," started Sarge. "From our first Thanksgiving together in those highly unusual circumstances after the collapse, we managed to join together each year to break bread and share the special relationship that has existed for centuries."

"Happy Thanksgiving, Mr. President!" said Art Peabody cheerfully as he raised his glass. Peabody was Sarge's strongest ally, although he was far less influential than Walter Cabot, because of his age, or Gardner Lowell, because of his assertiveness. Sarge was the youngest of the Brahmin, as he was younger than Gardner.

"Cheers!" said Endicott. The group raised their glasses once again and toasted one another.

"Please, everyone, take a seat and get comfortable. I have a couple of things to talk about and then we can open up the floor."

The men all took a seat except Gardner, who intentionally waited for Sarge to sit so he could position himself directly across the room. Sarge, who was not intimidated, continued.

"I only have eight weeks left in office. Traditionally, with Congress in recess, things are pretty quiet around Washington. The media turns its attention to the transition team and the plans the new president has for his administration. Oftentimes, the lame-duck president will return home or go on an extended vacation with his family. I have other plans."

"Like what, Sarge?" asked Cabot.

Cabot was never one of Sarge's enemies. He was very close to John Morgan and wholeheartedly supported the appointment of Sarge to head the executive council that fall of 2016. However, with Sarge focusing on his duties as president, Cabot was susceptible to a constant barrage of criticism of Sarge by Gardner. And as Sarge had just learned during the argument between Win and Gardner's grandson, his adversary no longer made any attempt to hide his feelings.

"Those of you on the executive council have various business interests that are closely intertwined with Washington. From shipbuilding to military armature, we all rely upon government contracts to enrich our companies and our families. As has been the case for years, the members of the executive council represent a who's who in the so-called military-industrial complex. While the goods and services we supply are often vilified in the media, it's the nature of what we do that allows Americans to sleep at night."

"Well said, Sarge," said Samuel Bradlee, a former Secretary of Defense and a direct descendant of Nathaniel Bradlee—one of the key participants in the Boston Tea Party. He was very well regarded among the group and was Brad's uncle. "I don't think any of us have issue with your direction over the years."

"Thank you, sir," said Sarge. "In my last weeks in office, I will be doing much more as my administration flies under the media radar.

From rarely used executive orders to new government contracts, I will set the tone for enhanced wealth for all of you for generations."

"This is why I was thrilled at Sarge's ability to take the highest office in the land," said Cabot proudly.

Sarge smiled and nodded his thanks as he took another long draw off his cigar. "Other members of the Boston Brahmin, who are not in this room, rely upon my stewardship regarding wealth opportunities in the health care, financial, and manufacturing sectors. They will benefit as well from these executive actions."

"I have to ask," Gardner interrupted. "You've had eight years in office to do these great things of which you speak, why didn't you? Perhaps we could have benefitted greatly for years, rather than the last two months."

Sarge bristled at the implication he had failed to adequately help the Boston Brahmin during his years as president. "Well, Gardner, every action I took in the White House was under a microscope. It's a job that requires finesse, not the arrogant wielding of power. While you might see my assistance as insignificant or miniscule, I can assure you the bottom lines of everyone in this room, including the Lowell family, have expanded greatly."

"No doubt the others agree with you, *Mr. President*," said Gardner sarcastically, emphasizing Sarge's title. "Frankly, I saw a number of missed opportunities over the years and elected to hold my tongue—*out of respect*."

Sarge could see that the members of the executive council were growing uncomfortable with the exchange. He couldn't decide whether to turn Gardner's arrogant hostility back on him or not. Just as Sarge was about to respond, Morrell knocked on the door and poked his head inside.

"Mr. President, I'm sorry for the interruption. I'm afraid it's urgent, sir."

Sarge stood and put out his cigar. "Gentlemen, I suspect I'm needed in the Situation Room, Please stay here and enjoy the cigars and the bar. I'll rejoin the conversation as quickly as I can."

Sarge managed a sly grin at Gardner, buttoned his jacket, and strode out of the room. *I'll be back to deal with you in due time. Count on it.*

CHAPTER 77

1:45 p.m. ET
Xindian District
Taipei City, Taiwan

"Grenade!" yelled Drew as he launched himself into the bedroom and over the back side of the king-size bed. The small distinctly spherical steel body bounded between Drew and Santa and landed in the grass outside the door. Santa fell to the floor and rolled behind the exterior wall while covering his head. The explosion of the fragmentation grenade outside the residence was deafening, causing the doors to be blown off the hinges and the door frame to splinter.

Santa quickly recovered from the blast and rolled into a crouch next to the back wall of the bedroom. Drew emerged from behind the bed, which was now covered with debris. His survival instinct kicked in and with it, years of experience and training.

Drew focused on the door's opening. Whoever threw that grenade would be peering around the corner to observe his handiwork. Drew had something for him.

Seconds later, a head emerged to sneak a peek at the damage. He was rewarded with a perfectly placed bullet in his right eye. The man stood as if suspended in animation, pieces of skull and brain matter sprayed on the hallway behind him as Drew's bullet tore through the back of his head. Then he fell to the floor in a heap.

"Moving," Drew said to his partner as the dust and debris began to settle to the floor. His focus was now twofold—find the ambassador and stay alive. He moved deeper into the house, carefully finding his way down a dark hallway toward the sound of gunfire.

Now he felt a sense of urgency. They were not located in one of the locations of Taiwan under siege by demonstrators, where gunshots and violence might have been the norm for several nights. This was a fairly upscale neighborhood where even suppressed weapons might be heard.

Between the heated gun battle outside, and now the explosion from the grenade, the Taiwanese military was likely to arrive at any time. Based upon what they had learned about Matsu and his potential involvement in the kidnapping, Drew couldn't count on the military being friendly to his operation. He had to work fast.

Santa slapped Drew on the back and the two continued until they reached a stairway leading to a basement location. On a hunch based upon experience, Drew worked his way down the dark staircase. He instructed Santa to remain at the top of the stairs to watch his back.

At the bottom of the stairs, a simple wooden door blocked his advance. He tried the knob, but it was locked. Most likely, this was the only way in or out of the basement. He hesitated for a moment as he quickly processed the possibilities. *What's gonna greet me on the other side of this door?*

Slowing his breathing, he pressed his back against the wall and listened. He couldn't hear anyone on the other side of the door, but he didn't need to. He was an assassin. He hunted others. They didn't hunt him. Drew Jackson was unafraid to enter any room because he knew his skills could take down any threats he faced.

He stepped back up two of the stairs and pointed his rifle at the door's deadbolt lock. With three quick volleys, the door was opened and a faint light illuminated his surroundings. A dark, musty basement greeted him except for the glow of the light from underneath another door.

The sound of gunfire and shuffling feet could be heard above him. Instinctively, he looked up the stairs to determine Santa's position. He was lying prone at the top of the stairs, firing his weapon toward the back of the house.

Drew doubted he still had the element of surprise on his side as he approached the light. Then he saw the shadows of feet blocking some of the light. Drew approached slowly, steadying his weapon as he debated whether to shoot the person behind the door.

But he knew he couldn't. If it was the ambassador, he'd never be able to live with the mistake. If he shot at the hinges, a guard on the other side might panic and shoot McBride. Drew weighed his options and opted for the bull rush.

He set his rifle aside and drew his sidearm. Drew took a deep breath and waited for the feet to stop in front of the door. Then he charged, lowered his shoulder and crashed through the door, knocking the person on the other side to the floor.

Drew lost his weapon as he tangled with the man. The guard pulled himself free of the wreckage caused by Drew and scrambled for his own weapon, which lay just out of reach.

Using his quick reflexes, Drew pulled his knife out of its sheath and brought it down hard on the man's wrist, causing him to scream in pain. With a twist, Drew withdrew the knife and forced it into the man's rib cage, which produced a gush of blood from the guard's chest, but it did not immediately produce his death. With one more effort, Drew closed in, yanked the knife out of the man's ribs and thrust it into his heart, ending the fight.

He scrambled to retrieve his gun and rolled against a wall to address any more threats. This part of the fight was over while the battle raged on upstairs.

"Ambassador McBride, are you here?"

"Yes, please help me," a man groaned from a dark corner of the room. Drew made his way to the voice and found the ambassador locked in a metal box. Using his knife, he pried the lock and clasp loose and the front popped open.

"Ambassador McBride, I'm Drew Jackson—Judge and Janie's son."

"Drew? I knew you when you were just a kid. Thank God, young man. Thank God for you."

"We're not quite out of the woods yet, sir. Are you ready for this? 'Cause we've still got some work to do."

Drew helped the older man to his feet. Ambassador McBride was still wobbly but managed to find the strength.

"Let me tell you something, Drew. It's like they say, I'd rather die on my feet than live on my knees."

"I heard that, sir," said Drew with a chuckle. "Can you handle a weapon?"

"I'm a country boy, young man," he replied. "Trust me, I'm so danged mad. Why don't you let me lead the way?"

Drew laughed and reached down to take the guard's nine millimeter. "Here you go, but I'll lead the way. Fair enough?"

"Fine, but I'm ready. Don't you worry."

Drew noticed the gunfire begin to die down. Another body sounded like it collapsed on the floor above them, causing dust to rain down on their heads.

"Control, Alpha One. Over."

"Go ahead, Alpha One."

"Positive contact on Golden Retriever. Repeat, positive contact on Golden Retriever."

"Roger that, Alpha One. POTUS says well done."

Before Drew could acknowledge the last transmission, he heard King's booming baritone voice reverberate off the walls.

"All clear. All hostiles KIA. All clear."

Santa ran down the stairs as Drew and the ambassador made their way through the doorway. "Hey, we're all clear."

"Yeah, I heard the bullhorn." Drew laughed, referring to King's deep voice. In the distance, now that the gunfire had died down, Drew could hear the sounds of sirens. "I think we've probably overstayed our welcome, boys. Let's get out of here."

"Roger that," replied Santa, who immediately hustled back up the stairs.

"Control, Alpha One. Please advise on extraction point. Over."

"Point of origin, Alpha One."

"Roger that, Control. Send my regards to POTUS and the VEEP."

CHAPTER 78

2:00 p.m.
The Oval Office
The White House
Washington, DC

Sarge and Brad were still hyped up from watching the assault on Ambassador McBride's captors as they entered the Oval Office. The entire thirty-six minutes played out on the monitors in the Situation Room through the lenses of the body cams on the Elite Eight.

As Drew and Santa began their move into the building, Sarge's eyes had darted between the gun battles taking place outside the house and video feed showing the catlike moves of the two operatives as they made their entry. It wasn't until the grenade exploded near the men that the danger associated with Drew's job struck home.

Afterwards, he pulled Brad and Donald aside and told them not to mention the grenade blast to Abbie. It wasn't their place to provide details of a mission to her when Drew was involved.

"Brad, I know you need to get back downstairs," Sarge began as he resumed his signature pacing routine. The Great Seal on the floor of the Oval Office couldn't withstand another four years of President Henry Sargent's foot traffic. "Both carrier strike groups are in position, correct?"

"Yes."

"Battle ready?"

"You betcha, Mr. President. So are the Virginia-class submarines. They're awaiting my orders to show themselves in the middle of the Taiwan Straits."

"What's your opinion of the Chinese troops' positioning?"

"Sarge, they're poised to strike. Now, our recovery of McBride may or may not impact their plans. There are a lot of things we don't know."

Sarge gestured for Brad to join him on the sofa. They made their way to sit when Donald returned with Abbie. She moved as fast as her pregnant belly would allow toward Sarge and Brad to provide them hugs of gratitude.

Wiping away her tears of relief and happiness, she said, "Thank you for not getting my husband killed on Thanksgiving."

"Abbie, I have to say, I've never seen anything like it. You can thank Drew for his coming home in one piece. The guy has an incredible sixth sense, an awareness, which enables him to anticipate what his adversaries have planned. We are very proud of him."

"Thanks for saying that, Sarge. I feel better."

"Now, that said," Sarge continued. "If I thought it was possible to tie him to a desk job at Aegis or even at 73 Tremont with me, I'd do it. But, frankly, he'd break free and then I'd fear for my life!"

The group joined Sarge in laughter as they released the tension caused by the entire affair. Sarge gestured for everyone to sit.

"Guys, the day isn't over yet," Sarge continued. "We've been closely monitoring the PLA's troop and equipment movements on Mainland China. Their intentions are obvious. Now, we need to gauge their seriousness. Brad, please summarize Beijing's plan for the invasion of Taiwan."

"The Chinese invasion threat has existed for years and has been war-gamed by their top military strategists with multiple scenarios. We believe they're in the early stages of their plan by using asymmetric warfare in the form of cyber attacks on the power grid in addition to destabilizing the Taiwan government through social unrest."

Abbie nodded in agreement. "Beijing has been using nonlethal means for years against Taiwan. Psychological, diplomatic, propaganda and informational warfare can all play a part in the undermining of confidence in the Taipei government. These orchestrated demonstrations seem to be the culmination of their efforts."

"Yes," added Sarge. "The cyber attack on the power grid cut the government off at the knees because half the country thought the administration should have embraced nuclear power as an electricity source and Taipei refused."

"How did the abduction of the ambassador come into play?" asked Abbie.

"This is still a mystery, but my guess is they would use him as a bargaining chip to force us to stand down during the assault," said Sarge.

"It's the only thing that makes sense except we wouldn't stand down," said Brad.

"That's right," said Sarge. He took a deep breath before asking Brad to continue. "Brad, the next logical step for the PLA is a missile attack, am I right?"

"Yes. The PLA would launch a preemptive missile strike directed at key military installations on Taiwan. This would be followed by an air blockade preventing the Taiwanese air defenses from engaging the amphibious beach landing with nearly a hundred thousand troops led by the Flying Dragons."

"Can our jets from the carriers counteract this?" asked Abbie.

Brad nodded and replied, "For a while until we can bring more fighters into the region. Make no mistake, this may have started as an invasion of Taiwan, but it will look like a massive naval and air battle between two major military powers."

"What about their missile attacks? How do we stop those?"

"A nuclear deterrent—our two Virginia-class subs, which are waiting for my orders to show themselves."

Sarge stood and walked toward his desk. Donald, Abbie, and Brad stopped talking. It was time for Sarge to make another decision. The Communist government in Beijing would be incensed that the United States had parked two nuclear-capable submarines barely fifty miles off their coast. With the press of the nuclear button, Sarge could annihilate Beijing and twenty-five million people in minutes.

"You know, if China parked a couple of nuclear subs fifty miles off Miami Beach, I'd be out-of-my-mind pissed off. By the same token, we're not amassing troops to invade Cuba."

"Been there and done that," mumbled Donald.

"That's right," continued Sarge. He leaned back against his desk and looked into the eyes of his most trusted friends within the administration. "We have an obligation to Taiwan and the rest of the world to push back against bullies. Brad, once I give the order, how long will it take the subs to surface?"

"Fifteen to twenty minutes," replied Brad.

"How long until they're seen by PLA intelligence?"

"They'll be in full view not later than thirty minutes from now, and the phones will be ringing off the hook in Beijing."

Sarge nodded and put his hands in his pockets. He stared at the Presidential Seal in the carpet before he looked at Brad. "We risk escalating an already tense situation, but it has to be done. This is not a time for détente. Power has to meet power. Give the order, Brad. Raise the subs."

Brad stood, followed by Abbie and Donald. "Yes, sir, Mr. President."

"Donald, contact State and tell them to keep the lines of communication with Beijing open. After the subs are raised and the gauntlet is thrown, I need to have a real frank discussion this afternoon with President Xi Jinping."

"You've got it, Sarge," said Donald.

"Now, I've got some unfinished business with another bully." With that, Sarge adjusted his tie and strode out of the Oval Office on a mission.

CHAPTER 79

2:30 p.m.
The Solarium
The White House
Washington, DC

Sarge entered the Solarium with confidence but encountered a room full of quiet, sour looks. The brandy snifters were empty and the cigars had been extinguished. The executive council of the Boston Brahmin were ready to get to the point, and so was Sarge. If he could stare down a Chinese invasion, he could abandon détente with this bunch as well.

Not unexpectedly, it was Gardner who stood and addressed Sarge as he entered. "We've been waiting for some time. There is an additional matter that needs to be discussed."

"Take a seat, Gardner," said Sarge sternly. "Actually, there are two matters. So please sit down. This won't take long, and then we can join the others downstairs."

Sarge sat first, but Gardner hesitated. He looked around the room until he faced Walter Cabot, who provided him a slight, imperceptible nod. Gardner dropped onto the edge of the couch across from Sarge.

"Let me address the matter of the Pacific Statehood Act first," began Sarge. "We've discussed the matter at length, both as a group years ago, and on an individual basis as my time allowed. We all reached an agreement prior to my re-election that returning the four states to the Union was a priority, but it was to be done without condition."

"Henry," started Cabot in New England dialect, "we're at the eleventh hour of your presidency. While I don't lay the blame completely on you for not accomplishing this goal sooner, we're at a point that the states must be readmitted. Frankly, and I think I speak for the group here, we're less concerned about these conditions than you are. The nation has evolved socially, and perhaps Washington should be forced to address these issues head-on."

"Besides," interrupted Gardner, "this is about economics, pure and simple. Our ability to control our business ventures through governmental contacts is greatly diminished when a state as big as California is excluded from the equation. The other three states are tagging along for the ride. The big prize is California."

"I don't disagree with either of you, but I stand firm in my belief that inviting the states back into the Union under these conditions is tantamount to blackmail," Sarge said, defending his position.

Cabot continued. "Henry, I'm sorry it didn't work out like you planned, but Congress has spoken through its passage of the bill. It's time for us to put the matter behind us and get back to our business as usual."

Sarge considered whether it was time to confront the issue head-on or use subterfuge to achieve his goal. He recalled the many conversations between himself and John Morgan during those days of isolation at Prescott Peninsula. The two were inseparable as Morgan mentored his godson in the art of wielding power and wealth. During those conversations, Sarge tried to maintain his own identity, refusing to believe that he could become his mentor.

But then, he never thought he could become his brother either, yet he did. On a day when he should've been celebrating the birth of Win and his inauguration as president, he channeled Steven when he shot a traitorous son of a bitch between the eyes in the basement of John Morgan's home. For years, he challenged himself to confront who he'd become in that moment, but each time he pushed it into the back of his mind.

As time passed, Sarge modified the popular bumper sticker to read in his mind, *what would John Morgan do?* His answer was not always consistent, as he was restrained by the magnifying glass that hovered over the presidency. However, in his dealings on behalf of the Boston Brahmin, of which he'd been the leader for eight years, he was more John Morgan than he was Henry Sargent. At least—not yet, anyway—he hadn't channeled his brother again.

He allowed the conversation to shift to discuss the future and business as usual, as Cabot termed their puppet-master activities across the globe. If they weren't going to press him for an answer on signing or vetoing the Pacific Statehood Act, then he wasn't obligated to tell them his plans. It was a mistake lawyers often make in trial practice. If you don't ask the question, the witness doesn't have to answer. A good lawyer should never presume the jury knows the answer.

"Yes, let's talk about our business together," started Sarge as he deflected. "Earlier, I outlined my agenda for the last two months of my presidency. The actions I'll be taking will benefit all of us greatly and for many years to come. Beyond my departure from office, I will continue my position as head of the executive council, fulfilling the wishes of John Morgan, whom all of you trusted with your life."

"We did," added Cabot. "John was a good man and his decision making always proved to be on the money, pardon the pun."

The room managed a laugh to ease the tension, except for Gardner. Sarge surmised this was not going as planned for him. He was going to like the next step even less.

"Let me state something that those of you who survived at Prescott Peninsula understand," continued Sarge. "It's most likely you are alive because of my efforts and those within my team like Mr. Endicott's nephew, Brad; Art Peabody's niece, Julia; John Morgan's daughter, Abbie: and myself. We're the ones who made the arrangements to provide all of you, or your families, food, medical care, and safety when the nation collapsed around us."

"Yes, Henry, and we're all grateful to you and the others," said Cabot.

Sarge pressed on. "John Morgan trusted me with that task, and after his stroke, he emphatically supported me to lead the executive council. Over these eight years, I've earned your support and trust."

"Absolutely, Sarge," said Art Peabody, who looked to others in the room for affirmation.

Sarge looked directly at Gardner. "Unfortunately, there are some among us who think they know a better way. A leader always has his detractors, I understand that. But in an organization such as ours, dissent can cause irreparable damage to our businesses and families. A politician may have to resign or lose an election. In our world, mistakes result in jail time and even deaths."

"That's a little overdramatic, don't you think?" asked Gardner.

Sarge shot back and made a point to the others at the same time. "Gardner, you are the newest member to the executive council and, as such, you're not experienced in the machinations of the Boston Brahmin and the strategies I employ. Know this, however. We have to be careful and work as a unit to avoid scrutiny. The shadows are our friend, and any attempt to work outside the group can result in daylight illuminating our activities."

"I understand that," bristled Gardner. "What's your point?"

Sarge had to hold back. Knowledge is power and he didn't want to expose Gardner to the others—yet.

"The point is none of us can enjoy the luxury of operating outside the group—going rogue, if you will. This group has been established to discuss our goals, but I've been charged with the responsibility of achieving them. Thus far, I've not failed any of you."

"I agree, Henry," said Cabot as he provided Sarge a thumbs-up. Cabot was coming around. Sarge could feel the hostility easing and the tide of support moving in his favor. He'd also effectively shined the light of discontent on one person, Gardner Lowell.

Sarge stood, adjusted his suit, and addressed the group. "Today, I'm seeking a vote of confidence from you. I will stand here as each of you simply votes yea or nay. If the nays have it, I will leave the room proud of my accomplishments and supportive of whomever you choose. If the yeas are the majority, then I want you to know I will diligently carry on the duties hoisted upon my shoulders by John Morgan during those dark days at Prescott Peninsula."

Walter Cabot stood and walked next to Sarge's side. "I've known this young man all his life. His father, John, and I were good friends. Henry has done nothing to lose my confidence or, more importantly, my trust. Therefore, I vote a resounding yea!"

One by one, the other members of the Boston Brahmin executive council rose and voiced their support for Sarge by saying yea. Finally, the last to rise, Gardner Lowell glared at Sarge but nodded his capitulation.

"Yea," was all Gardner could muster.

As Cabot and Peabody patted Sarge on the back, he thanked the group.

"Thank you all. There's still a lot of work to be done and I'm proud to have your support. If you will, please join me downstairs, as I have an important announcement to make to everyone regarding a matter of national security."

The Boston Brahmin filed out of the room and heartily shook Sarge's hand as they left. Gardner hung back, intentionally being the last to depart.

The room was empty when Gardner walked up to Sarge. He didn't offer his hand to shake. That suited Sarge just fine.

"I know what you did," Sarge leaned in to whisper as he looked his new nemesis in the eye.

"This is not over," Gardner growled in response.

"It is for today."

Gardner pushed past Sarge, who waited in the Solarium for a moment to gather his thoughts. He realized that he'd just made a powerful enemy who'd proven he didn't play by the rules, including the unwritten one established by the Boston Brahmin over the last two-and-a-half centuries. Sarge would have to become John Morgan, and his brother, if he was going to fight this adversary.

CHAPTER 80

3:00 p.m.
White House Blue Room
The White House
Washington, DC

Sarge was the last to arrive in the Blue Room. He was surprised to see Brad there as well. The two walked directly toward each other.

"Brad, that took a little longer than expected," Sarge said as he looked for Julia. She was in the corner with the children, Donald and Susan.

"That's fine. The timing couldn't be better."

"Well?"

Brad's smile was bigger than the look on his face when the United Nations had pulled out of Boston Harbor. "Mr. President, they're standing down. The Chinese have withdrawn their amphibs from the beach, and their jets are no longer patrolling their side of the Taiwan Straits."

Sarge and Brad immediately shared a bro-hug and spontaneous laughter, which immediately drew the attention of everyone in the room.

Sarge looked toward Julia, who was smiling, as was Donald, who raised a glass of champagne as a toast.

"Everyone, I'm sorry for my disappearance this afternoon, but there have been several important matters that pulled me away."

"We understand, Mr. President," said Stella Peabody.

"Absolutely, don't worry about it," added another.

Sarge motioned for Donald and Abbie to join his side. Sarge shook Donald's hand and hugged Abbie. The two of them stood with Brad as Sarge continued.

"As many of you know from this morning's news reports, our ambassador to China, James McBride, had gone missing following a signing ceremony in Taipei, Taiwan. What the news did not report was that we believe he'd been kidnapped by operatives loosely associated with the Chinese government."

The members of the Boston Brahmin and their families were shocked at this revelation and began to talk among themselves.

"Has something happened to him?" asked Art Peabody.

"He's safe thanks to the heroic efforts of our team on the ground in Taipei," replied Sarge, who purposefully made no reference to Drew. He was an asset that would remain hidden from all the Boston Brahmin, especially Gardner. "There's more."

Sarge nodded to Brad, who stepped forward. "The Chinese were mounting an offensive to invade Taiwan. The recent unrest and loss of electrical power were the first stages of a campaign to destabilize Taiwan before the People's Liberation Army crushed the Taipei government."

"This is the first we've heard of this," said Endicott, Brad's uncle.

"Yes, sir," Brad continued. "The PLA had amassed several hundred amphibious assault vehicles on the coast, with nearly one hundred thousand troops. Their next step was to launch missile strikes at key military installations and strafe the Taiwanese Navy with an air assault."

"Brad, how did you repel the attack?" asked his uncle, the former military strategist and general.

"Frankly, sir, it was the shrewd instinct of our president that prevented a war," replied Brad. He patted Sarge on the shoulder as he spoke. "This man saw the demonstrations and cyber attack that disrupted the power in Taiwan as a precursor to the invasion. He had the forethought to reposition our two aircraft carrier strike groups to flank Taiwan to the north and south. But the coup de grâce in the Chinese plans was the deployment of two Virginia-class submarines to a position between Taiwan and China. Upon Sarge's orders, the Virginia subs surfaced and stared down the ChiComms."

"Did they stand down?" asked Endicott.

"They stood down," replied Brad. "Our Commander-in-Chief boldly stood up to the Chinese and the crisis has been averted."

The room erupted in applause. Everyone shouted congratulations to Sarge and his team of Donald, Abbie, and Brad. Julia and the kids joined his side.

Sarge had a remarkable life. Professionally, the joy of teaching had provided him those moments of pride when his lectures made a difference in a young person's life. Marrying Julia and the birth of their children were personal moments that he would never forget. Naturally, winning the presidency twice was an incredible accomplishment. Today, however, he realized his decisions might have saved millions of lives in Taiwan as well as one ambassador, who was simply doing his duty for his country.

You're free to make your own decisions, but you're not free from the consequences of those decisions. Sarge owned the choices he'd made in his life, both good and bad. Those are the traits of a real man.

CHAPTER 81

8:00 p.m.
The Oval Office
The White House
Washington, DC

The media reports regarding Taiwan and the recovery of the ambassador dominated the rest of that Thanksgiving Day. Once the crisis had been diffused, Donald instructed the White House communications team to coordinate with their counterparts at the Pentagon to begin releasing information on the standoff with China to friendly news reporters.

Sarge wanted the world to know what China had planned for Taiwan so that it might act as a deterrent for years to come. In addition, his plan to pocket veto the Pacific Statehood Act required the attention of the twenty-four-seven news cycle to be directed elsewhere. After this evening's address to the nation, cable news outlets would focus on the Taiwan crisis and the world's response for many days. By Cyber Monday, the news would focus on retail sales and the strength of the economy. For the purposes of this evening's address, Sarge wanted to remind the nation he was committed to reunification, but not if it meant capitulation to the demands of these few states. In the end, he'd support what was best for the country.

He received a final touch-up of powder to his forehead, which tended to show sweat under the hot lights brought in for the camera. Sarge glanced to photos of Julia and the children for support as he waited for the countdown.

Three—two—one.

"My fellow Americans, this is the twenty-sixth time I'll speak to you from the Oval Office and most likely the last. We've been together through seven-plus years, and soon it'll be time for me to go. Before I do, I wanted to share some thoughts with you, some of which I've been saving for a long time, and others which were prompted by the week's events.

"It's been the honor of a lifetime to serve as your president. Many of you have written the past few weeks to say thanks, but I'm the one who should be thanking you for the opportunity to lead this country back from the darkest time in its history and on the road to recovery. Julia and I are so very grateful for the opportunity you've given us to serve this great nation.

"You know, one of the unfortunate aspects of the presidency is that you're always somewhat separated from the people you serve. As president, I spend a lot of time within the White House, and on precious few occasions, I'm able to travel across these great United States to talk with you and hear your concerns. Too often, I quickly move from point to point in a car driven by someone else, looking at all of you through tinted glass.

"I want you to know, I see parents holding up their children, who are waving a small flag. I read the handmade signs that read God Bless America. Every time I wave back, but by then I'm gone. You have no idea how many times I wanted to stop and jump out of the car to shake your hands or hug your child. Tonight, I hope to do a little of that from the Oval Office.

"The White House is where I work. The White House has served as the backdrop to the trying times we've endured as a nation, but also for the tough decisions that often characterize a presidency.

"But it's also our home, where Julia and I live with our three beautiful children. Win, who was born on my first inauguration day, is now seven and a half. My darling daughter, Rose, who was actually born here in the White House, is now five going on twenty. And our youngest, Francis, or Frank, is in the *throes of the terrible threes*, a phrase the First Lady hates for me to use.

"At night, when I get to tuck in our children and read them a story, I imagine myself doing the same for your children. When our son Win comes up to me and states something profound that he learned in school that day, I visualize you sitting down with your sons and daughters to hear about their activities.

"Like you, when a crisis arises in the world, or within our country, I fear for my child's safety just as I fear for yours. As president, my number one job is to protect the American people from harm, both within and without our borders. Unfortunately, there is evil in the world that manifests itself in individual, heinous acts of terror as well as in larger nations that impose their will on its smaller, weaker neighbors.

"Over the last several days, a threat revealed itself in a faraway part of the world, which may not have impacted your lives directly, but would've resulted in the deaths of countless thousands of human beings. I am pleased to report tonight the threat has been thwarted.

"The nature of relationships between nations has changed over the years. The defense of America and its citizens adapted to this change. As president, I rely heavily upon two groups. First, there are the intelligence analysts who study the activities of nations who some might call bullies. These exceptional, unsung heroes uncover and interpret the threats to America or other nations that we have pledged to protect.

"Then there are the men and women of our armed forces who are tasked with eliminating these threats. They are the real heroes in my mind. Their job is far more difficult and risky than anything I've faced.

"Make no mistake, our flag doesn't fly because the wind moves it. It flies with the last breath of each American soldier who dies protecting it. We don't enjoy our freedoms in America just because they're written in the Constitution. We are a free people because there are men and women of our military risking their lives to preserve those freedoms.

"Tonight, our ambassador to China is alive and the people of Taiwan can sleep peacefully because the brave men and women of our military stood up against a bully who was prepared to overrun the much smaller nation.

"When I took office, our nation was vulnerable to attack. We were at the weakest condition in our nation's history. Common sense told us that in addition to recovering economically, we had to become strong again to defend ourselves. We once again became the world's great superpower, which required us to step up to protect nations unable to protect themselves. Today, we kept our promise to Taiwan and sent a clear message to the world that tyranny will not be tolerated."

Sarge paused as he looked into the camera. He leaned forward to address the issue of Pacific statehood.

"I've been asked if I have any regrets from my years in office. Well, I do have one. I regret that I was not able to bring California, Hawaii, Oregon, and Washington back into the Union without political rancor and posturing getting in the way.

"I must admit I was proud of the American people for coming together the way we did following the collapse of our power grid. There was a period of time prior to my presidency when bad decisions were made regarding the rebuilding effort. I believe we set the nation on the course to regaining her former greatness and creating a climate of prosperity for all Americans.

"That said, there was still the issue of the four states who elected to abandon the United States and chart their own course. I objected to their decision at the time, and as president, I've tried to restore the Union to where it was before they left us.

"I wrote a book while I was still a professor at Harvard titled *Choose Freedom or Capitulation—America's Sovereignty Crisis.* The United States, as a sovereign nation, has the authority to govern itself. Therefore, it should not have to capitulate to the will of other nations being imposed upon it.

"Prior to the collapse, for example, the United Nations, an entity which seemed morally and ethically worthy on its face, used every opportunity to inflict its world view upon America. After the collapse, the UN occupying force intended to force its will upon our citizens, and we stood up against them. At the first opportunity, I withdrew the United States from the UN, a decision that was criticized around the world by some, but praised by those who counted the most—the American people. As I explained when the decision was made, America will never capitulate to the demands of others while on my watch.

"Well, the same thing applies with respect to bringing the four states back into the Union. I had to remind their political leaders of one simple fact—you left us. In our time of need, a time when America needed to come together as a nation, these four states struck out on their own.

"Now, like most of you, I was willing to forgive and forget for the sake of the nation and reunite these four to once again create fifty United States. However, our nation should not have to capitulate to the demands of these four states and adopt laws that are not consistent with the nation's as a whole. California, Oregon, Hawaii, and Washington are welcome to return, but we should not agree to any reunification that forces the nation to compromise its principles.

"This week Congress has acted on a bill allowing the states to return with all of their demands intact. This bill flies in the face of my stated goals and principles, which are consistent with the majority of the citizens in America. This bill will be presented to me for my signature next week, at which time I will have to make one of those difficult decisions I alluded to before. With prayer and input from all of you, we'll make it together.

"Many important decisions in any family, or a nation, for that matter, happen at the dinner table. Tomorrow night, I hope the talking begins between you and your families. Discuss what it means to be an American. Talk about freedom. Tonight, on this Thanksgiving, consider what the Pilgrims sought when they arrived in America on those wooden boats, looking for a home where they would be free.

"Consider the words of an early Pilgrim, John Winthrop, one of my ancestors, when he described America as a *shining city upon a hill.* President Ronald Reagan spoke of the shining city during his political life as an America built on solid rocks stronger than oceans, blessed by God and full of people living in peace and prosperity. That's how he saw it, and that's how I see our country as well.

"I'm proud to say I've done my part to restore our nation to her former greatness. When I leave the White House in January, I look forward to walking the streets of Boston and meeting as many of you as I can. And to each of you, as we reflect on the incredible accomplishments we achieved together over the last eight years, I'll say *my friends, we did it together. We made our shining city stronger, freer, and with hope for the future.*

"My friends, God bless you, always choose freedom, and God bless the United States of America."

CHAPTER 82

9:15 p.m.
The Executive Residence
The White House
Washington, DC

It was quiet when Sarge entered the Executive Residence. He'd already removed his jacket and loosened his tie. This Thanksgiving Day had been a long, stress-filled one. Before bed, Sarge always made it a point to reflect on three positive things that happened in his day. It helped him block out any negativity that might have followed him up the blue-carpeted stairs that marked the transition from working as President of the United States to Sarge, loving husband of Julia and adoring father of three. Saving the ambassador and standing up to China, thus preserving Taiwan's sovereignty and maintaining his position with the Boston Brahmin, made for a pretty good day in his book.

Julia emerged from Rose's bedroom and gently pulled the door shut. She approached him with a smile and hugged him tight. "Incredible speech, babe. I'm proud of you."

"Thanks, I didn't write it."

"Who did?"

"Nobody. I just spoke from the heart."

Julia took his jacket and pulled his tie off. "How about a drink?"

"Nah, I wanna look in on the kids. Who's still awake?"

Julia laughed as she tossed his jacket on a chair. "Are you kidding? They're all zonked out, even Win. He fell asleep right after your speech when the talking heads were explaining to all of us what you just said."

"Yeah," said Sarge with a chuckle. "I never quite understood that. I try my best to use proper grammar and words in most people's vocabulary. Why does the media feel compelled to take my simple statements and explain to the American people what they think I said? It's beyond me."

"Well, it's almost over," said Julia as she took him by the hand. "I've got a crazy idea. The world seems safe for the moment. Most of the White House staff has scampered off for some form of Thanksgiving festivities. Even the Boston Brahmin have departed the premises. Why don't you and I crawl into bed and talk."

"Talk?" asked Sarge, feigning apprehension. "Talk about what?"

"You know, talk about stuff," replied Julia with a smile as she tugged him toward the Executive Bedroom.

She provided her husband a schoolgirl giggle as she pulled his arm toward the room. Sarge pulled her back to him.

"Okay, okay, Mrs. Sargent, hang on. Come with me to look in on the kids first. Then we'll have your talk."

Sarge and Julia quietly checked in on their sleeping babes, giving each a kiss on the forehead before heading to the bedroom. Probably the greatest accomplishment of his presidency on a personal level was creating this beautiful family with Julia while being on display for the world to see. Their children were a testament to their achievements as parents.

Once in the bedroom, Sarge plopped on the ottoman at the foot of the bed and began to remove his shoes. Julia rubbed his shoulders as he spoke.

"By the way, how have things been going with the historian and his photographer?" asked Sarge. "I've barely seen them this week."

Julia laughed. "They've been spending a lot of time in the East Wing."

"Why?"

"I think it was part of Betty's plan to keep them out of your hair," she replied as she playfully mussed Sarge's.

"He asked me a question that I'm sure I'll get a lot in the next several weeks."

"Let me guess," started Julia. "He's asked me the same one several different ways to see if I'd respond differently, I guess."

"Yeah. If given the opportunity, would you do it again?"

Julia laughed as she slipped out of her clothes and into her robe. "That's the one."

Sarge pulled on his Harvard sweatpants and joined Julia at the side of the bed. "How did you answer it?"

She was quick to reply, "I finally said, jokingly, of course, *what is it about no that you don't understand?*"

Sarge let out a hearty laugh. "That's my girl. Here's the thing. Eight years ago, I was very idealistic about the opportunity the collapse afforded us. While I didn't agree with my godfather's methods, the reset allowed us a much-needed do-over."

Julia added, "We were all certain that Americans would set aside their petty differences and come together just as the colonists did in the beginning."

Sarge sighed. "Americans did after we showed them the way, but I'm afraid I see signs of the country slipping into that old way of thinking."

The two sat silently at the edge of the bed, holding hands. They were both quiet, contemplating how the presidency had changed their lives.

"We've done great things, Julia. I feel like we're turning over the reins with America in a better place than it was before the collapse."

"I agree. So how did you answer the biographer's question?"

Sarge chuckled and kissed his wife on the cheek before whispering his response.

"It was simple. I said I wouldn't wish this job on anybody, including myself."

THANK YOU FOR READING PATRIOT'S FAREWELL!

If you enjoyed it, I'd be grateful if you'd take a moment to write a short review (just a few words are needed) and post it on Amazon. Amazon uses complicated algorithms to determine what books are recommended to readers. Sales are, of course, a factor, but so are the quantities of reviews my books get. By taking a few seconds to leave a review, you help me out, and also help new readers learn about my work.

And before you go…

SIGN UP for Bobby Akart's mailing list to receive special offers, bonus content, and you'll be the first to receive news about new releases in the Doomsday series:

eepurl.com/bYqq3L

VISIT Amazon.com/BobbyAkart for more information on his next project, as well as his completed words: the Doomsday series, the Yellowstone series, the Lone Star series, the Pandemic series, the Blackout series, the Boston Brahmin series and the Prepping for Tomorrow series totaling nearly forty novels, including over thirty Amazon #1 Bestsellers in forty-plus fiction and nonfiction genres.

Visit Bobby Akart's website for informative blog entries on preparedness, writing, and a behind-the-scenes look into his novels.

BobbyAkart.com

READ ON FOR A BONUS EXCERPT from

DOOMSDAY: APOCALYPSE

Book One in The DOOMSDAY Series.

Free Bonus Chapters from *DOOMSDAY: APOCALYPSE*

PROLOGUE

Monocacy Farm
South of Frederick, Maryland
October 31

Any two of them rarely met in person, and only on one other occasion had they congregated as a group. Their backgrounds and ideologies were as diverse as the country in which they lived. Matters of race, gender, religion, and culture were irrelevant. Commonality of purpose was tantamount in their minds.

If the meeting were known to the public, one day it would be deemed historic. The gathering, located at a hundred-acre farm twenty miles south of Frederick, Maryland, was not called hastily. Hushed conversations and encrypted messages, starting several months earlier, preceded the clandestine meeting.

As fall set upon the Northeastern United States and the first Tuesday in November rapidly approached, the men and women began to feel a sense of urgency. The whispers grew louder—*a meeting must be convened posthaste.* October 31 was agreed upon.

The location sitting on the banks of the Monocacy River was a given, especially in light of its historic significance. One by one, they arrived at the mansion, a beautiful antebellum structure that had been in their host's family for generations dating back to its construction in the early nineteenth century. Sitting nearly a mile off the road, the stately home and adjacent barns were enveloped with sugar maple trees, whose leaves had mostly changed to golden yellow and brown. Interspersed around the property to maintain its privacy were enormous eastern hemlocks that managed to avoid a plague caused by the infestation of the hemlock woolly aphid, a blight upon the beautiful tree, which resulted in its slow deterioration and death.

The heir to the farm, who concealed his ownership through a blind trust, stood on the front porch despite the cool autumn air, and greeted his guests one by one. Although it was not intended to be a festive occasion, the attendees took the rare opportunity to socialize with their comrades by enjoying hors d'oeuvres and cocktails.

The staff who waited upon them were well trained and sworn to secrecy by more than a nondisclosure agreement that had become a worthless legal document in this day and age. No, they feared for their lives, for they presumed the tentacles of their powerful employer reached far and wide.

For the next several hours until midnight approached, they commiserated and debated. A consensus was reached, and then arguments began about things like moral high ground and sacrifice.

A plan was set forth to advance their goals, and countermeasures were adopted in anticipation of their enemies' reaction. All of them envisioned a high-stakes game of chess that history would prove to be unparalleled in the modern age of geopolitical stratagems and tactics.

As the evening drew to a conclusion, their host proposed a toast.

"I was once confronted by a man of great political power who stood in my face and said, 'You're not strong enough to withstand the storm.' Today, my friends, drawing from our collective strength and love of country, we have taken our stand. I would say to those who will condemn our actions—*we are the storm!*"

"Hear, hear!"

The group raised their glasses and drained them. Then their acknowledged leader stepped forward into the spacious living room that had hosted gala affairs and events over the centuries. He positioned himself in front of a massive stone fireplace containing a blaze that shot flames well up the chimney flue.

Before he spoke, he glanced up at the emblem carved out of granite that was inset into the stone. The skull and crossbones were fitting for their Halloween gathering. The numbers three-two-two carved beneath, were shrouded in mystery just as those who attended on this cold evening.

He slowly turned and looked around the room. "Messenger, are you ready?"

"I am," replied a younger, bespectacled man, who apologetically pushed his way through the group.

Their host addressed him authoritatively. "Read it before it's disseminated to your usual platforms."

The Messenger already had the screen open on the secured, data-encrypted application designed by him for this specific purpose. As the Messenger, he was responsible for communicating with other like-minded individuals around the world. He pressed the enter button, and the message was sent.

Their demeanor solemn, the guests quietly exited and returned to their homes and families, the weight of their decision hanging over them. Their host allowed himself another drink and poured two fingers of Glenlivet single malt scotch whisky into a glass. He dismissed the staff and walked out on the veranda overlooking the Monocacy River to be alone with his thoughts.

He gazed up at the full moon, that had taken on a somewhat bluish tint, befitting its significance. Historically, the first full moon of autumn, known as the harvest moon, allowed farmers extra time in their fields to bring in their crops. That had occurred earlier in the month of October.

On this Halloween night, this second full moon of the month, much to the consternation of soothsayers and zealots, represented the proverbial blue moon, the second full moon in a calendar month, which rarely occurred. The unusual astronomical event was coupled with the second moon of that October being designated the hunter's moon, so named as the next full moon following the harvest moon. The confluence of the three designations in the same month caused the cable news media outlets to take notice.

Throughout the month of October, psychics, clairvoyants, and prophecy pundits filled the airwaves. The media countered with scientists and historians, who roundly mocked the prognosticators as crackpots. Even so, many said the rare occurrence of the harvest, hunter's and blue moons occurring in the same month portended doom and that the apocalypse was upon us all.

They were right.

As if to confirm that the evening's events were real, he pulled out his phone and read the message appearing on the screen.

On the day of the feast of Saint Sylvester,
Tear down locked,
Green light burning.
Love, MM

And so it begins …

New Year's Eve

CHAPTER 1

One World Trade Center
New York City

It was cold in Manhattan as darkness overtook the city on New Year's Eve. A light snow had just begun to fall on the concrete jungle, which spread out one hundred four stories below them. The rebuilt One World Trade Center boasted the tallest building in the western hemisphere and the sixth tallest on the planet. It was America's way of giving the middle finger to the terrorists who had attacked the nation on 9/11. On this evening, a terror of a different nature was going to be unleashed on the world's superpower. One that would lead to an upheaval not seen in more than a century.

The SkyPod elevators carried them one hundred two stories to the One World Observatory in just forty-seven seconds. It was a remarkable ride to the top of the building that transformed the landscape with a herculean endeavor. Also known as Freedom Tower, the new World Trade Center stood proud at the heart of a forest of skyscrapers dotting the center of the world's financial markets.

The view from the observatory was nothing short of spectacular. As the snow fluttered from the blue-black winter sky, the visitors to the One World Observatory didn't seem to mind their view being obscured slightly. Many pressed their faces as close to the glass as they could, longing to reach out and touch the frozen snowflakes as they fluttered past.

The excitement of New Year's Eve added to the jovial mood of the visitors. This was the legendary city in which the ball drops in Times Square, to the delight of millions in attendance and many millions more watching around the world. On New Year's Eve, New York was more than a place of power for the world's financial elite, it was a preeminent city against which all others were measured.

Admired by most, envied and despised by others for what it represents, the Big Apple was more than a collection of tall buildings and financial brokerage houses. It was a cosmopolitan gathering of cultures, races, and ideologies—constantly in motion.

New York City was alive as people made their way to elaborate dinners or to find a place in New York's Times Square, four miles from the World Trade Center, in Midtown. From the observation deck, visitors could feel the surging energy throughout the island. Multitudes of office towers and apartment buildings were lit up as parties were in full swing, or revelers were readying themselves for the big night.

Many of the visitors focused on the beautiful panoramic views. They looked intently through the telescopes located around the perimeter of the observation deck. Their focus was on what was happening outside and not the two men who leaned quietly against a wall on the inside.

A gaunt-faced man in his fifties wore a black woolen trench coat with the collar turned up around his neck. His old, wire-rimmed spectacles contained lenses that made his eyes look larger than life. His flat cap hat resembled those worn by newsboys in the 1940s, those young street-corner newspaper sellers who helped their families make ends meet during World War II. The man was a throwback to the last century in more ways than one.

His associate, a much younger man built like the Incredible Hulk, was more out of place than the older man. Unlike his partner and the majority of the visitors, he wore khaki pants and a short-sleeve, black polo shirt. His chest and arms bulged, threatening to tear the shirt apart at the seams. The skull and bones tattoo on his right bicep seemed to come alive as his muscles flexed. The number 322 underneath fluttered like a flag atop a ship's mast.

The older man made casual conversation, not attempting to hide his native Irish accent. "I watched them tear it down, only to build it back up again, stronger and more powerful than before."

"Yeah," the young man replied. To the casual observer who might be eavesdropping on the conversation, his method of speaking didn't fit his stereotype. He didn't grunt his words or puff out his chest. His words were carefully chosen and articulate, befitting his Yale education. "It's a testament to American ingenuity and perseverance. When the new design was revealed, the architects proudly stated the structure would top off at one thousand seven hundred seventy-six feet—1776. Ironic, wouldn't you agree?"

"It is," replied the older man, pausing as a strong gust of snow enveloped the windows, to the delight of the tower's visitors. He removed a gloved hand from his coat and waved it toward the windows. "I assume you've checked the weather for this precipitation. Will it alter your plans?"

"The moisture is heading our way from the south, while the jet stream is pulling down cold air from Canada. There's already snow predicted from Washington to Philly to Boston for this evening. We'll get our share, but it doesn't materially impact our operation. The wind is a factor, but we've made the necessary adjustments in our calculations."

"Good." The man, who'd made a career out of killing, allowed himself a slight smile. He enjoyed the exhilaration of battle. As a young warrior, the dangers associated with combat never frightened him. He'd never admitted to anyone that war aroused him more than any woman had. The closer he got to taking another's life, the more enthralled he became.

In just a few hours, he would launch the biggest and most complex attack on the United States of America since 9/11, or even Pearl Harbor. It would not necessarily be the most violent, but it would certainly be the most memorable in American history, ranking alongside the *shot heard around the world* at Lexington and Concord, or the firing of cannon upon Fort Sumter in South Carolina.

A young boy interrupted his thoughts as he walked by with his mother. He pulled on her sweater sleeve and looked up to her. "Mom, is a storm coming?"

The older man managed a chuckle as he mumbled to himself, "It sure is, young man. A storm is coming."

CHAPTER 2

The Florida Panhandle

The incessant ringing of the phone had awakened him from a deep sleep that New Year's Eve. He'd had a crazy night of partying and carousing with other members of his team, blowing off steam from an operation they'd just completed in Venezuela. The handlers who employed him had plans for the Caracas regime, which had driven a once-thriving economy into the ditch. After their successes, the people of Venezuela would have a new slate of candidates to choose from while they mourned the old set.

After he cleared the fog from his brain, he digested the orders he'd been given. On the surface it was a simple op. Two-man team, plus one man with advanced training in a specific weapon to be deployed. He recalled the conversation with his handler.

"I'm not going to repeat this for you, so pay attention. You're tasked with delivering the shooter from point A to point B. Nothing else. Once the mission is accomplished, you extract and leave no trace behind."

It had sounded simple enough, although a thousand questions swirled in the operator's head such as when, where, who, and how. He'd learned years ago the *why* didn't matter. Somebody smarter than he was made those decisions. Besides, it didn't matter. He just wanted to get paid.

He'd also learned to check his emotions and morals at the door. When you worked in the dark shadows of the world's geopolitical underbelly, everybody was a target. Nothing, and no one, was immune from their manipulation of world events.

The four-hour drive from Atlanta to a desolate farm located in Florida's Panhandle was uneventful. He tuned in to the Liberty Bowl game being played in Memphis between Tennessee and Oklahoma State. He'd become a fan of American football, although it didn't compare to his beloved soccer matches. It was the emotion of the fans that first grabbed his attention.

The Vols were trying to recover from years of substandard play, while Oklahoma State was just coming off a probation by the NCAA for introducing potential recruits to *hostesses*, as they were called. When the sex-filled parties leaked to the media, *Sports Illustrated* in particular, the Cowboys' football program was almost given the death penalty.

The operator had a real name, but few people knew it. His travel documents and government identification would change periodically, printed to suit the clandestine mission. There were only a handful of operatives like him stationed on American soil. They were ghosts, living a secretive life, and only interacted with one another.

He followed the coordinates given to him on his GPS device. He was located in the middle of the Apalachicola National Forest outside a small town called Carrabelle. Dusk was approaching as he drove down a single-lane gravel and dirt road through stands of pine trees mixed with saw palmettos.

He checked the GPS again to be sure, and then suddenly a clearing appeared in front of him. He was surprised to see an Airbus UH-72 Lakota helicopter sitting alone. The chopper had been painted black, a divergence from its typical olive drab. In the past, the UH-72 was a light-utility helicopter utilized by Army National Guard units. As the U.S. Army moved toward the Black Hawk fleet, the UH-72s were sold to state and local law enforcement for police activities. The complete lack of markings told him this was privately operated, most likely by one shell corporation that was owned by another and so on. That was the modus operandi in his world.

He parked his car and walked toward several vehicles and a box truck, where he was greeted by another member of his team whom he'd worked with in Venezuela.

"Long time no see, mate," his partner said with a smile. The two didn't shake hands, a slight to the customary greeting in America.

"We could've come from Atlanta together," the operator lamented.

"Nah, mate. I'd already left for Miami when the call came through. I've been here for hours."

A third man, small and unremarkable, was seated inside the helicopter. Joining him in the cargo compartment was a long black case, the kind that was designed to carry a MANPADS. Man-portable air-defense systems were shoulder-launched surface-to-air missiles designed specifically to take down helicopters and punch holes in the sides of ships. The operator had used them in the Balkans years ago and was impressed with their effectiveness.

He turned to the member of his team who had proven to be a consistent and reliable partner on their past missions together. "Any idea of where we're going?"

"Don't be a drongo, mate. They haven't said a word," he replied in his thick Australian accent. He pointed in the direction of two men dressed in black pants, dark jackets, and navy-blue shirts. If they had not been so mysterious in their appearance, they might have been laughable. "And the men in black over there have been real tight-lipped. You wanna give 'em a try?"

He nodded and replied, "Sure. Who's the guy in the chopper? Is he wearing a wet suit?"

"No idea. He's cool as the proverbial cucumber. I tried to make conversation with him. You know, like, *what's in the case?* I got nothing out of him. And yeah, he's in a wet suit."

"I hate this crap," the operator mumbled as he pulled his shoulders back, hoping to relieve some of the stress from the drive.

Two pilots emerged from behind the chopper, with their helmets attached as if they were ready to go. He gave the pilots the once-over and then looked past them to a group of four mechanics who emerged from the back of the box truck. They were carrying a Zodiac MilPro rigid inflatable boat. A fifth man carried two duffle bags with black combat vests and headed toward him.

One of the men in black approached. "Gentlemen, we'll need you to get out of your civvies and into the wet suits. The combat vests will be supplemented with weapons inside the chopper. They've been cleaned, checked, and are ready for you."

"Got it, but we like to check our own weapons before we go into an op."

"You'll have an hour while in flight." The handler turned to walk away.

"Wait, what's with the Zodiac?"

Without turning, the man responded, "It's going to be strapped under the chopper."

The operator paused as the men approached the helicopter with the inflatable. The military-spec boat measured approximately sixteen feet long and six feet wide. From his experience, with the fuel bladders and the outboard motor in place, the weight exceeded four hundred pounds. They slowly positioned the Zodiac behind the helicopter and spoke briefly with the pilot.

"Hey," the operator shouted to the handler, "I'm not riding outside the chopper. You can forget that!"

The handler ignored him and approached the helicopter to give instructions to his team. As he did, the operator and his partner changed into their gear. Within minutes, they were loaded into the chopper next to the third member of their squad and the mysterious case.

The pilot joined them and gave them more information on their task. While the operators reviewed the packet of materials, the pilot explained the transportation apparatus.

"Your Zodiac will be strapped to the skids of the chopper using these harnesses," he began, showing them the heavy-duty straps similar to those utilized on a flatbed trailer of an eighteen-wheeler. "When we reach the drop-off point, there is a single latch release that will be located in the center of this compartment. Then you'll all fast-rope into the boat." *Fast-roping* was a technique using a thick rope to rappel from a helicopter onto the ground or, in this case, into a boat.

The operator turned to the smallish man, who hovered over the large case like it was filled with gold. "What about speechless here? I take it he's coming with us. What's in the case?"

"It is none of your affair," he responded with a French accent.

"Whoa, he does talk!" the operator exclaimed. "And he's a Frenchy. This is a true international op. Now, you wanna tell me what the hell is going on?"

CHAPTER 3

Undisclosed Military Installation

Human nature hadn't changed since the time of Cain and Abel. The act of war, however, had. In the minds of the world's military powers, drone warfare was considered to be *proximate war*. The notion was related to the concept of *proximate justice*. Proximate justice theory posited that something was better than nothing. It allowed us to make peace with the realization that some justice meted out was better than none at all. It allowed a victim's family to accept a life sentence as opposed to the death penalty for their loved one's murder.

Proximate war allowed those who wanted to inflict true bodily harm and death upon their adversaries to find some satisfaction in a lesser, albeit subdued, victory. Drone warfare accomplished that purpose. Modern military leaders fashioned themselves to be moral warriors. After World War II, after the atomic bombs were dropped onto Nagasaki and Hiroshima in Japan, the world collectively gasped, then paused to view the end result.

To be sure, the attacks hastened the end of the massive global war, but the civilian death toll was enormous. In America, after the dust settled and the country resumed its routines, conversations began among its leaders as to whether the use of atomic weaponry was overkill, pardon the tone-death pun. Talks began with the U.S.S.R. and agreements were reached. The concept of *mutually assured destruction* was born.

Those accords did not, however, prevent the world's preeminent military powers, which now included China, to develop modern, advanced weaponry capable of annihilating one another. Further, with new technologies, weapons of mass destruction were created that didn't necessarily take lives upon detonation like the atomic bombs of 1945, but the human toll was catastrophic nonetheless.

The rampant nuclear testing of the 1950s opened scientists' eyes to a byproduct, for lack of a better term, that, if harnessed, could be a valuable weapon in battle. An electromagnetic pulse, or EMP, was a burst of electromagnetic energy that occurred naturally during intense geomagnetic storms from the sun. As the atomic testing showed, the same result could be generated by both a nuclear detonation or a nonnuclear EMP weapon using nuclear technology.

The highly charged gamma rays, a form of light generated by the EMP weapon, slammed into air molecules, displacing electrons. Upon impact, the negatively charged particles circulated through the atmosphere at nearly ninety percent of the speed of light. It only took a fraction of a microsecond for the targeted area to be filled with the surge of energy.

The higher the detonation occurred above the earth's surface, the broader the area of impact. A low-altitude EMP could be more targeted, specifically intended to impact a smaller area.

The electromagnetic pulse could have a variety of devastating effects depending upon the type of weapon used. Today's modern electronics and computer devices are made up of tiny circuits that cannot withstand the powerful burst of energy. The power grid, phone and internet lines, and anything interconnected to electronics melts under the abrupt pulse of energy.

The United States, China, and Russia led the way in developing EMP technology. Once the capability was realized, then different and varied delivery mechanisms were sought. A nuclear-tipped intercontinental ballistic missile was the first, most logical means of delivery.

In the past decade, great advances had been made that allowed EMPs to be deployed by satellite, via directed energy weapons similar to ray guns in popular culture, and now launched from underwater, submarine drones.

Russia, with its Kanyon project, led the way, quickly followed by the United States and China. Soon, all three nations sought to expand their underwater drone capabilities, controlled from remote destinations around the world that could launch nuclear missiles of all sizes and payloads.

With the advent of drone warfare, nation-states could wage wars in places far from their own borders, all designed toward securing an advantage in small-scale skirmishes and counterinsurgency fights abroad.

In the U.S., the Pentagon refers to it as drone warfare. In the U.K., military strategists call it remote warfare, which includes both drones and cyber attacks. This was considered the means to wage wars of the future. For military leaders, it was an opportunity to accomplish a strategic military objective with no loss of life to their troops. Further, it meant less public oversight and internal analysis as to whether the missions themselves were achieving their objectives. Nothing raises public scrutiny more than body bags arriving at Dover Air Force Base, especially if the mission was deemed a failure.

As a result of this lack of oversight, in the U.S. and abroad, only those with direct involvement and knowledge of the operations would report back to the people who ordered the mission. In essence, a feedback loop of secrecy could be created, detached from criticism and accountability. The lack of transparency made independent verification of a nation's actions near impossible.

Plausible deniability ruled the day in a proximate war using drones.

CHAPTER 4

CityCenter Apartments
Atlanta, Georgia

"All right, gentlemen, let's make one thing real clear about this op." The former captain in the British Office for Security and Counter-Terrorism looked into the eyes of his three comrades as they prepared their gear. "We get in, place and activate our respective devices, and get out. There'll be no radio contact, so we're on our own inside. If you're caught, you're on your own too. We've all learned that the words *plausible deniability* have meaning, correct?"

"Yeah, roger that," mumbled one of the two Americans on his team.

"Use the commotion and mayhem to make your exits when the time comes. Don't leave early, because you're sure to be caught on camera. The rally point will be at Cleopas Johnson Park to our south. Avoid walking down Northside Drive; use the neighborhood side streets instead. The feds will react quickly once the call is made to the stadium offices, and the place will be crawling once we implement the plan."

"Chief, we've never worked with our man on the inside. I don't like trusting a mission to an unknown quantity," commented the other American operative.

"Yeah, I hate surprises, too." The first man echoed his concern.

"Our inside man is rock solid. He's been employed here for a couple of years and is fully aware of the ramifications of the mission. Now, remember, we have a limited window of opportunity to be at the Magnum Street loading dock. Your uniforms and credentials are in these duffle bags. They're designed to fit easily over your existing clothing, so you can discard them once inside."

After opening his assigned duffle, the Australian member of the team spoke up for the first time. "Very official looking. They've got the Mercedes logo on the sleeves and maintenance stitched across the pocket."

The team leader nodded. "They're actual uniforms. Like your credentials, they'll give us the cover we need to get in. Once you're in position, drop the uniforms and mind your watches. We've got this perfectly choreographed, so don't lose track of time."

The team leader checked his own watch. They still had over an hour to make the short walk from the CityCenter Apartments on the west side of Mercedes-Benz Stadium to the loading dock. The men would walk in pairs as if they were co-workers reporting for duty at the concert.

He looked at his hardened operatives, who'd performed so well under pressure for him in all corners of the planet. "We've got plenty of time. Any questions?"

One of the Americans spoke up. "Yeah, chief, I've got one. Listen, I'm a country music guy, and I've got no use for Beyoncé or her husband, Jay-Z. So don't get me wrong, I'd take issue with us screwin' up a Kenny Chesney concert. Why do you think this is the target?"

The leader walked away and ran his fingers through his hair. He was only able to speculate, but based upon the text message instructions he'd received, and the source, he suspected he knew the reason.

"Listen, you guys know the drill. It's like your old Budweiser commercial—*why ask why?* Our employers pay us well. They give us the latest in high-tech gear. In fact, it's stuff Her Majesty's Armed Forces know nothing about."

One of the American men began to chuckle. "I bet the chi-comms know all about it. Those hackers have all of our secrets."

"Well, maybe so," the team leader continued. "Regardless, I wasn't provided a reason, and anything else is speculation on my part."

The American shrugged and appeared indifferent. "I'm just curious, that's all. Regardless of the motivation, it's gonna fit a pattern of concert attacks in recent years. They'll be chasing their tails, pointing the fingers of blame."

The Australian spoke up. "You're right on that, mate. They never figured out the reasoning behind the Mandalay Bar shooting in Vegas. The Rascal Flatts concert in Indy was evacuated due to an anonymous security threat."

The Brit added, "And in Manchester, the Ariana Grande concert suicide bomber was identified as a bloody Islamist. For our purposes, there will be no discernible reason for the attack, so it can't be tied to us or our employer."

The men sat in silence for a moment as they contemplated his words. Then one of the Americans asked, "And do you have any idea who our employer is on this job?"

"I do, and no, I won't tell you. Trust me, you don't want to know."

The men shrugged and went about their preparations. They studied a printed map of the arena and confirmed their assignments. After a final sweep of the apartment that had been rented for them a month earlier, they gathered any trace of their personal effects and made their way through the parking lot of the apartment complex, systematically dropping trash bags of clothing, leftover food, and the map of the stadium into the dumpsters. Despite it being the New Year's holiday, it was a Thursday night, and the waste management trucks would be through to empty the dumpsters around ten o'clock. Any trace evidence of their presence would be incinerated just before midnight, when the fun began.

CHAPTER 5

Undisclosed Residential Location

The messages were always cryptic. Coded in such a way that certain sets of eyes could understand them all, while others were more compartmentalized based upon their sphere of influence. Everyone had a job to do. Some required physicality and military training. Others simply used the powers afforded them by way of their position. And then some, like the lonely young man sitting in the dimly lit basement of his home and surrounded by computer monitors, used their expertise. The common thread between them all? A sense of duty and the ability to respond on a moment's notice.

The message was short, but its words had a profound meaning.

!!!mG4VJxZNCI 12/31 19:34:28
As the snow cascaded downward,
The wild rides halted immediately.
One instance among many more,
As we seek Justitia Omnibus.
Fare thee well.
MM

He set his phone aside with the message on the 4chan chat board still in plain view. He reached to his side to pull open the desk drawer. At first, he hesitated, not sure if he was ready to fulfill his handler's wishes. He'd been paid well and given everything he needed.

But he'd contemplated his exit strategy on many occasions. He'd begun to stockpile supplies and cash. He had a vehicle that would go anywhere, under any circumstances. Although he was not an outdoorsman, he'd studied how to survive in the woods.

Not on these computers, of course. He was sure he was watched. His keystrokes monitored. Prying eyes were everywhere, and not just through camera lenses. His handlers were capable of anything.

The small black book had been given to him after he'd proven his loyalty. To be sure, he was once a rising star within the ranks at INSCOM, the United States Army Intelligence and Security Command garrisoned at Fort Belvoir, Virginia.

He had come out of high school as a broken teen. Constantly bullied as a nerd, and due to his being undersized compared to his classmates, the seventeen-year-old was not ready for adulthood. He worked on the Geek Squad at Best Buy for a while, but his real passion was not repairing computers. He preferred hacking them instead.

Just to be clear, he never engaged in criminal enterprise, at least not in his mind. Yes, he was guilty of accessing unsuspecting coeds' wireless cams on their laptops and watching them from time to time. Later, he decided to try his hand at cyber intrusions upon small businesses' computer networks. He was more of a gremlin than a full-blown hacker up to nefarious activities.

None of this paid the bills, however, and he soon became bored. With little going for him, he walked into the Army Recruiting Office in Tampa, Florida, and enlisted. It was a decision that changed his life.

He entered basic training and found himself overwhelmed by the rigors of the Army. In need of warm bodies due to attrition in recent years, the Army kept him in the program. One fateful day, he was having a conversation with another following their successful completion of the third and final field-training exercise known as the Forge, when he brought up his computer acumen as it related to hacking.

A senior drill sergeant pulled him aside and began to quiz him about his statements and expertise. A day later, he was sitting in the offices at INSCOM in Fort Belvoir, speaking with two of their technology personnel. The rest was history.

He moved on from basic training and took a position in the electronic and information warfare areas of responsibility at INSCOM. There, he was groomed under the careful, watchful eyes of the Military Intelligence Corps.

Four years later, he was at the top of his game, assisting Army Intelligence in their never-ending challenge to keep track of Chinese and Russian military assets. At one point he was brought on board to conduct *pen testing*, a term used by hackers for penetration testing of a computer's network, looking for vulnerabilities and security weaknesses.

He was in his element. He had a process, which he developed, that was ultimately adopted by others within his unit. He spent an inordinate amount of time conducting reconnaissance by gathering information about the targeted system. He would identify possible entry points, conduct several penetration tests, and record his findings for his superiors.

Using comparison models of other systems, he would eventually create a map, so to speak, of the target computer system. To look for weaknesses, he'd systematically test an organization's security policy compliance, the computer operator's security awareness, and finally, the target's ability to identify and respond to his intrusions.

The current administration turned the nation's cyber-warfare capabilities from a defensive posturing to being placed within its weapons arsenal. For decades, the Russians had used cyber attacks on critical infrastructure as a precursor to war. The Chinese preferred to steal military secrets with their efforts. INSCOM was tasked with following the Russians' method of military tactics.

He became an expert in accessing and potentially shutting down critical infrastructure on Russian targets, whether it be utilities, communications, financial markets, or transportation systems. In order to gain advantage in a military conflict, crippling one of these major components in a nation's critical infrastructure became a primary strategy in war planning.

He was becoming the best in his field, respected by his co-workers and appreciated by his superiors.

Then he was kidnapped.

It was never the intention of the kidnappers to cause him bodily injury. His life certainly wasn't worth ransoming. He was, as his kidnappers assured him, a potentially valuable asset. During the twelve hours he remained tied to a chair and blindfolded, he was assured that he wasn't going to be killed. They only sought two things from him, and he needed to understand their request was serious.

Cooperation and loyalty.

He asked if they expected him to betray his government. He insisted that he was a soldier and would never turn on the United States of America. He was assured that the plans they had in store for him would not require such a betrayal. He was simply told *trust the plan.*

So he did, and for the last nine months, he'd followed instructions and was paid handsomely for it. He still reported to duty at INSCOM, but he fulfilled his obligations to his nameless, faceless handlers. The ones who watched him.

And although he'd grown comfortable with the arrangement, he knew someday his time clock might be punched, or he'd have to disappear, hopefully on his terms.

CHAPTER 6

Undisclosed Residential Location

He opened his *little black book*, as he unimaginatively called it, and studied the initial sequence of codes and numbers. The first three exclamation marks indicated a level of priority, with one being the lowest and three the highest. The date and time stamp was generated by the chat board.

The message was encrypted as always, and he looked into his book to decode the string of characters and numbers. He underlined the ones of significance based upon the code sequence and key provided to him.

!!!mG4VJ*x*ZNCI 12/31 19:34:28
As the snow cascaded downward,
The wild *rides* halted immediately.
One instance among many more,
As we seek *Justitia Omnibus*.
Fare thee well.
MM

The number 4 represented the mode of delivery, in this case, the 4chan website, a social media site that allowed users to post anonymously. It was split into various chat boards discussing such topics as sports, entertainment, and politics. A similar site known as 8chan was also used from time to time. It differed slightly in that 4chan was moderated by administrators, and 8chan generally was not.

He thumbed through the sequence of letters and studied the sentences. Only certain words were considered important and part of a potential directive. To the casual conspiracy-minded observer, reading the post as a whole, they might point out the phrase *Justitia Omnibus.* This was translated from Latin to read *justice for all* in English. He also knew it by another meaning.

The Seal of the District of Columbia depicted Lady Justice hanging a wreath on a statue of George Washington. The motto of the District was Justitia Omnibus, justice for all. Others might arrive at this conclusion on their own, but only he knew it made the District the designated target of his activities.

He finished decoding the rest of the statement and set his glasses on his desk. He rolled his neck around his shoulders to relieve some stress and flexed his fingers. To his left was an undercounter refrigerator. He retrieved a miniature bottle of Tropicana orange juice and took a sip.

He spoke to himself aloud. "Last chance, pal. Whatcha gonna do, boy?" He could've shouted at the top of his lungs and not a soul on earth could hear him unless, of course, his watchers had their own form of listening device within his basement, which he affectionately dubbed the *Cave.*

After another moment consumed with conflict and introspection, he scooted his chair up to the modular desk and ran his fingers across his keyboard. He'd reached a decision.

This was a victimless hack in his mind. He wasn't directly killing anyone. In fact, in his mind, it was slightly humorous to derail the plans of the partygoers who were out carousing and enjoying adult beverages on New Year's Eve. He wasn't going to any parties, nor was he invited to any. There was no local pub nearby to ring in the New Year with a hearty chorus of "Auld Lang Syne." *Why shouldn't some other people be miserable like I am?*

His desk resembled the cockpit of a modern airliner with eight flat-panel monitors at the ready. He pulled up different sets of notes on his upper-level computer monitors, which were mounted directly to the wall.

One was labeled *AIRPORTS*—Reagan and Dulles. Another was labeled *AMTRAK.* The next screen was marked *BUS*

TRANSPORT—MegaBus, Battle's and Vamoose. The final screen was marked *WMATA*—DC Metro.

He studied his notes. He'd been tasked early on with pen testing of each of the major infrastructures of a dozen of the nation's largest cities plus Washington. Transportation, communication, utilities, and financial markets were all potential targets. Once he'd established a particular methodology for entering the computer systems of each of the subcomponents, like Reagan National Airport, he would conduct pen testing periodically to make sure countermeasures hadn't been adopted.

This was how he filled the extra hours of his day when he was away from INSCOM, in addition to monitoring chat boards and social media for instructions. Now he had work to do.

He set about his task. The keyword *Fare* in the post indicated he was to target transportation infrastructure that was ordinarily paid for with a fare.

The bus transport companies were the easiest to deal with. They were small companies with an unsophisticated firewall. It was easy for him to access their servers individually and schedule a DoS for the precise time indicated in his instructions.

He thought of the ramifications of his cyber attacks and others like them. The message had read *One instance among many more*. He was not the only one participating in this plan, which he was admonished to trust.

A DoS, or denial of service attack, was used to temporarily interrupt a web server's ability to connect to the internet. The common method of attack saturated the target network with external communications requests to the point the computer system was unable to respond to legitimate web traffic. The result was server overload and a shutdown of the entire system, creating chaos within the bus transportation network.

The servers at Washington Dulles and Reagan National airports would be attacked in a similar fashion, except the intrusion would involve the airlines as well. In this case, he would use a DDoS, or distributed denial of service attack, to completely weigh down the computer systems of the airports and the airlines that service them.

He would employ multiple servers around the world to remotely access the computer systems of the two airports and the three major airlines that service them—American, United, and Delta. Each of the remote servers controlled multiple computers, both public and private, around the world. All of them would simultaneously attack the servers at the two DC airports, bringing air travel to a standstill.

Amtrak would receive treatment similar to the airlines. The Washington Metropolitan Area Transit Authority, or WMATA, consisted of both bus and rail transportation. The bus transportation could be halted by a DoS attack easily enough.

The DC rail system was a little more complicated. Because the rail system encompassed such a wide area, he thought it best to take down the dedicated power grid for its lines. He was instructed to undertake a cascading failure of the entire rail system without creating widespread power outages throughout the District. It could be done, but he hadn't war-planned it.

The trains would be brought to a halt, and the power would be taken down in the stations and tunnels, adding an extra layer of chaos. He smiled as he added his own demented twist to the instructions he'd been given. He planned on creating a cascading failure by penetrating DC Metro's antiquated Windows-based servers.

He logged on to his VPN, a virtual private network, which prevented his identity being tracked by cyber investigators. His earlier pen tests had allowed him to sneak a peek without prematurely alerting the IT department at WMATA of his presence.

"Now that I'm in," he mumbled, "let's find their schematics and see what kind of software they're using."

He raced through the internal servers of the WMATA, his fingers clicking faster than the screen could keep up. After several minutes, he found what he was looking for. The WMATA used an Automatic Train Control software, which dealt with all aspects of train operations from routes, scheduling, operations, and communications. Most importantly, it provided safety and protection by monitoring life-critical functions of the trains.

"Hello, SCADA, old and out-of-date friend," he said with a smile as he dug deeper into the network.

SCADA, which is an acronym for supervisory control and data acquisition, was used by industrial utilities to provide interconnectivity across various platforms and networks throughout the utilities' network.

Many energy and transportation utilities around the world used SCADA despite the widely reported weaknesses and vulnerabilities the system was subject to. He reached for a USB drive and inserted it into a laptop that sat on the desk to his left. The portable computer went everywhere with him, you know, just in case he had to make a quick exit from public life.

His adrenaline was pumping as he navigated through the laptop in search of the perfect worm to insert in the SCADA system. Do-gooder companies like Symantec always professed to be one step ahead of hackers, but, of course, they were wrong. If they were one step ahead, there would never be a cyber intrusion, right?

The hacker community had a network, which he was part of. He rarely contributed anything of value, although he did post things from time to time to disrupt Russia's activities in Syria. On one such occasion, it got a Russian Sukhoi Su-24 shot down near the Syrian-Turkey border by a Turkish F-16.

The Turks swore the Sukhoi violated its airspace. What they were unaware of was the hack performed on their air defense radars that had temporarily moved the positioning of their border vis-à-vis the Russian aircraft. They thoroughly convinced the Russians that their military fighter had deviated into Turkish airspace, when it had not.

The hack, and the subsequent downing of the aircraft, created an international incident, with Moscow blaming Washington for not informing them of the aircraft's deviation. Washington never admitted that their data differed from Turkey's. Eventually, the matter went away.

He was applauded by the hacker community for providing the tools necessary to disrupt geopolitical affairs, and as a result, complex hacks were shared with him on a regular basis. He would deploy one of them that New Year's Eve to bring the DC Metrorail system, along with the entirety of Washington's transportation apparatus, to a screeching halt.

CHAPTER 7

Undisclosed Military Installation
The Philippines

The naval lieutenant eased back in a wooden office chair that was barely capable of remaining on its swivel base. The old facility in which he operated with the two junior members of his unit had been thrown together last summer. In the five months they'd been stationed there, they had done absolutely nothing except train on their simulators. They had minimal voice contact with their superior officers, instead relying upon daily directives and briefings via internal military communications.

The room the trio occupied stank of body odor and Thai food. The drab, vanilla walls surrounded three desks with computer stations enabling them to conduct training sessions and, if called upon, deploy the drone submarines that fell under their purview.

The lieutenant reviewed the newly received orders before he verbally passed them along to his team. The chain of command he'd been accustomed to had changed, but that was not unusual since their arrival. The new program was in the middle of an internal political struggle within the military that he wanted no part of.

He read the new orders again, which were marked *Top Secret Mission Sensitive.* From his experiences, when a mission was marked *sensitive*, it meant there were certain operational aspects of a task that were eyes only for the commander of a unit, albeit a small one like his. Since their arrival, every set of orders received fell under a classification that required no level of secretiveness.

He pushed his chair back from his work console and stood. He paced back and forth before speaking.

"What's the situation, sir?" one of his men asked.

"We need to clean up this room, now!" The lieutenant's demand was out of character for his normal demeanor. Ordinarily, he was able to joke with his team and even spend after-hours time in local bars, chasing available women.

"Okay, I'm almost—" one of his men protested, hurriedly finishing his meal.

"Now. I have orders and we need to get prepared. There's very little time before implementation."

The men scurried about, pulling a plastic trash can out of the restroom and shoving the take-out dinnerware into it.

One of his men began to question his lieutenant. "Is this a drill, sir? Are we about to get a visit from someone?"

The officer walked back and forth as sweat poured profusely from his brow. "No. At least I don't think so. The suddenness of the orders puzzled me, but they are authenticated, and that leaves us a job to do."

"What is it?" one of the men asked.

"Obviously, this is classified, but I'm going to tell you more than you should know. We're a team and our actions may have an effect on a global level."

"Tell us."

"It's labeled *Operation Ocean Aero.*"

"Are we at war?"

"Listen, I know as much as you do, but we need to focus. We only have a limited amount of time to position our AUV to hit a very defined target."

An AUV, or autonomous underwater vehicle, was commonly known as an unmanned submersible designed for survey missions like mapping the ocean floor, searching for sunken ships, or clearing possible obstructions to navigation for other vessels. Unlike an ROV, a remotely operated vehicle that is connected to another vessel by cables, AUVs had advanced technology to be controlled from locations on the other side of the planet via computer and satellite relay transmissions.

The proliferation of these underwater drones allowed nations that possessed them to park the AUV on the ocean floor, sometimes miles beneath the surface, awaiting orders from its controller.

Until now, no underwater drone in their fleet had been tested to fire an actual missile. The lieutenant and his crew conducted simulated war games daily, in part by orders from their superiors, but also out of sheer boredom. It was not unusual for them to pick locations to target all over the world, with varying degrees of difficulty and weaponry options.

If they chose to obliterate Israel, for example, they'd maneuver one of their drones into the Mediterranean Sea undetected and run a simulation of detonating a nuclear warhead over Tel Aviv.

Likewise, their AUVs were capable of attacking a ship or an airline with less destructive weapons. The arsenal at their disposal was as varied as the targets that they could be tasked to strike.

"Sir, what is our objective?"

"And what payload are we delivering?" asked the other man in the small unit.

The lieutenant continued to study their mission orders. He began to mumble as he read them. "One-megaton, EMP-tipped warhead. Just above the visual horizon," he summarized the orders. Then he paused, rubbed his temples, and considered the instructions. "Why is it so low? Targeted? None of this makes sense."

"Sir? Maybe this is just a drill."

The lieutenant shook his head and grimaced. "I don't think so, unless they removed the payload without our knowledge, which is impossible. Let's do our duty, gentlemen. Here are your coordinates."

He paused, and then he read them slowly to his team. "40° 0' 34" north latitude and 75° 8' 0" west longitude."

After several keystrokes were made at the terminal of one of the men, he took a deep breath and stated the physical location.

Philadelphia.

THANK YOU FOR READING THIS EXCERPT OF

DOOMSDAY: APOCALYPSE

—book one of The DOOMSDAY Series. The entire series is available on Amazon.com. You may purchase signed copies paperback and hardcover editions of Bobby Akart's books on www.BobbyAkart.com.

SIGN UP for Bobby Akart's mailing list to receive special offers, bonus content, and you'll be the first to receive news about new releases in the Doomsday series:

eepurl.com/bYqq3L

VISIT Amazon.com/BobbyAkart for more information on his next project, as well as his completed words: the Doomsday series, the Yellowstone series, the Lone Star series, the Pandemic series, the Blackout series, the Boston Brahmin series and the Prepping for Tomorrow series totaling nearly forty novels, including over thirty Amazon #1 Bestsellers in forty-plus fiction and nonfiction genres.

Visit Bobby Akart's website for informative blog entries on preparedness, writing, and a behind-the-scenes look into his novels.

BobbyAkart.com

www.ingramcontent.com/pod-product-compliance
Lightning Source LLC
Chambersburg PA
CBHW020935310726
48980CB00007B/778/J

* 9 7 8 0 5 7 8 4 8 4 2 5 9 *